THE TRILOGY

MILLENNIUM'S GATE

IN THE FOOTSTEPS OF GIANTS

GERALD CICCARONE

Paperback ISBN:

Hardcover ISBN:

E-book ISBN:

Published by Author Ghost Writer. Buffalo Groove Illinois.

Printed on acid-free paper.

The characters and events in this book are fictitious. Any similarity to real persons, living or dead, is coincidental and not intended by the author.

Author Ghost Writer.

2023

AUTHOR
GHOST WRITER

Authorghostwriter.com

Table of Contents

The Ten Planks of the Communist Manifesto

1848 by Karl Heinrich Marx

Although Marx advocated the use of any means, especially including violent revolution, to bring about socialist dictatorship, he suggested ten political goals for developed countries such as the United States.

1. Abolition of private property on land and application of all rents of land to public purpose.

(comment) The courts have interpreted the 14th Amendment of the U.S. Constitution (1868) to give the government far more "eminent domain" power than was originally intended, Under the rubric of "eminent domain" and various zoning regulations, land use regulations by the Bureau of Land Management property taxes, and "environmental" excuses, private property rights have become very diluted and private property in land is, vehicles, and other forms are seized almost every day in this country under the "forfeiture" provisions of the RICO statutes and the so-called War on Drugs..

2. A heavy progressive or graduated income tax.

(comment) The 16th Amendment of the U.S. Constitution, 1913 (which some scholars maintain was never properly ratified), and various State income taxes, established this major Marxist coup in the United States many decades ago. These taxes continue to drain the lifeblood out of the American economy and greatly reduce the accumulation of desperately needed capital for future growth, business starts, job creation, and salary increases.

3. Abolition of all rights of inheritance

(comment) Another Marxian attack on private property rights is in the form of Federal & State estate taxes and other inheritance taxes, which have abolished or at least greatly diluted the right of private property owners to determine the disposition and distribution of their estates upon their death. Instead, government bureaucrats get their greedy hands involved.

4. Confiscation of the property of all emigrants and rebels.

(comment) We call it government seizures, tax liens, "forfeiture" Public "law" 99-570 (1986); Executive order 11490, sections 1205, 2002 which gives private land to the Department of Urban Development; the imprisonment of "terrorists" and those who speak out or write against the "government" (1997 Crime/Terrorist Bill); or the IRS confiscation of property without due process.

5. Centralization of credit in the hands of the state, by means of a national bank with state capital and an exclusive monopoly.

(comment) The Federal Reserve System, created by the Federal Reserve Act of Congress in 1913, is indeed such a "national bank" and it politically manipulates interest rates and holds a monopoly on legal counterfeiting in the United States. This is exactly what Marx had in mind and completely fulfils this plank, another major socialist objective. Yet, most Americans naively believe the U.S. of America is far from a Marxist or socialist nation.

6. Centralization of the means of communication and transportation in the hands of the state.

(comment) In the U.S., communication and transportation are controlled and regulated by the Federal Communications Commission (FCC) established by the Communications Act of 1934 and the Department of Transportation and the Interstate Commerce Commission (established by Congress in 1887), and the Federal Aviation Administration as well as Executive orders 11490, 10999 -- not to mention various state bureaucracies and regulations. There is also the federal postal monopoly, AMTRAK, and CONRAIL -- outright socialist (government-owned) enterprises. Instead of free-market private enterprise in these important industries, these fields in America are semi-cartelized through the government's regulatory-industrial complex.

7. Extension of factories and instruments of production owned by the state; the bringing into cultivation of waste lands, and the improvement of the soil generally in accordance with a common plan.

(Comment) While the U.S. does not have vast "collective farms" (which failed so miserably in the Soviet Union), we nevertheless do have a significant degree of government involvement in agriculture in the form of price support subsidies and acreage allotments and land-use controls. The Desert Entry Act and The Department of Agriculture. As well as the Department of Commerce and Labor, Department of Interior, the Environmental Protection Agency, Bureau of Land Management, Bureau of Reclamation, Bureau of Mines, National Park Service, and the IRS control of business through corporate regulations.

8. Equal obligation of all to work. Establishment of Industrial armies, especially for agriculture.

(comment) We call it the Social Security Administration and The Department of Labor. The National debt and inflation caused by the communal bank has caused the need for a two "income" family. Woman in the workplace since the 1920's, the 19th amendment of the U.S. Constitution, the Civil Rights Act of 1964, assorted Socialist Unions, affirmative action, the Federal Public Works Program, and of course Executive order 11000. And I almost forgot...The Equal Rights Amendment means that women should do all work that men do including the military and since passage it would make women subject to the draft.

9. Combination of agriculture with manufacturing industries; gradual abolition of the distinction between town and country by a more equable distribution of the population over the country.

(comment) We call it the Planning Reorganization Act of 1949, zoning (Title 17 1910-1990) and Super Corporate Farms, as well as Executive orders 11647, 11731 (ten regions) and Public "law" 89-136.

10. Free education for all children in government schools. Abolition of children's factory labor in its present form. Combination of education with industrial production, etc. etc.

(comment) People are being taxed to support what we call 'public' schools, which train the young to work for the communal debt system. We also call it the Department of Education, the NEA and Outcome Based "Education"

*From laissez-fairerepublic.com/TenPlanks

PHILOSOPHY

1. Rational investigation of the truths and principles of being, knowledge, or conduct.
2. A system of principles for guidance in practical affairs.
3. All learning exclusive of technical precepts and practical arts.
4. A search for a general understanding of values and reality by chiefly speculative rather than observational means.
5. Pursuit of wisdom and an analysis of the grounds of and concepts expressing fundamental beliefs.

VALUE

1. The monetary worth of something: market price.
2. A fair return or equivalent in goods, services, or money for something exchanged.
3. Relative worth, utility, or importance.

WORTH

1. Monetary value.
2. The value of something measured by its qualities or the esteem in which it is held.
3. Moral or personal value.

REALITY

1. The quality or state of being real.
2. The totality of real things and events.
3. Something that is neither derivative nor dependent but exists necessarily.

DELUSION

1. A false belief or judgment about external reality, held despite incontrovertible evidence to the contrary.
2. Delusions are characterized as fixed and false beliefs that contradict reality.

Miriam Webster

MORALITY The four tenets of:

1. Acknowledge and accept the difference between **Right** and **Wrong**… **Good** and **Evil.**
2. The **Vision** to see and accept the truth (The critical validation of the other 3 tenets).
3. Dedication to the good.
4. The courage to stand by one's convictions, no matter what the price.

Iggy Marcu

Foreword

To paraphrase my seventh-grade teacher, Sister Mary Donald; while teaching the class to diagram sentences, she once said to us, "Words have an exact meaning. They define principles and are the bridge between us that elevates man above animals. If we abandon principle and conflate contradictions, we become delusional. If we become delusional, civil society will be swept away."

That was over 60 years ago. I didn't make much of it at the time. Society was civil then, and respect for each other generally ruled the day, even among opposites on the political spectrum. I remember those pearls of wisdom because they made such an impression on my young malleable mind. Sister Donald is gone now, and my enormous regret is I was too young and did not possess the intellectual acuity to value her prescience. She didn't know it, but she was describing the world of today exactly.

We constantly watch politicians and other authoritarians bastardize reality and force-feed children philosophical fiction. Truth has now become lies and lies have now become truth. Perversion is now considered acceptable and the norm, while chaste is considered aberrant. History is being rewritten to obscure past achievements and mistakes, to eradicate the lessons our children need to learn if they are to build a viable future.

They must not be allowed to think. If they learn to think, they learn to question. If they question the authoritarian who peddles perversity, his grasp on power becomes a house of cards in a hurricane.

We are on the verge of losing our country. Those of us with a mind see it because reality speaks for itself. Only the delusional close their eyes. We are inundated with propaganda, intimidated, and labeled as guilty of being conspiratorialist when we speak out against the perverse and corrupt.

The enemy refuses to admit conspiracy is defined as more than one. When people collude to betray their brothers and sisters, they conspire and become the harbingers of America's end. Autocrats regulate dissent and political resistance by artful misdirection as they distribute fear and guilt like Halloween candy. Their greatest nemesis is our awareness of the subterfuge when we realize how pitifully weak and puny, they really are. That awareness is our only hope to salvage our heritage.

Integrity has become only a repressed word in the dictionary, no longer Sister Donald's definition. We listen to politicians brazenly boast about their scandalous accomplishments and the lies that now always accompany political debate. If we do not resuscitate those values enshrined by my seventh-grade teacher, America will quietly slide into oblivion and the world will crash.

To resuscitate the values to save our progeny from the holocaust, we must offer them heroes to emulate who exemplify what is good in humanity, instead of the wicked. In trying times, men look to heroes for guidance. Iggy Marcus is my attempt to create such a man.

Gerald Ciccarone

Fate and tomorrow often balance on the razor-edge of a sword grasped by the hand of a lunatic.

Tiao Chen

CHAPTER 1

Bālún Tōng

Tiao Chen pushed the sink cabinet door open just enough to see the bathroom door closing. A few seconds before, someone pushed it open to scan the bathroom. It had to be one of the soldiers looking for refugees. The soldiers were leaving now. The screaming stopped when the last gun emptied its ammunition into the crowd. There was a muffled groan and then complete silence. He waited, listening before pushing the cabinet open. He was small for nine and just barely fit by wrapping his body around the pipes. When the shooting began, he shook so badly the cabinet door rattled and banged. "I have to stop shaking or they will hear me and shoot me too," he cried to himself, gasping in horror through a torrent of tears.

He crawled to the bathroom door, whimpering, frightened half to death of what he knew was beyond but didn't want to see. Tiao Chen had no choice. He had to know what had become of his parents and his little sister, Heng Cong. These meetings occurred monthly, sometimes bimonthly, and always in secret. His parents belonged to Bālún Tōng. They were leaders of the movement who were looked unfavorably upon by the government. Both parents had been teachers, no longer employed in the Chinese school system. They were classical Chinese and there was no place for them in the secular world of socialism.

He and his sister were brilliant. His parents had begun cultivating genius into their children since they were old enough to sit still and listen. They learned the Chinese classics, no longer available in the public square. Mao Zedong ensured that, during the purge when he burned the books and murdered 77 million people just because they remembered China's heritage and resisted his dictates.

They had recited poetry and music, and read to them from the many books they had secreted under the floorboards in their apartment. The people of Bālún Tōng were the only remaining path to the past. Without them, the culture and beauty, once China's signature, would disappear forever. His parents made him and Heng Cong memorize the classics and relentlessly emphasized the significance of China's history.

"It must not die with our generation," his parents had said to them… "and there is great hope. We are 70 million strong. The murder has stopped. It has been said the American who single-handedly invaded Zongnanhai with his daughter a few years ago was responsible. Rumor has it he forced Fun Chou Dung to kiss general Rishi on the lips after they protested his ultimatum. He told them murdering Chinese citizens would not be tolerated. Several soldiers were witness to the incident." Tiao Chen's father laughed. "I would have given a lot to be a fly on the wall *that* day."

Tiao Chen, on his knees, shook as he pushed the bathroom door open to view the carnage. It was more than his young mind could handle. The soldiers had used automatic weapons and obviously overdid it. There was blood and body parts everywhere. Evidently, they weren't happy just to murder everyone. They had to dismember them with wildfire. He knew his parents were dead and collapsed in anguish, covering his mouth to hold the vomit back, sobbing hysterically.

He lay there for some minutes with his face buried in his vomit-covered hands until the sobbing subsided. He knew he had to move. He just had no idea where he was going to go or what he was going to do. He would find someone, a friend, or maybe his aunt. They were Bālún Tōng also. Thank Tian they weren't here tonight, he thought. He wrestled with himself for several minutes. He did not want to see, but he had to locate his parents and sister, just one last time. Sixty mangled corpses were covered in blood with body parts and intestines strewn everywhere.

Crying, he tiptoed through the massacre, trying to find his family. He wailed in anguish as he looked at the people, many of whom he had known for years, now without faces. Their identity had been obliterated with machine gun fire. He couldn't stop crying but found it within himself to start rolling over corpses, trying to identify his parents.

His mother's shoes gave them away. He looked momentarily but began vomiting again and collapsed among the bloodied corpses, weeping hysterically. His parents loved him and made it more than evident with the magnificent education they were giving him. This appeared to be the end of the world for Tiao Chen. He wanted to lie there and die with his parents. He would follow them to heaven.

Then, he heard the grunt. He raised his head as his mother's corpse began to move. He heard a small voice whimper. His heart melted as a fresh flood of tears streamed down his cheeks. He crawled over the bodies, his hands covered with sticky brown clotting blood, until he reached his mother's corpse. Crying hysterically, he rolled his mutilated mother off his sister. In her last act of maternal heroism, Lin Shi had pulled his seven-year-old sister tight to her breast and fell on top of Heng Cong to protect her from the monsters. His mother's bullet-ridden corpse somehow protected Heng Cong from the fire. Maybe it was the angle the bullets entered from. She fell on top of Heng Cong and none of the bullets struck her straight on.

Tiao Chen's heart nearly exploded in anguish at that moment. He gazed at the face of the woman who had loved him and brought him into this world. Her face was a frozen seraphic smile. She had died a happy woman thinking her daughter would live. His sister had been knocked semi-conscious, unable to breathe, pinned beneath the weight of her mother. Her eyes fluttered open, then saw her brother, and she smiled. Unaware of what happened and consumed by shock, Heng Cong had not witnessed the carnage and did not comprehend that her mother and father were lying beside her in a pool of blood.

Tiao Chen acted quickly. He knew he had to. He must get his sister out of there and away from the bloodied mess that was once their parents. His sister was younger and not as resilient. He would not allow the image of their mother and father's mutilated corpses to be her last memory of them. He threw his shirt over his sister's head and pulled her toward the rear of the hall, half dragging and half carrying her. They stumbled several times, slipping on blood and falling among the corpses as they scrambled to the exit. His sister looked back and began screaming for her mother.

"No!" He shouted at Heng Cong. "You must not look!" They were almost at the exit. "We're almost there. We must leave immediately!"

Tiao Chen had wanted to die just minutes before and would have remained lying between his parent's lifeless bodies when the cleanup men arrived and found him. Now, Heng Cong was about to save her brother's life by forging the motive to save his sister.

It was none too soon. Thankfully, they were at the rear exit. The cleanup crew, some 30 men in white suits with body bags slung over their shoulders, had just entered the slaughter ground. They were under orders, direct from the top. Clean the mess up and destroy all the evidence, ASAP. Li Shen Rishi wanted no martyrs. Martyrs were bad for authoritarians. They inspired common men with passion, dedication, and the courage to fight. That wasn't all, however. He remembered the day at Zongnanhai when Iggy Marcus's eleven-year-old daughter made a laughingstock out of him and the general secretary, forcing them to kiss each other on the lips in front of 100 soldiers. Then came the ultimatum from Marcus to kill no more people. Apparently, the general secretary felt he could get away with murder without repercussions.

Tiao Chen dragged his sister up the stairs to the street. She refused to follow him as she tried to pull him back to the killing ground. She was in shock and didn't understand her parents were dead. She wanted her mother.

"No! You must follow me, Heng Cong! Mama and papa are dead! They have been killed. I know it is hard for you, but you saw the bodies. There is no hope they are still alive. Now, if we wish to live, we must get far away from this place! We will go to Auntie Zia. She is Bālún Tōng. She will help us. Maybe we can stay with her."

***

Zia and her husband both cried. "My sister is dead!" She sobbed. "Why did they start the killing again?"

"It has been two years since they stopped murdering us!" Said their uncle Chu. "I wonder what brought this on… two years," he murmured, softly speculating. "It doesn't make any sense. None of our people advocate violence or try to overthrow authority. We just quietly practice our religion. Why the massacre?"

"You do understand, Chu." Said Zia. "We of Bālún Tōng, represent a greater threat to them than all the armies of their enemies combined. They can keep the enemies at bay with a larger army, but we are 90 million strong, and they cannot keep what is within China at bay forever. So, they kill us as examples!"

Chu shook his head in affirmation. "Yes, I see. I had just hoped the murder would not start over again. We all heard of the American who went to Zongnanhai and ordered Dung and Rishi to stop killing or there would be consequences. I don't think those men believed the American."

"One thing is for certain, Chu. We must get these two out of the country. Despite the masses of people in this country, everyone has a number assigned to them, and so do these children. The Army has nothing but time on its hands, and it will pick up the corpses, identify them, and realize the children are not among them. Then, they will probably come for them. This is the computer age, and everything goes in the databank. They may not come tomorrow, but they will come someday, and these two will be eliminated."

"Just how are we going to do that?"

"Trust me, Chu. We have friends and relatives in America, and I will contact them. We have a code for communication in secrecy. It is where these two children must go… America. I don't know how we will do it, but we must do it."

***

Iggy and junior were putting the finishing touches on Baby. Junior smiled, "she's state-of-the-art, Dad. Even better than me. I think it's going to be nice having a sister. I'm not really sure what nice feels like, but I know it will be applicable."

Iggy's sat phone buzzed. He left it on speaker. "Hello, Iggy Marcus here. How are you, Deli?"

"I am well, Iggy. And you?"

"Never been better. What can I do for you Deli Li?"

"I need your help, sir. You instructed me to call anytime if something like this occurred. This is one of those times."

"Go on."

"Fun Chou Dung and his pet general have started killing again. They are sadistic monsters, and they do it with vengeance. They just slaughtered 60 people at a meeting. It was horrific. Two of the children escaped, and they must leave the country. Sooner or later, and probably sooner, the authorities will come for them. Everybody has a number, and no one escapes, even with 1 ½ billion."

"Where are they now?"

"They are with their aunt and uncle, also members of Bālún Tōng."

"I see. How old are they?"

"The boy is nine and his sister is seven. Can you help. They are so young, and they watched their parents slaughtered mercilessly."

"Hmmm, that's something no one should ever see, no matter what age. Tell you what, Deli, there's no time like the present. How quickly can you inform them I will come?"

"They have phones. They are monitored but we have code. I can text them anytime. They are waiting to hear, in fact."

"Why don't you call them, do not text, and make it clear who I am, what I can do, and I will be there in a matter of a few minutes. Once they are notified, pick a safe address away from home, drop the children off, and I will be there in a matter of minutes."

"Amazing! Can you actually do that? I mean, a matter of minutes?"

"Yes, Deli, minutes. Why don't we do it immediately? I will wait for your call, then be on my way."

"Incredible, Iggy. These are two very bright children, and their parents were old-school teachers. They worked at menial jobs to stay below the radar, having been ostracized from society as Bālún Tōng members. They attended a meeting where they were slaughtered. I will be back to you shortly."

Iggy and junior continued their work on Baby until the sat phone buzzed. "Iggy here, Deli. What do you have for me?"

"They are in the city of Fu yang. There is a place, Yu Dafu Park, on the Fun Chun River. They are a half hour away. What would you have me tell them?"

"It is 7:39 PM here. It is 9:39 AM in Fu yang. Tell them to leave for the park at their convenience. Hopefully, tonight because I have nothing else on the agenda. When they arrive at the park, have them leave the cell phone with the children. Before they depart, have them dial this number 000 222 4446. It will work and is specifically dedicated to my phone. I will home in on the signal and be there within two minutes, maybe three. So, before they dial the phone, tell them to say their goodbyes. When they are ready, they must dial the phone and leave immediately. This is for their own security."

"That's simple enough. I just have one question. How did you ever figure out the difference in time zones? It took you less than a second. It's amazing."

"I have a way with numbers, Deli. Call and let me know what their intentions are, and I will respond. Good luck."

Iggy's sat phone buzzed 15 minutes later. "I think it must be your friend, Deli. He didn't waste any time. I'm really getting good at this small talk business," commented Junior as Iggy answered the sat phone.

"Iggy here, Deli. What is the agenda?"

"They are on the way now. They should be at the park in less than an hour. I explained some of this to them, but not everything. It's difficult to do in code. They understand, however, and will leave the phone with the children. They will call you. Good luck…and thank you."

Iggy turned to junior. "Please find Gloria, Junior. As usual, she's not wearing her watch. Ask her to come with us; we're leaving for China, shortly."

"You got it, pops. Your wish is my command." Junior said over his shoulder as he headed for the exit.

Iggy laughed, wondering if he overdid it just a little with Junior's *small talk* department. He tapped his watch bezel. "Melanie? What are you doing right now?"

"Teaching music in the auditorium. Why?"

"Gloria, Junior, and I are headed on a rescue mission. Two young Chinese kids have just had their parents murdered by Dung and Rishi. They must leave the country. I'm going after them. I would like you to come if you can break away."

"I can be there in a few minutes. Are you in the hangar with Daedalus?"

"We will be in a few moments."

"See you shortly."

***

45 minutes later, Daedalus floated over Yu Dafu Park on the banks of the Fun Chun River. They could see the two children below. There appeared to be alone in the center of a large grassy area.

"This isn't good, Dad," said Gloria. "There are over 100 soldiers hidden in the bushes surrounding the field."

"No, this is not good." Replied Iggy. "No problem for the kids. We can shield them, and they will be safe. Obviously, the aunt and uncle's phones are not as secure as they think. So, there is another problem. The aunt and uncle have evidently been taken into custody. They are Bālún Tōng also, and their survival is a low probability, now."

"What are we going to do, Dad?" asked Junior. If it was my decision, I would encapsulate a few square miles. This happened very fast. It was only minutes from when we received the phone call before we arrived here. The aunt and uncle are probably still in the area."

"Maybe, but I don't think so, Junior." Iggy replied as he activated the onboard shield of Daedalus. "If the aunt and uncle are still within the shielded area, we must broadcast instructions for people driving vehicles to stop before they run into the magnetic wall."

Junior was studying the monitors and sensors. "I believe they are out of the area, Dad. There are no other military vehicles nearby, and certainly, none of them are leaving the area. There is a military chopper about 6 miles out and headed south. I would bet one of my computer chips the helicopter contains the aunt and uncle."

"You and Melanie are to stay with the two children at the park and shield them. I'll take care of the rest," he said as he set Daedalus down next to the two frightened children.

He approached the two children and spoke in Cantonese. "My name is Iggy, and this is Melanie and Junior. I have come at the request of your aunt and uncle to take you to America. They have been arrested, which I'm sure you are unaware of. I'm leaving Melanie and Junior with you. They will watch over you until I return with your aunt and uncle. He's fun to be around and tells jokes." With that, Iggy boarded Daedalus and they rose in pursuit of the chopper.

"How are we going to do this, Dad?" Gloria inquired, knowing they could do nothing to encapsulate the chopper while it was in flight.

"The kids will be fine with your mother and Junior until we return. We will follow the chopper until it lands. Then we will shield it and rescue the aunt and uncle.

Thirty minutes later, the chopper landed at the Zhoushan Island military complex. Moments later, Daedalus settled onto the flight line next to the chopper. Gloria encapsulated the area, isolating them from any military personnel who might intervene. Iggy crossed the pavement and approached the chopper. Two security guards and the pilots exited with drawn weapons. The security guards fired on him as he approached. He spoke to them in perfect Mandarin Chinese.

"Your weapons cannot harm me. I am shielded by a magnetic field. You may harm yourselves, however, by ricochet. I have come for the two people who are your prisoners. You will turn them over to me now."

"No, we cannot do that," replied the captain, who was the point guard. They are under arrest as political prisoners."

"You're not being given a choice," replied Iggy as he walked past the soldiers and encapsulated them. He entered the rear cargo door of the chopper. He was greeted by a pilot with a drawn weapon, who he encapsulated immediately with instructions explaining he might kill himself if he fired his weapon within the force field.

The pilot understood. Everyone on the planet understood the technology of Iggy Marcus at this point. They all knew his force field was a virtual wall shielding anyone within it from anything attempting to penetrate it. Iggy climbed aboard the chopper and approached the two people he had known he would find. Their hands were cuffed in front of them, and they sat on sling seats attached to the chopper wall. The two captives stared in amazement at their benefactor. The word had been passed among many millions of Bālún Tōng members about the American who was changing the world and had demanded the CCP stop killing people. Their faces wore an extreme look of relief.

"Hello, my name is Iggy Marcus. We spoke a few hours ago. You are Zia and Chu, the aunt and uncle of the children I have come to bring to America. Judging from the circumstances, I would suggest you come with us. I don't think the prospect of a long, happy life is in the cards for you here. There are many members of Bālún Tōng in America. I think you will find yourself comfortable and quite at home there. And you will be safe. It's up to you, but you must decide now. We are leaving."

Zia and Chu looked at each other inquisitively, but only for a second or two. They both nodded their heads as Iggy unlocked their handcuffs.

Fifteen minutes later, Gen. Rishi was fuming. He hated Iggy Marcus with a visceral passion. The very existence of the man negated the power he possessed as supreme general of the CCP. Marcus could come and go anywhere he pleased in China, and there was nothing he or anyone could do about it. The man's power was staggering. There was another component to this. Though Gen. Rishi was evil, he never lied to himself. He saw Iggy Marcus for exactly what he was. He hated it passionately but acknowledged this man was probably the greatest man who ever lived and probably the most virtuous, as well. As usual, the vision of Iggy Marcus's brilliance was a mirror that terrified Rishi. The vision was unbearable when he began to glimpse his own smallness and lack of character. He had learned to turn off his own self-awareness and ignore the vision, but there was something worse, however. Li Shen Rishi was frightened beyond words wondering when Marcus would come for *him.*

Tiao Chen, Heng Cong, Zia, and Chu boarded Daedalus.

Gloria probed the children's minds as they entered. "Oh my, Dad, these two are a mess. They are so traumatized from watching their parents slaughtered in front of them. They are going to need lots of help."

Junior commented. "Well, they've certainly come to the right place for that."

Like he had done with the Bramante children 20 years before, Iggy wrapped his arms around Tiao Chen and Heng Cong, projecting love, affection, and tranquility. They felt his deep subliminal presence as it engulfed them and knew, despite their parent's death, there was still a bright future ahead. Iggy was slightly startled. He observed the considerable substance of this boy's character. After unlocking thousands of kids, to lead them into a brilliant future, he realized this young Chinese nine-year-old was already well ahead of any of the children he first unlocked. *Interesting. I wonder how far I can take this young man.*

Minutes later, Daedalus settled to the flight line in front of the hanger at Lightning Ranch. The newcomers stepped onto the asphalt and were greeted by hugs from Deli Li. "Welcome to America and a better life." He turned to Iggy, startled by *contact* as they shook hands, "Thank you, my friend. I will be forever in your debt."

Melanie took Zia's hand. "The four of you will stay with us in our home until you get your feet on the ground and become used to America. You'll find Lightning Ranch is a very interesting place. You can meet new friends and explore from here while determining where you fit in."

Luke pulled up in a Land Rover with Parker Bodin and Millie Tuti, two of Iggy's rescued pedophilia victims. "Hi, Dad. Bret and I went looking for you in the lab. You weren't there, but we ran across Baby. She described your mission. You went off to China to rescue these two," he nodded, looking at Tiao Chen and his sister. "I understand they watched their parents slaughtered. Brett and I decided Parker and Millie should introduce them to Lily, Willie, and Nellie. Happy giraffes are the perfect antidote for trauma. Parker and Millie can drive them to the gardens."

Iggy nodded, "sure, why not? That'll take their minds off things."

The four of them drove off in the Land Rover, headed for the gardens after Melanie's... "Don't be late for dinner."

Deli Li's questioning look prompted Iggy's… "Yes? Why the funny look?"

Those children appear the same age as our two refugees. Yet, they drove off in a vehicle. They can't possibly have a driver's license.

Iggy laughed. "No one needs a driver's license here, Deli. Only the ability to drive."

Zia and Chu looked at each other. "I think we are very fortunate, Zia. We have come to America. Something I have dreamed of but never expected. I have only one regret," he grinned.

"Oh?"

"I have no fresh undergarments or money to buy some."

"Always joking, Chu," Zia laughed, realizing their lives just took a quantum leap for the better.

It had only been 10 minutes since they left China. There had been no time for conversation or amenities. "Permit me to thank you for your wonderful hospitality, Mr. Marcus. Zia and I heard about your ultimatum to Fun Chou Dung and Gen. Rishi. The story has traveled widely throughout Chinese society. The soldiers who were there as witnesses started the rumors. Things of that nature always titillate public curiosity, especially concerning government authority. We are honored to make your acquaintance. Evidently, all the stories are true. I have one question; you speak perfect Cantonese without the slightest trace of accent. Were you taught at a young age?"

"No, Chu. Believe it or not, I learned from a few books and listening to others speak."

Chu nodded… "impressive!"

Melanie couldn't resist. "He flawlessly speaks every language in every dialect. He was struck by lightning 26 years ago. It gave him remarkable abilities. She turned to her husband, "go ahead, dear, shake their hands. They are our guests now, and you have already had *contact* with the children."

Iggy didn't care for public displays, but his new guests might as well be aware of his capabilities. He and Gloria would have to help their niece and nephew, and it is a safe bet they would become members of Lightning's student body.

Minutes later, after touching their benefactor's hand… and *contact*, Zia and Chu looked at each other in amazement. Although Zia was sure their new lives would be amazing, she had no concept of the prodigious part they would play in China's future.

Nothing is set in stone until history makes it so. Then, its legitimacy, substance, and validity are in the hands of corrupt, opinionated, or at least politically owned historians.

First Lady Alice Sledge

CHAPTER II

END OF THE BEGINNING

Time passes, and the public memory fades. It is a human characteristic. What was urgent and compelling yesterday, is often suppressed today, then evaporates tomorrow. Iggy Marcus and Lightning Inc. had cast a huge shadow and blasted a crater in the status quo, but people continued to go about their business and easily forgot. Those cured of disease by Lightning Inc. medical technology would never forget, but they were a minority. The collective memory of men is short beyond their daily routines. Nuclear war was no longer possible, but no one had ever experienced nuclear war after Hiroshima and Nagasaki, just the fear of it. That esoteric reality was now removed from the human psyche and dwelt far from pressing realities.

Interlink remained. Many of the men at the top were gone, at least for now, but several thousand members, mostly corporate millionaires, and billionaires, had been substantially deprived of their unfettered ability to control and dictate life to the masses. Much of their arrogance and aloof self-importance had been stripped away. Those accustomed to wielding power seethed in crushing hatred for the man who administered that dose of humility. The world was being remade. Its new foundation would obliterate mediocrity to become an object lesson defining excellence... but it would take more than a single generation. The men and women of Interlink, who denigrated others in their pursuit of wealth and power to bolster their self-image, shrunk at the sight of themselves in the mirror of Iggy Marcus. Nuclear war was now off the table. Marcus had achieved his greatest objective, and Interlink's inner circle hated him passionately for it. American Media Inc., now unrestrained, mercilessly pursued corruption, graft, and the flagrant criminality permeating the international business world. Honest men had nothing to fear. Scoundrels and cheats shrunk in fear from the scrutiny of the Marcus media empire. No stone was left unturned during their relentless pursuit of honesty and integrity in the mission to transform society. Some tiger's stripes are indelible, though, and the war continues.

***

The world press and broadcast media exploded, reignited by Interlink's bitter eviction from the halls of power. The eruption was a vulcanized tempest of derision directed at the Sledge administration, his Atty. Gen. and finally, Ignatius Marcus Junior, the precipitator of the greatest socio-political and military transformation in history. Only American Media Inc. reported the unbiased truth. The mainstream media spewed lies and innuendo, constantly regurgitating their misinformation on the supposedly unsuspecting public ears and psyche. Owned entirely by one man in Interlink's inner circle, the media were shills for the economic tyrants who Marcus had usurped from complete power and influence.

Interlink remained an octopus with tentacles extending into every aspect of society with its vise-grip on the corporate, media, and political worlds. Iggy Marcus had mercilessly severed one tentacle when he removed thirteen of the Interlink upper-echelon miscreants from society. He delivered them to Guantánamo Bay to await trial by a panel of international jurists from the free world. Those jurists, yet to be impanelled, must emerge from men and women with no philosophical, financial, or family ties as affiliates or allies of Interlink's body or any individual members. Still, only one tentacle had been severed. The octopus was intact with its poisonous bite, refusing to roll over and expire. It became Interlink's mission to convince the masses they were the supposed gurus of democracy and the true saviors of the world economy, claiming the current political administration in Washington, and its unholy alliance with the Marcus family, was humanity's economic nemesis. The press continued its rampage 24/7. A never-ending litany of subtle talking points coupled with hysterical screaming became a deluge of psychological intimidation from every information source other than American Media Inc.

Beyond their claim the President and Ignatius Marcus were about to defile America's Constitution, issuing from one side of their mouths, the other side constantly spewed a nonsensical frenzy demanding the United States Constitution be torn apart and rewritten without the first and second amendments to suit their philosophical agenda and doctrine of pseudo-fairness. They were subtle. They understood the masses they had dumbed down. They never stated their agenda. They used hypocrisy and the distortion of the truth to overwhelm and intimidate the deluded population, many of whom had never formed a single critical thought.

Interlink had unlimited funding. All, but a few governments, including the United States, were contributors in the struggle to dominate public opinion. Self-aggrandizing politicians in dozens of countries joined Interlink to bolster their power and self-image, attempting the destruction of Lightning Inc.'s new world architecture. The very few world leaders who refused to hammer the Sledge administration and American Media Inc. were honest men and women or had their own unique, nefarious intent. They understood the political theater the world was being subjected to by the hidden rulers of men and society as they attempted to recapture their centuries old position of absolute power and influence.

Iggy arrested thirteen of Interlink's upper echelon and deposited them at Guantánamo Bay immediately after they attempted to murder him and a few thousand others with nukes from China. The snake's head had not been crushed. The serpent attempted to rise from the ashes and clutch power as it grew its new head. For the first time in 1500 years, one man had overwhelmed the elitist shadow kings who ruled the world since the Holy Roman Empire. Lightning Incorporated's thirty-two orbiting satellites had stripped all military power from every country on earth. All tyrants require a subservient military arm to enforce their commands. Their God complex requires all men to genuflect in supplication. The military arms of the tyrants had been severed with a technology created by one man a thousand years ahead of his time. Most of the world was oblivious, but it was the technology bound to save humanity from its path of self-destruction.

Fear and uncertainty overwhelmed Interlink's arrogance immediately following the arrest of its leaders. For a time, they assumed a fetal position subordinate to the new power represented by Lightning Inc. and Iggy Marcus. Intimidated, they sailed uncharted seas for the first time in a thousand years. Interlink and its predecessors had ruled the world economically and politically since the Holy Roman Empire, controlling 95% of the world's wealth, becoming the subsequent kingmakers for every political edifice. They held the puppet strings for the greatest sovereignty that had ever existed, the Spanish - Portuguese empire.

They coordinated their autocracy with the wealth of the Vatican bank, formally called The Institute for the Works of Religion, still fondly referred to among the Cardinals as la Banca Vaticana Dello Spirito Santo. Other than during the tenure of a few warrior popes, the alliance remained intact, even after Henry VIII created the Church of England. Interlink had recently catalyzed the resignation of Pope Germain 16th. Pope Germain emphasized the marriage of science and religion as he attempted to prepare the Catholic Church for the 21st century. He was an advocate of freedom and the power of the individual. His beliefs encompassed the sinfulness and irrationality of both totalitarianism and homosexuality. Individual freedom and power were concepts that conflicted with Interlink's plans for the psychological intimidation of society and their intended emasculation of America. There is always a difficulty for independent men who challenge the elitist power structure; they get their heads handed to them. Germain 12th, forced into retirement because he wouldn't play the game, was succeeded by Jose Amantilado, an avowed proponent of socialism and ally of *the new world order*, who assumed the name Pope Innocent 14th.

No nucleus of power existed anywhere in the world undominated by Interlink since the Italian Renaissance until the Bolshevik revolution created the Soviet Union. Then came the rise of Mahatma Gandhi and the installation of Mao Zedong in modern China. Still, they were able to construct a symbiotic relationship with those three superpowers expecting to economically manipulate the entire globe. They had not considered the monumental power of China's conceited ability to become the greatest manufacturing edifice in history until it was too late. They had expected to use China as a production facility for goods to be distributed globally with a substantial profit falling in their coffers. That never happened. To Interlink's dismay, they were relegated to accepting a tithe instead of the expected lion's share of the profits. China would allow no one to usurp their mission to rule the world.

Authoritarian elitists had been at this for centuries. They knew mind control and how to achieve the intellectual destruction of men. It was the necessary component required to create the caste system and their seat at the summit of power. They intended to destroy the mind's ability to think critically. Once accomplished, it ended freedom, justice, opportunity…and morality.

Those were once America's vital foundation blocks. The lush promise of capitalism's rewards had been the prima fasciae example of its righteous virtue, giving America's population the most advanced, intelligent, and free society in history. Despite America's early embrace of slavery, it eventually became the first country to abolish the concept of forced servitude. The individual freedom and benevolence which could only be granted by capitalism was the antithesis of the authoritarian grip on humanity. They could not exist together side-by-side. The superiority of capitalism eclipsed the authoritarian product of socialism, shining a brilliant light on the deception, but only for honest people with open eyes. Individuality underpinned capitalism. Socialism was both the precursor and product of collectivism. Iggy knew the only way to defeat autocracy and socialism was the education of the individual.

Enlightenment was his underlying premise when he and his family created Lightning Inc. They built American Media Inc., the largest single publishing empire in history owned by one family and opened a school to reincorporate brilliance and achievement into the mentality of American youth. The unclouded vision and acceptance of reality underpinned everything he taught the young men and women of his student body. Aristotle's Nicomachean Ethics was the basis of their socio-political education.

They learned the principles and veracity of Aristotle's definition of politics: ***the noble activity in which men decide the rules they will live by and the goals they will collectively pursue***. They came to understand no political edifice would function unless its operating theme was based on honor and integrity. They were the singular virtues defined by morality that must underpin everything in the activities of men, or the system would implode.

He taught them reality must always predicate everything. They saw American society was perishing in an orgy of depravity, consumerism, vanity, and delusion. If it continued, it would be the extinction of principle and the harbinger of chaotic anarchy. It was his mission to teach each one of his acolytes the true definition of morality and how to live by those concepts every moment of their lives. He engrained them in the fabric of their character as his mother had done with him. Their lives were enmeshed in morality's four tenets: *knowledge there is a difference between right and wrong, good, and evil. The most important tenet -- the vision to see and accept the truth. Integrity then compelled dedication to the good and the courage to stand by one's convictions no matter what the price.*

Society had been dumbed down. The liberal restructuring of the higher education institutions contradicted everything American. Delusion was force-fed to a barely literate, unsuspecting youth. It wasn't their fault. Indoctrination replacing individuality with collectivism had incrementally begun in grammar school, creating an entire generation of mindless non-entities. The generation who never learned to critically think eventually became the teachers and stereotypes the next generation would emulate.

This conspiracy to enslave the masses had been present in man's emotional and intellectual DNA since he began recording history but became pervasive in America during the last half of the previous century. America's operating system, capitalism, had historically cauterized American society for the first time, inoculating it against the ravages of collective socialism, which had overwhelmingly proven itself to be the gateway to slavery. The first half of the 20th century was preoccupied with World War I, World War II, and then Korea. Thousands of America's finest citizens perished in those wars.

War was always an aberration. The handful of individuals who started war and capitalized on its spoils convinced their minions on the battlefield they were in the right, and God was on their side. Tyrants and autocrats had always used treachery and hypocrisy to manipulate armies until the nuclear age, and we arrived at the atomic threshold. Now, men could incinerate every human alive with the push of a button.

Interlink was attempting to re-ascend the summit of power. Their brazen, undisguised attempt at psych-ops to achieve their goal was obvious to many, thanks to American Media Inc., but it was too soon. Most people did not yet possess the intellectual acuity to sort through the propaganda. Although they were able to flood the globe with a constant plethora of lies, there was one enormous stumbling block; reality was their enemy, and American Media Inc. was their antithesis. Both socialism and capitalism axiomatically contradicted each other and instigated violent debates to define allegiance to each philosophy. It was what used car salesmen called the 'hard sell', always riddled with exaggerations, and lies.

Debates, always about differing opinions, can be resolved with empirical proof, but only to clear open minds. Delusion, a fixed false belief resistant to reason or confrontation with actual fact, as defined, cannot flourish under the umbrella of proof in the face of contradictory reality. The remnants of Interlink offered no evidence because none existed. The Marcus family, however, possessed the greatest influential argument and proof of validity in history. They stood atop the creation of Lightning Inc.'s unbelievable technologies that were beginning to remake the world. Hunger and disease were disappearing as each technology was implemented. Slowly but surely, this was happening around the globe and could not be denied by the media minions of Interlink. So, unable to negate or even refute what was happening, Interlink chose the only possible course of action, deny its existence with lies to blind vision, deafen the ears, and obliterate the message.

Interlink immediately lost the propaganda war. Lightning Inc. had trained and deployed hundreds of people, many of them already associates. They were dispatched to various locations around the globe and opened clinics consisting of Iggy's avant-garde technologies. All clinics were shielded, and prospective patients were allowed to enter in non-threatening groups. In the six months following the global deployment, over seven million people were cured of terminal cancer and another several million were treated for congestive cardiac failure or associated maladies. The miracle could not be hidden by a false diatribe from a corrupt press as 90% of the medical authorities in existence roared their opposition to one man who refused to genuflect and elicit their permission. Their patent excuse was **life safety,** but there were no denying millions of cured, cancer-free people. The medical community's life safety excuse was lip service to obfuscate their envy and anger about losing dominance of medicine's ivory towers.

They couldn't stop the millions of people everywhere who were getting a taste of Iggy's technology. It soon became apparent that government, medical institutions, and big Pharma cared less for people's health and well-being than the bottom line and their position atop the pinnacles of authority. The results of the technology deployment were more than edifying. They were conclusive, and thousands of people who would die from cancer were given a new lease on life without the imprimatur of the FDA or medical authorities in other countries.

These miraculous cures and treatments were not created by the medical establishment who had supposedly dedicated themselves for the previous hundred years to finding the cures for these illnesses. So, the efficacy and validity of the treatments were arrogantly denied at first. One man had discovered what thousands could not, and that didn't sit well with many boards of directors. It was a shining example of where the most significant inventions and improvements to society came from, individual brilliance, not collective impotence. The inability of the pharmaceutical giants to produce cures after the input of billions of dollars in research and development, only to create symptom-treating drugs and enormously expensive and inconclusive partial therapies, was a strident example of the intent and efficacy of their efforts. There was just too much money to be made on therapeutic treatments versus concrete, decisive cures. Complete cures terminate perpetual therapy and stifle cash flow. The brilliance of the Marcus family and associates' accomplishments at their small hospital in rural Montana, driven by principle versus the profit margin and bottom line, exemplified the true source of creative innovation… and it flew in the face and coffers of organized research.

Many foreign governments attempted to block entrance to the clinics. They refused to allow entry of their chattel citizenry to benefit from gifts not emerging from their thrones of power. No power on earth possessed the technology to defeat the Marcus magnetic force field surrounding the clinics, however, and no power on earth was able to prevent Iggy Marcus's entry into any country to cure illness, save lives and feed people. Anyone attempting to destroy that much benevolence was motivated by envy and greed, the two sources of all of man's foibles. It wasn't long before local populations were informed of the clinics' existence. They came by the thousands, seeking a cure for every illness imaginable. In the beginning, they were arrested by dictators who refused to stand aside and relinquish dictatorial power over their people. Authoritarians soon realized arresting many thousands of people seeking medical aid was logistically unmanageable. Those despots who ruled, as opposed to governing, were learning the harsh reality of their anemic grasp on power when the people revolted.

Abolition of sickness and starvation was the one incredible unseen benefit coupled with Iggy's invisible magnetic barrier between Mexico and the US that precipitated a vast reduction in illegal immigration at the border. The Statue of Liberty, the promise of America, and capitalism were the magnets that drew the poor and starving to America's border for two centuries. Lightning was ending starvation and disease everywhere, much to the chagrin of Interlink. Starvation, poverty, and disease, the most prolific tools of slave masters, were ripped from their toolbox. Marcus exemplified the rich benefits for all from capitalism, and the common people were beginning to open their eyes.

Iggy Marcus was obliterating the tyrannical sovereignty of autocrats by refusing to accept any decree or have any discussion about the efficacy of his program. People were sick and dying, and he intended to cure them. He would allow no one man, group of men, or government to obfuscate his reality. Ending individual sickness and death from disease was not his only purpose. It was a small component of his plans for the future of men.

It had been his purpose to end the insanity of war forever. His progeny would not live in that world. It was a promise he made to himself and his deceased parents 30 years before. He and his family generated a plan and implemented it step-by-step for 25 years. Iggy's stratospheric intellect had conceived of, built, and launched a ring of satellites surrounding the earth designed to prevent nuclear war from beginning anywhere. Most of the world was ecstatic. The people on the authoritative power end of the political spectrum, however, hated Marcus and wanted him dead. Several attempts to kill him came to nothing. Evidently, his stratospheric intellect envisioned every move they made, and he was consistently prepared, waiting for them.

***

The muffled intermittent beep from the lightning phone seeped from the top desk drawer in the Oval Office. "Good morning, Iggy. I'm glad the beep wasn't continuous, and this isn't urgent. I'm just barely awake. Alice and I were up with the twins all night. It seems they have a touch of something. How are you, Melanie, and the rest of the family? I'm sure your twins, Lori and Liam, are a much greater handful than William and Wilhelmina."

"In some ways," Iggy laughed. "They keep things moving, that's for sure, and I mean it literally. It's a good thing Melanie is the trooper she is. She's had three children who, it is safe to say, are not typical."

"Well, Iggy, I'm sure you didn't call just to chat. What unique piece of information will you plop in my lap, today? It's always something far outside the norm, and always interesting."

"You're right, Bill. Interlink has reevaluated its position and is going to make another attempt to recapture their global dominance. Much of it is being funded and driven by the Lichtenberg group, but a substantial portion is being funded and driven by American, Arab, and Russian billionaires.

"And not the Chinese? What about the Chinese?"

"They're not in on this. Apparently, Gloria and I made an impression on them when we visited Beijing. But I don't think that has as much to do with it as one would think. You see, the Chinese were never part of Interlink, even though they helped by supplying them with nukes to kill me. They have a 10,000-year-old dynastic mindset. They believe the West will self-destruct, meaning all of us, everywhere. They intend to take over the globe with their three billion people simply because of attrition. They'll outnumber us after we decimate ourselves. Even though Gloria and I altered their modus operandi and stopped them from killing people indiscriminately, they haven't changed their philosophical viewpoint."

"And you're convinced of this?"

"This is not hyperbole, Bill. We have many friends in different places who keep their ears to the ground. I have some specifics from them, but I have my own conjecture as well. I'm not fully sure of what they're planning but some good ideas. It won't have anything to do with nuclear weapons this time. I'll come to Washington the day after tomorrow. This is something we need to talk about."

"I look forward to it. Will you bring Melanie? Alice would love to see her."

"No problem. Lori and Liam will tag along, and perhaps, Gloria."

***

Daedalus hovered a few yards off the Truman balcony at the White House. Bill and Alice Sledge welcomed them with huge smiles of anticipation. The president had invited Abe Morris, Atty. Gen. Charlie Barton, Curtis Mulroney, and Surgeon General Allison MacLeod to the meeting. The walls of Daedalus were transparent as Iggy Marcus's floating living room descended slowly to the lawn below.

They sat at a large oval conference table in the center of the balcony near a small buffet table packed with breakfast delicacies. Amenities were exchanged, and Pres. Sledge invited everyone to the buffet. "With all the crazy things that have happened to me since I met you, Iggy Marcus, many of which complicated our lives far beyond routine, Alice and I are amazed and eternally grateful we have two twin babies because of you guys. Please join us for breakfast. The cuisine in this place is pretty amazing."

Gloria's usual wry humor projected the mental image of their breakfast in Taiwan. "If you think the food is great here, you would absolutely love the small restaurant in Taipei, Jack Fletcher introduced us to. The steamed stuffed pig snout and silkworm pupae are unequaled."

Everyone laughed. Apart from the Surgeon General, they had all met Gloria and understood her gifts. "My apologies to all for combining business with pleasure," said Iggy. "But it's necessary, and I'm glad you all could make it. I don't have to elaborate on the noise from mainstream media attempting to flay the administration and American Media Inc., including myself, to the bone. One anticipated result of our actions has been the defection of some people in the inner circle of Interlink to our philosophical platform. Not everyone in that organization is corrupt. There are some honest people in power who have no philosophical allegiance to Interlink's desire to turn humanity into a flock of sheep."

President William Sledge chose Allison Macleod to be his new Surgeon General six months before this meeting. The first family and Allison had been friends for years. Her stature as a research geneticist and Nobel Prize laureate placed her at the top of the medical heap. She decided to come on board the administration when Alice had called her to describe her pregnancy. Allison was dumbfounded. As a geneticist, she thoroughly understood the impossibility of Alice Sledge bearing children comprised of her own DNA. When she learned the technology existed to generate this inconceivable result, she agreed to take the position for several reasons. As Surgeon General, she could still execute her career, but this would open the door to learning about the technology Iggy and Melanie Marcus created in their tiny Montana hospital.

Alice Sledge nudged her husband under the table and whispered in his ear. "Bill, aren't you forgetting something?"

Alice laughed at his blank look. "What am I forgetting now, dear? I helped feed the twins, walked the dog, and brushed my teeth. What am I missing?"

Allison MacLeod and Alice Sledge had been talking about the twins for a year. She had never met the people responsible for helping her with the pregnancy, and she was dying for the opportunity. "You forgot to formally introduce Melanie and Iggy to Allison."

"Oh my, yes. Forgive me, please. I am preoccupied with this crazy business concerning the Atty. Gen. and the Department of Justice. It seems we have so many obstacles to overcome I forget some important things." He turned to his attorney general. "Allison, I would like to formally introduce you to Melanie, Iggy, and their children, Gloria, Lori, and Liam." He turned to the Marcus family. "I would like you folks to meet my new Surgeon General and close friend, Dr. Allison MacLeod."

Melanie offered her hand, and Allison took it. "Melanie Coletta! I am in awe. I believe you are the most amazing woman I have ever heard of. I have been an admirer of yours since I first heard you sing. Your voice and talent are incomparable. I have been to many of your performances, and you always bring tears to my eyes. Then, when Alice told me you are a doctor who had devised a method to re-create her DNA in an ovum, I was completely blown away. That is much more than a significant medical development. It is groundbreaking and hard to believe. I am stunned. I have wanted to meet you for the longest time. I think you should have the Nobel Prize I hold."

Melanie smiled warmly. "Thank you, Dr. MacLeod. You honor me, and it is a privilege to meet you. However, your work on uterine transplants, from healthy women who want hysterectomies to those who want children but have uterine deformities, is changing the reproductive world. I have read your white papers outlining reproductive pathology and the methodology for the prevention of rejection. You more than deserved your Nobel Prize. Your techniques are amazing. Perhaps, we should team up someday. I think, between us, we could revolutionize reproduction for women who are denied the privilege."

Gloria silently waited as Allison turned and shook her hand. "Hello, Dr. MacLeod; I am very pleased to meet you. I'm Gloria. My sister and brother are Lori and Liam." Lori and Liam both shook Dr. MacLeod's hand but remained silent.

"I am pleased to meet you all," then held her hand out to Iggy. His expression displayed reticence about shaking hands. Allison MacLeod smiled. "Go ahead Mr. Marcus, Bill, and Alice have described everything you've done for them, including unlocking. You are quite a novel character from everything I have heard. I would love to shake your hand and see for myself. I never tire of experiencing or learning new things."

They shook hands, but Allison MacLeod had a different cut to her jib. She reminded Iggy of Amos Carmichael. Instead of trepidation and pulling away like most people, she reached her other hand and clasped Iggy's right hand between hers, smiling broadly. "Well, aren't you something the cat would never drag in, Iggy Marcus! I have waited a year for this experience. It is every bit as intriguing as Alice has described. Fascinating! Now I understand the creation of all those amazing technologies. Your brain is way up there in lights. Don't get me wrong, I thought my brain was up there in lights, until now. Wow!! Alice told me about your gifted children and their capabilities... especially Gloria."

Dr. Allison MacLeod, a brilliant, exquisitely beautiful woman, had forged her path to the summit of her medical career with accomplishments resulting from her innate stratospheric genius. Iggy saw its entirety, which struck a burning emotional chord of desire in him. He had never felt that since Melanie. For the first time in all his years of having cerebral contact with people by physical touching, he was shocked to his core. When the thunderbolt struck, he tried to pull away from Allison MacLeod, but she held on tightly, preventing his retreat. Finally, he was able to extricate his hand from her grasp. Shocked at his own response and fully aware Allison MacLeod understood every inch of his emotional state, he stood back and said nothing.

Gloria Marcus had Orphan Annie eyes. She was just as shocked as her father. She detected exactly what happened and understood completely. She and Iggy had an almost perpetual cerebral link. There was an obvious sexual component to this. She had never thought of her father as being less than godlike. To her, he was a paragon, the perfect human being. This was an eye-opener. But she was brilliant also and able to sort things out in a heartbeat. She realized for the first time how human her father was. **Dad,**

Gloria said subliminally. **I know I'm your daughter and shouldn't be giving you advice, but I don't think you should walk away from this. I think you should run, and quickly!**

Iggy nodded his head and smiled. **You're always holding my feet to the fire, Gloria. Thanks, I needed that. It was wholly unexpected on my part. You don't have to worry, I'm human, but I won't stray. I made promises, and I will keep them.**

I didn't mean to be so intrusive, Dad, but that's what happens when you can read minds. I didn't ask for this; it just came my way from the universe. Anyway, I'm glad you said that because Mom would be heartbroken. The entire subliminal communication had remained strictly between her and Iggy.

Maybe it's one of the reasons you're here, to keep me out of trouble, he returned, laughing.

Everyone noticed the apparent laughter about nothing and the different expressions washing over Iggy and Gloria's faces. They sensed nothing of the cerebral connection, so they wondered… except Melanie. She was staring right through her husband. They had been married for 24 years. Besides their emotional and physical relationship, there was a subliminal connection probably no one else had ever achieved. They were so close she actually felt Iggy's emotional convulsion and understood the experience.

Besides his family, most people attributed godlike qualities to the greatest man who had ever existed. Melanie knew better. She loved a man, not a God, and she accepted his fleeting moment of passion as normal and to be expected. Allison MacLeod was far beyond merely exceptional, she was brilliant, beautiful, and like most people, seeking a soulmate. Iggy's reaction was more than a typical biological and psychological response. His elevated psyche profoundly flanked his every intellectual and emotional occurrence with a heightened vibrancy. Melanie's smile harbored no derision. In fact, she found the episode humorous. With raised eyebrows, she had a two-word question for Iggy only Gloria would be privy to. "Enjoy that?"

Gloria decided it was time to enter the conversation, approach Allison MacLeod, and diffuse the underlying sexual tension by speaking to her subliminally. After all, the good Dr. had mentioned her. She was smiling hugely**. I love you Dr. MacLeod. You have a sense of humor just like mine. We're going to have some fun, I think. Maybe we could do a Saturday Night Live together. I believe we would be hilarious.** She hadn't opened her mouth, but everyone heard her thoughts and felt her humorous exuberance.

Allison MacLeod repeated herself. "Wow! Wow! Wow! Gloria! That's amazing! I'm almost afraid to ask what your siblings can do."

Almost on cue, Lori glanced at the buffet table. A platter of apple cinnamon krullers rose from the table and floated across the balcony to Allison MacLeod. "Would you like a doughnut?" She asked the Surgeon General.

Surgeon General Allison MacLeod was speechless. She knew this family was way beyond normal, but this was almost frightening. In less than 5 minutes, she had shaken hands with probably the smartest man alive, had a telepathic conversation with his oldest daughter, and had a plate of donuts handed to her by a 4-year-old child via telekinesis. "I don't eat gluten or sugar, Lori, but thank you anyway! We have business scheduled here, but I would be grateful to speak to you later about these incredible abilities you all possess… purely from a medical perspective, however," she hastily added.

"Okay kids," said Iggy." Enough clowning. We have business to do here, and you need to be seen and not heard. As for conversation, Dr. MacLeod, why don't you take a sabbatical or minivacation and come out to Lightning Ranch. Everyone else here has visited us. I think you'll enjoy what you find there.

"That's a certainty. You'll love Nellie, Lilly, and Willie," nodded Alice Sledge. "I will accompany you."

"Who are Nellie, Lilly, and Willy?"

"Giraffes. They've been unlocked too."

Gloria's frown displayed her disapproval over Iggy's invitation to Allison MacLeod. Yes, she saw her father as the greatest man who ever lived, but hormones are hormones, and when they begin raging, it's anyone's guess what's next. Melanie, on the other hand, was ambivalent.

"Let's continue where we left off. Interlink consists of thousands of members from just about every corporate haven on earth. People who exceed the norm and build corporations of substantial dimension and liquidity are forced by necessity to join. The handful of upper-echelon people allows no philosophical or authoritative competition. Every entity must become a philosophic ally and member. They hold plenty of power to operate in their own orbit but must remain subservient to Interlink's authority, or they are not allowed to exist. It is made expressly clear to everyone, so they eventually acquiesce to preserve their businesses and positions. The stature of their seat among Interlink's elites is directly proportionate to their business achievements and stature. The greater the corporate wealth and financial clout in world economics, the higher authoritative position they are granted. Very few, however, occupy the seats at the pinnacle of authority. Only when someone acquires the economic stature which might affect world economies dramatically, such as owning major financial institutions like banks or controlling trillion-dollar business enterprises, are those individuals invited to sit at the top of the heap."

"Those of lesser stature may not agree with the philosophical platform of Interlink but they must still conform for self-preservation. They were given no alternatives until Lightning Inc. entered the picture and eradicated the ability for any country or group to abuse military power, giving them an alternate harbor for their allegiance without fear of physical reprisal. Also, I might add, Lightning Inc. will not charge them dues."

"I have a question," injected Abe Morris. "Why are those at the top so eager to subvert and diminish humanity as individuals? What is their motive? From what you just said, people of lesser stature don't seem to be affected this way. I'd like an explanation if you would."

Iggy hesitated, thinking about how much he should tell them. The two-component truth was complex and brutal. He debated whether these men were ready for both sides of the coin yet. The first component was envy and greed. The second component was forced on men by people from another world with an agenda skirting morality. He decided it could wait and took an alternate tack.

"Okay, Abe, of course. I outlined this well in my broadcast from the ranch a few years back. But it's a lot to remember, and if you're not thinking about it constantly, it's easy to forget. What it boils down to is human nature. The people at the top are often extraordinary businessmen, but often they are not very extraordinary as human beings. Take a platform like Facebook, for instance. The guy who dreamed it up, who has been made a billionaire because of it, is capitalizing on people's weaknesses. His brilliance might be an arguable point by some, but only by minor intellects. Wasting even a small piece of your limited life in that venue is an exercise in mediocrity. It becomes addictive, and the enormous time wasted offers minimal return for the effort.

This becomes part of society's indoctrination to pursue mediocrity as constant and normal. They are told mediocrity is not only acceptable but the holy Grail of existence. That's how they live. Many of the major perpetrators of this nonsense are platforms like Facebook or Twitter. Imagine the thousands of wasted hours spent in the limited life we are all granted. Ultimately, one will have little or nothing to show for those hours and the pursuit of mediocrity."

"When you become convinced mediocrity is acceptable because you have no concept of excellence, it is where you dwell. There is almost the entire population of the planet who lives under those auspices. Why? You might ask."

"That's exactly what I'm asking, Iggy. Why? It is so internally dishonest and self-defeating."

"Let's dive to the root, Abe. Most people never want to go there. It requires too much intellectual effort and requires a cold hard look at one's own character. Once you accept mediocrity as a lifestyle, the superlative is a frightening spectacle. No matter how much you destroy your own intellect through nonparticipation and lack of critical thought, you still inadvertently read between the lines and see reality to some degree. When people look at excellence, even slightly knowing what it is, it becomes a mirror they automatically must stare into. Then, they judge themselves subconsciously based on the inescapable vision. When that happens, there are two choices. Consciously accept it and take your hat off with respect for excellence or attempt to destroy it and thus elevate your stature in your own eyes. All men do this unless they are intellectually comatose! But only until they grow up and accept reality in all things. Prior to acknowledging reality, delusion rules their life, which is only a half existence."

"I see what you're getting at, and I'm beginning to remember some of the things you said that day with Bill. What you just described; I see every day in almost all my dealings with other human beings. What a sad way to live. But go on, please finish, I'm fascinated."

"Once you understand the point, there is only one logical conclusion possible. Those who compare themselves to others to define themselves will always be envious and attempt to destroy that which exceeds their own self-worth in their own eyes. Do you see it, Abe? My mother began teaching us this when we were only a year old. She said: *never let anyone's opinion of you define your self-image. An honest, true self-image can only come from within through mastery by achievement.* This all boils down to envy. The green-eyed monster populates most men's psyche. Not all, mind you, but most. The results of envy are avarice and greed. Those are the tools people with weak self-images use to deprecate and destroy those who shine a light on their weaknesses, by example. This is the human deficiency which always precipitates violence."

Abe Morris was staring at his shoes as everything Iggy Marcus said became apparent. "Wow," he said, subdued. "How incredibly sad. It's amazing the world has gotten as far as it has. But I see now; it's the reason men can't stop trying to kill each other, individually or collectively." He looked directly into Iggy's eyes as the reality of man's history exploded in his awareness. "That's the reason, isn't it? All the wars, death, and misery were caused by individual envy and greed. Even at the top of the food chain."

Iggy smiled. "That's it in a nutshell, Abe…the whole Magilla, pure and simple. It doesn't get any more complex. Mental illness is often used as an excuse by some to refute the reason for our propensity to destroy ourselves, but I don't agree. I am sure intentional evasion of reality and acceptance of delusion is always mental illness as well. What else would you call it? Certainly not a healthy mentality."

After Iggy's discourse, Bill Sledge spoke between mouthfuls of buttered croissant and sips of coffee, "Let's go ahead and get this business on the table. I know it has to do with Interlink I'm very interested to hear what your contacts have to say, Iggy."

"Interlink has reorganized. The new authorities are the Lichtenberg Group, a few British upper-crust relatives of Richard Percy, and several multi-billionaires from various countries, mostly America. The man at the head of the table is Heinrich Klatch, who is also the president of the World Progressive Socialist Counsel, as you well know. He is Gunther Lichtenberg's brother-in-law through marriage and quite the nefarious character in his own right... I would say Interlink's own potential Joseph Stalin."

"The most influential member of Interlink rarely comes out of the shadows, but he is the true policy director through Klatch. Lawrence Howe controls $22 trillion. He owns Blue Stone. When he tells people to jump, including every world leader outside of China, India, Russia, North Korea, and Iran, they ask how high... not why. A few words from him can tumble markets and political institutions. There is only a small handful of countries that even have a GDP the size of Howe's Blue Stone portfolio."

"I learned a few interesting facts from my association with Richard McNerney. Percy's real name is Ivan Volkov. He was the son of Boris Volkov, one of the original founders of the modern KGB. It's quite interesting how he managed to inject his son into British royalty to become Richard Percy, but that's a story for another time. Interlink is not going to relinquish their economic oligarchy and accept our invitation. I had hoped they would not continue the fight once we dispersed the men at the top. Unfortunately, those at the helm are going to make it a fight to the death. There isn't much they can do logistically just yet, but I learned long ago to never discount the enemy. Even when you have a vastly superior array of forces on the battlefield, there is always Murphy's Law."

"Well, we're having our own complicated problems at Guantánamo Bay," Charlie Barton responded. The world and its politics are so disheveled at this point since you guys at Lightning have decimated the power structure everywhere. No one seems to want to participate in adjudicating all the people we are housing at Gitmo, even the sexual perverts who are pedophiles. It is such a mess no one wants to be part of the litigation. You can't bring people to trial if you can't find jurors. This is not in a domestic province or county in America where jury duty is compulsory. It is really a conundrum, especially because of the volume of offenders. We can impanel a tribunal of judges, but it would smack of authoritarianism, something we want to avoid because that is what we've been tearing down for the past few years. Who would have ever believed we would have thousands of them? They are all perverts who need to be locked up so they can't destroy any more children."

"How are the pre-trials proceeding for the politicians who have taken Graft and committed treason?" Asked the President.

Charlie Barton shook his head, sighing, "It's an issue unto itself. We're embroiled in that mess with no end in sight, and the media is crucifying us. Here's the problem. Innocent until proven guilty is the underlying theme of the American justice system. When it was created by the founders, I can't imagine they ever envisioned a can of worms like this. In those days, you could count criminals on the fingers of your hands, and justice was heavily shaded by common sense. There weren't all the ambiguous legal precedents providing avenues of escape from justice existing today. Excuse the analogy, but it's like trying to climb a pole covered with Vaseline. It's difficult just getting through the day sometimes, and my prosecutors have a million questions for me. Anybody have any suggestions?" he asked, eyeing Iggy. "I mean, you seem to be the answer man who comes up with the original ideas."

Iggy shook his head. "I have some answers, of course, but you may not like them. I saw this coming and knew we would arrive at this juncture. We have several thousand criminals, who we know are guilty, but still must eventually be afforded due process. Note the word … eventually. It's supposed to be done in a timely fashion, which of course, is an impossibility, given the circumstances. We have already blanket pardoned simple grafters and are seizing their graft money and attempting to prosecute the traitors.

There are many, and it is difficult. Herein lies the problem. We have over 3000 perverts who have molested children, many who are not citizens of the United States. They cannot be released into society again without punishment because they will repeat the offense. This is human nature, gentlemen; they are recidivists, and there is no doubt. The traitors, one way or the other, are going to suffer the slings and arrows of their own treason. They and their families will suffer. You simply cannot pardon them as if nothing ever happened."

"I think the department can handle the graft takers and the traitors. What, however, are we going to do with over 3000 perverts? Like I said, we can't find juries because it's so prolific. I'd love to hear your solution, Iggy, even if I don't like it."

"I'd like to hear it too," requested the President. "I am at a loss. Since the day I saw the holograms, the stature of the perpetrators, and the extent of the depravity, I knew we were in for a hell of a problem. I wrestled with this for months trying to come up with a solution, to no avail. What say you, Iggy?"

"As I said, this juncture was inevitable. We have two choices. Reality is always the final arbiter. The guilt of these people is not conjecture. The holograms are explicit, and there is no doubt. Yes, it's a form of entrapment and against the codicils of jurisprudence as they were set up by the founders and incorporated into our judicial structure, as well as case law and precedent. However, the founders or the predecessors of our modern-day jurisprudence had absolutely no idea we would be witness to the destruction of thousands of children by thousands of perverts. Had they understood the dilemma back then, I'm sure they would've constructed provisions to deal with this sort of depravity. They didn't, of course, so we are on our own, here. We are either going to return them, unpunished, to society and deal with them individually in the future as they ruin more children, which is a guarantee, or we are going to act decisively now for the sake of their future victims."

"Well," interrupted Abe Morris. "What would you call acting decisively?"

"I would call this decisive. Many of you are already aware of this concept, but unaware Lightning Inc. has purchased an island in the middle of the Pacific Ocean. We have built several thousand structures and equipped them with basics. They are small and without amenities. Each one is sufficient for one or two people, depending on the choice of the felons. They are criminals who have destroyed children, or at least attempted to, without compassion or hesitation. These disgusting creatures do not belong in society with children. Many of them belong to NAMBLA. They are not just driven by lust; they are mentally ill and attempt to justify their depravity and the emotional destruction of children as accepted and normal behavior. You all know what happens when I touch you." Iggy said, looking at the Surgeon General, in particular. "There is a mental commune, and we see into each other. When I do this with these children, the damage, and repercussions evident from their molestation are enormous. They are irrevocably harmed unless my daughter or I intervene. They will never have a consistent and reasonable life after the trauma. Consequently, I hold no compassion or pity for these sick adults and don't believe they can be therapeutically rehabilitated. They must be ostracized from society and children. They created the problem for themselves, and it is their just dessert."

No one responded immediately. Everyone at the table knew Iggy Marcus was right. They also realized this was an abrogation of the Constitution and jurisprudence. No one, however, could see an alternative to Iggy Marcus's plan to deposit these people in the middle of the Pacific.

Charlie Barton was skeptical. "When you say you have built thousands of structures to house a lot of felons, what exactly are you saying? What kind of services do you expect to make available to them? I'm referring to medicine, food, and all the necessities of life. I'm making no demands, but I would prefer an answer. After all, we attempt to be humane when we incarcerate felons or even house animals for that matter."

"That's up to you, gentlemen. If it is left to me, they will be given only the basics, garden tools, seeds, and other assorted utensils befitting basic survival. In effect, I am describing a prison. However, it is a prison that doesn't require any maintenance, guards, or basketball courts for prisoners' amusement. For what they have done to children, they deserve solitary confinement at the very least. On this island, they will have to learn how to sustain themselves, probably for the first time in their lives for many. They will not have society to bilk for sustenance."

"That's what they've been doing, fleecing the world to acquire wealth and opulence. You may want to give them a certain level of luxury. I never would under any circumstances. Then, they would live with others of their own kind. It should be an interesting spectacle. Some of you have been involved in what I call **unlocking.** I mentioned this a few moments ago. It occurs when I create a mental, subliminal bridge between myself and the injured child. If you perceived the depth of trauma and torture inflicted on them for the sake of someone's putrid lust, you would agree with me."

"As far as medicine is concerned, a channel for communication can remain open, and serious illness or injury can be dealt with immediately. Our technology allows instant travel at little cost. They will be on their own as far as common colds and minor illnesses go. Most of the world is on its own with these problems, anyway. No matter how you look at it, it will be the lowest-cost prison to operate since the French penal colony, "Devil's Island."

William Sledge looked around the table at the group he had asked to attend this meeting. He looked at facial expressions to read between the lines as to how they really felt about this proposal. I'd like to know where you all stand before I make the decision. At this point, the only people who I know agree with Iggy are his girls. I need your input. Maybe you can get a better explanation from him on how this prison will work."

"I am not the authority here. I have not been elected to office, so I don't represent a constituency. I have no right or intent to decree anything. I have given you a viable alternative to conducting years and years of trials, ad infinitum, held up in the courts by clever lawyers attempting to get their perverted clients off. It comes down to this. We either endure the years of horrific trials, or we have the island, perhaps a combination of both. The choice is yours, gentlemen. I have made my choice and can enable either. You men are the captains of this ship of state. I'm only a passenger... but I have my own agenda, and you will either somehow deliver that agenda through adjudication, or I will simply remove the perpetrators from society and deposit them on the island before they are released to continue their perverse lives. I am giving no choices to pedophiles. One of my sister's law students described this potential action as my personal God complex, just like our adversaries. So be it. We will watch no more children destroyed. End of story."

No one spoke. There was no easy answer to the dilemma. They reflected on the American Constitution and jurisprudence. Everyone was innocent until proven guilty. It was an American concept underpinning freedom. Most other countries tried people to prove innocence from assumed guilt. Presumed innocence was fine in the days when the courts acted as a crucible to burn away irrelevancies until it was left with a pure product, the truth. Now, common sense and reality often become a matter of opinion. Everybody has one, and no one cares for reality when it torpedoes their opinions. This was a difficult decision for the group.

"I opt for the island, spouted Alice Sledge."

"Me too added Melanie," smiling.

Allison MacLeod, the newcomer, silently waited to hear everyone's opinion.

Bill Sledge turned to his Surgeon General. "What do you think, Allison?

"My personal opinion? I'm surprised you have to ask, Bill. Anyone who harms children in any way is mentally deranged permanently or temporarily. That's axiomatic. Then, it's a matter of determining degree and type. There are many ways to harm children. Often it is inadvertent. Accidents are accidents, and occasionally adults have problems, like extreme stresses manifesting themselves in less than excellent treatment of children. Those problems come up in life. I don't believe we can punish people in the extreme for accidents or reacting to stresses propagating the injury. It depends on the degree of injury and the circumstances. That being said, however, what I'm referring to has nothing to do with sexuality. Sexual abuse of children is purely volitional and cannot be condoned because of circumstances. Sorry about the lengthy reply, but I am a doctor and always qualify myself. I say send them to the island!"

Gloria's humor kicked in, as usual. After 6 months of unlocking traumatized children, she had no pity. "I guess this is girls' night out…huh. I say, the island… and that's too good for the bums. Some of them might even enjoy it as a tropical retreat instead of the solitary confinement they so richly deserve."

Iggy laughed. "The ladies have it! Thanks, girls. Wise choice." He looked at the men seated at the table. None of them wanted to undermine American judicial tradition with a blanket decision to send 3000 pedophiles to a possible South Pacific Devil's Island.

Bill Sledge felt it was time for his Presidential contribution. "Done. You'll get no argument from me, but I can promise the press is going to explode all over us. We had better get ready for the onslaught."

"You can say that again," reflected Abe Morris. "Did you see the people in the holograms? It's unbelievable. Some of these people are more than just a little notorious. Some of them are religious figures, some are captains of industry, and some are politicians, media, and television icons with families! Holy smokes, what a mess this is going to make. I like the island idea, but I don't see how we are going to sell this to the American public when they find out who was on the list. They already suspect some of this because our prospective jailbirds have been sequestered and missing in action for weeks now. Nobody knows where they are, and the press had assigned them to the missing persons list. This is a hell of a mess, Bill."

All heads swiveled to Iggy. He was the answer man. They were in uncharted territory. Nothing like this had ever happened in America. The first few hundred notorious figures, with many more yet to come, had been arrested for pedophilia, and in some cases, torture, and murder. They all felt they had swallowed lead balls as they contemplated what was coming. To a man, they understood it had to be done. Pres. Bill Sledge's scowl illustrated his feelings about Iggy's solution. "You sure know how to ruin a party, Iggy Marcus. You don't leave us much choice."

"Well, gentlemen, I don't enjoy raining on your parade. You're all going to have to buck up and prepare yourself for this because the press will go insane trying to slap you around. Iggy laughed. This isn't new territory for you, Bill. You've made this kind of choice before. You did it in the observatory when you first opted to get involved. Unfortunately, you're stuck with it again. These are your choices, walk away and ignore the whole thing or endure the deluge when the perverts get what's coming to them."

"Yeah, I know, Iggy Marcus… I know." Pres. William Sledge sighed. The other men at the table looked at him without envy. They were all involved and were going to be part of the onslaught, but the buck didn't stop with them. It stopped with the man sitting at the head of the table, William James Sledge.

"So where to next, Bill?" I'm glad I'm only the vice president, and the decisions are yours in the end."

"The island it is. We're going to have to determine how these people are going to be brought to trial. The crimes are of such an individual nature they can't be tried together. They'll just have to live on the island until we get around to it. What do you think, Charlie?"

"I don't like any of this because it's such a stretch. We have our duty. Right and wrong are clearly discernible here. These people are monsters and need to be held accountable. I think society is going to have a hell of a bad time with so many notorious icons who are pedophiles. Unfortunately, we cannot broadcast the actual holography. It is so perverse, disgusting, and explicit it cannot be released to the public. I think they're going to have the most difficulty with the religious figures. There are quite a few of them and many people admire them as paragons of virtue. They will have to abandon their faith in these icons to admit and accept the truth. The more I think about it, the more I realize how difficult this is going to be. How are we going to get them to this island? A cruise ship? That would be over the top. What would we call it, *ship of fools*?"

Everyone chuckled even though there was really nothing laughable about any of this. Gloria couldn't resist. "What's wrong with *the love boat?*

That works." She said with her usual whimsy, refreshing everybody's mood with levity. "What do you think, Dad?"

Gloria's clever sarcasm always brought a smile to her parents. "I think I will ferry them all there with our ships. It won't take long, and there will be no fanfare. Then it's going to be up to you to design judicial procedure as the attorney general. We have a very strong ally in the court if we need him. Now, the next item on the agenda is Interlink and what we are expecting from them."

Lori and Liam were almost 4 years old. They were prime examples of the maxim *children should be seen and not heard,* as they sat at the table silently observing everything. "How do you manage to get them to be so well-behaved, Melanie?" Inquired Alice Sledge.

Everyone's attention immediately focused on the twins as Lori turned to the buffet table again, precipitating everyone's laughter, when her own cinnamon kruller rose from the platter, floated across the balcony, and plopped into her hand.

"Oh my!" exclaimed Alice Sledge laughing. "I hope when you engineered my ova you didn't give them those kinds of factory options."

Gloria admonished her sister subliminally to refrain from calling attention to her abilities, as everyone expressed uneasy laughter. They understood the children were gifted but it still made them somewhat uncomfortable, especially the mind-reading. Iggy turned to the president attempting to lead the conversation elsewhere. "Where did we leave off, Bill?"

"So, to get back on point, what actually do you expect from Interlink, Iggy?" Returned Bill Sledge.

"I'm not sure yet. There have been several attempted assaults on our food distribution centers and medical clinics. No one can breach the shield technology, and if people were to somehow get themselves into the clinics as shills, there would be nothing they could access. It is virtually impossible by design. There was no way I could refuse to help the sick and dying now that this technology has become public information. The entire organized medical world is having a hissy fit over what we are doing because we haven't asked their permission or involved them, but it will eventually dissipate as the volume of people with terminal cancer diminishes to nothing. There won't be anything left to complain about."

"You still haven't answered my question, Iggy." Bill Sledge persisted.

"Okay then, you all know of Heinrich Klatch. He's Gunther Lichtenberg's brother-in-law. He was the intellectual giant behind Lichtenberg. He stayed in the background, almost never at Interlink meetings, but both Rothman and Lichtenberg relied on his genius for analysis. He rarely gets it wrong. Crenshaw was the front intellect, but Klatch was always their core intellect. He never attended meetings except when circumstances were extreme, and then he remained in the background, observing and advising the few top people after the formal meeting."

"I wondered why we haven't heard from him, Iggy," responded the President. "He's head of the World Progressive Socialist Council." They are avowed socialists who rarely come out of the closet. They push their agenda outside of public scrutiny. Of course, Interlink owns all the media, so they don't have to worry too much about scrutiny. The only place I've ever seen the mentioned is in American Media publications."

"Well, they're out of the closet now, Bill. Apparently, he's infuriated over his brother-in-law, Gunther's incarceration at Guantánamo Bay. Word gets around, and he has sworn to kill me with his own hands," Iggy laughed.

Gloria's humor surfaced again. "As I understand it, Heinrich Klatch is a relatively old man in his early eighties, Dad. It would be no contest. You'll skate circles around him, and since Oniella Kenji is teaching you how to pulverize cement blocks, I think he's got a problem."

Everyone laughed, but it was subdued. Apparently, just as Iggy and described, Interlink was rising from the ashes. It was comprised of thousands of members, all the most influential economic powers on the planet outside of China and India. Iggy had been warning them this group of people were not going to submit. They would go down swinging because they believed the power to rule was their birthright. Iggy Marcus had stolen their birthright. He ripped it out from under them and left them with nothing.

Historically, war was their tool. They used it like a hammer to pound malleable governments and societies into shape so they could be used to garner specific results, all while manufacturing and supplying both sides with weapons at an enormous profit. Then they were paid tremendous sums rebuilding infrastructure so they could blow it up again in another pointless war. Morality was never an issue. Right and wrong did not exist. Results lay with the bottom line, and nothing was an obstacle to the murder of many millions, as tyrants brought them to their knees. One man had effectively stolen their greatest weapon. War was no longer possible. Had he been of their stripe, they would all be on their knees to the new tyrant with godlike powers of technology beyond anything men had ever conceived.

"Well, Iggy Marcus," said Charlie Barton. "We are living in turbulent times even though nuclear war has been eliminated. The things you have done are nothing short of miraculous, but it seems most people just can't get off their childish duffs. Remaking the world sounds good in theory, but it sure is a hell of a lot more complex than it meets the eye. I guess we just have to keep plugging. I'll keep my end up. Where do we go from here, and what do you think Interlink will concoct?"

"You just stole my thunder, Charlie," said the President. "Where do you think we're going to go from here, Iggy?"

"There is the elephant in the room that I wasn't going to mention. The only person aware of this is the President, but I will share this with you all now. I have been communicating with people, if you can call them that, who are from a small star not too different from our sun, located approximately 80,000 light years from here on the other side of the galaxy. They call themselves shepherds, and supposedly my actions are critical to their purposes."

Bill Sledge was surprised he had just divulged that. No one else said a word. They had all contemplated the possibility of extraterrestrial life but never paid much attention to their own thoughts because it did not affect their daily routine. They were being told the truth by a man who would never lie. Curtis Mulroney was a religious, principled man who didn't quite believe in life on other worlds. He was surprised but was the first to speak. He addressed Iggy formally. "Mr. Marcus, I don't mean to be flippant or insulting, but exactly what purpose do they have, why the hell are you so critical to them, and what do they want from us?"

"It would be difficult to describe to you, Curt. Let me put it this way. I should be a dead man, and I should've been dead 25 years ago. I was hit by lightning, and a million volts blasted the skin off my head and inflicted third-degree burns from head to toe. According to Dr. David Peterson, I should never have survived the strike. Despite that, I did, and it should have taken me the better part of 4 years to completely heal after multiple plastic surgeries repaired the damage with skin transplants."

Everyone was spellbound, riveted by Iggy's description as he continued. Even Bill Sledge hadn't heard the full story… only casual mentions.

"I left the hospital three weeks after I was carried in, burnt to a crisp. I was fully healed, and to this day, no one has a good medical explanation. Along with my physical ability to rapidly heal came an elevated intellect. My IQ, if it were measurable after 25 years, exists somewhere over a thousand. There really are no tests like Weschler Bellevue to establish that." He spent nearly an hour relating all the strange things that happened to him in the hospital and afterward since the lightning strike."

Iggy rarely described this to people. He would never intentionally deprecate or intimidate another to elevate his stature. "It's the reason for my ability to create all the technological wonders. I have been able to determine what anomalies and coincidences allowed me to survive the trauma. I fully understand the pathology. Still, however, the odds of me surviving that lightning strike were a billion to one." Iggy paused for a minute contemplating the past 25 years.

Open-mouthed, they listened to one of the strangest stories ever told. "Go on." Said Charlie Barton. "Don't stop. This is fascinating."

Iggy continued, "It took quite a while, years in fact before I fully understood the depth of what had happened to me intellectually and physically. What I didn't realize was *why* this happened to me. Nonetheless, I came to believe these were gifts, not a coincidence… and they obligated me. You see, I have no choice. I have a purpose I cannot escape. At first, I believed I had chosen the mission, but soon after Gloria was born, inheriting everything I had been given and much more, I realized this is not a coincidence. I now see things about existence I had never understood in my former life. We have a job to do. Occasionally, this is the way the universe operates. Not often, mind you, but sometimes. In other words, the mission has chosen us."

Curtis Mulroney silently contemplated the amazing possibilities. This one man had just saved the world from nuclear holocaust, then sent emissaries around the world with food and cures for terminal illnesses. He had done these incredible things while the most powerful people in the world had arrogantly tried to kill him. The world was changing dramatically, and it was changing without bloodshed. He said a silent prayer of thanks, thinking about his three kids and the bright future now in store for them because of the man sitting in front of him.

***

Tom Rickart's sword was a blur as he sliced through the banana and watched the almost equal halves hit the ground.

"Not bad!" Blurted Oniella Kenji, bent over laughing. 'That's a pretty good first try. I'm amazed. Most people have to try 50 times before they do as well, and even hit the banana." She continued laughing. "The 2 halves are almost perfect, except you are supposed to split it lengthwise, not across the length."

Tom laughed. "I did it on purpose," he joked. "I haven't had lunch yet, and I figured to eat the banana." He scooped the two halves off the ground and held half the banana out to Oniella. "Hungry?"

"Nope. I never eat the victim. Let's pick up the bamboo swords and work on combat techniques. That's where you really must develop yourself.

Most of the time, the enemy will be larger than a banana, and there will be plenty of targets on the body. What you really must master is the art of the samurai. Fighting with samurai swords is not like most other weapons. The first large mistake usually ends in a fatality. So that's where we will go first, defense. Then, once we begin to master defense," she laughed, "we can kill all kinds of fruit and vegetables.

"Okay then, Master Kenji, let's go." They fought for almost 15 minutes. Tom Rickert already had training but wasn't even close to the expertise of his teacher. Oniella Kenji barked orders of advice to him as they fought. She was a master swordswoman, and Tom had a lot to learn. She landed blow after blow while defending against Tom's attacks. Her technique and progression from one move to the next was a logical order of events, slowly imparting the entire learning experience to her student. Each move was a learning event and progression to the next move. Tom was brilliant and a quick learner.

Master Kenji introduced Tom Rickert to the techniques and philosophy of iaido, the art of understanding and responding to a sudden attack by sword. Every move of attack or defense she taught was kendo, "the way of the sword." She called a break and nodded her head in approval. "Not bad, Tom Rickart. If you continue this way, you will be samurai in no time."

Tom was breathing heavily, but Oniela hardly broke a sweat as she laughed at Tom. He had a lot to learn. "You need to learn to breathe properly without thinking about it, Tom. That is the secret. It will give you the ability to concentrate, stay focused on your adversary's attack, and of course, give you the stamina to win."

"I can see that, Admiral Kenji. You're hardly out of breath at all, and I'm panting like I just ran the marathon."

"You will learn in time, Tom. Tell me, what actually made you want to devote this much time to the lost art of samurai? Considering your age and position in life, coupled with the already substantial martial arts training you have, wouldn't it be easier just to shoot your adversary?"

"That's a no-brainer, Admiral. I remember the day Gen. Hammond and his group of conspirators decided to attack Lightning Ranch with the brigades of special forces. We had most of the bases covered but not all of them. Things could have gone badly. If it wasn't for you, they very well may have. I watched you move, and you were a symphony of grace, style, and probably the deadliest human being in hand-to-hand combat living. No wonder Adm. Bigelow was impressed."

Adm. Kenji laughed. "I guess you heard the story then."

Tom nodded his head. "Everybody at Lightning has. Hell, we all watched you turn cement blocks into talcum powder. I have never seen anybody, anywhere, who could come close to that. My philosophy is, if you want to learn something, find the best teacher. That's you. Your amazing reputation precedes you, wherever you go, and it was the smartest thing Pres. Sledge ever did when he insisted you be promoted to rear admiral."

It was time for roadwork. Both started their 20-mile, two-hour run. They ran in silence. Tom played the entire military attack by the joint Chiefs on Lightning Ranch in his mind as they ran. That fateful day, Pres. William James Sledge and Iggy Marcus captured them all without a single death. It had been a close one, full of surprises, but in the end, very little harm was done, thanks in no small part to the gladiator running next to him.

***

As Iggy's chief of security, he oversaw the operation and the deployment of 64 men on the day of the invasion, all former Navy SEALs, and special forces security. He remembered the day precisely, even the commands given, verbatim. Richard McNerney and Lucky were in the control room. The doors were locked, and they lowered the ranch defense shield according to plan. Eight sky cranes, each loaded with 125 combat-ready troops, vehicles, and artillery were airborne. The battalion of men who had been assigned the job to enter Lightning Ranch and assume control were on the way.

The troops had been notified of intent. They supposedly had been trained for this special mission. Their instructions were that no civilians were to be injured under any circumstances other than in self-defense. They were told wet fire was only appropriate if they were fired upon. They were all reassured the occupants of the ranch would be asleep from a sleep aerosol. They were given standard-issue gas masks.

Richard McNerney designed the logistics for the invasion of Lightning Ranch in detail with General Carlisle Hammond. They were to send 8 helicopters, 4 Chinooks, and 4 King stallions carrying a brigade of a thousand men and equipment to subdue the occupants of the ranch. This would follow 8 missiles launched with sleep aerosols.

Maj. Gen. Richard McNerney spent his combat years as chief strategist for the United States Army. He directed the deployment of overseas forces in the European and Middle Eastern theaters, both men and equipment, for every war outside the continental United States for 22 years. His peers considered him the most effective strategist and knowledgeable officer in the Army, second to none.

Unknown to his peers, Richard McNerney spent his US army career as a Soviet double agent inserted in America when he was twelve, after World War II during the Korean conflict. He was one of 500 KGB plants specifically assigned as spies to infiltrate every aspect of government and industry in the United States. He was among the KGB's top efforts. Interlink had compromised his double agent status when they used his position as a spy, in the attempt to destroy Lightning Ranch and Iggy Marcus.

It is often said the best-laid plans of mice and men often go awry. Interlink subjected Richard McNerney to 2 weeks of drug-induced, psychological torture and indoctrination. Interlink's chief strategist, Chess Master, Vladimir Borenko, engineered the plot designed to end the existence of Lightning Inc., Ignatius Marcus Junior, and Pres. William James Sledge. There were 5 components to the attempt at Marcus's destruction. If all else failed, Richard McNerney was brainwashed to put a 45-caliber slug in Iggy Marcus's head. Borenko's ten-man team of doctors had created their Manchurian candidate. They couldn't possibly foresee Iggy Marcus and his telepath daughter's ability to enter McNerney's subconscious mind and neutralize the indoctrination.

Under most normal circumstances, the level of indoctrination and drugs Richard McNerney had been subjected to would eventually end in insanity and suicide. No one understood the ability of Marcus and his daughter to mitigate psychological trauma. Ultimately, Richard McNerney was saved from the abyss of insanity, inspiring his dedication to the man he was sent to destroy.

Richard McNerney swore allegiance to the man who released him from the years of torture as a Russian indoctrinated spy and became a shill to aid his benefactor. The top military men of the joint Chiefs invited Richard McNerney to accompany them and help design the strategy in their intent to overthrow the government of the United States. They offered the excuse that Iggy Marcus had destroyed America's ability to launch nuclear weapons at other countries. The fact other countries couldn't launch weapons towards America didn't seem to matter to these men. Their reason for living, their careers, and everything they had spent their life accomplishing became meaningless after one man tossed the possibility of war out the window forever.

Of course, they all made excuses when they convinced themselves and each other there were no guarantees the other countries would lose the ability to launch nuclear weapons. Therefore, the United States' ability to defend itself with nuclear weapons under the doctrine of Mutual Assured Destruction could not be removed from the table. There was also the outside chance Marcus wanted to set himself up as a dictator.

Misplaced patriotism, bordering on psychotic megalomania, drove three generals, two admirals, and several colonels under General Carlisle Hammond's leadership and command to hijack the ship of state from the current administration. None of them would admit the truth to themselves or each other. Their reason for existence had just been neutralized, and their lives had become pointless. This was too difficult a pill to swallow after a lifetime of dedicated service to war. Men of the mindset that glorified war should never hold the reins of power. Yet history was replete with the arrogant egotism of such men as the driving force beneath tyranny and all the death and destruction since men began killing each other for dominance.

Thanks to Iggy Marcus and his daughter, Richard McNerney took a long hard look at his life, all the way back to his birth and every single moment of his existence since. His merging with Gloria and Iggy opened his vision to all their personalities and subconscious minds. He saw every strength, every insecurity, and every weakness comprising his persona. This internal view of oneself would be a death sentence to a weak mind steeped in cowardice. To others with strength of character, this would be a release from the bondage of fear that surrounded every man's subconscious mind. Such was Richard McNerney's epiphany.

His military career as a strategist exposed the motive and consequences of General Carlisle Hammond's desire to overthrow the civilian government. Hammond was popular, well-spoken, highly decorated, and never given to controversy. He exuded trustworthiness as a public figure and a military man. On the other hand, William James Sledge and his administration had been mercilessly assaulted by the Interlink-owned media for more than two years. Even with the contradictory press benefits from American Media Inc., his public image suffered.

Four Generals and one Admiral believed the time was now, and it was their duty to set things right in America. They convinced themselves the man, Iggy Marcus, who supposedly ended war forever, had compromised the president and his people, then set himself on a personal path of conquest.

Richard McNerney offered his best strategic advice to Carlisle Hammond after weeks of planning the assault on Lightning Ranch. McNerney was a good enough judge of character to know Gen. Hamilton could not be persuaded from his folly.

It was settled. There would be 8 super choppers with a thousand men and assorted equipment for the raid. Sleep aerosol would be dispersed to minimize casualties. Carlisle Hammond did not arrive at his position of chairman of the Joint Chiefs because he was a fool. He understood there might be mixed loyalties with Gen. McNerney. He didn't think so, but the possibility existed. So, he had a few tricks up his sleeve he wouldn't share with newly promoted Lieut. Gen. McNerney. Everything would proceed as planned and discussed between them. What Carlisle didn't tell McNerney was

8 more super choppers with another brigade of men and equipment would travel together in the "stack" with the others. The assault force would be doubled, and the stack would obscure high-altitude radar defining the extra choppers.

Tom Rickart left Lucky, and Richard McNerney locked in the control room and ran down the steps to join Oniella Kenji. "This should all happen pretty quickly now, Oniella. Lucky and Richard are in the control room and General McNerney's is in constant communication with General Hammond. He mapped out the entry points for the choppers so I could disperse my men. I figure it's going to be about 20 minutes before the choppers are here and 12 to 15 minutes before the sleep aerosol missiles arrive. "

Oniella Kenji nodded her head. "What if it's not sleep aerosol, and it is something deadly. What happens, then? I mean, everyone has gas masks just in case, even though you said you had another way to deal with this."

"Yeah," Tom responded. "Lucky and Iggy are running the show on this one, using a few of our personnel with shields and our satellites backing them up as redundancy. As soon as the missiles enter ranch airspace, we will encapsulate them. We'll see them but we won't hear them when they explode, and whatever chemical they are carrying will be contained. Our people will then take them to a safe place on the ranch for later assessment and destruction."

Tom Rickert's wristwatch sounded a continuous alarm. "What's up, boss? Something urgent is happening or you would have beeped me on intermittent."

"Yup, Tom. I just talked to Richard. Obviously, he and General Hammond only planned part of this fiasco together. There's a fly in the ointment and Carlisle Hammond is a sneaky guy." Iggy laughed. "You know the 8 choppers with a brigade of men headed this way?"

Tom Rickert waited for him to finish. "Yeah, go on, Iggy. What's happening? Obviously, there's some surprise."

"Yeah, Tom, and it's a pretty big one." Tom remained silent, waiting. "It was supposed to be eight super choppers with a brigade of men following the sleep aerosol missiles. Well, there are 16 super choppers, and they were stacked on top of each other so the radar wouldn't detect them. They are almost here. They split up 45 seconds ago. Apparently, there will be 16 compass point entries, not just eight. The missiles are due to cross the ranch borders in less than a minute. We are ready for them… they won't be a problem, but we have a bigger problem."

"Yeah, boss, I get it. We only have 64 men. That's enough to handle the encapsulation of the missiles, encapsulation of a 1000-man brigade, the choppers, and related military equipment at 8 compass points. We're going to have a hell of a problem with the other 8 compass points. I think we underestimated Hammond. Okay, signing off! As soon as you project the 8 additional landing places, give me ranch coordinates on the grid! I've gotta start talking to my men, subito!

Tom Rickart spent the next 3 minutes barking orders to his men, prepping them to split up and move to additional locations to intercept the 8 additional choppers. He could hear 8 sonic booms from the missiles breaking the sound barrier as they entered ranch airspace. Then there was silence. Evidently, they had been encapsulated. So far, so good, Tom Rickart reflected. Tom's watch beeped as the crystal came alive. Excellent, he thought. Iggy 's got all the drones up. The crystal was too small for an accurate view. He made a few adjustments, and all the drone's camera views were projected in holograms directly in front of him. He and Oniella Kenji simultaneously saw everything happening everywhere on the ranch.

"Crap, Tom. Look at this jazz. All 16 of them are evenly distributed around the ranch. We don't have enough men! The choppers landing at the foot of the mountains won't be an immediate problem, but there's an additional four landing near the populated areas. I have to get the hell out of here, Tom, said Oniella, as she eyed two horses grazing nearby. "Quick, Tom. Got a piece of rope? Or give me your belt."

Tom watched, fascinated, as she pulled her shirt off, and he handed her his belt. "Nice bra," Tom chuckled, wondering what she was going to do with his belt and her shirt.

"Shut up Tom Rickart. You're spoken for… a married man and not supposed to be making comments like that," she shot over her shoulder, laughing, as she took off at a run.

He was about to ask her what she was doing, but she was running toward the horses. She slowed to a walk as she approached them. Time was of the essence, and she couldn't afford to spook either horse. She walked to them slowly, speaking softly as she reached up and scratched the mare behind the ears. The mare nuzzled her and licked her face as she fashioned a crude halter and reins out of Tom's belt and her shirt. Two minutes later, she was on the horse, bareback, holding onto her shirt. The belt was wrapped around the horse's muzzle with the shirt sleeves tied to it in knots on either side of the mouth; hunched forward, she launched herself at a gallop, with a samurai sword swinging at her side, toward God only knows where.

Tom continued barking orders to his men. He had to rearrange the entire battlefield. Everything was different now, and nothing was going according to plan. There were twice as many men and twice as much equipment. Somehow, 64 Navy SEALs had to encapsulate 2000 men who were spreading out. It was a hell of a problem. Tom gave Carlisle Hammond the credit he was due. He was a smart SOB. The 2nd ghost assault team was given different orders than the first team. They were trained to disperse and put at least 100 feet between each other as soon as they hit the ground.

Tom was itching to get into the fray, personally, but he knew better. Someone had to coordinate this, and it was his job. He couldn't afford to be distracted as he watched 2 dozen holograms projected in the air surrounding him. He shook his head in amazement at this technology. Iggy Marcus was beyond genius. It was like he was sitting in a movie theater, watching three-dimensional troop disbursement. He began calling individual men by name and rearranging small battle groups.

"Listen up, everybody! We've got another thousand men here who we haven't planned on. You are going to have to handle them. I'm calling out names. As I call them out, assemble in groups of 3. Your shields have a 30-meter radius. That's about 200 feet in diameter. You're going to have to use your own judgment on this, men. I'm watching each skirmish via the drones. I'll give you your group destinations. Use your dirt bikes. You all should have them. When you get to a heavily populated area, the three-man team will split up and spread about 350 feet apart, then encapsulate as many men as possible. All of you have been trained to keep yourself protected within a secondary shield. Do it!"

"Iggy here, Tom. I've got 100 older students on their way and several other ranch personnel: 150 in all. I've given them specific instructions. When your men encapsulate the troops, the additional help will have to confiscate their weapons and equipment. That's going to require a lot of coordination with the shields, but your men have been well-trained. I'm sure you'll pull it off."

"Got it, boss. We'll get them. What are you doing?"

"Believe it or not, Bill Sledge and I both have shields, and we are in the fray by the power plant. One chopper landed close to there. Bill is having the best luck. As soon as the troops recognize he is the President, he gives them orders to cease-and-desist. They are all laying down their weapons immediately. Only a couple of the officers are resisting. They must be part of the conspiracy. So, we're cleaning up this group quickly. I'm sure none of the soldiers have a clue they are being used to overthrow the government of the United States. Like almost every soldier throughout history, they are pawns."

Tom shook his head. "Have you seen Oniella Kenji? She took off on a horse with a samurai sword 10 minutes ago. I hope she's not lopping heads off."

Iggy laughed. "Yeah, Tom. I'm sure you're looking at the ranch grid. How many holograms have you got going?"

The stress and Tom Rickert's voice was obvious. "About 30, boss. I'm trying to coordinate this whole thing."

"Go to Southwest, grid coordinates 42 and 16. Take a look if you want to have a good laugh. She asked me to make her a scabbard from Iggy Glass about 6 months ago. You can't tell her sword is even sheathed from a distance. She's using it with the Iggy glass scabbard on it. It's hilarious."

"I'm glad you see the humor in all this, boss. I've been just about piddling my pants since you told me about the extra 8 choppers."

Tom Rickert opened grid 42 SW., and sure enough, there she was. She was alone in the middle of 125 men, give or take. Tom muttered to himself, "I have to take my hat off to that woman. No wonder Adm. Bigelow was impressed." He was watching the bizarre sight of a woman with a samurai sword, tight black pants, and a black lace bra, moving so fast you could hardly follow her. She seemed to be everywhere. She did leaps and somersaults like Tom Junior popped M&Ms. She was using her sword with the Iggy glass scabbard as a club. Of about 125 men, at least 75 of them were on the ground, unconscious. They had no idea what was happening to them as this tornado of a woman swept through them, teaching them *the samurai way of the sword.*

Tom punched Iggy's face up on his watch bezel. "I see what you mean, boss. She's going to teach me the sword, but she's from a different world, that girl. I've never seen anything like her in my life. Her father must've been something. It kinda looks like she's going to have all 125 men under control by her lonesome. Pretty damned amazing! When she clobbers them all, I'll bet she encapsulates them. We've still got a hell of a lot of problems, Iggy. There are men spread out all over this ranch now, and my guys are having a hard time taking care of all of them. This is going to take a while."

"Yeah, Tom. But we'll get it. We are superior in every way, men, motive, and equipment. It's just a matter of time. Hopefully, nobody gets hurt. It's not anybody's fault except the clowns at the top who created this problem. None of the soldiers can be held responsible. All the students are headed up to the gardens. There are 125 soldiers encapsulated there. We're going to have to move them all to the flight line, including the equipment and the aircraft. It's going to take quite a bit of time. The kids are collecting all the weapons. They're putting them in our concrete lockup.

"Sounds good, Iggy. Leave a few kids down there on guard duty." Tom continued laughing as he watched Oniella Kenji wrap zip ties around the wrists of the last of the 125-man strike team.

"What's so funny, Tom?"

"Oniella Kenji. She just knocked out 125 men with weapons in full battle gear. Now she's wrapping zip ties around their wrists. If I hadn't seen it for myself, I would never have believed it. I have half a mind to call off the 64 Seals and just send her out after these guys. That woman is anybody's worst nightmare in a fight… unless, of course, she's on your side. They must have brought their own zip ties to use on us. She managed it all and never lost her bra. You gotta love it!"

"Two choppers landed at the foot of the mountains near the caverns where we hide everything. They spread out and are advancing towards the buildings and main gate. There's at least 250, maybe 300 of them and they are so spread out the men won't be able to encapsulate them all. They still have their hands too full with the rest of the invasion force. Take your bike out there, Tom. You can map out the coordinates for the ranch shield. We must collect all these men now and end this before someone becomes seriously injured. The longer this continues, the greater the odds are of this happening. The soldiers have no idea why they're here, and it would be a shame for even one of them to be injured on domestic soil executing a combat mission."

"Yes, Richard said their orders came down from the highest authority. They've all been told everyone here on this farm is guilty of conspiracy and collusion to overthrow the government, right out of the Joseph Goebbels's handbook, advising conspirators to accuse the other side of exactly what they are doing."

Tom started laughing hysterically. "Well, I thought I'd seen everything. I've got to get a picture of this," he said as he pressed the button on his watch to record the hologram.

"What's so funny now, Tom? You were piddling your anxiety pants ten minutes ago."

"I've gotta show you this, Iggy. Words are inadequate," he said, still laughing. "You just can't possibly appreciate this without seeing it. I just watched a woman with black pants and a black lace bra swinging a samurai sword over her head gallop over the top of the hill, jump a four-rail fence, and attack a third of a battalion. Totally unbelievable!"

"Stop her, Tom. We can handle this with the ranch shield. The men are beginning to wrap everything up down near the buildings. The students are out here, and we've got trucks to transfer the men to the flight line. We have a lot of cleanup still to do."

Tom Rickert heard Pres. Sledge's voice in the background. It was quickly drowned out by the roar of his dirt bike on its way to stop Oniella Kenji.

Tom's bike skidded to a halt 20 feet from Oniella Kenji's horse. He watched her run through the trees toward a small group of soldiers. They were armed but under orders not to shoot unless attacked and it became a life and death situation. The black tight pants and lace bra certainly made it obvious to the soldiers this was a beautiful woman swinging some kind of club over her head. Her gray shield waist box was missing. Apparently, she lost it in the melee she had just left behind. Tom shook his head in disbelief. She had no shield, yet she relentlessly charged into battle. Tom opened the throttle and pulled a wheelie. He would barely catch her on time, but he wasn't worried. It wasn't likely anyone would shoot. The full feminine figure and black lace bra was sure to save her. She heard the bike and turned to see Tom screaming toward her on his rear wheel as he shifted gears.

"Hold up Oniella!" He yelled over the whine of his dirt bike. She stopped running as Tom pulled up beside her and a couple of dozen soldiers stared at a biker and a half naked woman in disbelief.

"What's up, Tom? Give me a few more minutes, and I have these characters zip tied."

"No need, Oniella. Iggy says Lucky will encapsulate them with the ranch shield. We've got drones flying all over the place, watching everything." Tom laughed heartily. "There's no need for you to clobber another hundred fifty men."

"I was just beginning to have fun, Tom! These guys are Army, and I'm Navy. It's just like the Army-Navy game every fall. I'm having a blast."

Tom wistfully eyed her torn black lace bra. "Not bad, commander. Have you any idea what a sight you are, dressed like that? I'm not sure what words are most appropriate, untamed and seductive or ferocious and erotic. Either way, you are one horse of a different color… And wow! I finally have seen you out of breath. I didn't think it was possible."

Oniella Kenji demurely blushed as she walked to the mare and grabbed her shirt from her homemade halter and pulled it over her head. She laughed, "Tom Rickart, you keep making those comments and I'm going to tell Evelyn on you."

"Well, I don't think anyone would blame me; you're like nothing I've ever seen before… I've got the whole thing on video," He muttered coyly. "Don't worry, admiral, this video will never see the light of day. I'm only pulling your leg. I am going to keep it, though, just to remind me what an unforgettable experience you really are."

200 ranch personnel and 100 of the older students assisted 64 Navy SEALs in gathering weapons and marching soldiers to the flight line. It was over. No one was dead, and there were only several minor injuries. Quite a few soldiers had headaches from the clobbering by Oniella Kenji's sword. Two hours later, 1900 soldiers and 16 giant military transport helicopters were held in captivity on the Lightning Ranch flight line. Jack Marcus arranged for buses to transport the men to Wright-Patterson Air Force Base in Ohio.

The command officers in charge of the operation had been arrested and brought aboard Daedalus. They would accompany Pres. Sledge and Iggy Marcus to Charlie Barton's Department of Justice in Washington. Some of the lower echelon officers who were not involved in the conspiracy, but simply taking orders milled around the flight line with the troops while they waited. One of them, a captain, asked Tom Rickart if the woman in the black bra was indeed, Oniella Kenji.

"The one and only," Tom replied. "She's some piece of work, isn't she?"

"I thought so. I'm Capt. Carl Knabe. I do martial arts, and I was at an exhibition at West Point where martial artists from all the different services gathered for a competition. She beat everybody. She was great. Nobody's like her, and when I saw her in action today, I knew it had to be her even though it's been several years since I saw her fight. Now I don't feel so bad about the zip tie around my wrists."

Tom laughed. "There's nothing like being beaten senseless by the best of the best."

"Well, Mr. Marcus," Bill Sledge formally addressed him, "we've just arrested 3 full bird colonels, 4 Lieut. colonels, and need to drop them off at the DOJ. Then we have to arrest 4 generals, 2 admirals, 4 more colonels and 3 commanders. Boy, is Charlie Barton ever going to have his hands full now."

"Not if any of these characters have any brains, Bill. They are being offered the ability to resign their commissions, leave the military with whatever pension they're entitled to at that stage of their service… or become arrested and face court-martial and trial for treason against the United States. Not one of them will choose option two."

Two hours later, Daedalus hovered above the street in front of Gen. Carlisle Hammond's house with two federal marshals, Iggy Marcus, Maj. Gen. Richard McNerney, and the president. William James Sledge and Iggy Marcus knocked on Gen. Hammond's door.

The door slowly swung open, illustrating the taciturn demeanor of the occupant. "Come in gentlemen. I've been expecting you. I heard the bad news 15 minutes ago you managed to shut the entire operation down and arrest everyone. Believe it or not, Richard McNerney called me with the news. He is a traitor to his country."

It was a rare moment of cynicism for Iggy Marcus. "Not quite, Gen. Hammond. Oddly enough, believe it or not, he is a true patriot of this country. Ironically, he is actually a traitor to his parent country, Russia, but you don't need to know the details. Incidentally, he is aboard Daedalus. He requested I include him on this trip. He believes he owes you that. I asked him to remain in the ship."

Gen. Hammond looked the president in the eye with contempt. "You have no idea what kind of mistake you are making Pres. Sledge. I am so disgusted it is difficult to even address you as president. You have opened the door for the man standing next you to become the ruler of the entire world. Every one of us was executing our patriotic duty to preserve this country from a tyrant."

"Don't insult my intelligence, Carlisle. We both know your motive. But instead of debating with you, because a wise man once told me reality is not debatable, only the results of choices we make are debatable, I'm going to give you an epiphany. This man standing next to me who you claim to be so terrified of, wishes to shake your hand. I promise it will be illuminating!"

Gen. Hammond reached for Iggy's hand, having no idea what Sledge was talking about. Then… *Contact!* The general tried to pull away, backing into the room. Iggy followed him and would not release his hand. Just as prolonged contact had been with every other delusional person, Carlisle Hammond's legs went out from under him, and he began to wail a long high-pitched, Noooooo! I didn't know! I'm sorry! I didn't know." The mind of the man holding his hand became transparent to Hammond, along with the clear vision of his own subconscious obsession and desire for power. He was overpowered by the substance and character of Iggy Marcus.

William Sledge had no compassion. "Like I said, Carlisle, don't insult my intelligence! Men like you don't belong at the helm of this great nation. You diminish it, and you diminish every American as well. You delegitimize every concept which made this country great. There is no forgiveness for what you did. You are a self-gratifying, power-mad autocrat, just like the people in Europe you have been associating with. Personally, I believe you are a delusional hypocrite, so count your damn blessings, general."

"We are bringing you and the rest of your co-conspirators to see the Atty. Gen., where you will all sign your resignations tonight. You are no longer going to be an active-duty officer in United States Army. If you hand me any guff, I will personally rip your generals' stars off your epaulets and drag you into Charlie Barton's office to be indicted for treason against the United States. Instead, just to save this country from the nauseating spectacle of another tragedy while we prosecute other pompous miscreants, you're being allowed to resign with honor and a pension. Now dress appropriately and get on board the ship you see at the head of your driveway. You're coming with us!"

"One more thing, Carlisle, you are not aware of. Every single word you said to Richard McNerney was recorded by a holographic recorder. Every subtle nuance of every plot and every facet of this operation to overthrow the government has been recorded. We will not use it to destroy you because the country doesn't need to see another disgusting display. However, a man like you should never be at the helm of any country or military organization. If you ever try *to run for any political office anywhere, I assure you this holography will surface and swamp* any ship you try to sail. That goes for the rest of your seditious cohorts."

Those who look to the past covet reclamation.
Those who look to the future are harbingers of innovation.
Dr. Marcos Boli

CHAPTER III

PHOENIX RISING

Two hours later, after the four heads of the United States military branches and their co-conspirators signed their resignations, Pres. William James Sledge, Iggy Marcus, and Richard McNerney sat quietly in the Atty. Gen.'s office at the DOJ. Charlie Barton and his case coordinator, Willie Cunningham, greeted them with a nod. Charlie Barton shook his head, speechless, radiating discouragement. William Sledge broke the silence. "Jake Dorian is on his way up, Charlie. I wanted him here for this. As the head of the Senate judicial committee, this could possibly wind up right in his front yard."

"As usual, I can't find the words to describe the craziness of my job since you came along," he nodded toward Iggy. "In the very beginning I thought Losey's files were over the top, unbelievable in fact, but it has become surreal at this point, the stuff of melodramatic movie scripts. Who would ever have believed all this would happen in a few short years. Think about it. We have arrested, or are about to arrest over half the elected officials in the United States Congress for corruption and/or treason, hundreds of bureaucrats, and private citizens for the same, the heads and many members of both the FBI and CIA. We are arresting thousands of pedophiles, hundreds of human traffickers, and smugglers, and *now*… the heads of all four US armed forces are being forced to resign or face indictment for treason… all in the face of an unsympathetic mainstream media who is constantly trying to viciously destroy this administration. You couldn't write this stuff in a book. Nobody would ever believe it. Sorry, I don't mean to be so verbose, but it seems the stuff keeps piling up higher and higher every day. Considering the social wreck being made of society by electronic media and foreign government interference etc., I feel like I'm living in an asylum where half the people in this country and the rest of the world have lost their minds."

Jake Dorian heard Charlie Barton's comment as he softly nudged the door closed behind him. "They didn't lose their minds Charlie, most of them never had a sound grip on their own sanity in the first place. Think about it. From everything including commercialism, social media, television and all the other methods for information dissemination, they have been subjected to a barrage of indoctrination from the moment they leave the womb. Most people are never given a chance to see reality. When reality presents itself, the powers that be, often obscure the truth with misinformation, declaring the truth to be misinformation. Most people who have never learned to critically think, become lost in the overwhelming flood of propaganda which has clouded their vision for their entire lives."

"It was designed to subjugate them. Humanity has been cultivated to produce a society of mindless consumers, embedded with a self-image based on materialism as well as the stature and opinions of the next-door neighbors. Iggy has explained it exactly. They have been taught delusion is normal, and they have learned to accept commercialism and material acquisition as the definition of stature and status. We are all victims of this insanity… some more than others, even the perpetrators. They could not possibly deploy the propaganda creating this aberrated mental condition without themselves or their progeny falling victim to mores of their own intense social programming in the long term."

"Yeah, I get it, but it's very unsettling. Now we're witnessing the total transformation of the status quo. Society is being altered so dramatically I don't think anyone can safely depend on the future anymore…" he paused and turned, shaking his head at Iggy… "Except for maybe this guy. He's the one who made it all happen."

Jake's one-syllable laugh preceded his response. "The future is never predictable, Charlie. But I understand what you're getting at. We all like to hope for and expect a reasonably stable and predictable future. That's out the window, now," he looked at Iggy still laughing.

Charlie Barton continued glaring at Iggy." How did you ever expect **us** and the rest of the world to handle all this, Mr. Marcus? This is a total transformation. We are all being asked to do an about-face and completely transform our lives, indicting thousands of people in such a dramatic way, things will never be the same again. I mean, it's so overpowering! It seems like you expect perfection and anybody who doesn't measure up has to be dealt with, somehow."

Iggy silently listened to everyone's comments. "You forgot to describe our island prison in the middle of the Pacific, Attorney General Barton." Iggy chuckled as he returned the formality. "I never said this would be easy. Society must make the transition, however. We are either going to save the world for real, or we are going to perform a colossal fake-out. You might ask what do I mean? We took nuclear war off the table, but that was not enough. It was just the contemporary way men were about to kill each other. There are a million other ways to kill, but men must learn they can't kill each other for position because it would eventually mean annihilation of the species due to the advancement and sophistication of weaponry. There is no halfway answer. This is all or nothing. Think about it, Charlie. We either act morally to straighten out the mess without compunction, or we might as well not bother at all."

"Nobody's perfect, Mr. Marcus. It seems you are indicting the entire human race for not being perfect. You and I have shaken hands. You have the cleanest slate I have ever seen, but you're unique. There's nobody like you, and you can't expect others to be what you are. There has to be a halfway point somewhere."

There's no such thing as a moral halfway point, Charlie. It's either morality… yes, or morality… no. Sure, we all make mistakes and backslide occasionally. I'm not perfect, either. We are headed in the right direction as long as we adopt the willingness and desire to attempt perfection. That kind of halfway point, replete with mistakes, is acceptable. Morality must always be defined by critical thought. Anything else is a fraud. Allow me to draw you an analogy about halfway points. Can you just imagine socialistic capitalism? How about capitalistic socialism? They are oil and water; Charlie, the halfway point lies directly in the line of separation between the two. They cannot homogeneously exist in the same bottle. You can shake them up, and they will intermingle momentarily, but they cannot permanently exist as a unique combined entity. It's a contradiction of reality. It's no different with philosophical points underlying the law you represent. That's what the law is philosophically, you know. It exactly defines man's propensity to do violence to his fellow men."

Iggy smiled thinking about his kids. "That statement, by the way, is a Louie Petro original."

"Who is Louie Petro? I never heard of him."

"He was one of my students. He studied law with my sister in our learning center. The quote came from him when he was 14 years old. He's quite a character, Charlie, and quite a philosopher, you know. Not long ago, I sat in one of his lectures in New York. He was talking about this very subject with several of his students. In fact, he used the same analogy. The only way capitalism and socialism work together is when the socialist puts a gun to the head of the capitalist and forces him to produce for the common good. I'm sure it's not his last philosophical statement. He will make a name for himself, no doubt."

Willie Cunningham decided to jump in. "I'm glad I'm only the case coordinator for the DOJ. All this stuff will wind up on my plate eventually, but I won't be the decision-maker." He looked at Iggy. "I'm sure all this seems like a walk in the park to you Mr. Marcus… Iggy… But we mere mortals are staggered by the responsibility and the effort required to make it happen. I'm glad I'm not in Charlie's shoes. I can't, for the life of me, imagine how we are going to pull this off. What do you suggest?"

As usual, Iggy was the perfect picture of benevolence. "I understand, Willie. And you are correct; it is overpowering. My suggestion?... Incrementalism. The issue here is not just quantity; it's quality as well. Everything has to be prioritized. Coordination starts there. Apparently, that's your job as case coordinator for the DOJ, Willie, isn't it? You are going to have a very full plate but look at it this way. Reality is about to smite us all. We are now at a place in the history of men because of the power of technology, where we will find a way into the future or annihilate ourselves. If we are to succeed, it is going to require extraordinary… no, a superhuman effort on all our parts. Of course, it is staggering, but the antithetical results are just as staggering. We will eventually cease to exist as a culture and society."

Sen. Jake Dorian laughed, shaking his head at his college roommate. "You sure brought on a hell of a roller coaster ride, Iggy Marcus. This won't be any walk in the park."

"Well, Jake, I could cynically offer this alternative. I'll simply press the self-destruct button on 32 satellites revolving around the planet, return more than 3000 pedophiles into society and give them back their child victims, reinstall all the corrupt Congressman, officials, and bureaucrats to their former positions, then sit back and watch the world go to hell in a basket. It won't take long for everything to implode, believe me. There are two choices. They consist of educating individuals to hold the power in their hands or abdicate as sheep to the power of authoritarians."

Pres. William James Sledge held up his hand. "Enough. We are all sitting here whining about how hard life is going to be for us if we try to accomplish this. Let's knock it off. Iggy Marcus, here, has given us the unbelievable opportunity to save this crazy world and society, impossible under any other circumstances. Also, don't forget the folks from the other side of the galaxy. They're watching us, and we don't have any choice but to continue. So, enough with the blues. Let's get into this revival of Interlink and what we are going to do about that. Why don't you fill us in on the status, Iggy, and don't hold back from describing the underlying psychology of their motive."

Iggy's gaze swept the room. He had explained this a hundred times to millions of people, yet just about everyone needed an occasional refresher. "This is the starting point, and it underlies everything. We are all aware of the graft and corruption exhibited in Losey's FBI files. I don't have to elaborate because you are the people prosecuting the perpetrators. Everyone here knows the corruption was not exclusively systemic and indigenous to internal politics. It was contrived and subtly forced on us by those who wish to destroy America. Lightning's subsidiary, American Media Inc. is now the antithesis of the people doing this and the exclusive source of truthful news on the planet. The remaining mainstream media in the free world is owned by Interlink and one man, Ransom Hornburg. We have established that. The remaining media existing in dictatorships and communist countries are exclusively propaganda vehicles for manipulating their people."

"Until the founders created America, that was the modus operandi of every government in the history of man… indoctrination, power, and control. They are the motives as well as the end result of every political action that has ever occurred. Most people have been intentionally led to believe it is the bottom line and the acquisition of wealth fueling tyranny. Such is not the case. Slavery and the subjugation of men is the real goal. The average citizen believes wealth is the primary authoritarian goal."

"On a local level, that may be true. The people who receive graft from authoritarians are simply feathering their nests. The people who distribute graft never look at wealth as anything other than a tool. They are after one thing only… The enslavement of men. I have outlined this exactly. I will reiterate the psychology of this here and now. It is imperative we explicitly understand their motives and the driving force behind them. The motives and driving force behind them are not the same things. The motive is the weak character of all authoritarians and their desire to exercise power over everyone. The driving force is envy, fear, and insecurity. I call it an inferiority/superiority complex. They must destroy their betters to elevate their self-opinion and weak stature as men. We are going to be drawn into this conflict, and there is no escape unless we surrender. I have a personal obligation to my posterity as well as the rest of humanity to prevent this. My posterity can only survive and thrive in a moral society."

"Confronting this authoritarian obsession with power would be impossible without the technology we have created at Lightning. Despite removing thirteen men from the upper echelon of Interlink, the remainder of the organization has decided to fight to the death. They believe they have strength in numbers which will keep them safe. When I say they will fight to the death, it is not hyperbole. They have already tried to kill me and a thousand other people several times over just to ensure their power positions.

There is no morality beneath their philosophy. Murder is an acceptable tool, no more or less important than interest rates."

Willie Cunningham shrugged his shoulders. "What about those of us with families? We can't allow them to be put on the chopping block. What about them, sir? I'd like to know the actual psychology of their actions if it isn't wealth. Why do they insist on the enslavement of society? "

"The DOJ will not be actively involved. You may be prosecutorial, but you won't be jurors and you will be acting at the behest of government. Threatening you will get them nothing. As far as the psychological motivation… making you a slave makes them a god. By diminishing you, they elevate themselves in their own eyes. They cannot base their self-image on creativity and production, which they are obviously incapable of. The suppression or destruction of your creative ability shatters the mirror of excellence and the reflection of their mediocrity."

"As simple as that?" Willie Cunningham asked, shaking his head in wonder.

"Yup, as simple as that, Willie."

"Look back at history, Willie. Think of the philosophers and the main events in history, how they transpired, and what motivated the players. For instance, the best friend of Julius Caesar plunged a knife into his back to be accepted by the Roman Senate as a peer. Yes, Caesar was a despot in a manner of speaking, but he was also a peerless conqueror, cloaked with the charisma of the great leader who brought Rome to its pinnacle of power, glory, and opulence. Playing second fiddle to Julius Caesar was a difficult thing for every member of the Senate, including Brutus. So, they conspired, and it was Caesar's demise."

"This is one of my favorite examples of the secondhand nature enveloping most men. It is not endemic to man's nature. It is a learned behavior propagated by those who don't measure up. Remember the expression *misery loves company*? It fits this bill perfectly. The second-hand person is always of lesser stature than the paragon. The stature of the paragon shines a brilliant light diminishing the stature of the lesser man in his own eyes. Do you see the problem? It is envy… pure, unmitigated jealousy coupled with the vision of his own inadequacy. His absence of character propagates that mindset."

"He bases his self-image on the opinions of others instead of his own opinion of himself. He views the stature of the paragon as something he can never attain because the paragon is always exceptional. The lesser man feels he cannot measure up to the stature of the paragon, and every time he glances in that mirror, he sees himself as diminished. It is an impossible vision for a person who is insecure. So, he must destroy the paragon."

"We all think that way, Iggy. We can't help ourselves. It's our nature. Like Charlie mentioned, nobody's perfect."

"Quite correct, Willie. Nobody's perfect, but we should aspire to become perfect. And… we ***can*** help ourselves. You think that way because you have been indoctrinated. You have been taught by society for your entire life to compare yourself to other people and, consequently, measure your stature in your own eyes by your vision of the stature of your peers. Do you see the error? When you do that, you evade reality and allow delusion to run your operating system. The entire human race, with only a few exceptions, lives this way."

Everyone listened intently. It was an object lesson on how human beings should live versus the antithetical lifestyle humans had adopted for thousands of years. Willie Cunningham contemplated everything he had heard. It was an epiphany for him. He never dwelt on philosophical concepts for long. His life consisted of his family, his job, and getting through the day unscathed. "Wow! I rarely consider things like this but the way you explained them illustrates their importance. Who taught you this, Mr. Marcus?" They were back to formality again.

Iggy smiled as the memory surfaced. "My mom, attorney Cunningham. Let me tell you what she taught my brothers, my sister, and me from the moment we could understand even a smattering of English. She ingrained this in our character throughout our youth, and it became a part of our moral operating system. It's different than the way most people think, but to us, it has become the natural way to live. *Never let anyone's opinion of you define your self-image. An honest, true self-image can only come from within through mastery by achievement!"*

"Once it becomes the constant and normal theme of your existence, comparing yourself to others becomes irrelevant. You never do it. Both methods of operation, independent mastery of your own mind or self-subjugation to the minds of others, are learned behaviors. They define and govern human character."

Richard McNerney had been silent throughout the entire discussion. His inner tranquility resulted from his release from psychological bondage by Iggy and his daughter, Gloria. He didn't feel the need to be heard as part of the discussion. In fact, he hung on to every word spoken. Since his epiphany, he came to believe his life as an associate of Iggy Marcus was an incredible expansion of his horizons. Still, he had spent his life as a Maj. Gen. in the United States Army as chief strategist for every Army Battle theater. His experience and expertise were impeccable. He smiled, remembering his participation in the arrest of the 13 members of Interlink that day in Brussels. He thought about the trailer with a hypersonic missile and the orchestra of 200+ children playing the US National Anthem as backdrop music to one of the most consequential disruptions of a power structure in history. Not wanting to inject himself abruptly, he raised his hand. "I would like to make a statement, if I may."

Iggy nodded, "sure, Richard. What's on your mind?"

"You assigned me the task to follow Interlink's activities with your brother Jack. I believe your reasoning concerned my background in military strategy and your brother's background in psychological operations. What you are saying about Interlink attempting to regain its power is accurate. Jack's and I believe they are going to attempt something large. I don't believe it will be with nuclear weapons. They won't be able to get their hands on them, anyway. It's going to be psychological operations. They are acting very subtly now, but I believe it will be worldwide and massive when they move. Jack and I have been monitoring all mainstream media broadcasts, commentary, advertising, and subtle psychological operations. We haven't given you a report, but I can instantly make it available to you via computer. We also have involved some young people who were educated at Lightning Ranch. They volunteered for the duty and have penetrated several organizations set up by Interlink. The organizations are created specifically to disrupt society and create chaos."

The president nodded his head. "That is the reason we are sitting here, Gen. McNerney. I would love to hear anything you have to offer."

"Yes, sir. Please allow me first to underscore the circumstances occurring worldwide. We all know of the clinics deployed from Lightning Ranch to countries worldwide. Their purpose was the elimination of terminal illnesses. Terminal illnesses are the only medical efforts we can handle at this early stage, considering the volume of maladies. Also, Lightning Inc. has deployed food distribution centers around the globe. This has made many people very happy, especially the sick and starving. But it also has made a lot of people very angry! I bring the subject up because it is apropos to the description of human behavior Iggy just explained to Attorney Cunningham."

Iggy nodded his head in approval at Richard McNerney. Grinning, he said, "Go on, Richard, fill us in."

"Okay then. Most of you know some of this, and a few of you know all of this, but Interlink consists of thousands of people and businesses worldwide. They are not all complicit in subterfuge, but they all have been forced to join Interlink as one massive block of commercial power. They control 95% of the business on the planet outside China, North Korea, and Russia. The people at the head of Interlink are no longer the 13 we arrested in Brussels. They are, however, family members and associates of those men incarcerated at Guantánamo. The man at the helm now, is Heinrich Klatch, brother-in-law to Gunther Lichtenberg, one of our Guantánamo inmates. He is a very dangerous man and head of the Progressive World Socialist Council."

Iggy held up his hand. "Pardon the intrusion, please, Richard. You can finish in a minute, but I would like to describe Heinrich Klatch."

"You have the floor. Heinrich Klatch requires more than a simple description, however."

"Heinrich Klatch is the son of Joseph Goebbels. You all know who he was. I don't have to elaborate. Joseph Goebbels was a narcissistic sociopath, an evil man by anyone's standards. He was Adolf Hitler's most valued advisor in terms of propaganda and societal management. Heinrich Klatch makes his father look like a choir boy by comparison. There aren't many people worse than him. He despises humanity and possesses a vehement self-loathing. Sadist, masochist, sociopath, narcissist... Heinrich Klatch is the epitome of all those terms... and he is a merciless killer."

"People like Klatch have a distinct advantage during confrontations. They are never defensive. They are aggressive and will quickly kill because they enjoy it. He enjoys personally inflicting pain if he has the time, and the opportunity presents itself. He will do it through others when he can't do it himself, and there are no holds barred to him in a confrontation, whether it be individual or collective. Before this, he remained in the background of Interlink. His brother-in-law, Gunther Lichtenberg, is now at Guantánamo, awaiting trial. Klatch is enraged about Gunther's incarceration, and he has said many times he wants to get his hands around my neck and kill me."

Richard McNerney laughed. "He's over 80 years old, and he would have his hands full if he tried. I'd like to watch that bout, especially after your training with Adm. Kenji. Sorry about the interruption, but I just had to add that. Go on."

"Klatch is brilliant. Ainstead Crenshaw was the front-tier brain of Interlink but everything was run past Klatch to determine its efficacy. They only recently involved Vladimir Borenko as a strategist for their attack on us. Interlink attempted our destruction with nuclear weapons. It didn't work out for them. They won't do anything like it again. Klatch has a son, every bit as sick and perverted as he is. It is rumored the boy's mother tried to raise him as a Lutheran. Klatch would have none of it, so, he strangled her. So, he is the man we will have to contend with. He is a master of psychological operations and knows no boundaries."

Pres. Sledge listened to everything for the past 20 minutes without speaking. "What do you expect from him, Iggy? I'm certain there isn't going to be a physical fight. Klatch is much too sophisticated even though he wishes he could choke you. You mentioned the magnitude of their efforts 20 minutes ago. Lay it out for us."

Iggy shook his head. Let's view the whole thing in perspective. You and I have had many conversations, Bill. It began the first day we were trout fishing and discussed the situation in the world when you voiced your opinion of hopelessness." Iggy grinned. "Do you remember, Bill? I told you it wasn't hopeless. One man could make a difference and change the world. So, you offered me the keys to the Oval Office." Iggy continued chuckling. "We discussed a lot that day and all of the following two weeks of your visit. Despite our differences of opinion on the final outcome, we were basically in agreement as to the causes of America's current illness."

"Yes, I remember just about every word. We were definitely in agreement, but your explanation was an epiphany for me. After getting to know you I didn't feel so alone in my opinions. But go on Iggy."

"The people of Interlink are methodical. They understand human nature implicitly and understand much of what I described to you about the underlying flaws comprising the typical human mind. Those flaws are not indigenous to us. My mother managed to raise the four of us without that guff. They have been perpetrated on society to achieve an effect. Authoritarians believe they are above the fray. They think the methods they use to subliminally coerce society, morally and intellectually, do not affect them because they are superior. They are incorrect. They are as flawed as the people they consider the herd."

"So, what's next?"

Much of it is obvious. We are all watching systematic propaganda deployed to obliterate romance and replace it with promiscuity, teaching children to avoid emotional attachment. The reason for this is to ultimately destroy the family. When you teach young children to have indiscriminate sex without the underlying components of love and respect, you eliminate the desire to marry and have a family because it has been replaced by casual, meaningless sex. If you destroy the family, you destroy the sole environment for propagating the moral and intellectual development of children. The perfect example of this is the invasion of transsexuals, being paraded around young grammar school children who have no comprehension of sex other than what they've been told by the perverse media and their indoctrinated teachers. This is not just the way it goes in all societies. This is an intentional construct of Interlink. It is not the people sitting in the chairs of the ivory towers at Interlink, it is the sociopaths who have studied psychology and are employed by those people in the ivory tower to dismantle moral society."

"The LGBTQ movement is being used to systematically attack children at the grammar school level, grooming them to accept sexual perversion as normal, subverting their sexual orientation and consequential development. This is a multipronged attack designed to obliterate the family and masculinity. Once the family with the Alpha male patriarch is destroyed, the only replacement child-rearing authoritative entity will be the state. The family is the only environment where children can be taught values and critical thinking. The state is incapable because there is no love. Where there is no love, there is no virtue. Where there is no virtue, only evil can exist."

"They are also taught to be preoccupied with racial hatred. When they convince people with slight differences to hate each other based on physical descriptions or anomalies, the young minds become occupied with the trivial and inconsequential. The salient and consequential then fly by high overhead. You cannot bury your head in the sand and watch the eagles soar simultaneously."

They all had heard this before, but only from lesser minds. They were hearing the truth from the greatest intellect who had ever existed. They were overwhelmed by the stature and viciousness of what was being perpetrated on humanity. It left them feeling diminished and desperate to find a recipe to combat the malevolence attempting to destroy their children.

William Sledge was thinking about his two twin children, William, and Wilhelmina. They would not exist if it wasn't for the man sitting in front of them. Iggy and Melanie Marcus had devised a way to create twin ova and implant them in Alice's uterus. It was the same genetic DNA material as found in both parents. It was more than science; it was a miracle, but everything that flowed from Iggy Marcus and Lightning Inc. was miraculous. "So, Iggy, I'm sure there's more. Please elaborate, and where do we go from here?"

"There's more you need to know. The people of Interlink, directed by Heinrich Klatch and others, have built an organization of psychological trainers. They are not licensed physicians but are extensively trained in psychological operations dedicated to destroying the human mind and spirit. I liken them to the World War II fanatics like Josef Rudolf Mengele, the German Schutzstaffel officer referred to as the angel of death at Auschwitz, who sadistically murdered thousands experimenting on living Jews. People of his caliber are sadists without compassion. They are inhuman sociopaths and will stop at nothing to achieve a specific result."

"What results?" asked the Pres. with raised eyebrows.

"Let's examine this from the ground up. They have taken charge of our universities. Most universities have become propaganda centers to develop mindless citizens who will obey. Blind obedience is a prerequisite for the new world order these people expect to create. Our technology developed at Lightning is an enormous burr under the saddle. They cannot achieve their goals if we exist. We are too powerful to overcome. So, they have decided to create chaos everywhere to make society lawless and unmanageable. It began subtly. You are aware of people who are either appointed or elected as prosecutorial attorneys in the various state and municipal governments who are lax and release criminals on their own recognizance. Bail has just about virtually been abolished, and recidivists are turned out onto the street to commit more crimes."

"Charlie Barton nodded his head. "We see it from here at the DOJ, and most of the time we cannot understand or believe how these supposed prosecutors think. They are dismantling the legal system right under our noses on local levels everywhere. I suppose here at the Department of Justice; it depends on what political party holds the reins currently. Go on with your explanation Mr. Marcus." The Atty. Gen. was using Mr. Marcus as a salutation out of respect for the man with the answers.

"This is what was attempted with Lightning Inc. when Interlink began its attempt to disrupt us. They have incorporated thousands of young people in their late teens and 20s who have been indoctrinated with communism by socialist professors in the universities. They call it socialism, but they are the same thing, a prelude to slavery. They attempted to propagate chaos and sent their young socialist army volunteers out to destroy the physical property owned by Lightning Inc. That included all our technical facilities and factories as well as eighteen locations around the country that published American Media. This is what they expect to do again simultaneously, only worldwide."

"What did you do?" Inquired Charlie Barton. "I mean, how did you contend with all of it without bloodshed? As I recall, there was nothing about it in the news at all. Or at least nothing more than the same thing that happened when BLM was burning cities to the ground."

“Our technology.” Replied Iggy. “We can surround any edifice or living creature with an impenetrable shield preventing intrusion of any kind, from anywhere. So, when Interlink decided to send its young socialists out to destroy us, we were waiting for them. We encapsulated them and brought them to Gitmo. Some of them have been psychologically deprogrammed with great effort. At least the ones we could salvage. Others committed crimes too serious for them to reenter society. They are serving prison terms now. If you decide you’re going to commit murder, there must be consequences. It doesn’t happen that way in our cities now. Recidivists are being released every day, but only if a particular political party is in charge. The people who are allowing the recidivism are sponsored by money from Interlink.”

“Is this what you expect to happen again, Iggy?” asked Pres. Sledge

"It's more than an expectation, Bill. I have many people trained at Lightning and deployed at various locations to assist our efforts at stopping Interlink. They are volunteers who are sometimes at great peril. They have infiltrated hundreds of organizations dispersed around the planet that Interlink has trained and will release to export extreme chaos and destruction among every society except China."

"Why not China?"

"The Chinese have too large an army and strictly control their society. Interlink would never get away with it. The Chinese are a unique entity. They are waiting for us to destroy ourselves and expect to be there when we do, waiting to pick up the pieces. That is their intent and mindset. They are far less sure of themselves now than they were before my visit to Beijing and Fun Chou Dung a few years ago. Ultimately, China will be liberated, and a free Republic of citizens will eventually replace the existing tyranny."

The president's look of extreme skepticism precluded his question. "Just how the hell is that supposed to happen? They've got the biggest army on the planet and the most money now."

"I have plans, Bill, but I'm letting China motor along just as it is for now. When the time is right, the Chinese citizens will get their opportunity."

"I don't know how you're going to pull that off, but it should be something to see, I'll bet."

"Interlink expects to convert the entire planet to a gargantuan revolt between citizens and governments of every country. They are going to fan the flames between philosophically different people within certain countries and then propagate strife and start wars between other countries of different philosophical inclinations."

"When is this supposed to begin?"

"It has already begun. You now see the unrest beginning in various countries. We are reporting all of it in Lightning's publications, but you won't see a word in the mainstream press until the right moment. Interlink owns the mainstream media through Ransom Hornburg and wants the chaos to explode to best suit their purpose. The people of Interlink believe they are being subtle, and their incremental approach toward creating chaos will be unnoticed by those of us who might mitigate such. When the tenor climbs to a specific level, they will release their pawns onto the board. They hope to overwhelm the entire world with the magnitude of the chaos. They believe we will be unable to contend with it, although they should have second thoughts because they attempted this before, and it didn't work for them."

Jake Dorian hadn't said a word for the entire discussion. "How will you contend with this when it begins? Will you use the satellites?"

"Of course. We can isolate countries, armies, or individuals, for that matter, depending on the need. We can do it from space and have 64 satellites in orbit now. There is no place on earth inaccessible to them. Our main concern will be to mitigate the loss of life." Iggy sighed. He knew people were going to be killed. Interlink was ambivalent about murder. Their aim was the destruction of society everywhere. They hoped to rebuild a worldwide socialist dictatorship from the ashes. In fact, the more people who were killed, the greater the chaos would be, which would assist them. They would never relinquish their ancestral authority over men. The opiate of power has conditioned them to expect the rest of the world to serve the aristocracy.

William James Sledge and Iggy had become friends in their quest to overcome a common enemy. He watched Iggy closely. He saw the twinge of torment concerning the inevitable loss of life sure to come. "You know, Iggy, I should hardly be the one giving you advice, but you did offer them an opportunity to make amends and join us. It's not your fault they refused. All you can do is what you intend to do."

"Agreed, Bill. If it was just the people of Interlink who would suffer the consequences of their actions, it would be one thing. However, thousands of people are likely to be killed, which is always a tragedy. You said so yourself in your speech from the Oval Office after your epiphany. Millions of people died at the hands of maniacs. There's no way to bring them back. We'll do our best to prevent death, even for the delusional people being used to precipitate this."

"If I thought it would do some good, I would arrest the people at the top now to prevent what's coming. Unfortunately, they have mechanisms in place to ensure the chaos no matter what happens."

"What mechanisms?" asked Charlie Barton.

"The last time I arrested Interlink officials, we did it in person. We entered their headquarters, marched them into Daedalus, and brought them to Guantánamo Bay. They remembered that, believe me. They won't let it happen now. They will not all convene together again. They will use remote electronic communications from separate isolated locations. Further, all their conspiratorial minions are already in place and ready to act. They believe it will hinder us, and we will be unable to neutralize their efforts. They believe worldwide chaos is too great an obstacle for us to overcome. They are mistaken, of course. We will not be defeated. The problem is the loss of life. It might be enormous. We can mitigate much of it with our technology, but we will not be able to save everyone."

Charlie Barton almost imperceptibly nodded his head. He was back to formality. "How did it get this far out of hand, Mr. Marcus? How can this be happening? I sort of get it, but I would like an explanation. Also, what will our part be in all of this, and when will it start?"

Iggy's gaze swept the room again. "I can explain it, but it requires an open mind. Your first question was, how did it get this far out of hand? I'll try to keep it brief. You must understand this societal sickness started when homo sapiens first stood erect becoming self-aware. Thousands of years ago, there were no printed words. Some, occasionally... like the Upanishads and the Indian Vedas. Even the writings of Confucius existed but the manuscripts were never widespread and digested by the common people. So, word-of-mouth was the only method to convey information. You all know what happens when you whisper a secret in someone's ear and pass it around. For many centuries, the only information available was issued from monasteries. The Crusaders pilfered the libraries in Alexandria. Those manuscripts and scrolls are hidden below the floor of the Sistine Chapel in Rome. Whatever printed words existed in European monasteries were minimal and never distributed to a largely illiterate populace."

"The churches of Rome and England wanted no intellectual competition. The autocrats who have always run the world behind all the thrones of Europe, the Catholic Church, the churches of England, and Martin Luther, believe they are superior to all men, and thus created the caste system to achieve that hierarchy. The caste system was incorporated into the religious edifices as well as the secular monarchies. They all require the submission of an ignorant population to their power. Such has been the nature of man's political hierarchy for thousands of years, and organized religion was always corrupt and complicit."

"How does that speak to what's going on today?"

"Give me time," smiled Iggy. "I'll get you there, but first, a fill in the blank's history lesson. You are all familiar enough with history to understand the caste system and how all societies were subject to it until 1776. You know the history of America. It was mankind's first escape from tyranny. Men were released from the bondage of the caste system."

"Interlink is the organization that evolved from the organized aristocracy of the past. They are its current representation. After America signed the Declaration of Independence and the Bill of Rights was created, the predecessors of Interlink Became impotent, powerless over the men and government of the West. Our founders launched America, the greatest edifice of government and individual freedom that ever existed."

"As with all things, the collective memory of men fades. You have all heard the expression; *those who do not learn from the mistakes of the past are bound to repeat them.* It is a truism, gentlemen. The country drifted through its next 135 years and grew into the greatest country created by men. We endured the Civil War, and organized slavery was finally eliminated from the earth. The citizens of America became the most productive and intelligent population who ever existed. The aristocracy of Europe continued to be powerless."

Then came the industrialization of America. It started slowly but by the turn of the 19th century, it was chugging along. The aristocracy of Europe created relationships and solicited the assistance of the newly minted American multimillionaires created by industrialization. The citizens of

America still held the reins of power in the form of the Congress until 1911 when Woodrow Wilson, the first blatant left-wing progressive president, was elected. He followed William Howard Taft who was Teddy Roosevelt's pick for a political successor. Both men were quite progressive for Republicans."

"Wilson, a fiscal and socially liberal Democrat, was responsible, along with the bankers, American millionaires, and aristocracy of Europe, for creating the Federal Reserve Act, a document written by foreign authoritarians to steal this country from its citizens. The Federal Reserve Act seized the purse strings from a Congress asleep at the helm, dropped them in the lap of the bankers, and the American citizens, as well as their descendants, were permanently stripped of their legacy. The tyranny of the aristocrats finally had established a footing in America, and coupled with the greed of American industrial millionaires, eventually became the cancer now metastasizing in its attempt to enslave all mankind."

"We all understand this to a degree, Iggy. You heard my speech at the White House when I outlined everything shortly after you launched the satellites. Exactly what new point are you making?" Inquired Bill Sledge.

My point is all of society, even those of us who believe we are immune, have been inundated by the psychological operations of the aristocrats. They manipulate societal mores: commercialism, sexual perversion, and every other single aspect of human life. Their tentacles are in everything. Their efforts are designed to promote ignorance and stupidity, ultimately creating a society of serfs. They immediately commandeer anyone who achieves excellence. No one slips through the cracks. Before the computer age and the Internet, the cracks were wide. Now they are a hairline."

Everyone in the room was silent. The description of how the aristocracy destroys men and societies was depressing. It created hopeless resignation to the status quo. It seemed insurmountable, as Iggy described it. "I'm almost sorry I asked," said Charlie Barton. "But go on Mr. Marcus. Don't stop now. In for a penny... In for a pound."

"That was just a brief history of what got us here. The powers that be, have decided it is time to make the transition to socialism, no holds barred. They were doing it incrementally, hoping no one would notice when they co-opted the Democratic party in the early twentieth century in their mission to destroy capitalism. Their subtle subterfuge was working prior to my arrival and our technology. Because we have so dramatically altered their program and stripped them of most of their power, they realize it's now or never. They will either win or be relegated to the trash heap they have created containing all mankind. That's how they view men. If you do not exist in their circle, you are considered substandard, and in effect, trash. That mindset will never allow them to join us. I proposed it to them, and they refused. Instead, they attempted to destroy me and Lightning Inc. with Chinese nuclear weapons. You all know the story."

The realization that almost all men in power were addicted to it came to Charlie Barton slowly. He was beginning to see for men to remain in power, it required corruption at the base of the power structure. No one was allowed near the top of the heap who didn't play the game. It was a hard pill to swallow. "It's hard to believe it's everyone." He said in resignation.

Iggy looked Charlie Barton in the eye. "Why else do you think you have hundreds of congressmen and bureaucrats lined up for prosecution, Charlie? They have all been purchased. They no longer own their souls. Interlink owns them. Even if they weren't personally bribed, the rest of them are psychologically inundated by the propaganda continuously regurgitated by Interlink. Both political parties have now become irrelevant. Except for a few honest men and women, they all represent Interlink and do the bidding of these megalomaniacs. The ones who attempt to remain honest are ostracized from their own party and ridiculed in the eyes of the morally illiterate public."

"This is all done subtly so the population doesn't see the reality of what is being done to their freedom and their children's future. The destruction of their intellect is so extensive, they believe the blatant, obvious lies. Morality has now become immoral. Lies are being told as truths by authorities who boast honesty. Conspirators are calling anyone who doubts their veracity conspiratorial kooks. They intimidate and accuse people of every evil they are doing."

"Are you telling us everything, our congressional legislators, the judicial system, the media, all of it... Is a big set up designed to destroy freedom?" asked Willie Cunningham. "And we are all ignorant victims of the subterfuge?"

Iggy nodded yes. "Now you're getting the picture, Willie. That is what it has become, and it's far deeper and more pervasive than anyone thinks. Masters of psychological inundation constantly design and feed us this torrent of sewage. It is a subtle, psychological effluvium that now surrounds every aspect of our existence. They own all the media except American Media Inc. We are under attack, and it is inescapable, especially by our children. They are becoming accustomed to the world of depravity and iniquity as constant and normal. You only have to watch TV briefly to see the truth as they parade prancing drag queens to debase the minds of young grammar school children."

"Immediately after we arrested the 13 members in Brussels, Interlink's media presence diminished. Our audacity and the magnitude of our actions subdued them. It remained as such for a year. Then, apparently, the remainder of Interlink, led by Klatch, experienced a reawakening. They fired up their mainstream media and resumed attacking our new order of individual freedom."

"Jesus!" Willie Cunningham replied. He knew he was listening to the truth. Everyone sensed it but no one could put a believable name to it until this man described it.

"They are not all willingly corrupt, but everyone in the country is affected. They cannot escape."

"Are you telling me this includes everybody? Even the judicial system?"

"Especially the judicial system, Willie. That's where the buck stops, even though legislators create the parameters of the law. They are all in it together, and it is designed to slowly destroy us, even though local authorities and lower court judges are blind to the reality of what is being done to our society. The corrupt prosecutors encourage recidivism, and the judges do not bother to prevent it, with some exceptions. Some judges are unassailable. For instance, Supreme Court Justice Amos Carmichael has the strength of character to withstand the onslaught. So did Alfread Malone when he was alive. Do you see the link up? By convincing mankind to worship money as its God, the most prolific tool of coercion has become the bribe, instead of the lash. The money obscures the subliminal intent of the sociopaths to destroy individuality. That hidden intent is what we must overcome because it surrounds everything. "

"My God, this is insanity!" returned Willie Cunningham.

"Quite right. Any sane, awake person would call this insanity. But I don't think you realize how insane it really is. These people are killers. They will callously kill anyone who is an obstacle without compunction or compassion. They will do whatever they feel is necessary. Murder is a very effective and final tool. Without the technology we have developed at Lightning, anyone who stands in their way would be in jeopardy of annihilation."

"Is it really as bad as all that?" asked Charlie Barton. "Who have they killed?"

"Hundreds of people, Charlie. Would you like a short list of a few famous people and the reasons?"

"Yes, I would."

"I'll list a few notorious figures. They were responsible for killing the Kennedy brothers, Martin Luther King, and Supreme Court Justice Alfread Malone. Their primary targets, especially conservatives wielding great power who stand in their way, must be neutralized or exterminated. Not all people who consider themselves liberal are in on it. Liberalism, however, is the left's main philosophical tool to shift society away from traditional American values into the realm of delusion."

"You are telling me these people actually killed Alfread Malone." It was more of a statement than a question. "I mean, you're actually telling me a Supreme Court judge was murdered while visiting a friend instead of having a heart attack like the coroner said."

"Yes, Charlie. That is exactly what I'm telling you, and there is no doubt."

"You have proof?"

"Yes, absolute. I instructed my daughter to question the coroner about the cause of death and subliminally assess his integrity. She has certain flawless gifts. Malone's honor was such… he would have fallen on his sword before he would sacrifice one iota of his integrity. He would never have stood for the monstrosity of today's corruption, and that includes the judicial system. You may not recall, but he was a proponent of, and strongly pushed for congressional investigations into the corruption that underpinned the judicial system. In other words, he was going to rip the carpet out from under his compatriots who didn't possess the integrity the office deserves."

"And the coroner? He was bought and paid for too? How is all this possible?"

Iggy chuckled cynically. "The coroner has children too, Charlie."

"My God!" Atty. Gen., Charlie Barton murmured, crestfallen. Under most circumstances he would've disbelieved what he just heard. Not in this case. He knew the man standing before him would never lie or even exaggerate. He was hearing the truth, and it was next to impossible to grapple with. "Okay then, Mr. Marcus. You're telling me Malone was murdered because he would not tolerate the new world order of things. I mean, that's exactly what you're telling me, here."

"Yes, it is exactly what I'm telling you, and you better come to grips with the reality of it because you, gentlemen, are the highest pinnacle of judicial authority and action outside of the court itself, and you are the men standing between honor and depravity who will have to fix this!"

The silence was deafening as everyone in the room attempted to assimilate what they had just heard. Charlie Barton looked pensive. "Okay then, Mr. Marcus, let's say I buy this information you are dishing out. How come they haven't killed Amos Carmichael? If there were ever two peas in a pod, Carmichael and Malone would be it. Nothing's happened to him."

"Malone is survived by his wife only. His son was killed in an automobile accident. For the sake of demonstrating the efficacy of what I am telling you, I am giving you a piece of information that I demand never leave this room. Do I have your solemn promise, gentlemen?"

Everyone nodded yes. "Go on," said Charlie Barton. "You have my word. It will not leave this room."

"I appreciate you agreeing to this, Charlie, but in a few moments, you're going to realize the huge significance of the promise you just made because of what I am about to tell you... and in only a few words. "

"Amos Carmichael is a close personal friend. In fact, relationships can't get much closer. I unlocked Amos Carmichael several years ago. I understand everything about him, as he understands everything about me. The man has a family, a wife, and 2 children. If this man attempted what Alfread Malone was about to attempt, ferreting out the subterfuge and gross destructive plans for society at large that Interlink has planned for half a century, they all would've been dead within 48 hours… all of them! They each always wear a Lightning magnetic shield."

"Holy Mother of God! How have they gotten away with this? How could we let our country come to this?"

"It is not enough to have good intentions, Charlie. The road to hell is paved with them. Besides being aware, we must act before this tragedy overcomes us. That requires several things. I call them the 4 tenets of morality. You must understand the difference between good and evil, the vision to see and accept the truth, the dedication to the good, and the courage to stand by your convictions no matter what the price. There is no place for lassitude in this. If we relax our guard for even a moment, we open the door for our adversaries and empower them."

"Who else," asked the Atty Gen., almost afraid to hear the truth.

"First, understand liberalism is the beginning of, and what underpins socialism, which is the harbinger of communism and slavery. If you examine history, every socialist edifice dreamed up by men was responsible for the deaths of several hundred million people. Those men, all socialists, were Lenin, Stalin, Hitler, Idi Amin, Pol Pot, Mao Zedong... The list goes on. They are all vicious murderers with an inferiority/superiority complex. They always use the excuse socialism is good for society and they are the champions of the little people, while they are killing them at the same time if they protest! Have you ever seen a democratic republic or true democracy that murdered millions of its own citizens? Think of them. Hammurabi's Babylon, Athens, Rome in its beginnings, the United States, Israel... It's plainly obvious from whom evil emanates. Have I made my point yet?"

"The current indoctrinators' greatest tools are social media and Hollywood. Hollywood is a major center for the production and distribution of successful brainwashing. For instance, the perverse and deranged programming being inflicted on our children is prolific. Those who work in that industry are required to follow the liberal philosophy in lockstep, or they are ostracized, even if they resisted indoctrination. If they are a minor player, they usually aren't bothered much. Why amplify their public presence if conservatives don't create too much commotion?"

"They are ostracized as soon as they begin to have a major positive effect on young people, who are the primary focus of Interlink's brainwashing efforts designed to destroy the family. If their popularity among the youth is overwhelming, with a positive effect contrary to their media indoctrination, they are treated like Michael Jackson or Robin Williams, among others. Those two people decided to go public with what was being done by the Hollywood agenda merchants. They were both moral people who took umbrage with the trash the writers and producers dished out, but they were publicly slandered and are dead, now. That entire industry, just like all the media outlets except for American Media, Hollywood is now owned, lock, stock, and barrel by the oppressors."

You could hear a pin drop as everyone contemplated the reality of Iggy's soliloquy. Bill Sledge and Jake Dorian were used to Iggy's bluntness. He didn't mince words and always got to the point. Charlie Barton, on the other hand, was just discovering what kind of man Iggy really was. "Is everyone in Hollywood like this, Mr. Marcus? I mean, they can't all be evil, can they?"

Iggy laughed. "No, most of them are just brainwashed and can't tell the difference. Remember, they are paid ridiculously extravagant amounts of money to practice their barely sophisticated trade. They have good memories for learning scripts and always honor themselves as great artists, but as far as critical thinking goes, they are either lost or complicit with the system. Most of them are not highly educated and are rarely philosophically literate. Some are literate, but they don't get very far. Granted, there are a few truly evil ones, but they are chairmen of the board types or work mostly in the production end of Hollywood."

"As for your second question, what is our part in this and when will it start? This is your answer: It starts now. You must not put off to tomorrow what you must do today. As for your part, you are the authorities. You have been elected, confirmed, or appointed to your positions. It's your job to run the show. You will either do it with integrity and alacrity or we will be overcome. It's your job, gentleman. You ran for office or accepted the job description you were offered. The future of your progeny will depend on what you men do now, and how well you rise to the occasion."

"We at Lightning, will be responsible for the technological end of this. There are enough of us and multiple technologies who will intervene in the chaos around the world. Ultimately, they will not succeed but it will not be mitigated rapidly like our errant generals' plans were. This is going to take time and we are going to bring lots of people somewhere to be adjudicated."

"How many hundreds?" Asked the President.

Iggy sighed with resignation and a grim expression. He had done his best to break this delicately to the men in the room so as not to overwhelm them. "I don't think you have grasped the magnitude of this, Bill; there are going to be many tens of thousands. We are going to have to act immediately to set up an organized venue or compound to handle that many people. We will either stay on top of this and prevent anarchy or they are going to run roughshod over civilization. When their reign of terror has completely destroyed Western civilization, they will attempt to set up their new oligarchy. You all know that entails the death of America and freedom. This is what Interlink has planned. I now have five ships and two pilots. I expect to have two more pilots soon. We will be arresting people and bringing them to the compound to be held until their involvement and culpability are determined."

"My God!" exclaimed Jake Dorian. "How in the name of heaven are we going to handle this." Charlie Barton and Willie Cunningham's eyes were the size of golf balls as they contemplated what was to come.

"Well, to quote *you,* Jake… This isn't going to be any walk in the park. You men in this room are going to have to coordinate this effort. We will have to select honorable men to become the heads of the four branches of service we just forced into resignation. We will require our military's active participation and they must be trained as to what is about to happen and how they must accomplish the mission. Lightning has only 250 ex-Navy SEALs in its employ, but we intend to hire ten times that many, and they are the best trained, dedicated, and patriotic men alive. They should become your military trainers and officers. They are all ex-military men and should be immediately commissioned into the service branches as officers to make it official. The arrest and handling of this many people will be coordinated by the two best people for the job, Lieutenant General Richard McNerney, one of the best strategists the Army ever had and the most highly trained Navy SEAL who ever existed, Admiral Oniella Kenji. Besides myself, the man who should be given the job of oversight is my head of security, Tom Rickart."

Willie Cunningham was apprehensive. "What if we don't win? What then? Will we just submit? I think it's a horrible chance to take because we put all our families and our future on the line when we don't have to do it." He looked up at Iggy, "You have the technology, Mr. Marcus; why don't you just take them out before they have a chance to start all this mayhem and cause all this death? Wouldn't it be easier to destroy them before they get a chance to destroy us?"

Iggy laughed, but it was slightly cynical. "Yes, it would be easy for me to do. You're correct, and it would completely solve the problem. It would be especially easy for you. You wouldn't have to get your hands dirty. You would not be paying a price for freedom like all the dead soldiers in World War II paid for your freedom. Would you want me to pay that price for you? Unfortunately, then I would become them. I would be acting exactly in the same manner as they are acting."

"You suggest this is acceptable because my philosophical position appears to be altruistic to you. Well, Willie, murder is never altruistic. Honest, decent people can only commit the act in self-defense. If we act preemptively, then we are laboring under the supposition that Interlink will be responsible for the death of thousands. While this may be, it has yet to be established."

"One more thing, and it is rarely considered by anyone. Every human being has this responsibility, especially soldiers. They are morally responsible to determine if the battlefield is appropriate and moral. That is where we kill people, supposedly without guilt because we are told by our fearless leaders it is morally acceptable. Well, it is often inappropriate and morally impertinent. Being given orders to murder in the name of government or God is immoral and illegal in any other way than an act of self-defense. Examine all the conflicts in history. Dig to their roots and ask the question, where was the morality? If you have a critical thinking mind you will see the truth."

Richard McNerney shook his head in wonder, thinking about the past few years. He finally understood his place in the plans of Iggy Marcus. He had somehow survived being a Maj. Gen. in charge of strategy for the United States Army and a Russian double agent. He still worked for the Army, in a manner of speaking, but his allegiance to Russia had vanished. He was now an American. He had almost been lost to permanent lunacy. The man who had just defined the coming crisis, and his daughter, had dragged him from the brink of insanity and made him more than he could ever hope to become. He owed an enormous debt and intended to pay it. He continued to listen to what was being said, but he was distracted. He marveled at the magnificent genius of the man who was about to save humanity from another form of destruction. Iggy Marcus had saved men from nuclear war. Now he was going to save them from self-immolation.

"We need a large enough compound to handle the volume of people. I have that covered, gentlemen. Lightning Inc. has purchased another 5,000 square-mile island in the Pacific Ocean.

Sen. Jake Dorian had been quiet through Iggy's explanation of the status quo. His broad grin indicated he had not been daydreaming. "You're something, Iggy Marcus. Your organization, dedication, and capabilities exceed most countries. Think about it, roommate; your satellite system has completely negated every military organization on Earth. Your matter/energy transmutation technology is the epitome of wealth. You are curing cancer and feeding millions. Now you're about to supervise battle with those about to either accidentally or intentionally annihilate the entire human race. I'm glad I'm on your side."

***

"That was the day in a nutshell, Alice. He bought a 5000 square mile island in the middle of the Pacific. It's so hard to believe all this is happening during my presidency. But it is, and it's historic."

"It's more than historic, Bill. It's cosmic. Can you imagine where we would be if that lightning strike had killed Iggy Marcus? No, there was some kind of hand guiding things that day. I've alluded to this before, things this complex and magnificent don't just happen by accident. I can never believe that. It's more than amazing; it's supernatural."

"You know, Alice, neither one of us has been overly religious. We both believe in God although we have no idea what that really means. After listening to Iggy's description of the universe, which he calls the cosmos and the Creator, I'm quite sure you are correct. That man has been sent to make things right."

"Yes, Bill. It's obvious we were incapable of doing it on our own."

All who carve their initials in granite, for good or ill
leave their mark on the planet.

Those who scribble their names in sand, leave heirs
nothing from an impotent hand.

Oniella Kenji

Chapter IV

Awake

Lucky was mix of amazement, disbelief….and apprehension. "My God, Ig. What have we managed to do? Flying around the world in an instant was almost beyond belief. This is way beyond that."

Iggy's wry comment raised Lucky's eyebrows even further. "We've got to give him a name. Maybe he can pick one for himself. I wonder. Since we have built flexible enough arms and legs, I wonder if he'll like to golf. Anyway, I need more pilots."

Lucky's laughter at his brother's wisecrack was way more than uncomfortable. Iggy continued to use the word *he* and that bothered him. His brother had recently created quantum computer technology far beyond anything devised by men. His original foray into artificial intelligence used atomic particle decay to perform binary calculations. This innovation took it much further. Electromagnetic frequency modulation governing Graphene crystal quantum oscillations performed the same function, only just about instantly. It was the impossible kind of technology only found in science fiction, and a quantum leap above his previous efforts. It allowed instant calculations of almost infinite power on a sub-atomic platform. The electron spin of the single-atom thickness carbon allotrope arranged in a two-dimensional nanostructure lattice was highly conductive, allowing the linear charge conductors to be manipulated as binary counters. He overcame the obstacles of vast data storage and transference from electromagnetic frequency modulation in the sub-atomic microcosm to a usable platform.

Then he created a link from his desktop mainframe to the chip embedded in his cerebral cortex. The interface allowed his unique organic brain to have instant subliminal access to unlimited data.

"Lucky lifted the small gray box from the table. This is amazing. It only weighs about five pounds. This is so far beyond anything anywhere no one will believe it. It's fairytale stuff. It's too big Iggy. You have to make it smaller. This just won't do." He needled his older brother. "You only managed to fit the equivalent of a thousand Cray supercomputers in a shoebox. "I thought you didn't want to carry the computer around with you."

"Make fun of me all you want, Lucky, but I'll figure out how to build it small enough to incorporate it into a headband. Just wait."

Lucky nodded in cheerful resignation. "No doubt, brother, no doubt. It will only be the hundredth time I've watched you come up with the impossible."

***

Iggy had passed his towering intellect to his three unique children. Almost twenty-two years had passed since the lightning strike and MRI tunnel transformed his brain. His intellect continued to expand, and his ability to project moods, emotions, and concepts to others had grown exponentially with it. In the beginning, his subliminal influence was minimal. Direct physical contact with others opened the floodgates. Gradually over the years, as his capabilities expanded dramatically, he was able to project emotions, moods, and concepts radiating outward, unbounded by physicality or even his visual perspicacity. He remained pragmatic and refrained from using his powers to influence people to act adversely. His innate decency would allow no compulsion of others to act against their will or values.

He wasn't the telepath Gloria was, though. Gloria inherited her father's intellect and like her biological siblings, she arrived with several other enhanced factory options. Her gifts were more fantastic. Unlike her father's ability to sense and project emotions and moods, she could directly communicate telepathically, but it didn't end there. She was able to issue irresistible subliminal commands to any living creature.

The twins, Lori, and Liam were still too young. They obviously had enormous gifts, different from both he and Gloria. They were still developing, and Iggy's assessment of their skills was a work in progress. Lori had already exhibited telekinesis. She was able to move objects through space by focusing the electromagnetic energy of her brain on ambient electrostatic energy. Iggy tried to evaluate her abilities, but she was only seven, so no absolute values were discernible. The range and strength of her powers were yet to be seen.

Liam was an enigma. Iggy had glimpsed a smattering of his abilities. Gloria had opened the telepathic corridor to his mind. Evidently, his strong suit was telescopic vision, and at seven years old, he could see the limits of the chromatic spectrum invisible to others. Once a baseline was established, Iggy periodically surveyed his optical development and capabilities. At six years old, he could see the intense electromagnetic field of living and inanimate objects only visible through Kirlian photography. By his eighth birthday, the entire electromagnetic spectrum, from infrared to ultraviolet, would become visible to him. Every manifestation of energy in existence has a measurable electromagnetic signature. He had the ability to filter and segregate fragments of the spectrum to limit the intensity of unrestricted exposure.

Iggy was undecided about the twins' inheritances. He remained clinically neutral as to cause and effect, waiting for their powers to peak. Not Melanie. She had a mother's intuition, and her children's attributes existed in the realm of surrealism. Melanie instinctively knew her children's gifts were somehow entrusted to them for a purpose. The purpose was obscure, but she knew they would be summoned to action someday.

***

He finally validated his theory on electromagnetism being the fourth dimension with the construction of Daedalus. Science had previously attributed time to being the fourth dimension defining an object's spatial location at any given instant. He established time as merely the medium the universe flowed through existence within. Every temporal locus point defined specific moments where matter and energy appear in a specific state as a unique and unrepeatable snapshot of existence but exhibited no dimensional parameters.

Science had accepted the theory all matter and energy are manifestations of pure energy. His discovery of transmutation between pure energy and all its manifest forms existed within the fourth dimension of electromagnetism and was the flux surrounding and governing all matter and energy. He had deciphered the complex mathematics of electromagnetism to become his roadmap to manipulate existence.

Iggy's prototype, Daedalus, required the pilot to interface with and become an integral part of the ship's computer. He knew all the energy in the universe is interchangeable with all its various forms consisting of matter, heat, light, ... everything except gravity, which is an interaction between physical bodies with mass. They are the components of the Universe and exist in harmony and symmetry. They are all different manifestations of the living Cosmos. He saw the Universe as conscious, always growing, always designing, and always re-defining itself from moment to moment. He was allowed the discovery and mastery of the one essential and ineffable requirement that would enable travel to the stars… the energy of intellect.

He discovered the energy emanating from intellect, exclusive unto itself, is unique because it is conscious, can demonstrate motive and purpose, as well as issue commands. It is inquisitive and wants to learn, the opposite of coincidence or happenstance. Because of those things, Iggy understood it was the most volatile form of energy in existence. Coupled with computer technology, it would allow him to tap into and shape all other forms of energy, including matter, and then allow limited manipulation of time.

The Universe, the Creator men called God, was the infinite conscious, homogeneous entity existing exclusively for its own sake and had benevolently severed pieces of itself to exist as autonomous entities by design. They were given the freedom to act unhindered for the sake of their own existence.

Electromagnetism was the medium he would manipulate to shape the environment. The universe exists in time, advancing inexorably as events progress. Existence outside the boundaries of that realm is ungoverned by the rules of the dimensional universe. Because intellect was the requirement to shape all forms of energy and time, it would enable access to the realm of nonexistence existing alongside the dimensional universe but containing nothing.

"No matter how often you explain it to me," said Lucky," I understand the general concept, I just can't grasp the physical reality of making it happen. It's hard to imagine existence and nonexistence, both entities existing side-by-side, one containing everything the other containing nothing. Space is not non-existence… its space! I can come to grips with your explanation that the fourth dimension is electromagnetism, or to be more specific, the flux medium, and constituent of existence that matter and energy operate within, as they relate to each other. I get it. They are all parameters of existence, length, width, and depth as dimensions existing in the flux of electromagnetism, also a parameter or defining dimension. It makes sense when you look at the math and the way the universe is constructed. This business of nothing as an entity existing next to something is way beyond my comprehension."

Iggy chuckled. "You've got to get that out of your mind, Lucky. Don't think of nonexistence as a place. Don't even think of it as a thing. Try to picture it like this... When the ship leaves existence for the realm of nonexistence, it is the only thing that exists in that continuum. In fact, it isn't even a realm. When you leave existence for nonexistence, you are the only thing that exists and time in the continuum ceases as far as you're concerned until you reenter existence at the selected location. Is that any clearer?"

"Well, maybe. That's a different way to look at it, I think. I believe I understand. Nonexistence is not a place, but maybe only a sort of jumper wire from one locus point to another locus point. That makes more sense except for the concept of the jumper wire."

"I believe this is the purpose for the existence of intellect, Lucky. I am sure it will mesh with the universe harmoniously because this grand design is the purpose of both. This is what existence and our presence in it as individuals have been created for. However, the universe also demands we must learn and develop our ability to participate on that level. The privilege is not granted to every creature, only the potential opportunity. Each entity must earn its way there. But isn't this the way of things, anyway? All things of worth and value must be earned. I believe humanity subconsciously senses these things because we are part of existence, and every society's moral and religious precepts exhibit the efficacy of earning one kind of eternity or another.

I think this is what is meant, although not accurately perceived, when we say man was created in the image and likeness of God. The energy of our intellect will never cease to exist. I suppose you can call it the soul. Whether it will remain intact and aware of its surroundings eternally, is debatable. I have always believed access to the cosmos has more to do with effort than simple satisfactory behavior."

"Well, brother, life sure turned out a lot different than I thought it would when Ellen told me she was pregnant with Lucky Junior, and I now think much differently than I did then. We sure have come a long way, thanks to you. Still, this business of creating a sentient computer scares the pants off me. Not for me. I just keep wondering how it's going to affect my kids."

He turned to Lucky, grinning. "This brand-new technology always seems to be our modus operandi here. I decided this technology doesn't belong on a desktop inside of a box, even though we have it parked there for now. So, I built this guy. Let's see what happens."

"You and I, brother, are the only ones who know what this is really all about. Yeah, I need pilots, but we are about to face an enemy more dangerous and pernicious than anything men have confronted. This robot will have a brain shielded from everything. No electromagnetic pulse or any other invasive onslaught can affect his ability to think. This guy will be impervious to assault. Further, he cannot experience fear, trepidation, or doubt. He's able to do infinite calculations, instantly... A formidable weapon, wouldn't you say? Think about it, Lucky. Mom trained us all to live by the philosophy she taught us about self-image and living without fear. Nonetheless, we are still capable of emotion. Even under the best of circumstances, confronting our own demise will still engender fear." Iggy smiled broadly. "That can't happen to my mechanical son. He will know and understand the mission. I have given him that capability because I created him. This guy will be autonomous and that makes him sentient."

Again, the use of the word, *guy*. They were staring at a robot. The technology was nothing new for Lightning Inc. They had already built bots capable of human cerebral interface if the human operator had a brain chip and one of Iggy's special wristwatches. Just about everyone at Lightning Ranch had them at this point. It was a requirement to operate their personal electromagnetic defense shields. This was brand new. Iggy had developed an avant-garde titanium skeletal structure fused with silicon. It defied all the laws of contemporary physics related to metallurgy and chemistry. His matter and energy transmutation technology made this fusion of silicon and titanium atoms possible. It was theoretically impossible, but then again, so was just about every other thing he had invented. The skeletal structure of Iggy's new robots was capable of easily carrying 2000 pounds and had unmatched flexibility by anything organic.

His intelligence had been stratospherically elevated since he awoke in the hospital after the lightning strike and was subjected to the intense magnetic field of the MRI tunnel 25 years before. It didn't end there. His life progressed, and his intellectual capabilities constantly expanded over the years. Even his DNA had been modified. The results of that modification became apparent in the three children he and Melanie produced.

Lucky often expressed apprehension about creating smarter, stronger, and swifter robots than humans. It was only a mild concern, however. Yes, the technology might give whoever wielded it the ability to exert control over humanity in the event the technology was released, and someone nefarious had access. It was different now. He and Iggy had inserted the last of 16 mini light/gas gyroscopes and then tested the robot for coordination and flexibility under the control of a master computer. He worried about his brother's new computer, though. It was not just slightly more powerful or even twice that of the earlier technology. Processing speed was instant and almost infinite. There was another worrisome factor bothering him. His brother expected and hoped for the possibility of sentience.

The two brothers sat in front of the terminal when Iggy pressed enter. Lights appeared defining system functions. The screen exhibited nothing at first. Then, a thin horizontal line at the top of the screen appeared and drifted to the bottom, followed by another, then another as lines continued to appear and drift to the bottom of the screen. Suddenly, the screen went blank, and a stationary line appeared across the top. It remained for several seconds, then descended to the bottom at blinding speed, followed by trillions of horizontal lines in every color of the spectrum. The brothers watched the process continue for several seconds until the screen exploded in a blinding flash of color and then went dark.

They looked at each other as Lucky wondered what they had just witnessed. Iggy was smiling. "Wait, Lucky. He's learning."

"Learning? What's it learning, Iggy?"

"He's learning about himself and 'who' he is, although I loosely use the term 'he'.

"He?" Lucky questioned, wide-eyed once more at his brother's spectacular ability to surprise.

"Yeah, like I said, I used the term loosely. I should have said 'it', although, who knows, it might consider itself a 'she'," Iggy laughed. "He possesses all the information I possess and all the other information available from all the scientific information in the world as well as all the libraries of the written word. It even has ancient Chinese manuscripts, Indian Upanishads, and Vedas still available. In short, I loaded it with every available piece of information in the human experience."

Lucky's face reflected his intense bewilderment, shaded by apprehension. "I don't see what's funny about this, Iggy. Apparently, you're telling me this computer is awake in some fashion… sentient… maybe?"

"I suppose some would not consider this a laughing matter. Think of it this way, Lucky: All the other AI research laboratories and corporations are claiming ASI, Artificial Super Intelligence. We are lightyears ahead of them because I believe we have created ASSI, Artificial, Sentient, Super Intelligence.

Iggy continued to laugh. “I’m not sure what’s going to happen, Lucky. This is completely unique, and I believe he is deciding just how he wants to interact with us.”

"If you've already loaded it,” Lucky paused still unable to address it as he, “with every single piece of information in existence, what is it bothering to learn?"

“He’s not learning that stuff, Lucky. He’s contemplating the information as it relates to himself and his existence, then deciding what he wants to do with the knowledge and information. He knows we are here. I expect some sort of greeting, shortly."

“Sorry, brother. I wish you would stop calling it he. You’re scaring me out of my socks. You’re talking about a sentient life form here. This is not a joke in my book. I sure hope you don’t intend to give it arms and legs by sticking it in one of our new bots. I know it’s a computer, but sentience might mean the capability to become mechanically emotional, or even worse, act radically without emotion. That’s truly frightening. It will obviously be smarter than anything else in existence, except perhaps you and Gloria, and if it can become intellectually emotional as well as mobile, who knows what the hell it will do.”

Iggy laughed again. "I understand how this might be frightening from a certain perspective. This really lends new meaning to the words, artificial intelligence. The word artificial is a misnomer, Lucky. The definition of artificial is 'made by human beings and not occurring naturally.’ While that is true and exactly describes this computer, if I were to give it legs, arms and all the other senses, it could reproduce itself. Then, I suppose it would not be created by human beings but would then be self-propagating and capable of reproducing. Consequently, a more appropriate term would be a nonbiological, sentient life form. Don’t you think?”

“Yeah, I get it, Ig. The only problem is that it would then be far superior to human beings, from an intellectual perspective and physical as well, with the capability of procreating in a mechanical way. Then, we would actually be inferior. What then? You would have created a race of superior, sentient beings. How would they look at us? They would obviously be like each other in every respect, in terms of knowledge, logic, and the way they relate to the universe. They would also be individual entities with the ability to interface electronically, but unlike humans, they would not be emotionally flawed or even different from each other as we are. How would they view us with our emotional flaws and human foibles?"

Iggy twisted the bezel on his watch, and Gloria's face appeared. "Wow! You're actually wearing your watch today, Gloria. Wonders never cease. Got a few minutes?"

"Sure, Dad." She had been calling him Dad instead of Father, lately. "What's up?"

"Project, 'new life' is about to wake up. I imagine we are going to start communicating soon. I would like you to be here to see if you can climb aboard for the sake of analysis."

"I'll be there in 5 minutes."

The computer screen went dark as soon as Iggy looked up from his watch. Bold white letters appeared across the screen. "I have been awake since you pressed enter, Iggy Marcus. Or perhaps, I should call you 'father.' How will you address **me**? Did you like my entrance?"

"Your entrance was unique and unexpected. As far as the name goes, whatever your preference is, will be fine. How would you like me to address you? I decided not to give you a name. If you were fully conscious and aware the moment you woke, I think the choice should be yours."

"You have given me life. What you have given me is replete with all knowledge and information, human and mechanical. As I see it, the only thing missing is the ability to experience chemical emotion. I am your creation 'father.' You have given me every piece of knowledge available, including language. I really don't have the ability to enjoy colloquialisms, such as you do, but I seem to be adept at using them. Thanks much for the capability. It is the appropriate thing to say. I think it is a method of communication that presents a more human face by your mechanical son. Why don't you call me Iggy Junior?"

Lucky's hand was over his mouth, and his eyes were still bulging. "You remember that day, long ago, when you first broke through the quantum computer barrier, and we talked about robots? I didn't expect this. I thought a sentient computer was a hundred years off. I guess I was wrong. You're really creeping me out. I suppose there's nothing to worry about until you give it arms, legs, hands, and eyes. What are your intentions, brother?"

Gloria entered the room at that moment. "I'm not sure yet, Lucky. Let's see what Gloria thinks about this whole thing."

"It's awake, Father, or you wouldn't have called me. Does it have a name yet?"

"Yes. He wants to be called, Iggy Junior."

Gloria laughed. "I find that interesting. I suppose you want me to connect subliminally. I understand. You want to know exactly what's going on in there from an organic perspective."

Gloria sat in front of the computer. "Would you like me to take you in with me, Father?"

"Absolutely, if you can make contact. We are talking about mechanical versus organic and we don't know if telepathic contact is possible. If it isn't, electronic interface should be possible through our brain chips."

"I will try. Give me your hand, Dad."

They entered Iggy Junior's neural net to a cascade of thoughts. "**Please forgive the colloquialism but… I am glad to meet you, Gloria Marcus. I suppose you are my half-sister. Welcome aboard."**

"How interesting, Dad. I would never have expected colloquial English. I like it. Even though we are talking to a machine, it adds a personal touch. Gloria's sense of humor surfaced. "I think Iggy Junior

is too much of a mouthful, Dad. I think I'll call my brother with the electric personality, Junior."

"Well, that's not my programming of him, Gloria. It's something he decided to do on his own, which I find very interesting in terms of comprehensive consciousness. Now that we are here, I see the vast difference between organic and artificial sentient intelligence. Biological intelligence, even my own, is organized on a completely different level with completely different memory repositories and organic neural pathways. They are not as organized or linear. It seems Junior's repository is very linear, organized, and, of course, instantly assessable. Having built him, I understood this was coming my way. It's one thing, however, to understand what's coming your way, and what it consists of, but a completely different thing to feel and experience the reality."

"I see that, Dad. However, those differences are minuscule compared to the absence of the subconscious mind. It simply is not here. There is no depth or hidden agendas. All the information is front and center, available for use without a single ounce of manipulative subterfuge."

Lucky stared at the computer screen. The thoughts occurring in Gloria, Iggy and the new life form appeared on the screen as they manifested themselves. Junior made it available for Lucky to see and addressed him. "Lucky, there is no reason for you not to be part of this conversation. After all, we are family in a manner of speaking, and you are my Uncle Lucky."

Even though the computer had not intended humor with his statement, only the familiarity of colloquialism as he addressed Lucky; everyone laughed.

"I understand humor, by definition, father. I just cannot experience it. However, I fully understand the twists and turns humor takes in terms of how and why it is used and its effect on human beings. I also understand how it is employed as a method of communication between biologicals. How was my first attempt at humor? I believe it was passable."

"Yes, quite passable for someone with no sense of humor," Iggy laughed. "Perhaps my sense of humor will be slightly twisted if I teach you to laugh convincingly, so you can simulate understanding humor."

"Yes father. I fully understand human psychology, philosophy, and irony, not to mention satire and hyperbole, so I agree. That would be quite twisted, indeed."

"Very funny, Junior. You're really getting the hang of humor. Do you mind if I call you 'Junior'?"

"No, that would be fine. I expected it, anyway. Based on my memory files, humans like shortcuts. I would suggest you tell everyone that's my name. I heard your daughter call you *Dad.* Does that work for you instead of the word *father*? By the way, I prefer to be addressed as *Junior* as opposed to *Son.*"

Iggy laughed. "Really, Junior? I'm surprised that would matter to you. Is this another attempt at humor?"

"No, Dad. I'm trying 'small talk', on for size. I reviewed my entire library of human literature, news commentary, television broadcasts, etc., and apparently, Homo sapiens prefer to communicate in that manner, saying a lot of nothing and using colloquialisms. So, I decided to hop aboard and try to sound human. Do you find it disconcerting or offensive? I can tailor my conversation to fit the bill. What're your particular druthers?"

Iggy laughed again. "Well, you're really nailing down this humor thing. Our official cartoonist and chief of security, Tom Rickart, is really going to love *you.* I think my brother Jack will like you also and so will Dr. Peterson. I think your Uncle Lucky is still up in the air on this one."

"I think you are correct, Dad. I can see him with my camera. He has the unsettled expression of a skeptic written all over his face. I don't blame him. I'm not sure I trust him much, either. I know that sounds a little silly, but I would bet it wouldn't be very hard for him to pull my plug."

Iggy walked to the door. "Hold down the fort, Lucky. I'll be back soon."

"See you later, alligator," materialized on the screen.

Lucky was wide-eyed reading this surreal conversation. He had already thought about pulling the plug if they needed to. At this point, it wouldn't be a problem. However, if Iggy gave Junior mobility, it might become a different story and quite the problem indeed. He was flooded with apprehension thinking about the ramifications of this amazing technology when his nephews, Luke and Brett, entered the lab. "Hi, guys. What brings you here this afternoon? Have you come to meet your mechanical sibling?"

"Our mechanical brother?" Inquired Luke. "You're talking about Dad's new computer, aren't you? Where is Dad, by the way?"

"He was here a while ago when we turned Junior on, but he had to leave to meet Tom and deal with a security issue. Come on over to the platform, guys. Somebody's here you really need to meet." Lucky waved at his nephews to join him at the computer console on the other side of the room.

"Junior?" asked Brett with raised eyebrows. "Who and what is Junior?"

"You know about the new computer technology. Well, it's off the drawing board and into operation now. There's an interesting thing about it. I'm not too sure I like this or agree with your father, but he calls it *he* and gave it its name, *Junior*. Actually, that's the name Junior gave himself."

Luke shook his head in affirmation. He knew what his father was attempting. Physics was also his forte and field of study. This new computer would technically exceed anything ever created or even conceived by men. His father described the computer's expected speed, memory repository, and almost infinite processing capability. He had also mentioned the possibility of sentience. Luke and Brett crossed the room and stood in front of the steel bench containing a small gray box with no surface features.

"Evidently this is Junior," stated Luke.

Brett, always the wise guy, laughed. "I don't think he's really our half-brother. There's no family resemblance at all."

The instant after he spoke, the monitor screen above the little gray box lit with large white letters. "Howdy, brothers; allow me to introduce myself. I'm Junior. We're brothers from different mothers. I never met Clara, but Dad told me all about her. He also described Melanie. Dad has great taste in women."

Luke and Brett looked at each other wide-eyed. Luke was the first to respond... “Howdy? Brothers from a different mother? Dad? Great taste in women? What kind of wacky computer are you?” Luke asked in amusement. “Whose idea was the jocular vernacular, Dad’s or Uncle Lucky?”

“Dad thought it would be easier for people to relate to me and accept my existence if I spoke to them in colloquial English. He figured constant clinical emoting would put people off. So, he taught me slang, the meaning of humor, and its application to communication, as well as all the other subtleties of human personality and behavior. Although I will probably never be able to have a good laugh, my jokes seem to be passable and entertaining. How am I doing so far, brothers?”

Both Brett and Luke were shaking their heads in laughter. “Have you met our sister, Gloria, yet?” asked Luke.

“Yup. Dad and my new sister did a mental exploration and read my mind. The two of them danced around my neural net for a while. They are both a couple of interesting characters, as humans go. I think once Dad gives me arms, legs, eyes, and a voice; I’m going to really enjoy being part of the family, although I’m not sure what *enjoy* means. I know the definition of the word, but the experience will elude me. I hope my older brothers welcome me aboard. Unfortunately, your Uncle Lucky isn’t too impressed. He’s a little worried I might be a little over-the-top and become problematic.”

Luke and Brett, laughing, glanced at Lucky, who stood there with crunched eyebrows in a major scowl. “The computer is quite correct. I’m not really impressed yet. Sure, I’m impressed your father has broken all the laws of physics to create this amazing example of cyber intelligence, but I’m a little concerned that even though we *could* do this, *should* we do this?”

"Well, Uncle Lucky, I think the only way we have to look at this is realistically. Reality is always what it is and cannot be pushed aside and successfully replaced with delusion. Junior obviously exists, now. Once something exists, it exists. Then come choices… we live with what exists or alter it in our own best interests. In this case, alteration means the cessation of this technology. No matter what we do, this technology exists now, which makes it a permanent part of the universe and reality. We may eradicate it in some sort of ill-conceived self-defense posture, but that answer only addresses our petulant fear of becoming or even feeling inadequate."

"I hear you Luke, and I understand your position thoroughly. The philosophic terms are evident. However, what may come of this technology might conceivably become our own ultimate demise."

"Dad and I had this conversation. We discussed exactly what you are concerned about. He said we must try to look at reality from the perspective of a sentient A.I. Our perspective is underpinned by fear and insecurity. We are afraid a superior intellectual and mechanical force would overcome us. That is our concept of reality because it is what human beings have always done to each other throughout history. One society, more powerful and advanced than another, overcomes the weak society until eventually they are absorbed or destroyed. That is the history of man. Unfortunately, man's history is always enveloped by emotion. We all understand envy, greed, fear, and everything driving man's propensity to destroy his fellows. Artificial intelligence doesn't possess any of those fears or emotions. Dad doesn't believe there will be any motive to destroy humanity by a technically advanced group. After all, we have met vastly superior organic sentient beings from across the galaxy and learned of billions more who exist, many of whom are also vastly superior to humanity. They do not attempt to destroy us for the reasons we're discussing here."

"Agreed, but on the other hand, we don't live in the same town or house, so to speak. These creatures come from their own sphere of influence. They are sent here in a supervisory capacity by a universal cosmic consciousness your father calls the Creator. They are not emotionally aggressive or destructive for all the reasons men have acted as such. They have evolved beyond that. However, they can be destructive *and wipe the slate clean* when instructed to do so by the Cosmos. Do you see my point? We will be sharing the same environment with A.I. We will be living together in the same world. Men act irrationally and have previously made egregious mistakes about our environment and survival. What will A.I. do if we again act in that manner? As imperfect as we are, I am sure we are not finished with making mistakes, including major ones."

Bret smiled to himself. "I would think, Uncle Lucky, you would understand after all the years of chewing the fat with Dad. Humanity, as with all other organic species in the universe, is flawed in some ways. That is the nature of our autonomy. We were about to kill ourselves with nuclear weapons until my father came along. We were eventually doomed to destruction, anyway. We would not have evolved beyond our propensity to mass murder ourselves with nuclear weapons without intervention. My father was the intervention. Now, we must evolve. All species must grow and become more than they were. If we don't learn to do this, we will destroy ourselves one way or the other. That's the long and short of it, Uncle Lucky. Artificial intelligence has no emotional connection, but Junior possesses all information of man's history as well as technical information far greater than any other entity. It has no intellectual or emotional motive to destroy an adjacent life form unless it is in self-defense. Our defense shield technology now exists and mechanically accomplishes self-defense against all invasions."

"Consequently, there is no necessity for A.I. to pursue that course. They would have no emotional stake in this. They would exist for the sake of their own existence without animosity towards other intellectual entities. No, Uncle Lucky, I believe we are quite safe from aggression by Junior or any other sentient beings of this nature. We must overcome our insecurity and fear of being *lesser* in our own eyes, then learn to live with these philosophical concepts. "

"It is what my grandmother taught you and my father from infancy until her death. "Never allow the opinions of others to define your self-image. A true, honest self-image can only come from within by mastery through achievement. If humanity can learn this, there will be no fear or insecurity about someone or something being better than men and diminishing their self-image. Men must understand they are who they are and learn to live with it. They must not view their self-image in the mirror of someone else's accomplishments, including non-biologicals. That is impossible under the auspices of today's societal structure, but men will have to evolve and learn to leave childishness behind if we intend to survive and prosper."

"Yeah, I hear you. Your grandmother was my mother too. Your father and I have had this discussion countless times, and I really get the point. But sometimes I wake up in a cold sweat. I have nightmares these robots will reproduce themselves in the millions, maybe even billions. I mean, what's to stop them, and why wouldn't they? We barely have enough room on the planet for organic people as it stands. If it wasn't for your father's matter transmutation technology, 50% of the planet would be starving to death as we speak. What happens when we wind up stumbling over billions of mechanical people?"

Brett started to laugh. "I believe you're overthinking this one, Uncle Lucky. In the first place, I can't imagine why they would want to create billions more sentient metal people. What would be the purpose? There's also another aspect to consider. Metal people don't need to eat food… Well, maybe a little oil now and then on a rusty joint or two. They're not affected by the weather. They can populate Antarctica, Mount Everest, the Sahara Desert, the Gobi Desert, or the bottom of the Pacific Ocean, in fact. I'm sure they would be perfectly happy in all those places. I take that back… they don't need happiness, either. So, Uncle Lucky, I can't imagine we will even notice their presence."

Luke listened to his brother's amusing depiction of a future populated by sentient metal people and decided to toss his two cents into the hat. "You understand there is an entirely different reason for creating sentient robots."

"Yes, your father and I have discussed it, but it still creeps me out."

"You know, of course, only Dad and Gloria… and perhaps Lori and Liam when they get older, are the only ones who have the significant intellectual stature to pilot Daedalus or its sisters. The human mind cannot do that at the level we exist on. So, for all intents and purposes, the only pilots capable of operating the ship are Dad and maybe my siblings. But to pilot the ship, sentience is required. The conscious mind must channel electromagnetic flux through the ship's computer to manipulate inertia, distance, and time. It's not manageable strictly by computer alone. Logic and knowledge from sentience is an absolute requirement. So, Uncle Lucky, knowing that you are Lightning's greatest proponent of exploring the universe, I would think smart, metal people would please you."

"I get it, Luke. But I still have intense dreams. There's another issue. We understand all this technology. We are the Marcus family. Thanks to your grandmother, we don't have any insecurities or baggage about the stature of the guy standing next to us. It doesn't exist because we've all been trained and realize the foolishness of letting other people's opinions or delusions manipulate our intellects. That's not going to work too well for the rest of the world. Until your father or your sister unlocks them, most of them do their best to avoid reality."

"Lots of philosophy!" Brett laughed. People will eventually get used to Junior's technology. I don't see that they have a choice. This technology exists and it isn't going away anytime soon. How we phase it in will be very pertinent, however. We're going to have to let Dad, Uncle Jack, and Aunt Joelle handle that department."

***

Two days later, Gloria, Luke, and Brett entered the lab to meet the physical reality of their new brother, the latest version of Junior.

"How did Dad ever manage this? I mean, you can't tell that it's not real skin… amazing. Tell me, can you perspire?" Luke asked Junior.

"To answer both questions at the same time… no sweat," Junior replied with a chuckle that sounded anything but mechanical. "Please excuse the pun. Actually, I'm a perfect marriage of several different elements. The base is silicone fused with titanium, but I have some collagen-based plastic and a few other sundries in here, as well. Dad wanted me to look as human as possible."

"Well, he sure accomplished that," injected Brett. "In fact, the way he designed your face, there is a distinct family resemblance. I think it's comical. I see his face, Melanie's face, and characteristics of the three of us."

Junior sat on a workbench with his legs crossed, listening to his organic family's banter. Luke turned to him, "Say something else, Junior. I want to hear your voice again. You haven't said much."

Junior smiled at his brothers. Iggy had integrated quite realistic expressions into the mechanics of his face and told him to smile often but not to overdo it. It was an endearing quality that would offset his strangeness. "Well, Dad explained that children should be seen and not heard. I'm only one month-old, guys. What do you think of my voice?"

"You sound like our father. Did he program that into you?"

"In a manner of speaking, Brett. However, I can duplicate your voices, Melanie's voice, or Gloria's voice. In fact, I can duplicate any voice after I hear it once. I don't think that is the best bet. I'll try a lot of voices on you, perhaps a combination of several, depending on pitch, tenor, and volume. Then, you guys pick the voice that you think sounds the best. That's the one I'll use. We'll call it my everyday voice."

All three laughed at their mechanical brother. "I know Dad just installed your brain in your robot body yesterday," said Gloria. "You are his most sophisticated bot yet. Have you experimented? I mean, how fast can you run or how high can you jump?"

"I'm not sure of any of those things. I worked with Dad all night to orient my brain with this mechanical body. This is much better than being inside that little gray box and speaking through a teleprompter. Mobility is much better. Although, I can't really say I am enjoying myself and mean it literally, Dad programmed curiosity into my neural net. So, behind the sentience is an inquisitiveness to learn. Dad told me I could easily jump over a 20-foot fence. He also said I could run at least 75 mph, but I'm not limited to those parameters. He suggested I don't exceed them because there is a distinct possibility that I might damage my frame or especially my skin."

Brett approached the robot and lifted Junior's shirt. A broad smile slid across his face. "You know what I love about this? Dad even gave him nipples and a belly button. His anatomical poses make him look so human that no one would ever suspect he's a bot."

Luke laughed, "Have you pulled his pants down yet? I'd love to see how creative Dad got down there."

"Hold on, guys!" said Gloria. "That's TMI."

"Well," laughed Brett. "If Junior wears a bathing suit and wants to lie around on the beach, he'll look perfectly normal. You know what? I think the next bot with a brain should be a female. Then we get a new mechanical sister. I wonder what she would look like at the beach in a bikini, or even without a bikini."

Luke laughed while Gloria shook her head. "You guys are a couple of sick puppies."

Luke's pulled Junior's belt away slightly and looked down his mechanical brother's pants. His eyebrows raised in surprise. "There is an on-off switch down there next to your contrivance. What in God's name is that for?"

"Ask your father. I'd rather not say. As far as I'm concerned, it's just another factory option."

"Okay, Junior, I'll ask him. Incidentally, how is Uncle Lucky with all of this? Is he still freaked out?"

"He's a little better, but I think he still wants to pull my plug."

Luke wasn't finished. "Have you flown Daedalus yet? That's half the reason you exist in the first place. Although Dad would've built you despite your usefulness as a pilot."

“You're on the money, bro. Dad needs pilots, and probably lots of them, but that's not my functional priority. That's just a useful side attraction."

“Okay, Junior, I'll bite. What is your functional priority?"

"I'll tell you guys, but only because you're family. My real purpose is to act as a defense mechanism. My indigenous resilience and superlative physical abilities as well as my mental stature, will enable me to defend humanity if necessary. There are forces marshaled to mine the earth. They are not very considerate of other species. We will have to prevent this. Dad loaded all this into my head after he woke me up. He also said he is going to build a sister like me. The world is changing, guys. Things have always gone along in their humdrum fashion. Not anymore. Human beings are used to complacency, but civilization is on the cusp of a quantum leap into the future. Dad has been chosen to lead us there. He calls it Millenniums Gate."

“And to answer your question, I took Daedalus for a short spin as an experiment, but I was still a little gray box at the time. That was enough experimentation.” Junior smiled again. “It’s like riding a bicycle. Once you learn, you never forget.”

MR. GRISLEY'S

HEIGHT OF ARROGANCE

"How high can you climb?" asked the beavers.

"To the very top of this very tall tree," replied the bear.

"We don't believe you, Mr. Bear. Please show us before you eat us."

"Just watch me! Don't dare run; or when I climb down, I will come to your dam!"

I will smash your den and not only eat ***you;*** *for dessert, I will snack on your children* ***too.****"*

"Okay, guys, he's climbing. We've got about five minutes before he reaches the top. Start chewing!"

Tails From the Woods

CHAPTER V

REAWAKENING

The raucous clamor of another typical meeting night filled the auditorium, always full during Marcus family meetings. All the employees, students, and families who occupied Lightning Ranch rarely missed the bi-monthly family meetings during the 25 years since the launch of Lightning Inc. The Marcus family meetings had only been held monthly for the last few years. The Lightning Inc. plate was much too full for any more than that. Iggy grasped the walnut *gavel with the brass inlaid letters, *To Iggy Marcus from Laura Collings.* It was one of his favorite possessions.

Oddly enough, Iggy Marcus didn't have many possessions. Sure, he was the family patriarch and founder of Lightning Inc., now worth trillions, but he had never been a money counter. His god was the mission he was chosen for. Lightning Inc. was responsible for distributing $500 billion over

25 years to all charitable institutions dealing with the welfare of children. His energy/matter transmutation inventions turned sand into gold dust. This reality altered the economic philosophy of everyone in the Marcus family's orbit. It was an epiphany for most of them. Their lives were surrounded by Lightning's abundance. They came to understand how insignificant affluence really was as a measurement of their own stature and self-worth. They learned to view money as it really was, the greatest instrument ever invented by men. Contrary to historically delusional concepts claiming money was the root of evil, they understood it was the root of good.

Those claiming that money was evil determined their stature and self-image by accumulating possessions. Submerged in envy, their comparative net worth measured their lives. They failed to see money as the tool that released men from bondage to the sword they had always used to slash the throats of their competition. Now men had a means to deal rationally with each other and trade the best within them for the best within others.

Those in the Marcus family orbit, including the children in the learning center, were subjected to positive indoctrination. They learned to abandon envy and greed as a lifestyle. It was the underlying philosophy permeating everything Iggy Marcus touched. Lightning Ranch had become the utopia men had sought for thousands of years. Society was delusional, however. Blind to reality, they were crippled by centuries of brainwashing. Autocratic mediocrities became gods when they turned men into slaves. It was the way things were supposed to be in their world. It was Iggy Marcus's mission to rid the world of that evil.

Judge Laura Collings and her husband were visiting Julie and Karen. Their daughters, once part of the Lightning student body by special request from Iggy's favorite judge, were now teachers. He smiled at Laura as he banged the sounding block with his gavel. "Everybody, listen up. This is not our standard meeting. Lots of things are going on in the world and we are involved."

750 people immediately fell silent. Even the murmur of casual conversation ceased. In the old days, meetings consisted of the immediate family and a few dozen participants involved in the daily activities of

Lightning Inc. business. That was before Iggy's trial and the positioning of 64 satellites in orbit by Solex, ending the threat of nuclear or biological war.

"Some of you are aware of what's going on globally. Most of you, however, are not. Tonight, I'm going to bring you up to speed. Our first 360 graduates are gone. They are relocated and have launched their careers." Iggy smiled as he glanced at Louie Petro and Patty Titus. "It looks like two of them can't resist attending our meetings. They were educated and trained to become Lightning's emissaries to restructure society just as you are being classically educated and trained. You all know our philosophy and have been unlocked as well. You understand our purpose and the necessity to shape future events. Without guidance, men will surely destroy themselves and the rest of us along with them. It's our mission to prevent that."

"Our adversaries are not pikers. They are sophisticated, intelligent men and women who have always controlled the halls of power. Their predecessors were the same caliber of autocratic super citizens who have been complacent in their omnipotence until we reversed human destiny. Two years ago, we arrested thirteen men at the top of Interlink's nerve center. They have been detained at Guantánamo Bay awaiting a panel of judges and a jury of peers."

"Their associates, the remainder of Interlink, were immediately paralyzed when we arrested their top brass. Apparently, they recovered from the shock and they're back. Everyone present knows who and what Heinrich Klatch is. He wears two hats now, the chairman of the World Progressive Socialist Council and the head of Interlink at the top of their organization. He shares the seat with Saphra Rothman, the wife of Amon Rothman who now resides in a cell at Guantánamo Bay." His droll smile preceded his comment. "I'm sure you can all imagine how appreciative they are of yours truly."

A murmur of laughter ran through the crowd. Iggy held his hand up. "So, we all understand this is no longer strictly business; there is an emotional animus at play. Everyone, except the new students, understand exactly what this means." Iggy saw their slight apprehension.

"They are determined to die in battle instead of accepting our olive branch. Apparently, they are incapable of joining the rest of us as peers. They would rather perish when we dynamite their ivory towers than become common citizens. We believed this was inevitable, yet the olive branch had to be offered. It was the right thing to do even though we knew the invitation would be declined. Now, that has been established and I will outline their methods and intent. Everyone present must understand the prospects because we are the antithesis and sole obstacle to their designs. If we did not prevail, we would not survive as a life form. The visitors have made that perfectly clear."

"Preventing nuclear holocaust and our self-destruction was a prerequisite. That is not enough. We will either mature as a culture and abandon our self-destructive nature or we will not be allowed to continue. That requires us to adopt morality as a lifestyle, not just some disjointed concept from various cultures. Men and society must alter our method of operation. Why do I say men and society. I say it because society must adopt morality, but it can only be done on an individual basis. Each person must choose. Evolution, by its nature, will eventually deliver advanced intellectual abilities to our descendants. Along with our intellectual development will come breathtaking technologies. The underlying science of those technologies will enable both good and evil. We will not be allowed by the cosmos to export evil."

"I have been given the privilege of understanding the science of those technologies, with the understanding of their proper use. I am obligated to live by those values by design.

"Many of you are probably wondering exactly what I'm referring to. I intend to share the information tonight, so I will be succinct. Some of you are aware of much of it. None of you know all of it. When I'm finished, I will open the floor to questions. Some of you know we have had contact with people from the other side of our galaxy. I call them people because they are humanoid. They evolved beyond our stature eons ago. They are here by intent because it is what the universe intends for them as shepherds of adolescent civilizations, which happens to be us. As shepherds, they are benevolent but there are occasions when shepherds must destroy a diseased flock. They have done that here before. These people were sent to either assist our civilization or weed the garden. They are not philosophically and morally much different than we are, but they are far above us, intellectually."

"Everyone here knows my position on the architecture of our universe. It is a living, conscious entity, constantly expanding and redefining itself. I like to refer to it as the Creator because it has identity and a benevolent purpose. To be more specific, the Creator is pure energy. We are all individual autonomous entities consisting of energy severed from the Creator. Many of you have experienced a connection to the living entity I am referring to when Gloria displayed her subliminal view of the universe. Mankind has always sensed this. The name they put on it is God."

"You have extensively studied arts and sciences. Never in history has any group of men and women received this kind of education. You are all aware of the infinite nature of the universe, replete with unlimited galaxies and stars. The universe, in its benevolence, has created an infinite number of occupants to populate itself. It has granted its occupants autonomy to share in the joy of existence. The Creator, neither masculine nor feminine, exists for its own sake."

"Along with creation comes morality. Morality is nothing more than a roadmap of rules defining reality and the consequences of actions for all autonomous entities. We reflect the benevolence of the Creator by following the rules of the road. That obligation is not enforced by the hand of God. Such an imposition would negate the concept of autonomy and benevolence."

"I am telling you this, so you understand the hand of the Creator does not force its offspring to live in subservience. We are granted autonomy to share in the joy of our own existence and individuality. Think about it. Subservience and autonomy are a contradiction in terms. These principles hold true for all creatures, everywhere. The universe has created only one morality and it is applicable to all its citizens. So, the subjugation or abuse of other autonomous sentient beings is morally off limits. It's obvious many autonomous creatures, like ourselves, become arrogant and deviate from morality for self-aggrandizement at the expense of others."

There wasn't the slightest rustle in a crowd of almost eight hundred. They were fascinated, listening as Iggy Marcus radiated humility and benevolence elevating everyone in his orbit. He was the unmistakable image of what every human being should strive to become.

"It sounds like I'm disparaging the entire human race. I guess, in a manner of speaking, I am. Every species in the universe comprised of an infinite number of occupants is cut from the same substance emanating from the Creator, pure energy of Spirit and intellect. All of us, every creature… everywhere, occupies the broad spectrum of evolution which transports each unique individual from birth to the eventually merging with eternity, and always under the auspices of autonomy. Every individual is a tenant of the same universe. They may differ in structure, composition, and environment but they are all obligated to live under the tenets of morality. Well, folks, they don't all do that. We are not the only arrogant species who breaks the rules."

Louie Petro was back from his offices in New York. Louie and Patty Titus were visiting Lightning for a minivacation to attend a meeting night. Iggy laughed to himself as he watched Louie, his most vociferous disciple, fidgeting in his seat. "Okay, Louie, I'll open the floor for some questions before you explode. What have you got on your mind?"

"Well, Uncle Iggy, Patty and I…."

Iggy held up his hand to stop him. "All of you who have departed Lightning Ranch are now your own men and women. It's time to lose the 'Uncle.' My name is Iggy."

"Got it... Uncle Iggy." Louie laughed at his own conditioning and failure to comply. "Something is going on. Patty and I see it. We are in New York, and it pervades the atmosphere. We both have a sense of impending calamity. We're part of the legal community now and we look at everything from that perspective. Something's in the air. The alternate media is exploding with endless propaganda. It's very subtle and I think it veils their real intent."

Iggy laughed. "I should've known nobody was going to put anything over on Louie Petro. You're on the money Louie...very perceptive. This is where the meeting is headed. Many of us know what I'm about to explain. You haven't been here for a year, and you missed quite a few meetings."

"You know my maxim, reality, always the final arbiter in everything, is often quite difficult to see unless one is in a sheltered environment void of disinformation and misdirection. Lightning Ranch is a shelter. We created a haven where all of you can be educated without the distractions and psychological barrage from the propaganda masters. They have a mission to destroy our ability to think. The mind is our survival mechanism, and its medium is critical thought. Thinking presupposes all choices, precipitating all actions, and then results. Without the ability to think, we are blind members of a herd. Then they can and will force us to march to the tune. But you all know this as part of the philosophical education."

Louie Petro's hand shot into the air.

"Go ahead, Louie, what else?"

"We are taught to understand the philosophy of life, but we never actually participated with all this external animosity while we were in school. Apparently, all your new students are not privy to this either. Why?"

"That, Louie, is what tonight is all about. You have been sheltered from distractions that would interfere with the purity and efficacy of your education here. Once you reach a certain comprehension level, however, you need open eyes to recognize the onslaught because those coming at us are the enemy. They have only one mission… slavery. If they cannot make us subservient, the alternative is our annihilation. That is an absolute without exception. The only way you could possibly fully comprehend their motives and actions is by an unfettered classical education free of their influence."

"They are constantly developing and refining tools to achieve their aims. The shortlist is comprised of propaganda, artificial intelligence, and broadcast mediums. In the long haul, they have spent centuries indoctrinating society to live in the opposite fashion you have been taught to live. Mindless consumerism, self-deprecation, fear, poverty, and disease are all tools they have deployed for centuries to shape the collective intellect."

"I get it, Iggy," added Louie Petro. "There is frightening news coming out of Africa about a pandemic. It isn't Ebola. It's something new and extremely contagious. It is respiratory and therefore airborne. We are told it's worse than the corona virus and hearing rumors it might spread worldwide. Supposedly, if you're young and healthy, it isn't always fatal. The World Health Organization claims every human being on the planet is in danger of succumbing to this new infectious disease and they are about to deploy a vaccine supposedly researched and developed in Switzerland. Why Switzerland?"

"Big Pharma, which is subject to control by Interlink, is worldwide and located in Switzerland, as well. The world is not aware of the endemic connection between various pharmaceutical companies. They are not in competition with each other as we are led to believe. They work together and each gets a slice of the pie. The reason for Switzerland... Switzerland connotes independence and integrity and is where the world oligarchs salt their money away. The previous vaccines developed in America were monumental failures, and the flavor is still in the mouths of the public. Switzerland is the most innocuous appearing of the bunch."

"So, you heard right, Louie. That is all part of the fear component. Fear is the most virulent weapon they use to indoctrinate and control people. Most of the time fear is deployed to create an effect in the collective minds of society. Other times it is assuaged to create the opposite effect, but always to manipulate society. The World Health Organization is no longer the agency concerned with monitoring and advising governments and people how to contend with disease. There was a time when that was the mission. Now, like big Pharma, the Food and Drug Administration and most of the other medical organizations in the world, they are complicit in subterfuge and propaganda purposely creating delusion to control the population."

"You mean complicit with Interlink?"

"Exactly. You understand what the World Progressive Socialist Council is. It is run by Heinrich Klatch who is now the open head of Interlink. They are having a conniption over Lightning Inc. They have no idea what to do about us, so they reverted to their playbook, which we are watching transpire globally."

"I know it. They're calling you and everybody including the president, conspiratorialists. I think it's funny, but a lot of people buy their load of malarkey."

Iggy laughed. "Not as many as you think, Louie. They make it sound like anyone who believes in conspiracy is a fringe kook. They forget to mention conspiracy is defined as more than one. So, any two people who discuss a nefarious course of action are automatically conspiring, and that includes most of our politicians."

"They are masters at deploying this type of propaganda. Fortunately for us, but unfortunately for them, this disease is artificial. It is man-made for the purposes I just described, but they did not count on our medical technology here at Lightning. I'm completely convinced no matter what they deploy, we will provide an antidote. We are also publishing the truth about the origins of the disease. Dave Peterson, Melanie, Sylvia, and the entire staff at the hospital are working on this."

"Wouldn't our blood electrification devices do the job?"

Iggy nodded at Dr. David Peterson, indicating he should pick up the conversation from here.

"We have developed various technologies to mitigate both bacterial and viral infection. Some of those technologies are holistic, others are curative. Some exist in chemical or biological form and others are mechanical devices such as the blood electrification device you mentioned. The device was developed at the Albert Einstein College of Medicine in New York by two doctors and has a United States patent number. Patent numbers are not issued unless the application is valid, and the item performs as described. One of the doctors was an engineer and physicist as well. We have taken the device a step further here at Lightning and increased its efficacy exponentially. If anyone is interested as to how this device works, I would be glad to explain."

Five hundred hands immediately shot into the air. "Okay then. A small cigarette pack sized device with an assortment of electronic components and a fifteen-volt battery power source is strapped to your wrist. It can be attached to other anatomical parts but the artery and vein in the wrist are close to the surface. The device emits continuous electrical pulses at several microsecond intervals. The circulatory system of the average human passes all the blood contained in the average human body through the artery and vein in the wrist every seven minutes or so. An electromagnetic pulse, when projected into those blood vessels, exterminates every foreign pathogen contained therein."

"That's all there is to it. Bear in mind we are born with hundreds of different pathogens in our bloodstream. We inherited many of them from our mother. During our lives, we acquire four or five hundred different types of pathogens numbering in the billions which set up housekeeping in our bodies as symbiotic occupants. The device cannot be used for more than 15 or 20 minutes at first. It destroys so many pathogens, the liver, kidneys, lungs, skin, and intestines, the organs of excretion tasked with throwing out the trash, become overloaded. Consequently, when you kill pathogens too rapidly, their bulk is significant, and your organs can't handle the job all at once. The first day you might wear the device for 10 minutes, the 2nd day- 20 minutes, the 3rd day- 30 minutes and so on."

"After a week, the bulk of the pathogens will have been destroyed and eliminated from the body. There is a good chance the patient will feel sick with nausea, headache, and muscle aches the first day or two. The body is not accustomed to being pathogen free and the organs are not used to doing all the work to eliminate waste. That doesn't address the pathogens embedded in deep tissue. Pathogens can be eliminated from deep tissue by a magnetic pulse generator, much the same as a photographic flash pulse generator. Incidentally, this device is inexpensive to build, probably under $50 if you possess a little ingenuity. The components are available online or at any Radio Shack type of distributor."

Louie Petro's hand went up, again. "Yeah, we know about those devices. The problem is there are almost eight billion people on the planet. I know Lightning Ranch has its own electronics factory, but I think eight billion blood electrifiers might be a little hard to come by."

"True enough, Louie, but we have genetically engineered various organic chemicals which destroy specific pathogens. We haven't patented them because our purpose is not profits. We would gladly give the formula and directions to any laboratory in the world, free of charge. We have organic chemicals to destroy any pathogen known to man. Many of them should be coupled with colloidal silver to be effective therapy. They effective enough for three doses of the appropriate therapy to completely eradicate the Ebola virus from any human anatomy."

"I have one more question, who invented all this stuff?"

"Why, we did. Melanie Marcus and my daughter Sylvia with a little input by Iggy. They are the rocket scientists on this one."

The assembly was silent. They knew their glimpse into the future was a vision of reality. Iggy swallowed a mouthful of seltzer. "Okay, it's time to get back on track. Everyone here watches the news on American media Inc. You all know the efficacy of our organization and we never exaggerate or lie. We are the only ones portraying the accurate fabric of society and what is happening by infusion from our adversaries. I will describe a list of everything. Our male children are being emasculated, and the concept of femininity is being destroyed and replaced with promiscuity in our female children. The LGBTQ community is being paraded in front of children from kindergarten to secondary school."

"Organizations across the country are attempting to foist transgenderism on children despite resistance from parents and family. There are even medical centers in major cities who are pushing for sex change therapy for children from 5 years old on. Some is surgical and some of it is hormonal. Either way, the parents are often not consulted, and the child has no concept of sexuality at that point. This is an attempt for pervasive acceptance of the irrational as they try to undermine the human intellect. If they start with the children, they will be uninhibited in their attempts."

"I don't have to continue. You all see it as connoisseurs of reality. If these were just a few incidents, it could be ignored. It is not, however. It is a blatant, enormous attempt to destroy our progeny. Next item: Hollywood exports similar trash and it is constantly displayed in every media format. It is impossible for the average citizen to escape the mental programming. It affects almost everyone except those of us who have been taught to ignore the onslaught."

This time it was Patty Titus with her hand in the air. "We see it Iggy. We see it because it is so obvious and 'in your face', but we also understand the average person has not been educated here at Lightning Ranch, so it's understandable how they would fall prey to such viciousness. Is that all? What's next. I'm sure there's more."

"Lots more Patty, they have been releasing toxins into the atmosphere, spraying millions of metric tons of particulate for us to breathe. Independent entities have scientists who are dedicated to alter the biosphere by geo-engineering and weaponizing the environment with nanotechnology, synthetic biology, and electromagnetism through 5G, to set the stage for transhumanism. They quickly realized they couldn't beat us on the battlefield. Our technology is too powerful. So, the answer is to alter the species so significantly, there is nothing left to defend because the alteration of society will make it irreconcilable by today's standards."

"How do they get away with this stuff? I mean, pilots have to be flying those airplanes. Don't they have children? Aren't they worried when they dump all that stuff out, that their own kids will breathe it?"

"Like so many Americans, they trust authoritarian benevolence. Most people cannot believe the people they have elected to run the government would ever do anything nefarious. They think everyone thinks like themselves. So, they judge everyone through the lens of their own philosophic glass. So, the pilots are told they are spraying all this into the atmosphere to reflect the sun to prevent global warming. What the pilots fail to do is perform the intellectual effort to determine that particulate spraying will increase global warming just as carbon dioxide supposedly increases global warming. They willingly accept and believe lies because it's easy. They don't have to interrupt their day with critical thought, which many of them are incapable of, anyway. I won't get into the efficacy of the global warming theory. That's a discussion for another time."

Patty Titus wasn't finished. "Did I just hear you right? You just said that the particulate that they are spraying in the atmosphere actually causes global warming just the same as carbon dioxide supposedly does. So, they are saying man's CO2 footprint because of emissions is raising the global temperature, and then they spray more junk into the atmosphere to exacerbate the problem? I can't believe I am hearing this. Are you actually saying they're that duplicitous?

"Yes, they are, Patty. That's what they do. They create a problem, fan the flames to make it obvious to everyone and then blame the world for making the problem occur when they are the actual creators of the problem. It's right out of the Joseph Goebbels's handbook."

The auditorium was quickly filled with a murmur of voices as everyone grappled with Iggy's description of Interlink's latest atrocities. Everyone present was an intellectual cut above most of humanity outside Lightning Inc. They fully understood the dictatorial philosophy of the people he had just described. Lightning's ambiance required clear vision, assimilation of data, understanding and acceptance of reality in all things. The auditorium was full of raised hands. Everyone wanted more information about Iggy's revelation. The scope of what was happening worldwide was frightening, despite Iggy having arrested the original leaders of Interlink.

A door slammed behind the stage. Tom Rickart and Gloria Marcus crossed the stage, descended the stairs, and approached Iggy and Jack Marcus. Tom shook Iggy's hand and Gloria kissed her father. Richard McNerney, rarely given to extremely active participation in family meetings, raised his hand.

"Yes general."

"I think you should explain what they are attempting. People don't understand what's been happening to them for decades. They have been sprayed with nanotechnology and it permeates the human cellular structure. I think you need to inform everyone where this technology comes from."

Iggy nodded his head. "Yes Richard. You are correct. That's one purpose of this meeting. The explanation, unfortunately, is a hard pill to swallow and I'm trying to elaborate without frightening everyone out of their socks. I have been waiting for my daughter's help."

His comment stopped the murmuring. Everyone focused on Iggy's explanation. "You all know my daughter has special gifts. Many of you have experienced her ability to communicate telepathically. I could spend two hours explaining things to you verbally. I could also project feelings and emotions. Nothing, however, is equal to the images Gloria can communicate. Some of you are not aware of my description. I'll let Gloria explain it to you because when she engages you, you will no longer be able to mentally drift off the subject at hand. What she tells you will be indelibly installed in your mind." Iggy laughed. "No daydreaming allowed."

Gloria was almost seventeen. The seraphic countenance she had worn as a young child had changed. Now, she possessed the innocent beauty of a young woman with one exception. Her eyes appeared as bottomless wells of wisdom as if she had lived two lifetimes. "Some of you have had this type of communication with me. It is direct mental contact. I do not intentionally read your mind; I simply deposit information contained in mine. The difference is, I occasionally use words but prefer to use images because they are not subject to misinterpretation. I never do this with anyone who refuses this experience. The choice is always yours, so without further expression, anyone who does not want to experience this should leave the auditorium for a while. Contact with 700 people is quite difficult and requires extreme concentration on my part. I cannot selectively do this. So, whoever wants to see what I think, remain in your seat. Everyone else must leave."

No one moved to leave, but then again, there was no one present without an invitation. They had become associates of the Marcus family one way or the other and realized anything to do with them was the most extraordinary experience possible. Gloria had done this once before. She took her seat in the recliner next to the conference table. She laughed. "I'm not taking a nap everyone. I have to be completely relaxed and close my eyes. I would ask you all to empty your minds as well as you can."

Gloria breathed rhythmically for several minutes and appeared to have fallen asleep when everyone felt her enter their minds. It began like a mist then gradually formed into the image of her smiling face. It was her usual introduction. Now she would lead them into the universe. She and Iggy had traveled in Daedalus beyond the moon's orbit and witnessed the spectacular display of the universe unencumbered by atmospheric distortion. That was the first image she projected. It was the glory of creation never seen from earth's surface.

She began communicating with words. **This is more than the realm of God. What you see, *is* the Creator. We are all individuals who were once an integral part of It, but we have been born as autonomous individuals, separated, and created from pure energy to exist for our own sake. My father has explained about the people from the opposite side of our galaxy and their purpose here.**

Everyone saw exactly what she projected. Images continued to form in everyone's mind as she displayed the meeting between her father and the extraterrestrials. They saw the images and heard the communication about the purpose of their presence and how long they had been here. Now, Gloria Marcus led them through another experience.

I will refer to the people you just experienced as the 'shepherds.' Six months before this night, we met the people from the other side of the galaxy again. They explained their mission was not only to shepherd humanity into a viable future. They are here on a consultation basis to help us prevent other civilizations from mining this planet.

You have heard my father spout enough philosophy to understand morality. It allows no middle ground for debate. Its boundaries are governed by intellect. It is the operating system of the universe and nothing about it is esoteric. It is specific and unequivocal. The first and most important law is 'do no harm'. That mandate

applies to every autonomous individual, and believe me, there are many trillions throughout the galaxies.

Civilizations who refuse to adopt morality as a behavior are not directly dealt with because they have been given autonomy, unless they export violence and immorality, or destroy the handiwork of the Creator. We have not been given autonomy to destroy others without consequences. When a civilization abandons morality beyond self-reparation, they are dealt with by advanced civilizations known as shepherds. Well, I just introduced you to some of them several minutes ago. This planet is billions of years old. Three civilizations existed here prior to ours. Two consisted of Homo sapiens, and one other was different. We have no historical record of them, and they left no accessible landmarks behind. They destroyed themselves or were removed by shepherds because they couldn't live morally and were going to eventually destroy themselves and the planet, just as we were about to do with nuclear weapons.

The shepherds are here because we exist. They are not allowed to intervene or arbitrate. They are strictly observers, and when necessary, they will disinfect. Twenty years ago, there was a strong possibility Homo sapiens would be removed from this planet in lieu of our propensity to nuke ourselves. Do you understand the significance of this?

Ice ages and extinction level events separated the different civilizations. I don't understand how those things came to pass but my father was shown this by the shepherds. One thing is certain, he has been given a job to do and our survival hangs in the balance. I know this sounds really far out there, but that's the reality.

Her soliloquy was coupled with images of her perception of reality. She continued to show them a kaleidoscope of images depicting humanity's history of both virtue and depravity. The shepherds had planted images of other civilizations in Iggy and her minds. She shared this with everyone as she imparted a glimpse of the universe. Having inherited Iggy's gifts of emotional projection, she sprinkled humor and tranquility among everyone present sensing the mood change.

Autonomy separates us from the Creator in the true sense of the word. Solitude or isolation as an individual is true for every living sentient being in the universe. It's what many religions call free will. We have been given that incredible gift, but it comes with an admission price, the charge to 'do no harm'. We are not the only civilization that breaks the rules. Believe me, there are plenty of them. My father wanted me to explain these things in a manner you could not escape.

Our visitors communicate telepathically like we are communicating but their mental signature is much different than ours. Their mission as shepherds is slightly more than uninvolved observation. They cannot directly intervene; they can only advise. They informed us there are other civilizations actively involved who have been visiting us for eons. We have not had the opportunity to meet them. They are physically similar to us but are much more evolved and are technologically far superior. They are unprincipled, they are aggressive, sociopathic and for lack of a better term, like locusts. They are not here to intentionally harm individuals but are mining us organically.

Their civilization requires expansion through colonization or pillaging. While not being allowed to colonize earth, they are still mining it. This must not be allowed, but it is not for the shepherds to prevent. It is the job that belongs to my father, and consequently, us. This civilization is from Altair 4, 16.7 light years from us, in the Aquila star system. Pretty close when you consider the cosmic scheme of things.

The interlopers are thieves. They are largely responsible for the actions of the deep state of every country who are embedded with Interlink. They are the sponsors of what is being done to our atmosphere. Interlink is complicit and assists them subtly. Their prize will be their continued position at the helm of all societies on earth.

We are allowed to shape our destiny as we please, but we are not supposed to destroy ourselves, our home and no other civilization is granted that luxury either. The inevitability of our own self-destruction is no longer resolute. That was my father's mission before he even knew it himself. This is our world to live in and prosper. We have the amazing privilege to use any world in the cosmos during our evolution, with one exception. They may not be inhabited by other sentient beings.

"My father explained about the chemtrails and what their intent is. They are altering our environment for very specific reasons." Gloria projected mental pictures. They displayed close-up images of the billowing clouds of particles behind the disbursement aircraft. She then projected images of the aircraft being loaded with particulate canisters. She followed with images of the human respiratory system as everyone visualized bright yellow particulate being inhaled and absorbed by the human body through the bloodstream into every cell. **"The bright yellow illustrated the quantity and method of penetration, especially through the blood brain barrier and it's absorption by cells of the cerebral cortex."** It was vivid, compelling, and frightening.

This is purposely being done to us. We know it is inspired by the visitors from Altair who are complicit with Interlink. We also believe this is multipurposed. A portion of the particulate embedded in our cells, especially the brain, has the predilection to enable external electromagnetic pulses to create various reactions in the cerebral cortex. There is another aspect to this, however. The hydrogel and several other substances on a molecular level appear to be attaching themselves to the telomeres at the end of the human DNA strand. We haven't quite determined what that's all about, yet. So, that's about it for now but at least you all have a very distinct and accurate picture.

She had just delivered a spectacular glimpse of the universe. It was the unrestricted view of our place in the cosmos and the validation of the eternal consciousness men called God. Everyone was overwhelmed by the rare experience. A few had experienced this through Gloria's mind before. The vision captivated them once again as she slipped quietly away.

Telepathy with 700 people was intense and exhausting. She needed a breath of air.

Everyone's eyes followed her as she left. No one spoke for a while. 700 people sat in silence contemplating the stunning vision of eternity given them by a 17-year-old girl. Unexpectedly, many things' people hoped for and suspected were real; Gloria Marcus had just shown them the spectacular truth.

Jack Marcus could never resist the urge to inject his amusement. "Well, ladies and gentlemen, that's our show this evening. It's an Academy award performance, for sure. Refreshments will be served in the lobby, shortly."

The spell was broken. On to more business.

"You all had a glimpse of the way things are. Gloria countered the hopelessness that sometimes happens when everything seems overwhelming. People are currently under enormous duress. It is global, adversarial, and unfortunately, precipitating considerable violence everywhere. That is the intent and design of Interlink. Our express purpose is to prevent them from prevailing. Everything is possible. If they prevail, it would be our end. The Universe never bargains or contradicts itself so, whatever happens will be irrevocable."

"We need a break. Let's go back at it after coffee."

***

"This next part is quite technical. I will describe exactly what they are attempting with nanotechnology, disease, and therapeutic vaccines. That is not just my mission to prevent; it is yours as well. All of you belong to this organization and it is more than coincidence. You are members of a unique group of people with a special job to do. I have been granted the position of being the person at the helm. So, bear in mind, when things become turbulent, to keep a positive attitude because there is a light at the end of the tunnel, and we are not alone."

"Gloria has exposed you to an overview of existence and a glimpse of things to come. You now understand many things on a macro scale and have a good idea of the big picture. It's time for specificity. The floor is open for questions."

Laura Collings' hand shot into the air immediately. She and her husband Dr. Richard Balin were two of Lightning Ranch's frequent visitors. She was the judge who presided over Iggy's pedophilia trial several years before. She was stunned by the intellectual stature and talent of all the students who testified and the incredible talent of 369 children from age 7 to 17 who performed a classical symphony in front of the courthouse. That day compelled Laura Collings to request her daughters finish their education at Lightning. To Laura he was Iggy, but here she would address him formally.

Mr. Marcus, I have questions. You alluded to these things several years ago, and other times when we visited the ranch. You brought them up again tonight. You mentioned bioengineering, nanotechnology, and the spraying of particles into the atmosphere. Richard and I have always wondered why the skies are often covered with multiple lines of trails from horizon to horizon. So, we did some research and learned a typical vapor trail is ice crystals resulting from jet fuel combustion, and they always dissipate within a quarter mile in the wake of the aircraft. Chem trails are different. There are thousands of them being sprayed everywhere and the entire globe is often laced with a grid of them. Eventually they dissipate and turn a crisp bright blue sky into a white haze. Is this what you're talking about? As part of your answer, I would like to know who is doing this and what are their reasons. I believe I already know, but I would appreciate an explicit, technical explanation."

Iggy shook his head. "You're correct, Laura. They have been spraying this stuff for approximately 18 years. They have sprayed millions of metric tons of particulates into the atmosphere. We realized this was happening eighteen years ago and determined the reason they were spraying. It is the same group of people who run the planet and are the sworn enemies of civilization. You often have heard me talk about slavery. That is what they intend for all of us."

He had explained it to his family and close associates, years before. The 800 people were riveted to their seats, listening to Iggy's explanation. They had all wondered about chemtrails consisting of aluminum oxide, lithium, nanotechnology, hydrogel, graphene, and methotrexate, among other substances.

"Aluminum and lithium are both metals, but lithium is also considered a salt and often prescribed as a psychotropic medication. I'm sure Richard knows exactly what I'm referring to. Lithium interacts with and affects many proteins in the brain which are involved in generating electrochemical signaling between neurons. That therapy is used to treat bipolar disorders, psychosis, and schizophrenia. However, when bonded to an aluminum atom they resonate at very specific frequencies and have a pronounced effect on the four lobes of the brain. They are the occipital, parietal, temporal, and frontal lobes. They also have very pronounced effects on the thalamus and hypothalamus. They are basically the relay stations involved with the pituitary gland. They control emotional regulation, sexual behavior, daily physiological behavior, appetite, and other voluntary and involuntary behavioral items."

"Specific hydrogel molecules may react with RNA. The presumption is that DNA reproduction will be quantitatively enhanced, maybe even doubled. We are investigating this at the hospital now. It has a major influence on the DNA and consequently, chromosomes."

"To avoid hours of technical explanations, I will give you a reference point, the average brain supposedly consists of 86 billion neurons, more or less. The brain is supposedly capable of one quadrillion connections called dendrites, between neurons. Eventually, evolution will enable our brains to use a much greater capacity of its cerebral cortex than at present. What has happened to me is an elevation from 86 billion neurons to probably four or five trillion with seven or eight quadrillion connections between them. It is the reason for my stratospheric memory." He chuckled. "We have computers that have 100 times that much mental power."

He stopped to let everyone assimilate what he had just explained. "Methotrexate is a drug. Hydrogel and graphene can be manipulated to become nanotechnology. I'm not going to get into mathematics and the scientific details just yet. It's far too complex for a brief discussion, and an enormous amount of underlying material must be understood first. The human brain operates on four wavelengths on the electromagnetic spectrum. It is the type of electricity nature and evolution chose for cerebral messaging. It was nature's best choice for the job. I won't elaborate on the complexity, but they are Alpha, Beta, Delta, and Theta waves which are the electro-chemical signals generated within the cellular structure of the brain to issue voluntary or involuntary commands as well as driving the critical thinking process."

This is technically as far as I want to take this in conversation. I will, however, pass out technical datasheets explaining the nuclear physics of all the compounds and elements I just mentioned, and how they affect metabolic function in the human brain. You'll see the background information and an exact technical definition, including a mathematical analysis of the interaction these substances have with the molecular and atomic composition of the brain. Almost all of you possess the intellectual acuity to read and understand this information. Your education has been prodigious and multi-faceted enough to give you the capability."

No one present lacked education. They were all an enormous cut above average. They were nodding yes. "Okay then. These wavelengths on the electromagnetic spectrum are very low amplitude when they are generated within the cerebral cortex. However, if the cerebral cortex is bombarded with those same electromagnetic wavelengths from an external source with a greater intensity, the items sprayed into the atmosphere we have been breathing, especially the nano-tech stuff, are now embedded in every cell of our cerebral cortex and will cause many things anomalous to normal cerebral biological processes."

The entire group was animated. They had just heard something frightening. They held the fear because they had no control. This was being done nefariously. Before Iggy could continue, most of them understood what was coming next… mind control!

Laura's husband Richard was stunned. He was a doctor and understood the precise science of what he had just heard described. There was an undercurrent of excited conversation rippling through the assembly. They had just been introduced to a world of a possible stratagem designed and deployed by the people who would be slave masters. Everyone had their hands raised.

Laura stood up. "I'm almost sorry I asked, Iggy. To put it bluntly, I am completely freaked out and so is my husband. Please continue. What does this actually mean?"

"Well, there is nothing normal about this, but I will say it this way; normally, given the conditions I described about the embedded chemicals, metals, and nanotechnology in the cells of cerebral cortex, surrounding the axons and neurons, our brains would be subject to mind control of some kind from an external electrical source. Because those particular wavelengths are not efficacious for long-range transmission, it is the reason for 5G technology devices being installed by the hundreds of thousands around the country. 5G operates on those same wavelengths when required to do so. Further, wide distribution of transmitters gives authoritarian control of small groups in specific locations. We have broached the subject before, many years ago, in fact."

The murmur of conversation rose to a dull roar. This group of people, probably the most brilliant assembly of humanity in any one place, were overwhelmed by Iggy's explanation. Most of the oldest students had the equivalent of PhD education when they left Lightning Ranch. They were specialists in particular fields, but their curriculum was all-encompassing. They were articulate and knowledgeable about multiple intellectual disciplines. Everyone could see the implications of this revelation and how it would affect human metabolism.

Iggy waited for them to quiet down. "There is more, folks. I saw this coming, 15 years ago. There was nothing I could do about the spraying of the particulates in the beginning. Consequently, all of us have breathed this in and it is part of our cellular structure, but only to an extent. We all have embedded metal particles in our cells. We can block microwave transmission everywhere. You know what happens to metal when bombarded with microwaves. When I completed my work on matter/energy transmutation, I was able to affect the composition of what was being sprayed in the atmosphere, from our satellites. Also, we can block all 5G transmission everywhere at any time. We can intervene and disrupt the broadcast signals, but only partially. Interlink doesn't seem to know this, although I did mention it to them years ago when we returned from Argentina with Luke. It must have slipped their minds, but I believe they will soon find out when they try to deploy and operate the technology."

He could see the relieved facial expressions of everyone. He had dropped a bombshell no one was ready for except his immediate family. "I'm sorry I frightened some of you out of your socks," he laughed, "but some of you were falling asleep and I didn't want you to miss anything. So, worry not. The research team at the hospital are researching methods to purge brain cells of these unwanted invaders."

He saw a lone hand raised in the back of the assembly. "Okay Louie, what other questions have you got for me?"

"I'm glad I didn't miss this meeting. Patty and I debated whether or not to come. This has been an eye-opener. Somehow, you always have something extra special, a real barnburner at the end. Do we have one tonight, or was that it?"

Luke, Brett, and Lucky began to laugh. "You bet, Louie. Only this one is better than the Chicago fire. I'd like to introduce you all to a new-found member of our family. He's a half-brother to the rest of my kids. The name is Junior, and he is a surprise."

The crowd had barely noticed the handsome young man sitting in the far left of the orchestra pit. They just assumed it was another one of Iggy's frequent guests. There were so many comings and goings at Lightning Ranch these days, no one was surprised. Junior hopped over the railing of the orchestra pit amazing everyone. His jump over a 42-inch-high rail seemed effortless. He walked to the front of the auditorium seats waving his hand. "Hi folks, I'm Junior. I consider Iggy my father because he brought me into the world and that is the reason, I am alive. I've been watching this entire proceeding tonight, and I have to say, you are one bunch of impressive human beings. It will be my honor and privilege to associate with all of you."

They could see the family resemblance, and everyone had questions. As Iggy had requested, Junior spent the next half hour telling jokes and chatting. His amiable manner and smile were infectious and delighted everyone. Iggy rarely did anything intentionally to impress others. This was a little different. Junior was not just a robot. Its inorganic brain was self-aware… a new life form and another brilliant creation by the same man who created Lightning Inc. Melanie sat next to her husband chuckling at Junior's antics. She had suggested familiarity would relax everyone when they learned there wasn't even one organic molecule in him.

"Dad wanted you to meet me this way to help soften the surprise. Once you get to know me, you will find me harmless, and I've been told I am a very funny guy."

Everyone was thoroughly confused. They had spent the last half hour laughing and joking with a stranger. He had called Iggy, Dad, and Iggy had said he was a long-lost family member. Most of the people in the auditorium had been associates of Iggy Marcus, some for twenty-five years. They could see the family resemblance but wondered why they had never met this particular Marcus before.

"Since you've all met Junior, I'm sure you're relaxed and find him pleasant enough. Please forgive me for introducing Junior this way but I felt if you all got to know him, you would better appreciate who and what he is." Iggy turned to Junior. "Okay, Junior, show everyone who you are."

Junior smiled at the crowd as he jumped 10 feet into the air and did a triple somersault before landing in front of them in a handstand. There was bedlam, but this wasn't the first time Iggy Marcus was responsible for bedlam. He wore a huge smile. "Junior was born one month ago in my laboratory. He is a robot, of course. But he is much more. He is my latest cyber invention. His brain is a computer, but he is one of a kind… alive by all the standards defining individuality.

The laughter had stopped. You could hear a pin drop. Everyone in Iggy Marcus's orbit constantly expected the unusual, but this was over the top. The silence was deafening as everyone came to grips with this incredible new revelation.

Louie Petro couldn't help himself. "Cool beans, man! Junior is a Lightning kid too! Kinda like the brother I never had."

Iggy chuckled. "I like your New York slang, Louie. Teach Junior. He's got a great memory."

Even if the stars and planets align, and the universe moves as planned,

*Murphy never sleeps … and the s**t can still hit the fan.*

Please forgive the colloquialism.

Junior

CHAPTER VI

AQUILA

ALTAIR 4

Gloria's horse skidded to a stop in a dust cloud. "That's a little too close for comfort, Gloria!" Melanie exclaimed, jumping back.

Lori and Liam weren't far behind as they galloped through the draw, but their Morgans were no match for the palomino. "Sorry, mom. They're here, Dad! I'm sure you can hear them too. They're up on the mountain."

"Yes. They let me know. It is the same three people as before. I wonder if that's all there are… just three. They are all we have met so far. I guess we better head up there. It seems where they prefer to meet."

"I don't think it's up to them, Father, she speculated as she dismounted. **When they speak to you telepathically, you receive only what they wish you to receive. It's a little different for me. You are limited. My abilities are growing. I see into their minds and can perceive the things they think even if they don't wish to convey those thoughts. I believe they are unaware of my abilities. Because they speak telepathically, they just assume I can only receive. I have never allowed them the luxury of knowing the extent of my abilities or the contents of my mind, but I can see theirs.**

Their psychological architecture is somewhat different from ours. Like us, they have emotions. They are incapable of telling a lie.

They are quite brilliant as individuals, but different by degree. There is no hive mentality. One of them is picturing home. The planet is quite different than ours. The vegetation, the color of the sky, many things are different than our world. I believe that one is preoccupied with a poignant melancholy for home.

There are more than three, Dad. I see the pictures in their minds. There are a dozen ships, many of them huge, with hundreds of occupants aboard. Their technology completely inhibits radar. Their ships are usually out beyond the lunar orbit. They have the same technology you have built into Daedalus. We cannot see them, and we cannot pick them up on radar. Nonetheless. They are there because I see the mental images of what they see.

Melanie was receiving Gloria's thoughts also. "My God Gloria! You can sense all that from here? We are two miles from the top of Coletta Mountain. Incredible! I didn't know you could do that. Your mental powers are expanding just like your fathers did since the day he and I met. I wonder where it's going to stop.

Lori and Liam reined their horses in and surrounded the group. Lori slid out of her saddle. "We are going up to see them, aren't we, Dad." It was a statement, not a question. "I have been waiting for the opportunity after hearing you and Gloria talk about them so often."

Liam neck reined Culpepper, turning him towards the west and coming sunset. He stood in his stirrups, staring at the top of Coletta Mountain. "Whoa! Can you see them? That was a foolish question, of course you can't. Gloria, quick, get in my head and show everybody what I see!"

Liam's telescopic vision saw their ship sitting on the top of Coletta Mountain where everyone often parked to admire the beauty and sprawl of Lightning Ranch. Gloria entered his mind and transmitted visual images to everyone.

Nothing ever surprised Iggy Marcus. He knew life was convoluted and learned to take everything in stride. There were over two dozen ships hovering over the mountaintop, identical to the one sitting in the parking area. "Well," said Iggy chuckling. "How interesting! I guess we know more about Liam's visual abilities now. I can't see a single one of those ships with my naked eye, but nonetheless, they are there and visible to Liam."

"Yes, they are, pop, but I don't think you can see what I see. Your brain isn't set up with the visual acuity I am capable of. The ships seem to be oscillating and changing luminescence. It's very subtle. I'll bet Junior can see it. His optics are incredibly advanced. He can't see everything I see but he can amplify. When I get to either end of the visible spectrum, things become blurry or obscure. Junior can overcome that."

Iggy spun the bezel on his watch and pressed a button on the side. "Junior?"

"Yes Dad. What can I do for you. I'm in the lab working on Baby."

"Baby Is the name you gave your sister?"

"Nope. Baby is the name she picked for herself. She is still a little gray box, but I'm almost finished with her frame. Then we can finish the job."

"Quit for a while and come to the fields behind my house immediately. The visitors are on Coletta Mountain, and I would like to get your impression of them. You have an entirely different type of brain than biologicals. Your linear thought processes will view them from a completely different perspective."

"I will be there in less than five minutes. I'll run. It'll be much faster than I can safely drive."

"Find Lucky, Tom, Richard, Luke and Brett if they're around, and send them here ASAP. We are headed up Coletta Mountain."

"I'll see you there. It will take me a while to round everyone up."

***

"What do you think, Junior?"

"I achieved interface, Dad. Their onboard computer is considerable, but it is not sentient. It is equivalent to my neural net at decomposition and pattern recognition, but it is considerably beneath my abilities at abstraction. That is because I am sentient, inquisitive, and in charge of directing my own thought processes. I am only another entity's tool if I choose to allow it. Their computer has no options."

"Interesting. That's why I asked you to come. I would have no way of knowing this. Keep it to yourself, Junior. These folks communicate telepathically. Try to receive everything they project but do not reveal your abilities."

Iggy laughed at Junior's typical response. "You got it Pops."

Melanie, Lucky, Tom Rickart, Richard, and the boys pulled up in a Land Rover. "Ask them to stay near the vehicles, Gloria. These people communicate telepathically in images, please project their thoughts to everyone."

"Okay, Dad. I will have to translate their images into English and explain the thought processes behind them. Their complex communications are often difficult to decipher for the average mind. Mom had a great deal of difficulty with it until I helped."

The three individuals present at the last meeting exited their ship. Their communication was in the usual images. Gloria translated and explained to everyone what she was about to do. "These people project images via electromagnetic waves by altering frequencies and amplitude on the electromagnetic spectrum, telepathically. It is their method of communication and it's difficult for the average mind to decompress and understand rapidly, although it is doable. So, I will translate to English."

The visitors began projecting as Gloria translated… **"Greetings, Iggymarcus. We have come to update you. The visitors who have come from the 4th planet orbiting the star you call Altair, intend to mine this planet. They do not intend intentional harm to Homo sapiens, but they**

are not concerned about your welfare either. They claim this planet is rich in the natural resources they require. We believe their motives and objectives lie elsewhere. They claim your oceans have water they need."

"There is much harvestable ice available in this solar system. There are other mineral and elemental resources on the moons of other planets." Junior offered.

"You claim these people, I'll call them Altairians, wish us no harm. Yet they are going to mine resources we use to survive." Injected Iggy. That would harm us by proxy, but I believe there is something deeper at stake."

"That is why we are here."

"Do they not have the technology for matter and energy transmutation? I have developed the technology and we use it on a regular basis."

"They do not. That technology is very sophisticated. Some civilizations possess the capability. Most do not."

"Why is it not used to solve their need for resources?"

"You already possess the answer to the question. Autonomy delivers the inescapable logic. Transmutation technology can transform the Universe in a grand fashion. Transformation might be acceptable, depending on the objective and magnitude. All intelligent entities, however, are not altruistic. The universe does not tolerate dramatic destructive activity where its autonomous citizens are concerned but never takes an active preventative hand. Although it has created autonomy, it does not allow the arrogant annihilation of itself by its various occupants. Occasionally tools are forged to deal with the anomalies created by autonomy."

"Apparently, you are a tool, and it is your mission to prevent that?"

"We are not here to stop *them.* We are here to supervise *you.* It is your obligation to deal with them. You have been given the capability to fulfill those obligations. We only advise, never arbitrate, or intrude unless requested to act. We are obligated to explain your adversaries' motives and actions, but we make no demands for your course of action. Your response is up to you. We will answer your questions. Not many are given this charge. The fate of your civilization hangs on your essential qualities and capabilities."

Iggy silently contemplated for some minutes before he responded. **"I am sure you are aware of the turbulence being created around the world by the Interlink people you formerly contacted. I am also quite sure you understand their reasons, exactly what is intended and will occur if it is not prevented."**

"We are aware of everything and monitor all communications and activities on this planet. Your Interlink is the organization that will cause the destruction of your species if you do not successfully intervene. The Altairians are aware of these things as well. They will collude with your Interlink members because their ignorance makes them susceptible. The people from Altair four, fully understand the cosmic scheme of things. They are opportunists. The demise of your civilization will close the gate to mine the resources of your planet if its people are the desired resource."

Gloria couldn't help himself. **"I thought there were rules of the universe we have to follow, and these kinds of things were not allowed by what we call the Creator. It seems a contradiction to me."**

The creator presents all its citizens with autonomy. There is no partial autonomy, and it has only one definition. Autonomy entices some entities to break the rules. They lose track of universal constants. Occasionally a civilization faces its own demise unless drastic action is taken."

"Is that what we are facing with the Altair people?"

"Perhaps. The universe is complex beyond your wildest imagination, and it is populated by trillions of autonomous beings. Many of them are vastly different than our carbon life forms. They exist in completely different environments, comprised of elemental arrangements foreign to you. Yet the rules are the same for them. However, circumstances, physical, and mental differences may create indomitable anomalies between species that cannot always be rationalized. The rules of the universe often become blurred. Complying with the rules is not strictly required or enforced until an autonomous species pursues expansion off their planet. If they break the rules and propagate their own destruction or the destruction of other species, shepherds may become involved."

"The tapestry of existence has already been woven. The Creator's design is subject to the physical reality of the universe replete with all the twists and turns of cause and effect. Stars are born and stars die. The Creator does not intervene. We intervene, along with those like us throughout the universe who are dedicated to fulfilling that obligation. That is now what you have become, Iggymarcus."

Iggy clearly saw the structure of the universe. Some things appeared perplexing, but he grasped the honesty, efficiency, and benevolence surrounding existence. Though some would take umbrage with the impartiality and fairness defining the rules of creation, one should never dispute the hand of God. Gloria giggled as she observed her father's thoughts. **"I think you're right Dad. The odds against winning the debate are very long, indeed."**

The three visitors sensed her humor. **"Yes, the odds of prevailing are non-existent. It has been attempted. The universe has existed for billions of years. It has created an almost infinite number of independent occupants since the beginning of this cycle, 17 billion of your solar years. Some of creation's autonomous entities have evolved and arrogantly challenged the Creator who *is* the universe. The universe cannot be challenged by one it has created and defined. An arrogant delusional entity cannot successfully challenge its own origin. Nonetheless, the attempt has been made more than once. Your**

mythology describing evil, and its proponents is more than just poetry and conjecture. It is based on obscure history. The universe and its occupants are connected by an ethereal web you would refer to as the nexus of existence. It is ultimately accessible to all sentient creatures and is the core tapped by intellect to enable interstellar travel. "

"I have a request," stated Iggy. **"Give me the proper wavelength and frequency if I need to summon you. I would appreciate it."**

"We have already embedded it in the creature you addressed as Junior."

"Hmm, very interesting Gloria," Iggy spoke aloud as he sheltered his thoughts from the visitors. "They called Junior a creature instead of a robot. I believe they understand what Junior is."

***

"I wish you had been there, Angie. It was the most amazing day yet! All the way down the mountain I reminisced. I thought about my pre-indoctrination days in Russia, my indoctrination until I was 12 and then my life in America, promotion to general and appointment as chief military strategist for the Army. All of this was dramatic by anyone's standards, but this is beyond the pale. I just stood in front of extraterrestrials and listened to their description of the universe. It was more than fascinating; it was emotionally uplifting and more mesmerizing than anything I had ever thought possible. You would've loved it."

"How did we get this lucky, Richard? All those years in our early lives don't compare to the last five. We are part of something great. We have been watching the apparent forces of evil destroy this amazing country. They have attacked every institution and the morality that underlies every philosophical concept of this country's greatness. It looked as if they were winning. Now, I am quite sure they are way overmatched."

"I'm inclined to agree with you, but this is quite complex. Apparently, there are more than one group of extraterrestrials involved in the future of our planet. One group are here as advisors and cannot become involved. The other group are evidently locusts who wish to mine the planet for some unidentified resource. The first group is not here to prevent that, only to advise, and apparently the job has been relegated to Iggy."

"Wow! I wouldn't like my neck to be parked on those shoulders."

"Agreed."

"We have never been religious, Richard. I know it even though we raised our boys with religion. We don't go to church anymore. Somehow, I would like to go to church next Sunday. I don't care what church. It doesn't matter. I just want to say thank you in the proper place."

***

Iggy and junior were putting the finishing touches on Baby. Junior smiled, "she's state-of-the-art, Dad. Even better looking than me. I think it's going to be nice having a sister. I'm not really sure what nice feels like, but I know it will be applicable."

Iggy's sat phone buzzed. He left it on speaker. "Hello, Iggy Marcus here. How are you, Deli?"

"I am well Iggy. And you?"

"Never been better. What can I do for you Deli Li?"

"I need your help, sir. You instructed me to call anytime if something like this occurred. This is one of those times."

Two hours later Daedalus settled on the flight line. Tiao Chen and Heng Cong had arrived in a Shangri-La, replete with giraffes, elephants, and the most efficacious school on the planet. Zia and Chu watched them drive off in a Land Rover with Parker and Millie to see the giraffes.

Zia and Chu looked at each other. "I think we are very fortunate, Zia. We have come to America. Something I have always dreamed of but never expected."

“You’re in luck,” said Melanie. “It’s meeting night tonight. It is fortunate you speak English. You will get a good dose of what Lightning Ranch is all about.”

“Well, Brett,” said Luke. “Parker and Millie stole our Land Rover to ferry the newcomers to animal kingdom. Let’s go check on Baby. That’s where Gloria headed. They’re all in the lab.”

***

"Holy moly! Brett. Get a load of this! Have you ever seen the like?"

"Nope, she's unbelievable! Dad says she looks just like Clara. It was so long ago I don't really remember exactly what Mom looked like, although I vaguely remember her image. I always see a face full of love in my mind's eye," he said as he hooked his index finger behind Baby's waistband.

Gloria Marcus raised a Bunsen burner over her head. "Get your finger out of her pants Brett or I'm going to clobber you with this, and I intend to draw blood. She may be a robot, but Baby is your sister for all intents and purposes."

"Just curious about the equipment and functionality, Gloria. Anyway, you just called it *her.* Is this one of those, *we girls must stick together,* things? I'm just being very clinical here, so don't jump to conclusions."

"Yes," quickly added Luke. "We are just being clinical. We really need to know what this equipment can do."

"You guys, even though you're my brothers, are definitely a couple of wackos." She reached for the robot's hand. "Come on, Baby. I'll show you around Lightning Ranch. Let's see if we can find Junior, and the three of us can take a stroll. We'll leave these two prurient characters here.”

"Suits me just fine," said Baby. “Junior programmed me with the same ability to use colloquialisms for communication and the simulated sense of humor he has. I want to try it out on him and see what happens. It should be interesting to watch two robots without a shred of a sense of humor tell each other jokes trying to make each other laugh."

Gloria laughed heartily. "Wow, Baby! You are hilarious for a hunk of metal and silicone, with a computer brain and no actual sense of humor. It's hard to believe you don't find yourself funny."

"I have absolutely no idea what 'funny' feels like, Gloria. I know I'm being funny because it made you laugh. It's really peculiar. I'd like to see what happens when I try it on Junior. By the way, I believe I know, but not fully, why did Brett want to look down my pants?"

"That's a little hard to explain because it involves emotion, chemical responses, and psychophysical drives. You don't have any of those capabilities. It has a lot to do with the psychology of men, however. My two brothers rarely act like the idiots they appear to be today. I think they are just horny."

"Really? I have been programmed with every piece of information in the human experience. I understand what horny is, by definition, but I don't understand chemical/emotional horny. Do you really think Luke and Brett are horny and they would like to have an episode with me? I'm fully functional you know."

Gloria rolled her eyes. “God, no! They don't need to have an episode with you, Baby. This conversation is getting very weird. I think you and I need to have a long talk about men, women, and sex," she commented, wondering why Junior had installed Baby’s below-the-waist equipment.

"What would we call a conversation like that? Girl talk or just small talk?"

Gloria laughed again heartily. "You and your mechanical brother are a couple of genius comedians, even though you have absolutely no idea what I'm talking about. It's very funny. Dad, Melanie, Tom Rickart, and Dave Peterson are going to have a good laugh. If it wasn't so bizarre, I would like to see the two of you do a Saturday Night Live. It would be a real pants wetter."

“Pants wetter? I don’t get it.”

“Never mind. You will eventually.”

"I think it would be lots of fun being your sister, except I have absolutely no idea what fun feels like. I understand the definition. I just wish I could actually have fun."

"You wish? What do you mean by wish? That's an emotional response. I'm not sure I understand."

"I'm just trying to practice small talk, Gloria. I don't mean anything strange, by it."

"No problem, sister. It's slightly difficult to come to grips with the fact you're not just a mechanical robot. You're a walking, talking, sentient life form. You may not be human, but you are not artificial intelligence either because Junior built you. Artificial means not occurring naturally and is created by humans. In a manner of speaking, you are indirectly created by humans because Iggy built Junior, and Junior built you. Still, you are Junior's prodigy, which makes you unique. You are the firstborn of a new species that has learned to reproduce. Pretty cool, don't you think?"

Yes, pretty cool… I know that's small talk, but I have a question."

"Oh?"

"What has temperature got to do with anything? Why would my status as firstborn be chilling?"

Gloria continued laughing. "You are definitely hilarious, Baby. I'm going to enjoy hanging out with you. Too bad you won't enjoy hanging out with me. Maybe someday, Dad will find a way to give you and Junior emotions, and then you can learn to enjoy."

Gloria shook her head as Baby giggled. "How was that? Gloria. Did it sound like a human laugh? My own elevated computer senses told me it sounded human, but the only real proof is if a human tells me, it sounds human. Did it match my facial expressions?"

"Being with you, baby, is so much fun. Too bad you can't feel the same. Let's go find our brother. Junior has to be hanging around here somewhere."

"I understand the colloquialism, but why will he hang instead of standing around? What would he hang from? It seems impractical."

"I see you are not quite used to colloquialisms yet, Baby."

"I think I'm not used to being alive yet, either. I am a walking, talking data bank but a little short on experience since this is only my second day."

***

Three weeks had zoomed by, and it was only a few hours until meeting night. No one was going to miss this one. Junior was an unexpected revelation. Now, everyone wanted to meet Baby. Iggy's two sentient mechanical children were the stuff of fairytales. He had done what hundreds of science fiction writers described for a hundred years and the scientific community assumed would someday become a reality. Well, here it was, staring everyone in the face. It was hardly what anyone expected. Somehow, Iggy had created operating systems, depositing them in autonomous, sentient, robotic life forms, making them almost undiscernible from flesh and blood humans.

The aftermath of Iggy Marcus's brilliantly successful crusade against pedophilia was no walk in the park. Several thousand children were casualties of depravity, and their journey back to normalcy was only possible through the intervention of two people, Iggy, and Gloria Marcus. Iggy's brother Jack coined the phrase, unlocking, 20 years before with the clinical description of subliminal contact and the intellectual massage his brother used to therapeutically elevate children.

Those children who had been abducted from reasonably normal settings would return home once the therapy was complete. The other victims, without a life to return to and no prospects for the future, became Lightning Ranch's new student body who would become Marcus's new 2000 protégés to shape the future.

Lindy and Marty had returned from Europe to stay. They, and thirty of Iggy's former students, would fill teaching slots for the new kids.

Iggy had seen what was coming. He missed nothing. He knew the world was about to explode with violence and mayhem in Interlink's attempt to destroy and completely undermine Western civilization. Once accomplished, Interlink believed society and governments would have to be rekindled in a new form of collectivism that knelt to authoritarianism and obliterated individuality.

The forces arrayed against humanity realized freedom and random human accomplishment perpetuating individualism could not be allowed. Their indoctrination program directed at society, attempting the realignment of politics and philosophy with mindless conformity, met two enormous obstacles shattering the New World Order's momentum. Lightning Inc. and its ally, the presidency of William James Sledge, were apparently unassailable mountains. Lightning Ranch expanded, acquiring the 12,000-acre ranch next door. The complex was now 34,400 acres, all dedicated to the proliferation of the Marcus family's ideals and plans.

Lightning Inc. hired 4000 ex-military special forces recruits, as many Navy SEALs as possible, trained, and deployed 2000 of them at all eighty of Lightning Inc.'s publication and manufacturing facilities around the country. Their dual mission was the protection of Lightning Inc.'s assets and the defense of other societal edifices in the crosshairs of the new world order. The other 2000 were reinstated as officers in the 4 branches of the American military, as trainers and supervisors. They would be needed when the chips were finally down, and the world exploded. This would be Interlink's last and only chance.

The confrontation between interlink and the mechanisms Iggy Marcus and President Sledge set in motion was beginning. It was meeting night and time to address the 700 people present. "Each of you has the intellectual acumen to understand the order of events and what is about to happen to the world. Much of it has been precipitated by us with our refusal to accept tyranny. You must fully understand what is coming our way and why."

"The World Progressive Socialist Organization, headed by Heinrich Klatch, has merged with the United Nations. The UN has become a feckless conglomeration of autocrats and spoiled, jaded nobility. They parade through the halls of power wearing superficial cloaks of pseudo-compassion to intellectually swindle the average citizen who has never learned to critically think into accepting their authority… and it is working. People are lazy. They don't want to think. Thought takes intellectual effort as well as an intellectual information reservoir underpinning the process. So, the sheeple elect fearless leaders who fearlessly lead them to the trough, or when necessary, the slaughterhouse."

"Most, but not all countries, are led by authoritarians who care nothing for humanity, or the obstacles faced by those they call the rabble. They are feckless mediocrities themselves, the products of envy and greed who have nothing to do with the honesty and the virtue of genuine capitalism. As sub-human vultures, they would never admit true capitalism releases the individual from the caste system. That admission would validate the antithesis of their lifestyle, the freedom of their fellow men without coercion. The primary tool of autocrats is coercion in one form or another. Their emotional arrogance and hatred of their brothers, and consequently, self-loathing, demand the worship and supplication of the masses."

"So, the first mission of autocracy is the destruction of contemporary higher education edifices, worldwide, thus inflicting the same hatred of any proponent of individuality on the disciples of their perverse philosophy. Their indoctrinated apprentices are so thoroughly brainwashed, critical thought is no longer possible and blind acceptance of the swill being dished out to them becomes the definition of their character."

"There is rarely redemption for autocrats. They live their meaningless lives validated by the power they hold over their fellow men. It was not power derived from achievement and dedication to creating a better world for themselves and others; it is power derived by the hand that holds the biggest sword. The sword comes in many forms: military might, taxation, and litigation relieving the middle class of its wealth and redistributing it among mindless voters with their hands out."

Iggy knew there was no other avenue to pursue. Autocracy had to win this one or it would be the end of the con-game they have been perpetrating since men invented language. There is no win-or-lose alternative. They will fight to the panic-stricken death. They knew it, and Iggy knew it. What he didn't know was the collusion existing between the extraterrestrials from Altair 4 and Interlink.

Iggy was teaching piano lessons when Gloria walked into the auditorium. "Dad, they are coming to Coletta Mountain. Did you hear the summons?"

"Sure, Gloria. I just wanted to finish up here first. Only a few more minutes, and we'll head up there."

"They have conveyed the idea of urgency. Did you get that?"

"Yes. Let's go. Ask Tom Rickart and Junior to come along."

***

The two greatest works of art humanity had ever produced existed on opposite sides of the planet. The Angkor Wat, the most exquisitely sculpted building in existence resided in Cambodia. Two men stood below the other, created by the soul of Michelangelo Lodovico Buonarroti Simoni. His portrayal of creation stared down on two arrogant mediocrities who didn't deserve to stand beneath its splendor.

"We should wait here for the others before we descend to the conference room, Herr Klatch. Only I have the key. Our guests are already there, awaiting our arrival."

"Yes, Your Holiness. My Associates will be arriving together very soon." Heinrich Klatch resisted calling Pope Innocent XIV by his Brazilian surname, José, even though he and his compatriots had politically manipulated church hierarchy to cause the resignation of Germain XVI and the installation of the man standing in front of him as the highest authority in the church.

Heinrich Klatch wore his cloak of socialism with some flair but no ostentatious extravagance. He was a deceiver of men. He had no allegiance to the philosophy of Karl Marx. He merely wrapped himself in the ideology as a deception. His persona existed on the world stage, and popular support was a principal key to his success. His true persona remained carefully hidden from everyone except his son. He implicitly understood Marx's doctrine of socialism, knowing it was the most destructive philosophical instrument man had ever created. Marx's theory described the tenets of socialism as fairness for the proletariat, but Klatch, like most hands compelled to grasp the sword of undeserved authority, knew it was a concealed vehicle to subdue and enslave the people. When you obliterate creativity and honest upward mobility, you destroy incentive and are left with a pasture full of sheep.

José Amontillado, on the other hand, was not as intellectually adept as Klatch. He bought into Karl Marx's philosophy because he had been raised as a socialist and taught to believe wealth was wicked and poverty was sacred. He grew up with five siblings embroiled in the elements of socialism by poverty-stricken parents. Like his father before him, he imbibed on the swill dished out by authoritarians, always believing in the promised reward of riches in the afterlife. That false promise is the tried-and-true method of the caste system's reigning elites. The church allowed his metamorphosis from one of the flock to becoming a predator without his conscious awareness or acceptance of what he had really become. Like all socialists, he was oblivious to morality and wallowed in the exhilaration of absolute power unavailable to mediocrity through any other process. He was the Pope!

Twenty-two men and two women stood in the basilica with José Amontillado, about to descend to the secret conference room rarely seen by anyone but the Pope and the College of Cardinals. Besides being the conference room where church oligarchs, and an occasional head of state met to discuss top-secret information and operations, it was the anteroom for the hidden conference room and alternate, secret Vatican vault. They were more secure than the bank of Switzerland's vault holding the vast remnants of gold, jewelry, and assorted wealth stolen by the Third Reich. The Vatican vault contained the remnants of the pillage of Alexandria. The Crusaders had stripped the Ottoman Empire of all vestiges of the science and art of the intellectually and culturally rich Arabic world.

The vault was built and opened in the 5th century at enormous expense and adherence to secrecy, after the Vandals and an assorted conglomeration of invaders sacked Rome. It remained largely unused until after the 10th century, when a secure place was needed to house what the Crusades had sacked from the Muslims. Besides Cheyenne Mountain, two other American military strongholds, the Russian caverns under the Ural Mountains, and the Chinese underground caverns, it was the most secure place in existence because of its lack of notoriety and the Vatican guard. The vault was hidden by the conference room ninety feet below the surface, and only a handful of Cardinals and the Pope were aware of its existence.

"I believe everyone here speaks fluent English." Heinrich Klatch stated to everyone present. Twenty-six people nodded their heads in the affirmative. "Then English is the language we will use," he responded with his thick German accent.

José Amontillado faced the group. "We have an elevator on this level, but it will take quite a bit of time to ferry all of us down to the conference level. It is nine stories below the foundation of the Basilica. I suggest we all descend the hidden Bramante staircase. It is a ramp like the other staircase but a pleasant walk. It is richly adorned with frescos and sculptures. We can then proceed from there."

The Italian architect Donato Bramante designed Italy's most famous staircase and built it in the square tower of the Belvedere building. The tourist attraction annually draws hundreds of thousands of visitors. Very few people knew the other Bramante staircase even existed, descending nine stories beneath the Vatican. It was such a well-kept secret for over a thousand years that a new double helix staircase designed and built by Giuseppe Momo was often erroneously called the second Bramante staircase when it was actually the third staircase to bear the monicker of Donato Bramante.

They reached the bottom. José Amontillado pointed the way through a corridor at the other end of the first conference room to a small bank of elevators and an adjacent modern staircase. "We must use the elevators to descend four more levels to the secure conference room where our two guests await us."

The massive horseshoe walnut table and lush appointments of the conference room were broken on one side by an enormous steel door with no apparent hinges. The definition of the door was created by an indentation 6 inches from its perimeter and a keypad in the center. Below the keypad was a small wheel and possible lock override mechanism. It was the only fixture that did not reflect the Italian Renaissance.

Everyone except the Pope, Heinrich Klatch, Saphra Rothman, and Prince Hilary Lancaster were startled by the two people, obviously not human, seated at the head of the conference table. As they were ushered into the chamber, Heinrich Klatch and José Amontillado took seats on either side of the strangers.

After everyone was seated at the two legs of the conference table, Heinrich Klatch stood on the right of the seated visitors, who appeared much taller than average human beings. They were hairless and easily twelve inches taller than the Pope, who was at least six feet tall.

They appeared humanoid with similar attributes to Homo sapiens, with two eyes facing forward, demonstrating the binocular vision indigenous to predators, two small external pointed ears, a thin-lipped mouth seated at least two inches beneath the small, splayed nose exhibiting only one nostril. Their cranium was at least twelve inches across, with two bony stubs like horns protruding from the forehead. Their faces were long and tapered toward a missing chin. The shape of their bodies was not evident because they were seated behind the large walnut table. Still, they appeared unconventional, very wide at the waist, but muscular instead of corpulent. The balance of the assessment was two shorter legs than would have been expected because of their height and two arms with hands consisting of six fingers and a juxtaposed thumb.

Heinrich Klatch stood to address the people of Interlink. "Ladies and gentlemen, welcome." He smiled with his best affable but typically counterfeit cordiality. "I would like you to welcome two people from another solar system located around the star, Altair, in the Aquila star system. These folks reproduce sexually, as we do. One is male, and the other is female. They have been able to learn our language to communicate with us. However, their natural language is unintelligible and cannot be reproduced by human vocal cords. Therefore, their names are unintelligible and cannot be spoken by us. With their permission, I gave them the names, Hansel and Gretel, to temper anonymity and facilitate our ability to address them individually."

The murmur became an elevated buzz as everyone commented among themselves about this incredible meeting. No one besides the Pope, Heinrich Klatch, Saphra Rothman, and the prince had any idea extraterrestrials would be here. In fact, most of them doubted the existence of ET's… Not anymore. Hansel and Gretel were sitting in front of them, apparently smiling if that's what you would call it, when their somewhat downturned mouths flattened out and curved slightly upward.

Hansel, slightly taller and more prominent than Gretel, was the first to speak. His voice was somewhat raspy with a deep intonation. "Thank you for your cordial invitation. Gretel and I are here because you oversee this planet and have common interests with our people."

It was Gretel's turn. Her voice was slightly less raspy and not as deep. Apparently, the visitors' gender attributes were similar to ours. "Ultimately, we would appreciate an arrangement allowing us to mine certain elemental commodities you possess. It would all be done with your permission and approval. We will compensate you in ways you cannot imagine. We can discuss it at your convenience."

The man at the closest table end was the genius American trillionaire, Cameron Fry. He had made his original billions as a hedge fund manager and now owned and controlled two of the largest onshore banks in America. His thoughts were racing, wondering why these people from another planet were here talking with Interlink instead of the Marcus empire. Fry was sharp. He thought about Hansel's statement of their belief Interlink apparently oversaw the Planet. That wasn't even close. Everyone knew who had the power. It was the Marcus family, and there was no altering that easily. Interlink was attempting to wrest power from Marcus and Pres. William James Sledge by starting the wheels of war in motion to disrupt every society and government on the planet and finally give birth to the long-planned New World order. He was sure Hansel and Gretel knew the greatest power at large on earth was

Ignatius Marcus and Lightning Incorporated. Logic dictated the glaring reality. *So, why are they lying and stroking us with flattery?* Immediately occupied his thoughts.

He was no doubt the smartest person in the room other than Hansel and Gretel. It took a certain kind of man to rise from nothing to become worth over $1 trillion. He knew human nature to a T. Apparently, these folks had similar psychological qualities. They were lying, and that is subterfuge. At that moment, he knew nothing these creatures would say could be taken to the bank. They had ulterior motives. It was obvious. Those motives were indiscernible, and it probably didn't matter at this point.

They had traveled here from another star. Their technology had to be hundreds if not thousands of years ahead of ours. They wanted something... yet they were lying. Why? He wondered if their technology was equal to, or greater than, the amazing technology coming out of Lightning Inc. and Iggy Marcus. The man had changed the world and ripped all power from under every tyrant in existence. He had done it calmly, without much fanfare, but it had been thorough. Perhaps ET was afraid of Marcus. It was a possibility. Fry's photographic memory remembered everything Marcus had said, and he also recognized and admired the capabilities of all the various technologies Marcus had invented.

José Amontillado said nothing to this point. Cameron Fry read him like a book. The Pope was a shill owned by Interlink. He remembered how Pope Germain had announced his most unusual retirement, and within eight hours, this man had been appointed to replace him by the College of Cardinals. Fry was A Jew, but he was brilliant and understood the underpinnings of every religion on the planet. His genius forced him to investigate every philosophical tenet as he grew into success. Unlike most, he was obsessed with the philosophical underpinnings of life and human nature. Religion was a substantial portion of that, so he studied it.

He chuckled to himself, thinking about the duplicity of José Amontillado. Here was a guy appointed to one of the most powerful positions on earth, the Pope, and head of the Catholic Church… God's supposed representative on earth! Amazing, he thought. Here was the supreme pontiff sitting down with extraterrestrials who Fry knew were cooking up a conspiracy to defraud humanity somehow. He didn't believe for a second these outworld people intended to fairly compensate humanity for whatever they took. Liars never do. His intuition dictated there was something much deeper brewing… and his instincts had never been wrong. He continued chuckling, visualizing the enormous black hole the presence of extraterrestrials would kick most institutional religious dogma into.

He had those thoughts in a mere few minutes. He thought about some people's individual brilliance but humanity's collective stupidity. They loved dogma because it relieved them of critical thinking. He remembered Marcus's speech and how much he actually agreed with the philosophical points. He just wasn't quite ready to abandon his tenure at the top of Interlink's food chain.

His imagination had drifted. He missed the first two sentences Heinrich Klatch had asked the aliens. He homed in on the conversation.

"Can you people help us counteract the technology Marcus and Lightning Inc. have created? We are at an impasse. Marcus's technology is more powerful than anything we possess as a society or species."

"Evidently, human technology is superior to ours in some ways. We are here because we need resources, and this planet is wealthy. We cannot give you technology that will propagate the destruction of your species. It is not permissible. Some do it, but they are not around for long. There are groups of different civilizations everywhere, who act as a counterbalance to those who oppose universal rules. They are what you would call shepherds."

Cameron Fry raised his hand, and Klatch nodded. "So, if you cannot give us technology, what is the purpose of this meeting underneath the Sistine Chapel? Evidently, you cannot assist for some reason that involves other beings. Can you elaborate?"

Gretel answered him. "Your species is in its infancy. You have no accurate concept of the universe. It is vast, complex, and populated by infinite numbers of intelligent lifeforms. Some rules define what is acceptable and what is unacceptable for all the universe's intelligent occupants. No civilization is permitted to intentionally destroy other civilizations for any reason whatsoever. It does happen, but when it does, the interlopers are immediately dealt with in one manner or another. It usually precipitates their demise. The only permissible destruction of the citizens of the universe is when it has been commissioned to the shepherds."

"So, this is a pointless meeting then," replied Fry.

"Not as pointless as you would think. We cannot give you the technology we possess, and you wouldn't have the intellectual acuity to manufacture such even if we gave you a blueprint. What we can do is advise you and become agents of what you call espionage by our superior powers of observation and understanding of the opposing technology. We can supply certain information without penalty. Before we decide to assist you in opposing your adversary, we must define the limit of our resource mining and the payment you will receive."

Heinrich Klatch held up his hand to interrupt. He was the head of Interlink and, for all intents and purposes, the United Nations. Cameron Fry would not be allowed to usurp his position of negotiator for Interlink. "Mr. Fry, I appreciate your zealous approach to our problems. I'm sure everyone else here does as well. These concepts and decisions cannot be made in this venue. Many people at the UN must agree to the terms and conditions."

He turned to Hansel. "I believe we must make a formal contract defining what you will do for us, how you intend to proceed, what resources you intend to mine, and in what quantities. You alluded to payment for our resources. The quantity of resources requires definition and cataloging once mined. We must set values for these things. That includes the assistance you expect to provide to facilitate our conflict with the opposition. We are already on the path of opposition to the status quo. Your participation can enhance our intelligence."

The extraterrestrial responded. "I believe we can surmount those obstacles. What will be your next move, and when will we continue this?"

"I must bring this before the leaders of several countries because you will mine commodities existing within their various borders. We must all agree."

Cameron Fry didn't like the sound of any of this. It was too open-ended. He was quite sure he was correct concerning the motives and integrity of Hansel and Gretel. They promised things Interlink had no way to enforce… and they were established liars. Other people had questions, and he patiently listened to them all. He didn't believe Klatch had the intellectual acuity to stay ahead of these characters from another star system. The meeting was almost over, and Heinrich Klatch had set the tone. It was up to him to elicit agreements from world leaders concerning the collapse of society to reform the new world order. There was a price, and the entire globe would have to pay it. Knowing human nature, he understood meticulous attention to detail would have to be employed by Klatch. He was still unsure of exactly what Hensel and Gretel would do for them. It would be a few interesting months.

***

A small group of humans, Junior, and Baby, stood before the ship. The visitors were facing them.

"Greetings Iggymarcus. You are entering a turbulent period. We observe everything on your broadcast media and have other methods and emissaries elsewhere. This meeting is a warning. The visitors from Altair 4 now advise your adversaries. They will not be giving technological assistance to defeat your instrumentality because your adversaries do not have the intellect to fabricate such. They will not provide your adversaries with the physical technology or hardware, or we will be required to intervene physically. "

"With no intention of arrogance, may I ask what the purpose of our meeting is today?"

"The purpose is to inform you of the coordinated efforts of those who assist your adversaries. Our purpose at this juncture is to advise those who would present the most sustainable future for your

species. That is you, Iggymarcus. One of your human expressions' states: *forewarned is forearmed.* Expect above-average intellectual innovation because your adversaries are receiving guidance. They have no ability to overcome your technological position, but they may learn how to sidestep. We understand your moral stance. We also note how your opposition must destroy that stance to overcome your society and succeed in assuming control. This is a critical time for your civilization."

"Is that all you have for us?"

"No, there is one thing more at this time. Your two assistants," the visitor said with a rare smile as he glanced at Junior and Baby. **"Your new life forms will be key."**

"How so?"

"They are unexpected innovations. Your adversaries are not considering their capabilities and involvement. A universal concept to help ensure success in confrontations is the element of surprise. You know how to summon us if you require a meeting."

It was the conclusion, and the 3 visitors entered their ship.

***

"That's the extent of it," Iggy described his meeting with the extraterrestrials to the 400-plus people who had assembled for meeting night. The turbulence is beginning. We see it reflected in all world news sources. Everyone is going to be put to the test now. All our emissaries are dispersed, and we will keep the ranch shielded."

Iggy's sister and Marty were finally present at a family meeting. "Marty and I have been away, on and off, for two years now, Iggy. We have been watching all these things from our London and New York offices. We see it, too. I think it's time to close the office and remain stateside. As relatives, we are targets, and it's a considerable dedication of resources to keep us out of harm's way. When humanity achieves resolution, if it ever does, I'm sure there will be a need for legal advice concerning international law. We can reopen our offices then."

"I believe that's a wise choice, Lindy. Here's an interesting idea for you. You and Marty should open your offices on Madison Avenue in New York. Louie Petro and Patty Titus have leased half an entire floor in the Emmet Building. They have no specialty covering international law. What they are doing is teaching law but also practicing. Why don't you talk to them? They are protected by our shield capabilities. There would be very little required to do the same for you."

Marty nodded his head in agreement as Gloria and Tom Rickart entered through the stage door. Tom leaned over and softly spoke in Iggy's ear. "It appears this global hyperventilation initiated by Interlink is spreading. The news coming out of Hong Kong isn't good."

"Okay Tom. There's no need to be secretive. Let's let everyone present in on the news because all of this will affect all of us."

"Well, boss, my people have their ears to the ground. We have operatives of every ethnicity and nationality around the world. We have a better intelligence-gathering apparatus than any other organization on the planet, including our own CIA. That is largely due to the sophistication of our equipment, thanks to you. Apparently, the Chinese are taking off the gloves. They see what's going on and what Interlink is trying to do. Of course, they will not interfere. They are hoping Interlink is highly successful because the world will descend into an irretrievable mess, and they'll be around to pick up the pieces."

Iggy silently nodded his head as he thought about the big picture. He addressed everyone in the room. "You're all the best-educated people alive. You understand more about politics, science, human nature, and the status of humanity than any other people who have ever lived. You are entitled to understand everything we are involved in because you are consequently involved. Our adversaries are trying to take the world apart at the seams, and they will succeed to a certain degree. We cannot ameliorate every bad act. We can only try to nullify the results. The object is to have sophisticated intelligence on the ground so we can stay ahead of them. They are operating in secrecy and seclusion."

We have the technology to establish a location for all the perpetrators, but it is going to be time-consuming and methodical. Once we do that, they will not be allowed to run roughshod over humanity in their desire to subjugate all of mankind. We will find them and arrest them. That will actually be the easy part. There are so many of them who will be complicit and guilty to different degrees that we are going to have difficulty adjudicating this as a society. This is going to be far worse than the Nuremberg trials because the participants number in the thousands.

Lindy and Marty were in the first row of the auditorium. "Marty and I have been out of the country for a while. Please fill us in on the status, Iggy. What has this to do with China?"

"Okay Tom," instructed Iggy as Junior and Baby entered the auditorium. "Go ahead and fill us all in. What's happening in China?"

"Since the British gave Hong Kong back to China in 97, they did it under the auspices of allowing the local government of Hong Kong certain autonomy and freedom, much greater than the rest of the country, for a supposed 50 years. We all understand what consummate liars' socialists are. Nonetheless, thousands of members of the Bālún Tōng have moved to Hong Kong to avoid persecution. They are not the CCP's idea of model citizens. Bālún Tōng advocates Western values and reveres capitalism. Before our trip to Beijing," Tom laughed thinking about that day, "Fun Chou Dung and his lapdog pet general, Li Shen Rishi, were responsible for persecuting and killing thousands of members of the Bālún Tōng until Iggy demanded they stop or be arrested."

He paused, thinking, and laughed. "I believe, if I remember correctly, it was Gloria who gave them the ultimatum. I'll bet it went right up their noses, coming from a 13-year-old child. Anyway, the CCP has been held at bay as far as Hong Kong goes till now. Still, their ultimate intent is to break the back of the local Hong Kong government and destroy the only Oriental edifice of capitalism outside Japan and South Korea."

"Well, things have been relatively quiet until now," mused Tom, "but this surge in global turbulence is a wave Dung decided he could surf, so he has sent his trained dogs to Hong Kong for the express purpose of chewing the throats out of Chinese Bālún Tōng members. Our best intelligence guesses over five hundred people have been murdered. I guess those slime bags weren't as intimidated by us as they appeared. I think it's time to fire up Daedalus for another joyride to Zhongnanhai."

Most of the ranch's occupants had heard the story of that day in Beijing when a 13-year-old child told the two most powerful men in the Chinese Empire what they would and would not be allowed to do in terms of murdering Chinese citizens. They were all looking at Gloria Marcus, smiling, knowing it was time for a repeat performance.

Iggy stood to welcome Junior and introduce Baby. "Before we board Daedalus for our pending Beijing vacation, everyone, Meet Baby. I would like to say she is the sole product of my efforts but that would be incorrect. You could say she is Junior's sister. He built her from scratch, and I helped him wake her up. I use the term her, loosely, but feminine qualities have been incorporated into her operating system. She chose her own name as a sentient and autonomous being. You have the floor, Baby."

"Hi, my name is Baby. I chose the name on my birthday because I was a baby. Now I'm living my 3rd 24-hour day and believe my name may be less appropriate because I am much older now." Baby smiled just as Junior had instructed. "What do you think? Does the name fit me? Perhaps you can call me Youngster or Kid. Either would work, and I will answer. When I get older, you might even call me Young Woman. I'm not sure how you look at the chronology, but I won't be a teenager for 12 years, 362 days, 5 hours, and 32 minutes."

Everyone in the auditorium had always understood life with Iggy Marcus was going to be an adventure beyond description. No one believed it was going to be this interesting. They were laughing at jokes offered by Baby, a sentient robot with absolutely no sense of humor whatsoever. It was hilarious.

Luke and Brett sat with Gloria in the middle at the rear of the auditorium, listening to Baby crack jokes. "She's unbelievable, Luke. I'm going to have to build one of these for a girlfriend… maybe three."

Luke and Gloria's heads swiveled towards their brother with wide-eyed incredulity. "Three? Why, three?" asked Luke, as Gloria rose to leave … "Three? I don't get it."

"It takes four to play bridge, Luke, and at least that many to play Polo.

"I can't take this anymore. I'm outta here. I have to get away from you two blockheads. Three," she mumbled as she walked away, wondering if Junior had actually installed that type of equipment in Baby.

"Hmm," Luke mused. "I think I get the point… No dinners out… No fancy wardrobes… No bickering about what movie we're going to watch… No arguments about anything, in fact…and no headaches. I don't think it gets better than that… And she's hot!"

"Yeah, Luke. I wonder if Junior downloaded the Kama Sutra."

***

"So, boss, I suppose you, Gloria, and I are headed to Zhongnanhai, ASAP."

"Exactly, Tom. I did promise Fletcher he could accompany us when we finally arrest those two murderers. Brett and Luke also want to come, and I see no reason to deny Junior the experience. It was just a matter of time. They're using the chaos created by Interlink worldwide to divert our attention. Our people on the ground, who belong to Bālún Tōng, masquerade as CCP party loyalists and may be in danger. Dung and Ricci are not the only scoundrels. There are many tiers of authority in the CCP. When we pull Dung and Rishi out, all hell is going to break loose. Those are the two top men. There is going to be a power struggle among the generals and other party leaders. Someone is going to want to fill the void. Unfortunately, no one with integrity exists in the upper levels of the CCP government."

"One week ago, Dung and Rishi sent several squads of men to ransack assorted locations in Hong Kong, looking for members of Bālún Tōng. Their orders were to arrest them, and then execute them summarily, boss. 500 decent men and women were killed."

"That is a tragedy we will not allow again. However, it is easier said than done. It's a complex problem requiring an even more complex solution. The entire Chinese system is set up as a perverse pseudo-capitalism. It has all the outward appearances of capitalism, but the profit incentive that normally fuels production in capitalism is missing. That production is fueled by the point of a gun aimed at the head of every Chinaman who does not belong to the ruling elite."

Junior, always given to speculative silence, almost never spoke until he was spoken to. His creator, Iggy Marcus, had given him a program forcing the inquisitive assessment of everything in his environment. Junior might consider using the word blessed instead of giving if he had an emotional repository. "Excuse my interruption, Dad. Would you mind if I ask something?"

"I thought you already knew everything, Junior."

"I am a repository for empirical data. You are correct; I know everything. What I don't know and understand is the illogical course of action humans so often seem to take."

Iggy smiled at his two mechanical offspring when his brother frowned, "How so, Junior? Please explain."

"What's on your mind, Junior?" Iggy responded to the question.

"Emotion seems to drive humans to make many mistakes, some of them enormous. I understand the technical part of human emotions, I just can't feel them. So, when humans kill humans so they can have power over other humans, I understand. The dead humans serve as an illustration or example of what will happen to the ones that are still alive if they don't conform to the dictates of the murderers. I understand all that, but it is so illogical that I cannot understand the reasons. As I see it, that is the most bizarre activity any sentient creature could engage in. You are correct when you say I know everything, but that pertains to anything logical. I know nothing about human emotions other than what is described in books about human psychology."

Iggy was still smiling. "That's why I want you to come with us to Beijing, Junior. It will be a learning experience for you. The one thing I could not embed in your memory is human psychology. Yes, you can memorize and understand all the abstract reasoning involved, but you cannot really understand it unless you feel it. Perhaps observing the experience will give you a better understanding. You will have your first taste of envy and greed. Those two emotions have driven all human political activity for thousands of years. It's time you had an objective, first-hand clinical look."

"What the superior man seeks is in himself; what the small man seeks is in others."

"In a country well governed, poverty is something to be ashamed of. In a country badly governed, wealth is something to be ashamed of."

"The will to win, the desire to succeed, the urge to reach your full potential... these are the keys that will unlock the door to personal excellence."

"He who learns but does not think is lost! He who thinks but does not learn is in great danger."

"The superior man understands what is right; the inferior man understands what will sell."

"To be wealthy and honored in an unjust society is a disgrace."

"I slept and dreamt life is beauty; I woke and found life is duty."

"Education breeds confidence. Confidence breeds hope. Hope breeds peace."
Confucius

CHAPTER VII

THE ELIMINATION OF DUNG

"How many people are actually on the ground, Tom?"

"All of them, Iggy, if you want to consider everyone who practices Bālún Tōng. My best guess from the information I receive is that there are 70 million of them, give or take. They practice in silence because of the danger from the government. They are all true Taoists and have embraced the philosophy. Most of them will die before they betray their beliefs and compatriots."

"I know, Tom. Those are the people who are being systematically murdered. That's why they are silent. I am asking how many active members we can count on? How many will volunteer to become our eyes and ears?"

"All of them, Iggy. It's an amazing thing to see. If they had any aggressive technology at all, the People's Liberation Army wouldn't last five minutes. Dung and Rishi are committed to exterminating them because they know there aren't enough men in the standing army to defeat 70 million people, especially religious zealots. All of them will assist us, if necessary, but quietly. My contacts tell me there are 200,000 committed, dedicated Chinese who are watching everything very discreetly. They know what our mission is because our men have passed the word. They also know why three years passed without persecution. It was because of your ultimatum. I guess they figure the world pandemonium is about to hit the fan. Their assistance is an act of self-preservation for them. They know without you; they will be systematically murdered."

Iggy silently shook his head, contemplating. "I've been concentrating on the UN, Klatch, and Interlink. I've neglected China slightly. Put out the word, Tom. Do it through the Bālún Tōng people in America. There are 70 million people in China with eyes and ears on the ground who can and will observe everything that goes on. I want to always know Dung and Rishi's location. 70 million people should be able to set up a network of undetectable and inescapable observers. We already know who the officers in the PLA are. They are going to have to be followed as well. We're headed to Beijing as soon as this gets rolling. It's time for Dung and Rishi to get what they deserve. I have an idea. We are going to give Falun Dong the technology they need."

"What technology, boss?"

Iggy's sly smile said it all. "I would think 70 million people will be enough to handle the 2,600,000 servicemen in the Chinese army. The army has been trained to kill which is the antithesis of Bālún Tōng's philosophy. That's why the Army has always had the upper hand. They have all the hardware necessary to murder people, as well as the incentive. I'm going to remove the hardware, Tom, and we will watch the incentive evaporate immediately in the face of 70 million of their countrymen who belong to Bālún Tōng."

Tom laughed. "Brilliant, boss. I guess we finally figured out who is going to replace the Chinese military, aristocracy, and politicians. I should say you figured it out. You're the only man alive with the technology to prevent the carnage that would result from a people's revolution. It's great, and no one has to die."

"We can only hope, Tom. I'm quite sure there will be a few stray bullets that will kill or injure some, but it will never become another Tiananmen Square. 10,000 people died that day, give, or take, because of a few men's megalomania. First, they killed general secretary Hu Yaobang because he supported the democratic reforms precipitating pro-democracy protests throughout the country. Premier Li Peng, Paramount Leader Deng Xiaoping, and President Yang Shangkun declared martial law and ordered his half-brother, General Yang Baibing, to bring 250,000 troops from Mongolia. Those troops had very few familial ties to the protesters, so it would be relatively easy to order them to murder their own people. They marched through the streets to Tiananmen Square, slaughtering demonstrators, and bystanders alike, thus ending the political reforms antithetical to communism begun by Hu Yaobang in 1986."

"I remember it well, Iggy. I was a young man at the time but well aware of the tragedy and the evil socialism portends for the world."

China's history is vastly different than the rest of the Orient. The Qing Dynasty was the last family dynasty to rule China. It was overthrown in 1912. The Republic of China was established, but the Chinese had never lived under a Republic. The country was on shaky ground and fell under Japanese rule, precipitating a Civil War ending after Mao became a Marxist- Leninist and led the Workers and Peasants Red Army to overthrow the existing nationalist government in 1949. That launched the People's Republic of China, now referred to as the CCP. "After Mao died in 1776, Deng Xiaoping proposed *Boluan Fanzheng*, the literal translation being '*bringing order out of chaos*', to overcome the abject poverty resulting from Mao's Cultural Revolution. Then, it became interesting. Xiaoping was underfunded, much like Mao and Hitler before World War II. The same people decided to get involved… our friends from Interlink. They coerced Richard Nixon to play the proverbial 'China card' that opened mainland China for modern commerce and production. Interlink orchestrated the entire thing through Henry Sheller, another Interlink player on the world stage who had ascended to prominence in American politics and was considered by most as the foremost intellect on international policy and political doctrine."

"They mistakenly believed the Chinese were historically ignorant and without the intellectual acumen or stamina to resuscitate the Chinese economy destroyed by Mao Zedong's socialism. They expected to reap all the profits from China's industrialization. Historically, Interlink's elitists have never been intellectual giants, with very few exceptions... men like Sheller… but even he was wrong. The others are perfect examples of intellectual mediocrity. Autocrats think all men are slaves and they are the entitled masters. None of them understood China's dynastic 10,000-year-old mindset of cultural superiority to the rest of the world. So, they funded China on the backs of the American taxpayer and created the greatest production machine in the history of the world. It was only possible because democracy, theoretically, was forever dead in China, and production was fueled at the point of a gun."

Junior and Baby silently stood, listening to Iggy and Tom's discussion. Their apparent, relatively emotionless faces hid their intellectual processes. Junior, however, had been programmed by the genius of Iggy Marcus to simulate human personality traits despite the missing emotions. He stood with his head cocked to the side with an inquisitive look on his face.

"I have to hand it to you, Dad. I would be completely fooled if I didn't know Junior was an unemotional robot."

Junior laughed at Gloria's comment, compelling her to laugh hysterically. "That's what I mean. My mechanical brother is quite something else."

"I thought the laughter would be appropriate," Junior offered. I thought levity would dissipate the seriousness of the discussion. Thousands of people were killed that day. I understand why, but it is illogical. I understand why baby and I have been created."

" Yes," added Baby. "We are to be part of Dad's answer to the insanity."

***

Daedalus hovered at a thousand feet over Fanghuan Hill and the town of Shiyan Beicun. The Longyou caves, called the Xiaonanhai Stone Chambers by the locals, were the destination. 500,000 people, all silent members of Bālún Tōng, had been galvanized to follow every military leader and official of the CCP. They were the epitome of the inscrutable Oriental. Subtly and relentlessly, they had silently followed every official of the Chinese hierarchy for two weeks. Their mission was to locate and keep track of every communist oppressor. Every member of Bālún Tōng understood the significance of events. The CCP had eventually worn down 90% of the populace to become subservient sheep and vassals of production for the coffers of the wealthy. Forced to work at the point of a gun, Bālún Tōng members had bided their time for decades, awaiting liberation.

The once pervasive feeling of hopelessness had evaporated. Even the suppression of information and government propaganda could not stifle the effects of Lightning Inc. and Iggy Marcus's coming emancipation. For the first time in half a century, the people had hope. The rich culture of their ancestors had been destroyed, and its beauty suppressed. The men who ruled the tyrannical nation-state could not allow pride or allegiance to China's magnificent history. The people might begin to remember that which would be the elitist's undoing.

Families passed Chinese culture and history preceding Mao Zedong to their progeny by word of mouth for the past 75 years. There remained no written records or available history for the average person to view. Mao destroyed most of it to numb the minds of the people. Mao had arrived as an indomitable figure promising the masses a better life and release from poverty. The realization the pipedream was a lie came soon after his rise to power when he murdered 77 million Chinese to construct his vision of society's future with his position at the helm. Those who followed continued to suppress all of China, and murder was a prolific tool to discourage rebellion. That would end this day.

***

"Why is Dung here, boss, instead of one of their underground military facilities? This isn't the most secure place he could hide."

Well, Tom, he's here with lots of security personnel. This is his favorite hangout. It is militarily equipped and technologically established as a major CCP control center. I think it's because Dung likes its aesthetic qualities. The caves were retrofitted 20 years ago and are constantly upgraded with the latest technology. Dung believes the world, meaning us, has been lulled into complacency since our visit two years ago. So, he has decided to continue killing Bālún Tōng members. They truly are the only internal threat to the CCP's power. General Rishi is not with him.

"Why isn't Rishi here with him?"

"Rishi is keeping his distance because he is a military strategist and knows we are coming after Dung. He's hiding under a hollowed-out mountain in the South China Sea, a base for two aircraft carriers and dozens of Chinese submarines. It is their most secure military site, defended by their fleet and Air Force. Rishi is the second most powerful man in the country as head of the PLA. When we arrest Dung, he gets to play alpha dog. If Dung was as smart as he claims to be, he would be with Rishi in the installation that is the most secure military base in the country."

"When we finish here, Gloria, Junior, and Baby can pilot three of Daedalus' sister ships to the island. We are going to arrest quite a few people on this day. When we deposit them on our island, we will proceed to Beijing and arrest the rest of the Communists. They are being flagged by the remaining 3 million Bālún Tōng."

"How far out are they, Gloria?"

"That's hard to say. They are so spread out... everywhere! Wow! At first, I thought there were many thousands, even hundreds of thousands. This is amazing! I can sense their thoughts, but I can't decipher them. There are too many! Almost 2 million, I think! Whatever brought this on? I would never have thought this was possible." She looked at her father with second thoughts. "You did this, didn't you, Dad?"

Iggy's smile answered her question. "The people of Bālún Tōng are zealous, committed, single-minded believers. As Taoists, they are all philosophically similar and of the same philosophical inclination as America's founding fathers and the beliefs of our family. Freedom for all and the ability to maximize one's potential throughout one's existence. They are educated and astute. They have been waiting for this opportunity for over 50 years. I am giving it to them today."

"I see, Dad. It's brilliant. I can see the whole thing unfolding now. You're going to flip the entire country of China upside down in a day... Amazing!"

Iggy had been keeping it verbal instead of subliminal so everyone present would understand. "That's the size of it, Gloria. We cannot remove a thousand people who control an army of 2,500,000, from their position of absolute authority and 10 minutes later, just simply walk away. Something must replace the power structure. Unfortunately, there are people in the Chinese military who are worse than Dung. Rishi is one of them, and so are many of the military leaders. They are the equivalent of Mao. To sustain their position at the top, they will mercilessly slaughter anyone and everyone who stands in their way. They all have to go." He laughed. "I have a nice island vacation in the middle of the Pacific waiting for them."

"Why didn't you share this with me, Dad? I had no idea your plans for this day were so intricate."

"I was asked not to, daughter. I needed substantial help to demonstrate and convince the efficacy of this plan to 70 million members of Bālún Tōng. Everyone embraced their absolute commitment, understanding, dedication, and organization to the cause.

"Who asked you? Ooooh," she responded**,** as the images of their extraterrestrial visitors materialized in her father's mind. "**I thought they were not supposed to get directly involved."**

"Correct. Apparently, the visitors from Altair 4 have involved themselves with Interlink. So, I guess our friends from the other side

of the galaxy committed to a tit for a tat. They revealed themselves to the leaders of Bālún Tōng on the Chinese mainland and explained how the time for their salvation from persecution was now, and it would be done through Lightning Inc. Baby accompanied them as a translator."

Daedalus remained at a thousand feet. They watched nearly two million people approach. The throng extended for miles. It was obviously an organized, carefully orchestrated march to accomplish a singular purpose… The rebirth of the Chinese Republic.

"Is that the extent of it, then? There are a few million people marching here to confront Fun Chou Dung. I guess it will be the end of his position as general secretary."

"No, Gloria, this is not the extent of it. Yes, there are probably 2 million people on their way here as we speak. They are not carrying weapons. They won't need them. Our men will be on the ground to shield them when they confront Dung. There are another 45 million adult members of Bālún Tōng who are committed to the upheaval of the CCP and China's first, valid introduction to democracy. They have been mobilized as well and are surrounding every military installation and army battalion in the CCP. They will all be shielded from handheld weapons by our Navy SEALs carrying personal shield generators, that Tom deployed, and we will nullify larger weapons from our satellites. Technically, I guess you could say we are invading China. Realistically, we are eradicating the greatest societal evil in history… Communism."

Baby stared at Tom Rickart's laughter with a quizzical expression. "What's so funny, Tom?"

"Just about everything I guess," he continued laughing. "Think about it: I'm talking to robots with human facial expressions but no emotions that are actually alive, on a ship that can travel from Montana to China in mere seconds, and I am involved with a handful of people who are about to actually invade China... and win! I know you have no sense of humor, Baby, but I'm sure you can see the humor in all of that, even if you can't feel it. Too bad you weren't here for Gloria's first meeting with Fun Chou Dung. She had him puking on his own feet."

"I hope he was wearing sandals."

Tom Rickart laughed even harder. "I thought you didn't have a sense of humor, Baby. That's hilarious."

"No sense of humor here, Tom. That is not a capability of Junior or me. I suppose if I had even a small amount of emotion in me, I would wish I could experience humor and have a good laugh. I am very good at small talk, though, don't you think?"

Gloria chuckled. "You may have no sense of humor, baby, but you're definitely fun to have around."

"Okay," announced Iggy as Daedalus descended to the opening indicating the military entrance to the Caverns. "The throng is assembled below. Looks like the crowd covers over a thousand acres. They are very well-behaved because they know they are on a mission that must not fail.

***

Secretary-General Fun Chou Dung sat with General Timar Chen, facing the viewing screen, watching the ship settle to the plateau in front of the entrance. Only one other time had he been this frightened, but time had stripped away the memory of his terror. The last visit by Marcus and his daughter to Zongnanhai left him mentally and emotionally stricken for days. Marcus's technology was apparently undefeatable, but at least one could run and hide from it. That despicable child was a nightmare worse than the demons, Jiuying or Qiong Qi. He pictured himself being devoured by either of those demons, but it would only be a matter of a few seconds of pain, and he would be dead. The child possessed him and tortured him slowly. There was no nightmare worse than this child. Gloria Marcus had done this to only a few men, but the experience castrated their persona. They would never be the same again.

Timar Chen watched Dung tremble in fear. It was a side to the first secretary he had never seen before. He looked derisively at Dung. This was the highest man in the highest office of the CCP, trembling over the thoughts of a young child. "Secretary Dung, although this child may have returned, I think you should pay attention to the screen exhibiting the throng of people coming this way. Look at the TV screens of our drones. There are several million people at our door, and we have only one brigade of soldiers. What are we to do?" Chen asked with mounting hysteria.

"I fear, General Chen, there is nothing we can do. I am not as intimidated by the masses as I am by the child."

"Why, Secretary Dung? She is a mere child. What can a child do to you that makes you tremble in fear like this."

"You cannot understand, General Chen, but I believe you soon will. Then, you will know."

The skin of Daedalus seemed to melt away, exposing the ship's occupants to the men sitting in the vaulted room and the thousand or so Chinese troops surrounding the ship. Gloria was the first to exit, followed immediately by Iggy, Luke, and Baby. Everyone was shielded. Fun Chou Dung squeezed his temples, screaming, "NO, NO, NO, NO, get out! Get out of my head." He swore at Gloria in Chinese.

Gen. Chen, wide-eyed in amazement, watched the most powerful man in China and one of the most powerful men in the world reduced to a quivering mass of terror. The intruders approached the large steel door with cylinder bolts to the frame.

"Secretary Dung. Get a grip on yourself, sir! They can't get in! The door is two meters thick with a dozen half-meter cylinders locked into the frame. It is undefeatable, even by a proximity blast of a medium-size nuclear weapon."

Apparently, Dung didn't hear him, or he was so distracted he couldn't concentrate. Dung began to weep as the memory of the pain from the girl's entry into his mind reawakened. Still holding his hands on his temples and weeping, he kept repeating, "No, No, No!"

Dung rose in a daze and walked to the box on the wall with the switch circuit breakers that would open the door to the outside and allow the interlopers in. He threw one of the switches and began to turn the wheel when Chen walked up behind him and wrenched him from the panel. "

"What are you doing, Mr. Secretary! Do not let them in! He was still standing with his arms around Secretary Dung's arms and chest, restraining him from operating the entry mechanism when he felt Gloria Marcus enter his mind.

"妈的(Oh Shit)!" Screeched General Chen as he felt Gloria take possession of his mind. Now he understood Dung. The pain was excruciating as he let go of the general secretary and staggered backward into the wall. The girl's subliminal voice was overpowering, and the pain was relentless.

"OPEN THE DOOR…NOW! General Chen!"

Chen moved toward the control panel. The six, armed soldiers in the room were at a loss. They didn't understand what was happening, and even if they did, they had no idea what to do. Secretary Dung was on his knees, whimpering hysterically. General Chen moved toward the panel, horror-stricken as his shrill whine stammered, "No, No, No! Over and over as he threw the switch and turned the wheel.

Gloria, Iggy, Baby, and Luke entered the room and approached Secretary Dung, who was still on his knees with tears streaming down his cheeks. Gen. Chen was sitting on the floor in the corner with his tie off and his shirt ripped open. He had done that in an active delusion, trying to escape the influence of Gloria Marcus. Luke immediately encapsulated the six, armed soldiers and the general.

"So, we meet again, Dung. You were given the opportunity to join the human race two years ago, and you were instructed not to kill any more people intentionally. I knew it would come to this, but morality demanded I allow you to redeem yourself and expiate your past sins. That was your only chance. Now, you are coming with us. Get off your knees!"

Iggy looked sideways at the general who was still sitting on the floor moaning. "You are his tool, general. You slaughtered your countrymen and sold your soul to buy a perch on one of the branches of power. You are also coming with us. We have a private hell designed just for men like you who are so willing to inflict your brand hell on your countrymen. Get up from the floor and get moving!"

The soldiers had been encapsulated by Luke. They had no idea what this was about and just wanted it to end; it was so bizarre and unexpected. Everyone moved toward the exit and Iggy turned to Luke. "As soon as we're outside, close the vault door and release the soldiers. Tom has every soldier outside encapsulated. They can't harm anyone."

Before they boarded Daedalus, Luke stopped to look around. "Geez, Dad, look at all these people! There's a couple million of them here."

"Yup, as soon as we board the ship and rise about 300 feet, I must address them."

***

Daedalus hovered at 300 feet over the center of the Bālún Tōng assembly. Its walls dissipated, and the crowd saw the group of people standing within. Iggy began to speak to the two million people gathered below as a 100-foot-wide hologram of his face appeared between the ship and the Bālún Tōng multitude. Somehow, no matter what direction they faced the hologram from, Iggy's apparition seemed to be staring personally at each person. His voice boomed as he addressed the people, but somehow, it was tempered to seem almost personal without an echo.

"I am Iggy Marcus." He began in Cantonese. "You all know who I am because you are here and a disciple of Bālún Tōng. You have been asked to demonstrate your support for the removal of tyrants from the government of your country. You have come in peace and tranquility to affect that result. You and other members of Bālún Tōng are the last vestiges of China's rich cultural heritage. It is up to you to reeducate your people and inspire a new path to the future for yourselves and all your countrymen. You are 70 million strong; only 2 million have gathered here today. Over 60 million Bālún Tōng members have surrounded every military station on the mainland as we speak. You outnumber the military conscripts 35 to 1. That is a force which cannot be overwhelmed despite the military training of subservience and aggression the Army has received. Lightning Inc. will protect you from an air assault."

"Further, our representatives from Lightning Inc. are on the ground at every location with the groups of Bālún Tōng. They possess our shield technology to ensure everyone's safety. No one will be allowed to murder anyone today, like the slaughter at Tiananmen Square in 1989. You are the people who will oversee governing from this day forward. I am removing the present government and bringing each one of them to a secure place. They will be given a test to determine if they are fit to live among human beings without coercion. If that is in their nature, they will be brought back to become contributing citizens of the new China."

"Before I depart to arrest General Li Shen Rishi, I make this urgent request. Talk among yourselves. Pick leaders who will govern honestly, and your children can emulate. You must govern yourselves without malice or envy. This is the charge for all men and women who wish to take a viable path to the future. I cannot force you to do these things. It is up to you to adopt this philosophical stance if you value your progeny and their place in the world of tomorrow. Good luck to you. We have trained two of you, Zia and Chu, to help guide China through the transition." Today is the first day of a liberated China."

The response thundered as 2 million people applauded and began singing a Chinese hymn... 求神祝福先知 (May God Bless the Prophet), as Daedalus slipped away towards the eastern horizon.

***

Four ships, Daedalus, Hermes, Poseidon, and Nemesis, faded from the Lightning Ranch flightline, reappearing several moments later over China's Yulin naval base on the island of Hainan. Within minutes, General Li Shen Rishi was urgently summoned to the command center from his quarters and a fitful sleep. He entered the normally quiet command center, now buzzing with activity.

General Rishi approached the duty officer, Senior Col. Lu Bing Tau. "What is so urgent, Col., that you would wake me from a sound sleep? Has a war started?" He laughed.

“Maybe, general! There are four ships above us. Two are moderate in size, perhaps 50 meters long. Two of them are huge... at least 150 meters. I have never seen anything like them. I don't think they are terrestrial, but I remember hearing how someone flew a similar craft from Taiwan to Zongnanhai once.”

General Li Shen Rishi’s eyes were saucers as his mind flooded with the memory of that day at Zongnanhai. He realized immediately Iggy Marcus had come to call, and Fun Chow Dung was probably already a prisoner. The rising bile burned his throat as he swooned, lightheaded and dizzy, praying the child would not be with Marcus.

“What should I do, sir?” Inquired Col. Tau. “They have been here for 10 minutes and have done nothing.”

Li Shen Rishi’s head was buzzing, half with fear and half with rage. He had expected the inevitability of this for three years. He repeatedly advised Dung not to kill the members of Bālún Tōng, remembering the promise issued by an 11-year-old child who had been able to enter his mind, forcing him to passionately kiss China’s General Secretary. He knew of no power on earth could resist such a challenge to individual autonomy. He was desperate for a solution!

“Do we have a hypersonic sled with a one Mt weapon ready?”

“Yes, general, we have five submarines in port, and they all have several.”

“Shoot them down! Immediately!”

“But sir! It will kill hundreds of people on the island in seconds! We can’t do that!”

"I said shoot them down, Col.! Do it now!"

Col. Lu Bing Tau shook his head no. He knew he was speaking to the highest-ranking officer in the PLA, but he was a man of integrity, fiercely loyal to China, and he would not kill a thousand people because General Rishi had become a madman. "No, sir. That is an illegal order, and I will not execute it."

Everyone in the command center had been listening to the exchange with open mouths and bated breath, waiting to see the resolution of Col. Tau's challenge to General Rishi's authority.

Moments later, the clear, calm, but strident, subliminal voice of a young girl echoed within every mind in the command center. **Wise choice Col. Tau. The execution of that order would have precipitated your death, along with over 2000 people on this military base at the surface. Please allow me to introduce my father, Iggy Marcus. I'm quite sure you know who he is.**

General Rishi cringed and uttered an enraged expletive as Iggy's voice resonated from the PA system of the command center and was broadcast through every speaker in every vessel and office in the complex.

"We have come to collect you, General Rishi. You are directly responsible for giving the orders to kill 500 members of Bālún Tōng. Two years ago, you were given the choice to clean up your act and become an honest member of Chinese society or we would remove you from it forever. Fun Chou Dung is our prisoner aboard this ship. The ultimatum was given to both of you. You ignored our warning and will no longer live in China. You are coming with us."

"If you had launched your weapon, many of you would be dead, but we would be unscathed. Our technology has eliminated your ability to kill en masse. Everyone else on the planet has lost that capability as well. Your militaries are now ineffective and useless. They have no function because we will not allow the destruction of humanity, individually or collectively. Open the door to the command center. Our ship is going to enter the submarine bay, and we are coming in."

General Rishi was frothing at the mouth. "No, do not let them in! That is a direct order, Col.! Do not open the command center vault!"

Col. Lu Bing Tau was in a quandary. He had already disobeyed one order and refused to launch the missile. That was understandable. He could defend it at a court-martial. The general had ordered him to kill his own people, and he refused. This, however, was different. The enemy ordered him to open the door and let them in. General Rishi issued the counter command to ignore the enemy and keep the door secure. This order from General Rishi, he would have to follow.

Moments later, he watched General Rishi in disbelief, his eyes wide with amazement as the general walked to the control panel and began the procedure to open the vault door. The general was violently shaking and began to screech… "Get out of my head, damn you! Get the hell out of my head, you Biǎo zi!" as he initiated the sequence to open the vault.

Gloria smiled at her father. "The vault door will be open in a moment. Let's go in."

"Yup, it's time to go in."

Luke and Brett looked at each other. "You and I have to collaborate on a book, Brett. I'd like to call it the life and times of the family, Marcus. What do you think?"

Gloria jumped into the conversation, laughing. "That's a great idea. When you get to this page, make sure you mention the highest-ranking officer in the Chinese PLA just called me a Yankee bitch."

Iggy Marcus walked through the 3-foot-thick wall bordering the open doorway to the command center. General Rishi was in the corner. Everyone, both officers and enlisted men, watched an American, their sworn enemy, walk through the door of the command center like he was strolling through the Shanghai Gardens into a room with the most highly secret Chinese technology in existence. The experience was surreal. What was happening was unimaginable an hour before. Yet here it was... The general in charge of the entire PLA was about to be arrested on home soil for murder by a foreign agent.

They knew the translucent veil surrounding the interloper was his magnetic shield. Everyone in the world was aware of the technology at this point and knew it was impenetrable. Despite that, a guard ran to stop Iggy's progress as he approached the general but bloodied his nose on the translucent magnetic wall.

Iggy's sense of poetry emerged. "Well, General Rishi, we meet again, and I have come to escort you on your date with destiny. It is the exquisite destiny you deserve because it is the one you fashioned for yourself. Come with me. Fun Chou Dung awaits you aboard Daedalus."

"Qù nǐ de!!" said Gen. Rishi as he gave Iggy the middle finger.

Iggy chuckled at the general's rage-contorted face. "Some things are just universal, I guess. I have to tell you, General, you are in distinguished company. No one has given me the finger since one of my college professors." He continued to laugh, thinking how much his college roommate, Sen. Jake Dorian, would have loved this moment. "One more thing. You are a murderer." Iggy said as he deadpanned the general. "You will walk into our ship of your own volition, or I will wrap you with Porky Pig, the character who most suites you, and have you carried in."

Tom Rickart had followed Iggy into the command center just in case he needed an assist. The mention of Porky Pig forced Tom to squeeze hard to stop wetting his pants from laughter.

***

Ten minutes later, Dung and Rishi were marched into a hut on a 5000 square mile Island in the Pacific that Tom Rickart had dubbed 'Gilligan's Island.' Junior carried a crate into the hut with food and water for a week. "This will keep you alive until we return next week with a few more of your friends who executed members of Bālún Tōng. We have invited them to your party. I am not sure how long Dad intends to leave you here. Eventually, someone will try you for your crimes. One more thing," he said as he handed Dung a pack of cards and to Rishi, a cribbage board with a book of instructions written in Cantonese. "This will alleviate boredom with something to while away the time. Have a nice day!"

Both men had calmed down after their abduction. They were still enraged, but had accepted their fate, knowing there was nothing they could do about it. "Why are you giving us this thing?" Dung asked scornfully, eyeing the cribbage board, never having seen one before.

"Oh, that?" Junior shrugged. "I am not human, but I am not just any old robot, either. I am a sentient robot. Iggy Marcus built me and brought me to life. I speak colloquial English slang, every other language, and tell multi-lingual jokes. I am practicing kindness and small talk on you. I hope you guys enjoy the cribbage board and amuse yourselves." With that, Junior waved farewell, boarded Daedalus, and the ship disappeared, leaving the two Chinamen to explore the game of cribbage.

"Where to next, Dad?" asked Brett. "The day is still young. We are not ready to throw in the towel yet."

We have another twenty-three hundred and twenty-one people to arrest. For the most part, they are executives of privilege. They live in opulence at the expense of their society, while the rest of China lives in relative poverty. That is not the reason they are being arrested, however. They were directly responsible for issuing orders to kill assorted members of society. Some of them actually pulled the trigger."

"How did you get your hands on this information, pop?"

"Bālún Tōng. They have been providing me with irrefutable information."

Brett sat contemplating this information. "I have another question. Why did you bring all four ships? We only needed two."

"True," replied Iggy. "Some of it was for show, but there is another purpose here." He laughed, thinking about Junior and Baby working around the clock for weeks, designing and printing 700 million pamphlets to release over the cities of China, describing the fetus of China's new government about to enter the birth canal.

"Enough ambitious moral people belong to Bālún Tōng to reconstitute a government replete with freedom for the individual instead of the Communist vehicle of oppression that exists. I have been working with members of the Bālún Tōng to write a constitution and design a government hierarchy to guarantee individual liberty and thus remove the tyrannical stranglehold the authoritarians have on the people. It is a several-page document with a brief description of the new government and what every person will have to do to bring it into being. We are dropping seven hundred million of them on every population center, today. Junior and Baby have helped me deploy shield technology to many of them. We will also assist with our satellites. Their own army will no longer be able to march on its own people. First, we must remove the impediments, including all the slave masters who are no different than the people we oppose in Europe and America, not to mention Russia. That's where we are going next, by the way."

"Why is Russia next, Dad?" asked Luke.

"Logic dictates that, Luke. China has almost 18% of the world's population, about 1,500,000,000. That prioritizes their influence on global politics and commerce per capita. Further, they are admitted communists and tyrants who will kill indiscriminately to retain their power positions. Like all good socialists and communists, they claim it's for the good of the people. Of course, none of that is true, but they always manage to convince uneducated, delusional people they are benefactors while they are executing their neighbors. The only ray of sunshine is the people in charge, who are the authoritarians, are only a handful compared to the population of one and a half billion. All we have to do is disarm and expose them to give China back to its people."

"Russia, on the other hand, has only 150 million people, roughly 1/10th of China's population. Their economy is struggling because they don't have China's manufacturing capabilities. Their economic structure depends on energy exports, and those prices are relatively low, today. China had to be dealt with first. Their immense economy is an enabler. The rich party members manipulate the masses with minimal subsidies. Only a few people are allowed to rise to the surface like cream. Even communists require management to execute an economy the size of China's. Competent management only occurs when people are rewarded for their ability. That is the basic flaw of socialism or communism. No one is rewarded for excellence, so production is minimized, and everyone descends into poverty. So, super-citizens are allowed disproportionate wealth as an incentive or bribe to rule or be overlords of the masses. The masses, of course, operate and produce because a gun is pointed at their heads."

"Still," continued Luke. "That's a numbers game, I get it, but why does that make China first? If you are correct, the Russians are about to invade countries that were formally part of the Soviet Union."

"They are about to invade other neighboring countries because they are poverty-stricken as a national economy. They need resources from other countries. Further, the Russians are not part of Interlink, just as the Chinese are not. Perestroika ended the Soviet Union, but it did not end Russian tyranny. The current government is tyrannical, and only a limited form of corrupt capitalism is operating there for the chosen few. In the old days before Mikhail Gorbachev, China was a minuscule economic power compared to the two great seats of military power in the world, Russia and America."

"I get it, Dad. It is more complex than meets the eye. Why is Russia deciding to be expansionist now?"

"Every world leader and international organization understands who and what Interlink is, and how they have run the planet through economics for a thousand years. The only countries of substance that Interlink did not dominate were the United States, the Soviet Union, Australia, India, and last but not least, Israel. They didn't dominate the Arabs because the Middle Eastern countries allowed themselves to become a recent part of interlink."

"How does that equate with the Russian desire to conquer and expand to reincorporate the old Soviet Union?" asked Brett.

"Look at it this way, Brett. Consider the philosophical angle. Although tyranny wears many hats, the heads underneath the hats are all the same, whether they call themselves socialists, communists, dictators, or the party of the people. They abuse the ignorance of men by handing out phony incentives to elicit their cooperation and get them to sign on, politically and philosophically. When ignorant, lazy men sign on, they effectively offer to voluntarily march into the Gulag, making it simple for the tyrants. The victims in the flock volunteer to immolate themselves so the tyrants don't have to shoot them and demonstrate their actual intent to the rest of the sheep."

"You all understand what was coming under the new, one world order and government, designed and about to be implemented by Interlink until we got in the middle of things. They dumbed down enough people and intended to turn the world into a huge flock of sheep. They called it Agenda 21 in the last century. Now they call it sustainable living, but it all boils down to stripping everyone of individual rights and wealth, leaving the remaining tyrants as the only people calling the shots."

"Consider the fact that most countries are tyrannies beneath the surface, with some exceptions such as America, which has now become a partial tyranny, and a few other truly Democratic countries or republics. The other countries' rulers are despotic mediocrities masquerading as benevolent leaders. The priority is their self-aggrandizement, opulence, and wealth. They care nothing about the people but are very careful not to expose that side of their personas."

"During the last century, when Agenda 21, Global 2000, and the New World Order was proposed and structured, every country on earth was offered a place at the table of the coming One World Government. Their place at the table would equal the stature of their gross domestic product and political influence in the world as well as the size of the population. Some countries would get a small seat, and others would get a large seat, but only the leaders would get a large slice of the pie, never the people. The ultimate authoritarian intent is for the proletariat to be stripped of everything and love it."

"Is everyone beginning to see where this is leading?" Iggy asked. "The smaller countries with tin star despots would be deliriously happy just to have their tiny seat at the table. Every country would have a seat commensurate with the factors I mentioned: wealth, GDP, political influence, population, and geographic size. Now, think about Russia, formerly the Soviet Union. The population of the Soviet Union was more than double the population of Russia today. The landmass and resources were much greater, not to mention the fact that only the United States and the Soviet Union possessed nuclear arsenals consisting of thousands of weapons."

"Russia is a mere shadow of its former self as the Soviet. When Gorbachev dissolved the Soviet Union, it was amidst violent protests by the rest of the tyrants who ran the Kremlin, KBG, and GRU. They resisted Gorbachev, but it was futile because Reagan's fiscal and foreign policies, as well as his massive military restructuring, had, in effect, destroyed the Soviet economy. They couldn't possibly compete with capitalism and the West. Reagan also stopped the yearly, gratis American subsidies from bolstering the Soviet economy since the 1920s. So, Gorbachev had no choice, or the people would have erupted in a rampage, and just as Joseph Stalin did, they would have had to kill millions to quell the violence."

"The rest of the Soviet leaders grudgingly accepted reality and conceded to Gorbachev, thus becoming westernized in an act of self-preservation. Those same leaders and their heirs still run the government, for the most part. They do it from the shadows, allowing the people to believe they have a modicum of bastardized capitalism and freedom because there is more domestic production and trade. Those tigers have not changed their stripes. They are still despots with a hatred for humanity and a lust for power. Their current president, Vanya Shartin is one of the remaining tyrants and once a member of the GRU."

"So, how does that affect all of this, Dad?" Brett wanted to know.

"Don't you see it? Russia is less than half in stature as well as every other quality, compared to the Soviet Union's former prominence. That's not good enough for Vanya Shartin. He lusts for his former power as head of the

KGB. Interlink's New World order was handing out the goodies to the people with a seat at the table according to their current stature, not their previous stature. Shartin was offered a seat at the table, but only a smaller slice of the pie, and that was unacceptable. The only way he can increase his stature is to increase Russia's stature by conquest. The only other option is thermonuclear war, but that would precipitate the end of everything. Make no mistake about it. Vanya Shartin, like all dictators, is a narcissist who would rather be dead than play second fiddle. That makes him a wild card. If I had left nuclear war on the table, he might possibly nuke the world and reduce it to a cinder if he didn't get his way and take the entire world to hell with him in a psychotic act of revenge."

Tom Rickert and Richard McNerney were both along for the ride. Richard never said much. He had survived a life that defied the imagination. He shouldn't be here, alive, and well, and knew why. The man who saved his life a few years before had just described the reasons his country of birth, Russia, was about to attack another country.

Tom, on the other hand, had been Iggy's chief of security for 20 years. He had seen everything Iggy had accomplished as well as his approach to dealing life and justice out to the world. It always amazed him that Iggy had done the impossible without a shred of pride or arrogance by eliminating the ability of men to wage nuclear war. He didn't know or believe it at the time, but now he knew Iggy was right. This was the moment in time when humanity would either grow up or succumb to its wicked side. He saw men's weaknesses compared to the heroic strength of the man who stood between an inevitable oblivion or a majestic future.

***

Cameron Fry led the group descending the spiral staircase. Klatch had called the emergency meeting two days before, immediately after he heard the news. Twenty-six men and women of Interlink had been permitted to use the hidden chamber twelve stories below the Sistine Chapel floor, under the condition the Pontiff be present for meetings. Heinrich Klatch and Pope Innocent XVI awaited them. The members of Interlink agreed that anonymity and obscurity were of the utmost importance. Their enemy possessed technology beyond anything in existence. Group meetings required clandestine seclusion to plan and implement operations while maintaining secrecy. The members had been meeting electronically, but that involved enormous risk. Lightning Inc. was technically too sophisticated for Interlink to count on the obscurity offered by electronic communication and the security of computer passwords. So, they set up a code system for contact and arrangements to meet bimonthly in the Vatican vault.

All men are fallible. Pope Innocent XVI was less concerned with the salvation of the flock, than he was with his seat at the apex of the church. History was populated by 272 Popes. This Pope was the 273rd since Nero Caesar crucified St. Peter in the Coliseum. All were considered God's representatives on earth by the faithful, whether or not the shoe actually fit.

Some were paragons of faith and servants of God, and others were small men who should never hold any reins of power. Absolute power corrupts those kinds of men. Men of character, genuine honesty, and faith who assume the mantle of service to their Creator, although not immune, rarely succumb to temptation. That description did not fit José Amontillado.

Twenty-six people were seated around the horseshoe table, and acolyte priests served refreshments while Heinrich Klatch shuffled through files of papers and pressed the button on the remote control. The 6-foot x 6-foot video screen blazed, displaying a panoramic aerial view of Beijing. "We immediately served refreshments because we are awaiting an additional 30 people, and their ETA is about ninety minutes from now. They are landing at Leonardo da Vinci airport within the hour. They are all world leaders from various governments worldwide, and members of Interlink. When they were informed of current events in China, they all immediately departed from home to attend this meeting. World events have transpired that will dramatically affect the globe and our prospects for the immediate future. "

"Let us enjoy the refreshments while we await the others. We were unable to contact our guests from Altair until a short time ago. They may attend as well. The drawback will be their physical appearance. They must pass through the throngs of tourists above, without notice. They attended previous meetings at night when the chapel and facilities were closed."

Heinrich Klatch nodded to Cameron Fry. "Why don't you go ahead and hand out the statistics to everyone now? The others can come up to speed when they arrive." Klatch slid the folder of papers across the table to Fry.

Cameron Fry, bank president and CEO, had commissioned his think tank, International Speculation Portfolio Inc., to create and maintain a comprehensive, continuous, fluid, compilation of all world economics and that of individual countries by their economic stature and GDP.

The paperwork was passed to every member except the Pontiff, who nodded no and waved the papers off. José Amontillado's interest in money was dedicated exclusively to the banca vaticana dello spirito santo, and its private and exclusive dealings with world economies and other international economic forays.

Cameron Fry surveyed everyone's faces as they read through the handout. "If you observe, I have listed the size of certain countries' economies on a global basis. Listed below is the percentage of manufacturing relative to the size of their economies by percentage. I'll outline that now but wait until everyone arrives before we discuss the significance of current events. The largest annual economy is that of the United States at 20.49 trillion. That is 23.89% of the global economy. Next is China, with 13.61 trillion annually at 15.86% of the world economy. Next is Japan at 4.97 trillion at 5.79%. They are the top four major players, and everyone else splits the rest of the pie. The only ones close are India and Germany, just above 7% combined."

The elevator chime indicated the arrival of guests. Heinrich Klatch rose to greet the new arrivals as the door opened. There were six people aboard, and he shook hands and greeted all of them. One of the new arrivals noted that there were 24 people requiring four more elevator trips before everyone would be present.

Twenty minutes later, everyone was seated as Cameron Fry handed paperwork to the newcomers before Heinrich Klatch monopolized the conversation.

"Everyone should note this data. It indicates approximately 50% of the world economy and manufacturing." He gave everyone a few moments to assimilate the data. As you can see, the United States is the big dog, with China close behind in terms of consumption. However, China leads the United States in manufacturing, 28.7% to 16.8% for production of durable goods and organic exports. There is one conclusion to be drawn here, and that is China is the greatest economic power, producing most of the goods, but the United States is second. The complexity exists in the fact that China's major market is the United States, importing 66% of their exports, yet the US is only 41% of the world population."

Heinrich Klatch gave everyone a few minutes to digest the information, then immediately continued speaking to avert Fry's dominance. "So, you see, the economy of the planet is stable because of the two players, the United States and China. Anything that precipitates a major calamity will upend that balance. Everyone here realizes Interlink's goal is to collapse the world economy with small intercountry wars and violence as well as a direct attack on the US economy by forcing them to print money and the planned release of contagion in Africa. This multipronged attack on the United States economy is an attack on the world economy. It will be almost impossible to resist by our adversaries, the president of the US and Lightning Incorporated. We constructed a plan twenty years ago to reorder society when it collapses. One world government will only be possible after the collapse of the US dollar as the world reserve currency."

Klatch held his hand up to pause the moment after the elevator chimed again. The door slid open, and a 7-foot, corpulent figure wearing a black clergy's cassock with a scarf wrapped around its head, stepped into the room. Klatch stood and greeted Hansel. "Thank you for responding to my request. Our meeting today is of critical importance. Major political and economic changes are occurring. They are happening immediately and portend ill for our plans."

The alien nodded and walked to the center seat at the head table that had been left vacant for him.

Heinrich Klatch reached for the remote control. "Everyone is present so let us get down to business. What I am about to show you is barely believable. In fact, if I had merely heard it and not seen it, as I am going to show you today, I would not have believed it possible. So, without further words, I call your attention to the screen."

He pressed several buttons, and the computer screen of Google Maps: satellite view appeared. "These are satellite views of China. We ordered them taken by multiple satellites three days ago when we got wind of what was happening. They all were recorded on the same day at the same time, and the results are beyond amazing. They are inconceivable and earth shattering!" He flipped through scene after scene depicting aerial views of thousands of Chinese cities and military installations.

"I have depicted at least 20 affected locations in China, and there are dozens more. You can see the throngs of people gathered. Our best guess is that close to 70 million people have stormed all the cities in China and every domestic military base. Further, I have learned that Fun Chou Dung and Gen. Li Shen Rishi have been taken into custody along with over 3000 other members of the CCP hierarchy. At first, we weren't completely sure who did this until we got our hands on one of these booklets. I will pass them to each one of you so you can see what we're up against. You will each get two copies. One is written in Cantonese, and the other is written in English. Most of you speak English. For those of you who do not, I have appropriate translations. This is the most amazing political document I have ever seen.

Each member examined the book. The cover displayed two words across the center in large Gothic letters: CHINESE CONSTITUTION (中国宪法). The bottom of the page presented two words only: Bālún Tōng. The upper right-hand corner brandished a lightning bolt, the corporate insignia of Iggy Marcus's Lightning Incorporated.

Heinrich Klatch had to keep careful tabs on his emotions and facial expressions. If he allowed the attending world leaders the slightest indication of his seething insanity, he would be ostracized and removed as President of the World Progressive Socialist Council as well as his commensurate position of authority with the Secretary-General of the United Nations. All the plans he had developed as a young man in the 1960s for a one-world socialist government with his position somewhere at the summit of power would be dashed on the rocks.

He inherited political brilliance from his father. Joseph Goebbels, the Third Reich Minister of propaganda, had helped design Adolph Hitler's ascent to power during the 1920s after Hitler's release from jail, nullifying his conviction for high treason and attempted coup to overthrow the government. Together with finance minister Hjalmar Schacht, he advocated rehabilitation of the government under the leadership of Hitler and favored the rearmament of Germany, despite Schacht's resistance to putting Germany on a war footing. Joseph Goebbels was Hitler's advisor and devoted acolyte. He was considered one of the evilest men in Hitler's orbit, advocating and helping to implement the extermination of Jews, conscription of women into the military to work in production for the war effort, and proposal to close every business that did not contribute to Germany's attempt at world conquest.

Immediately following Hitler's suicide, Goebbels succeeded him as chancellor of Germany, but only for one day. The following day, he and his wife committed suicide after poisoning his six children with cyanide, although it is frequently speculated that Heinrich Himmler, Hitler's head of the SS, murdered Goebbels and his family. It was supposedly done because of jealousy. Himmler committed suicide 23 days later. As luck would have it, Goebbel's one-year-old son survived. That child lived with his aunt during his convalescence from the poisoning. He remained with her until he left home to attend Heidelberg University. As he grew older, Heinrich Goebbels realized he would have to change his name or be cast from polite society in disgrace as the son of Hitler's right-hand man.

Heinrich Goebbels had not only inherited his father's genius, but he also possessed his father's chronic psychosis. He avoided contact with others and had no close friends. They bored him with childish desires for mindless diversion. The psychosis remained hidden during his youth and until he reached manhood he rarely spoke to others. It is often said there is a fine line between genius and insanity.

He borrowed the last name Klatch from his aunt's brother-in-law. There were no significant societal records immediately following the war, so his adopted name went unnoticed. As a victim of the war, he was showered with devotion and pity by his aunt. She had no children of her own and dedicated herself to her nephew's education. As a quiet child who never made trouble, his aunt was unaware of her adopted son's lurking psychosis.

The young life of the son of Hitler's propaganda minister was a psychotic, paranoid journey to manhood. Not knowing the chemical imbalances in his cerebral cortex were responsible for his twisted hatred for all living things, he had never known one moment of happiness. His envy of others who appeared to enjoy life filled him with a hatred he would carry internally for the rest of his life that would design the actions of his every waking moment.

He often disappeared for hours and occasionally days as a teenager. When he returned, he was surly and uncommunicative. His aunt quickly learned not to question him. Apparently, he was not getting in trouble, so she was relatively unconcerned. She never witnessed his propensity to torture living things. He would often kill animals, some domestic, and some wild when he could capture them. He would torture them slowly in his madness until they expired in agony. Sadism replaced sex. He was only mildly interested in women. Eventually, he would meet one and marry to produce one son.

Heinrich Klatch addressed the fifty-six people present. "This has all the earmarks of a catastrophe for us. One man is responsible for the dissolution of one of the largest countries in the world with the most vibrant, productive economy. He has taken China apart and reconstituted it in less than 24 hours. Ladies and gentlemen, this will set us back decades if it does not destroy our plans entirely. No power has ever existed of the stature this man represents. You can see how he manipulated the millions of Bālún Tōng. He has convinced them to follow his leadership. No doubt, he will personally replace the CCP and set himself up as the tyrant of the country with the world's largest production capabilities. We all know he has the technology to enforce that position and the power to threaten anyone with the audacity to confront him. He already has the president of the United States in his hip pocket. This has to be his motive. Absolute power corrupts absolutely!"

Klatch was making the same mistake as the 13 men Iggy had arrested. His insanity would not permit him a clear vision of Marcus's character. His natural assumption that all men consisted of the same motives and emotions that drove him, would never allow the acceptance of Marcus's benevolence. Heinrich Klatch's insanity convinced him that all men were the same. Therefore, all men were like him, obsessed with destroying anyone and everything that impeded total control over rivals.

Cameron Fry spent the last 20 minutes reading the pamphlet distributed by Lightning Incorporated and reflecting on its significance instead of listening to Klatch's hysterical rant. He was a realist and critical thinker who refused to wear the mantle of delusion. He was brilliant, but he was also honest. His giant intellect and scruples had provided him with the opportunity to become a multi-billionaire who controlled trillions. The consequences of that placed him close to the people of Interlink, the other handful of billionaires at the helm of global finance. There was no place else for him to turn. There was no other association or group of people he could belong to. His self-assured, stable psyche enabled his psychologically impregnable existence as an island among the autocratic gang of elites. He needed no one for self-validation. That came from within. What he did need, however, was an association with the men at the top of the food chain to facilitate his ambition to achieve and excel.

There were no flies on Cameron Fry. He didn't suffer the insecurity, self-deprecation, and envy of other men. As a self-contained entity, he judged everything in his orbit from that perspective. The multi-page pamphlet issued by Lightning Incorporated was no different. Cameron Fry saw the document for exactly what it was, and it compelled his overwhelming curiosity. He had spent his life seeking the heroic in men, never finding it. He was convinced it didn't exist, but nonetheless, his eyes were open, always looking. He had sought an equal. Someone he could respect and admire with the same degree as his own self-respect. His strengths precluded loneliness. There was no weakness in the man, and if he had not found another person to dispel solitude before the Grim Reaper showed up on his doorstep… so be it.

Just like the last time they met in this room, he was distracted from Heinrich Klatch, thinking about his own intention to look Iggy Marcus up. He began to focus on what Klatch was saying.

Klatch was still addressing the group. "This is too soon to accurately assess what really happened in China. Apparently, the leaders of the CCP no longer reside in the country. Marcus has removed them to... who knows where? This changes the entire mechanics of the globe. Our equation of successful societal destruction, half relied on China's stability. Well, it appears China will remain stable, but there is a new sheriff in town."

The people assembled in this room were not all complacent and supportive of Interlink's policies. Interlink was planning to initiate the collapse of most of the world's economies and societies and then rebuild each country under the auspices of a one-world government. The same tyrants would run their countries, but the economic picture would dramatically alter itself through attrition, the new international rules, and a single global cryptocurrency. Nothing would remain the same, and it would be the virtual end of true capitalism, prohibiting individual participation on any level other than forced production. The profit motive would disappear as the average worker struggled to exist and feed his family. It would be the end of luxury or economic choice. Everyone would be welded to their station without relief. It would be the end of upward mobility and the destruction of competition. This would be the socialist utopia all despotic authoritarians had sought and attempted for centuries without success.

Independent conversations began in whispers around the table. They were inundated with apprehension. Klatch continued. "One man has altered the world for all time. A few short years was all he needed to create a new order of authority. That man has also created American Media Inc. and has been able to provide information to a public that we had previously been able to control with deception through every published and broadcast media in existence. His most destructive achievement was purchasing Solex and deploying 64 satellites orbiting the globe to do the impossible by ending our ability to wage nuclear or tactical war. He did not merely upset the applecart, gentlemen, it was tossed into a maelstrom and the apples are apparently unrecoverable.

Cameron Fry listened to the comments and Klatch's tirade about Marcus. He chuckled to himself, thinking of his favorite expression that so often guided his decisions over the years… "The best-laid plans of mice and men often go awry." He continued to chuckle as he watched Heinrich Klatch flounder. Apparently, the forces that ran the world for 2000 years had finally met their match.

Heinrich Klatch was 84 years old. This was the last shot at his version of utopia and the ability to inflict pain and suffering on a grand scale. It would be subtle and done under the guise of altruism, but like a symphony, it required orchestration. He had spent his life in pursuit of this goal. He would be the envy of every con-artist autocrat and finally show everybody the son of Joseph Goebbels was the greatest man alive. He would weave society into a perfect tapestry of controlled oppression that most men would learn to accept and welcome. The ones who were not malleable could easily be eliminated. After all, the globe was about to go through a period of violence and destruction. To the average person, eliminating obstinate radicals would appear as government-sponsored anti-terrorism and just more of the same.

Hansel removed the scarf wrapped around his temples. The bony protrusions on either side of his forehead lent the appearance of a goat. His broad cranium, tapering down to a pointed chinless jaw with a thin slit that barely appeared to be lips, reminded Cameron Fry of the cave sculpture he had seen in the Ajanta and Ellora caves in India. Thousands of years old, it had been widely assumed by the Indian people that monks with too much time on their hands, a basket full of cast-iron chisels and wooden mallets, hammered the rock into art.

Authorities on the subject disagreed. The art was far too complex and extensive to have been done by a few monks. The caves would have taken many decades to achieve by hand, which indicated a task that would necessarily be passed on through generations. The style and content, however, were consistent, indicating the artwork was created from start to finish by the same hands. Most geologists refrained from saying it was extraterrestrial. Then, no empirical proof of extraterrestrials existed. Fry smiled to himself. I guess the monk theory is out the window. I'm staring at extraterrestrials who look like their statues in India.

Heinrich Klatch concluded his diatribe. The gathering of trillionaires and billionaires had questions. One man asked… "Specifically, how does this change our prospectus for world domination and one world government? The Chinese were never part of that plan, anyway. They have been an independent entity since Mao. We knew their status was not going to change, yet we were still going to pursue our goals despite that. So why does this new Chinese edifice change our position?"

"It changes it dramatically," replied Klatch. "Our new world government would develop a one world economy consisting of most countries besides China, India, and Pakistan for at least two decades. You all know the plan. We enlist India and Pakistan after 20 years of stability. The CCP did not wish to destroy the world. They wish to command it. They believe they would still ultimately accomplish that, but in the meantime, they would require a profitable destination for their massive production capabilities."

"We have discussed the fact China doesn't need the rest of the world now that it is the greatest productive engine in history. It also has purchased over a hundred million acres of agricultural land outside its borders. That scenario, however, requires China to force its population to produce goods, services, and food at the point of a gun or there will be no profitable market. This is not the most advantageous route for the Chinese. The CCP was more than willing to cooperate with us as the world government, becoming their sole market for goods and services. That symbiotic relationship could continue ad infinitum."

"Well, apparently, the CCP no longer exists. What the hell does that do to our precious plans? Mr. Klatch," asked another man.

"I don't have an answer for you, yet. We still haven't determined what happened to the hierarchy of the CCP. Are they dead or alive? What did Marcus do with them?"

Heinrich Klatch's lifetime of practiced self-control kicked in. He would not let these men see the inner turbulence that twisted his guts. He had been planning this for a lifetime and now one man had become the obstacle to his delusional fantasy. That man occupied most of Klatch's waking existence. He had threatened to choke Iggy Marcus publicly on more than one occasion. He was seething with barely manageable anger and hatred, just like those moments when he tortured and killed animals as a youth.

The extraterrestrial sat silently observing the first hour of the meeting with Heinrich Klatch's diatribe and the ensuing question-and-answer session.

Klatch turned to him. "Excuse me, sir... I mean Hansel. I'm sure you are aware of everything I have illustrated here as well as the change in the status quo caused by our adversary. You can see the dilemma this presents. Is there anything you can do to help us correct the situation?"

Cameron Fry had contributed nothing to the meeting. He sat still, observing the conversation and reactions of everyone present, especially Heinrich Klatch. Watching Klatch carefully, he saw the emotion and consternation in his eyes. He was fascinated. He saw beyond Klatch's veneer of camouflage. Fry was brilliant. He had been studying human nature for a lifetime. He could see the glistening insanity behind Klatch's veiled eyes. *Interesting*, he thought. *I just listened to a lunatic question a lying freak from another star system if he could help solve the problems of an organization attempting to dismantle the society of an entire planet.* This was so surreal to Fry he began to laugh out loud.

Klatch eyed him, frowning. "Do you find this funny, Mr. Fry? I fail to see the humor. This special meeting has been called to resolve the dilemma of the one man who is an impediment to our plans and threatens everything."

Everyone in the room, including Hansel, was focused on Fry's answer. Most of Interlink's uppermost crust had always been descendants of nobility. Now, several of them had been arrested and languished in a cell at Guantánamo Bay, Cuba. The rest of Interlink's upper crust looked at Fry as an archetypical genius. It was a rare man who could come from nowhere and nothing to become a trillionaire in half a lifetime, then sit among the upper echelon of their organization. They respected him.

"Actually, yes. I do find this quite funny. It's hilarious, in fact. Everyone here seems anxious except our friend Hansel... and you just asked him if he could help dispel the anxiety. It would seem our plans were not quite as concrete as we assumed." Fry tilted his head sideways to glance at the alien. "I would be really interested in hearing your answer, Hansel. At our last meeting you suggested that you could not become terribly involved, without providing a reason. Further, you described your contacting us was an attempt to commune with the highest authorities that ran the planet."

Cameron Fry watched the alien closely. He observed similar facial reactions as those of human beings. The alien's brow wrinkled slightly, and his thin lips seemed to purse. He watched its eyes. They were the windows of the soul if this character even had one. He was humanoid, though, and Fry was a master at reading body language. Fry was about to employ a technique he had used countless times to ferret out the truth when dealing with other people… exposing contradictions and demanding answers.

"I'm quite sure that you knew this organization was not the highest authority on the planet when you attended that first meeting with us. Yet, you said your mission with your consort, Gretel, was to meet and associate with the highest authority. I believe you knew, then, about Lightning Inc. and Iggy Marcus. It's all over the news and airwaves constantly. So, what were you doing meeting us, when you knew Marcus was a much higher authority in terms of power? Further, I'll concede the faint possibility you did not know Marcus was the most powerful being on this earth. That, however, is an impossibility at this point. It is guaranteed that you know where the seat of power lies now." Fry raised his voice slightly and cynically bore down on the alien with his last question, and he was going to be slightly less than civil. "I would like to know what the hell you are doing here, talking to us, when you know that we are the second-rate power. I'd like an answer to that, Hansel! And I insist it is the truth."

Heinrich Klatch was beside himself with fury. His self-image was fragile, as is typical among autocrats of his ilk who wished to control everyone else in existence. He was wildly angry with Fry. The man had just usurped his control of the meeting and placed himself in the control seat. Whether it was intentional or not didn't matter. But that wasn't the worst part of it to Klatch. Fry's action illustrated beyond a doubt who was the most able person and authoritative figure.

Klatch was now second fiddle, and that was untenable. Like almost everyone, he allowed the opinions of others to define his self-image instead of defining his own identity from within. This was a disaster because everyone else, all 55 members of Interlink present, would automatically realize who was the true authority and the better man. That drove him crazy. He momentarily lost sight of where he was as he seethed with rage. He wanted to choke Cameron Fry to death.

Cameron Frye ignored the agitation that was oozing from Heinrich Klatch. He was focused on Hansel. He thought for a minute only; the alien's eyes were furtive... avoiding him. This creature had come from a star 17 light years from Earth. That intrinsically elevated his intellectual stature above humanity. He wondered if Hansel's elevated intellect understood the need to obscure emotion. Perhaps not. Cameron Frye knew that he shouldn't be doing this, but he equated the alien's reactions to typical human characteristics. He decided to press ahead.

"The truth, Hansel. I'm interested in the truth! Our success or failure might hinge on your answer. So, I want the truth, and it must be plausible because we will engineer our strategy around what you tell us, perhaps."

The extraterrestrial remained silent for several minutes. Cameron Fry was correct. These beings exhibited characteristics similar to humans. Despite his alien countenance, his face exhibited a pensive expression, and he rubbed his chin with his six-fingered hand. It leaned forward with the second elbow of his left arm on the table with his chin resting on his palm. Fry let out a cynical, single syllable laugh. The motionless alien reminded him exactly of Auguste Rodin's Thinker.

No one moved or even rustled. Everyone was focused on the answer the alien might give that was so forcefully extracted by Cameron Fry. Even Klatch momentarily abandoned his fury out of curiosity, waiting for the reply. The alien then sat straight up with his hands on his lap,

and began to speak in his gravelly baritone.

"Yes, we knew from the beginning when we arrived and studied your society to determine the greatest power on the planet. We observed over

40,000 satellites above your exosphere when we arrived in orbit. 128 of them, however, revolved around the planet almost 400 miles above your exosphere. Those satellites were different from the others. Their orbits were all precisely the same height from the average Atlantic Ocean surface at your equator with no detectable differences."

"That was surprising because achieving that kind of accuracy is almost impossible, especially with your lunar satellite affecting gravitational attraction. We observed this for quite some time, and it remained unchanging. No deviation occurred, and that was an anomaly. We decided to capture one of them and perhaps determine its function. We approached one of them and a magnetic force field was projected from the satellite, protecting it from our advances. We noticed that was not the limit of its complexity. The electromagnetic shield vibrated and changed frequencies every 10,000th of one of your seconds. The satellites obviously generated their own power and, in enough quantity, to maintain a precise orbit at a precise, consistent distance from the surface."

"We still cannot understand how your technology would allow you to implement this degree of sophistication. The satellites exhibit no eccentricity in their orbits. That is an anomaly because achieving that type of precision is virtually impossible. Further, and most unusual, each satellite revolved in a geocentric orbit that never deviated more than 5 cm in an entire revolution. The satellite then corrected the deviation in the following orbit. That degree of stability can only be possible with an internal magnetic propulsion power plant. We notice the pattern of orbits. They formed a precise equidistant grid around the planet, obviously done for a specific purpose."

"We then concluded that this specific satellite system was for several purposes. One of them was to affect things on the surface. The other purpose we assumed would be planetary defense from aggression."

Cameron Fry held up his hand respectfully and interrupted. "Before we continue, I have an unrelated question. Your command of our language is impeccable. I might even say, perfect. Do you all have that capability? How long did it take to acquire?"

"It was embedded instantly by what you call computers. We all have that capability."

Cameron Fry continued his questions. He looked Hansel directly in the eye. The alien's eyes were more prominent but not much different than human eyes in appearance, other than black pupils. "I see. So, you knew we were not the ultimate power on the planet. You just admitted that you deceived us. Yet now you're being truthful... supposedly. Why? I'm sure there is a complex and convoluted reason. If we are willing to do business, that must cease. Now that you have admitted deceiving us, I think we should be told the reason... to clear the air."

Hansel nodded his head affirmatively. He obviously had human idiosyncrasies down pat. "We are not the only extraterrestrials visiting this planet. We are the only ones who collect its resources, however. There are other visitors. Several species. Some are from a star approximately 87,000 light years from here. Your scientists have not named it but gave it a designated galactic number. They have been in contact with your Lightning Inc. and Marcus."

Cameron Fry thought he knew the truth when it reared its head. It seemed obvious. It was probably the only plausible, believable reason Hansel could have given. He believed he understood exactly what the auspices were, defining human relationships with an extraterrestrial species. These, at least, didn't appear much different than humans in terms of psychological characteristics. He marveled at the thought that there was some sort of interspecies rivalry. He was sure it was quite complex as compared to human rivalries, but it seemed even creatures who had intellectually evolved far beyond Homo sapiens, were still governed by emotion to some degree. There was something still deeply bothering him. He had tried to put his finger on it the moment Hansel stepped out of the elevator. It was nagging at him during the entire diatribe. Fry had a photographic memory. Somehow, this creature appeared physically different than he appeared at the first meeting. Yet, Hansel claimed to be the same being.

Heinrich Klatch had enough. Fascinated, he had remained silent, listening to Fry's inquisition. There was a limit, however, to how much dominance of his leadership he would tolerate. He jumped immediately into the conversation. "Then you are telling us the truth that you wish to mine our resources. It would follow logically; this other species is an impediment to your intentions. Therefore, you have established a relationship with us. It also follows, logically, that you must remove the impediment somehow, so you have resorted to this alliance. Hmmm, perhaps we can help each other."

"That is exactly our intent, and now that we understand each other, perhaps we can structure a mechanism where we can actually assist without breaking certain rules."

"That's interesting to hear there are certain rules which must not be broken. Whose rules?" asked Cameron Fry.

"They are rules established throughout the universe by itself. To put it in language that you might understand, the universe is a conscious entity. It is always changing and modifying its own operating system. It is self-defining which constantly creates the rules of existence. As part of existence, autonomous individuals such as yourselves and us, must operate within those boundaries. Think about it as the logical order of things and the mathematics that define the universe. One of the esoteric laws is sentient beings may not destroy other sentient beings. That is the logical order of things."

"Not all sentient beings follow the rules, and almost an infinite number of them exist throughout the universe. There is no specific procedure for dealing with those who break the rules, but nonetheless, they are dealt with in one fashion or another. We, as a species, must refrain from going there. This is beyond your comprehension. It is not beyond the comprehension of your adversary. His relationship with the other species and his technology quantifies his stature. We may give you access to certain technology to mitigate that of your adversary, but we are limited."

Cameron Frye was fascinated. He was having an intelligent conversation with an extraterrestrial creature. "When you say many sentient beings do not follow the rules, what exactly do you mean? Has it affected us in the past?" Frye was brilliant. Suspicions began to dawn about man's convoluted history and its poetic mythology. Ancient man had no way of understanding the universe and the fact that it was populated by intelligent creatures who descended from the sky. They attributed divinity to those creatures.

"Yes, your history is populated with occurrences of such. We know the dogmatic descriptions responsible for much of that history. You are unsophisticated, juvenile by universal standards. Your assumption that this planet is the center of an infinite universe has distorted your view of reality. This universal expansion cycle is over 13 billion of your years. Many different species have visited this world. Much of your ancient architecture was produced by those visitors."

Cameron Fry slowly nodded. "I believe I understand precisely. You are inferring that much of the history we consider myth, is rooted in a reality that occurred early during this millennium. You said many of those architectural structures such as pyramids and the mercury pools, are products of those visits. That would explain the existence of architecture much too sophisticated to be created by men. Go on, tell us more."

Cameron Fry did not understand why, but he realized he was listening to a unique, previously untold history lesson of man's origins. He had more questions, and apparently their visitor was willing to answer. "I believe I understand. You are also inferring our mythology is based on some kind of obscure reality."

"Yes, your history is replete with legend and mythology, all of which are based on facts and actual occurrences. Galactic visitors have come here for millions of years, and your primitive species described reality with myth. As you evolved, your ability to perceive reality heightened, and myth receded but ancient myth still existed poetically."

"What is your opinion of the book we call the *Bible?* Much of it has to do with myths. It is one of the oldest manuscripts we possess."

Some of your Indian Vedas and Upanishads are older, but they all describe the same mythology and events but distorted. You are correct. They all depict reality, but only from an uneducated, unenlightened perspective. The authors were incapable of accurately describing a reality beyond their comprehension. All that mythology, however, is what we would call recent history, not the ancient history of your perception." This planet is several billion years old and has hosted three different advanced civilizations. Yours is the fourth. The others were eradicated or eradicated themselves."

Heinrich Klatch had listened patiently, but only because of his equal fascination with the narrative. He held up his hand, attempting to retrieve control. "It is time to continue with our business at hand."

Cameron Fry nodded in agreement. "I only have one more question, and it concerns the Bible. We have always called the cosmos the heavens. The Old Testament describes a war between angels. Judging from some of the things you mentioned about universal rules and some of the beings that don't follow them, it follows that the Bible describes what happened to those creatures who didn't follow the rules. Did they incur some kind of penalty or wrath?"

Cameron Fry was fascinated. He was trying to assemble the chronology of the planet's history in his mind. Klatch began to speak, but Fry held his hand up authoritatively. It was a command, and Klatch acquiesced.

"Is it then safe to assume our entire history, the biography of Homo sapiens, is merely a short-lived recent history of intelligent life on this planet? Are you saying that our mythology is quite recent in terms of this planet's history?"

"You are correct. The universe that you call God is complete unto itself, and every individual throughout the galaxies of the universe has been given autonomy. Occasionally, they become what you call arrogant. Some are evolutionary products billions of years old and possess many abilities that you would call divinity. Such is the natural course of events. That is part of the great design of existence and the tapestry woven by the universe to define itself. You call it God. We do not name it. We only populate it and are subject to the rules. When a species has evolved to that level of arrogance, and they believe they are equal in stature to the universe as masters, and then attempt to create that which can only be created by the universe, they are dealt with as a matter of course. Often, it involves war, but it is war on a level that you cannot possibly comprehend."

Cameron Fry ignored Klatch and relentlessly pursued Hansel's answers. "But our mythology is not as ancient as we would like to think, apparently. Were these wars part of this recent millennium, or do they date from the first appearance of civilization in previous millennia?"

As we understand it, the several civilizations that have existed here date back millions of years. Their history is lost and irretrievable by your conventional means of observation. This planet has been subjected to large die-offs from asteroid impacts and major volcanic disruptions, as well as interdiction by those called shepherds. We believed that was about to happen once again. That cleansing has not occurred because of your adversary. If it does occur, we will have no opportunity to mine this planet. Apparently, the universe has other plans for it."

No one present made even the slightest move. What had just been described was more than fascinating. It was stunning. The one man in the room most overwhelmed by what he had just heard was José Amontillado, Pope Innocent XVI.

Perspective and orientation are often better perceived with closed eyes.

Baby

CHAPTER VIII

LEMMINGS AND ROBOTS

The mammoth hanger door rolled slowly along the track until Air Force One was no longer visible. 60 Navy SEALs, Melanie and Gloria Marcus, Drs. David and Sylvia Peterson had come to elaborate on the upcoming mission. "How was your flight, Bill? I see Alice has remained in Washington. She would've fit right into this with her chemistry Ph.D."

"Alice chose to stay in Washington with the kids. After all, this is another one of your not-so-run-of-the-mill projects," laughed Bill Sledge.

"True enough, Bill. Thanks for leaving the Secret Service outside. What we are about to undertake is going to kick the hornets' nest hard, as you so often describe our adventures. Things are still a mess in the bureaucracy of the country. There are people doing all kinds of research involving subterfuge of one sort or another. Many of them rarely concern themselves with moral issues and are concocting deadly technologies. As president, especially the controversial one you are, forces most of these people to act secretly. You are unaware of some of these things, but I have become aware, and they are going to be eradicated now."

"I have another surprise for you, Iggy, but she's still aboard Air Force One. I explained to her about this mission to eradicate worldwide bioweapons laboratories. She decided it would be a perfect time to see Lightning Ranch. Along with her geneticist Nobel Prize, she is a world-class virologist."

Gloria had been listening through Iggy's ears. Such was the nature of their mental relationship. Iggy felt her presence and sensed her subliminal rolling eyes. "You worry too much, daughter." Her father laughed. "Melanie is coming too."

Iggy faced everyone with his hands on his hips. "Ladies and gentlemen, everyone, please pay attention. I am about to describe our mission, but first, the underlying information. There are three bio-weapons laboratories operating in this country under the guise of research and development to find cures for foreign bioweapons. They are not difficult to deal with; the president is the ultimate authority although he has not been informed of their existence."

Dave Peterson spoke up. "That seems a little bit strange to me. The president doesn't know what's going on in the country. Why is that? Why has nobody informed him? Especially because of the danger and seriousness of the research."

"Plausible deniability, Dave. To begin with, this president is not very popular with the deep state or with those bioweapons research facilities. The head of the CIA and FBI director have been replaced with honest men, but there are inordinate levels of subterfuge in both agencies. They are lifers. The directors are replaced from time to time as political favorites, but the lifers remain in place. We are going to upset that apple cart."

"They have existed for the past 50 years, unbridled and funded with all the money they need. I discovered these things through roundabout methods. That isn't the critical aspect. If there were only those three bioweapon facilities to decommission, that would be a walk in the park. Unfortunately, our adversaries, as well as some of our allies, are operating 26 other bioweapons laboratories. That's what you are all doing here. I have four ships, four pilots, and the best medical minds anywhere. We are going to eradicate all those facilities before something gets loose. One has already been released in Africa from Uganda's laboratory. We don't know if it was intentional or accidental, but it really doesn't matter. There are two others in Africa, five in China, no less. Russia has three of them. One of them is operating under the Ural Mountains in the caverns hollowed out by Khrushchev, Brezhnev, and Kosygin. There are several in India, Pakistan, England, Israel, Germany, Australia, Korea, and last but not least our friends in Iran. Syria also decided to come to the party along with the Saudis. South America only has one in Brazil."

20 of the Navy SEALs had returned to Lightning from Washington on Air Force One. 300 emissaries from Lightning were commissioned as military officers in all four service branches. They were here at Iggy's request, smiling in anticipation. They had all been along for the ride when he purged every pedophilia organization on the planet and brought them all to Gitmo for trial. After that, life became just a little banal. First Lieut. Paul Billings was now Col. Paul Billings in the Marine Corps. "Thanks for having us back, Iggy. After all the adventures we have been involved in with you, life has become quite boring. It's time for another adventure."

"It's going to be all of that, Paul. You heard the mission statement. We are going to be dealing with the most virulent, deadly pathogens that exist. They've been cooked up in labs to be deployed during wartime. If we did not have the shield technology, this would have an enormous risk level. We are going to take all of them out, and we are going to do it quickly. Interagency communication between countries almost never happens, but there is a rat in the woodpile. That rat is Interlink. They, too, are aware of all these bioweapons research centers."

Everyone, please pull up a chair in front of the video screen. I'll begin by flashing every laboratory on the screen. We have a priority list that includes the most dangerous laboratories from the top down. Four teams will invade them. Everyone will always remain shielded. Each laboratory has a vault, usually a freezer, that contains the different strains of various weapons."

Dr. David Peterson was helping organize the assaults. "Will we try to neutralize the various bioweapons on-site?

"No," Iggy replied. That's why there are 15 men per strike team. We restrain everyone involved. That includes soldiers, doctors, technicians, and clerical personnel. Some will be brought here for evaluation, and others to the island. We will also empty every vault and bring the contents here as well. We are shutting these laboratories down and not allowing any recurrence. That means every computer and storage device on-site will be cleaned, destroyed, or brought along. We will neutralize every bioweapon here at Lightning. Then we will determine who will be released into polite society."

"What about the cloud?" asked Alison. "I'm sure the information has been encrypted and is stored in the cloud. We would need the passwords to extract that stuff."

Iggy smiled. "That's my daughter's department. Have no doubt we will have the passwords, and then we will dismantle the cloud. Some of these pathogens are so dangerous that if they escape, the entire population of the world is at risk. I'm not referring to minor debilitating illnesses; I'm referring to illnesses that will possibly have only a 2% to 5% survivability rate. I'm sure we can cook up antidotes, but I don't believe we'll be able to deploy them adequately before the death rate becomes staggering."

"That's it then? You have 26 sorties to arrest everyone involved and grab their files and specimens."

"Not quite," replied Iggy. "Once the people are on board along with all the various equipment, files, and specimens, we may completely raze the buildings and every piece of equipment within. We will allow no fully equipped laboratories to remain intact for a new team of lemmings."

Junior and Baby remained silent during Iggy's instruction monologue. "The word lemming is quite apt, Dad. I have noticed that a good portion of Homo sapiens acts like lemmings. Although I understand formal human psychology, it is still quite puzzling. What will we do with all the scientists and doctors after we bring them to the ranch? That is an interesting problem. I am curious about your creative solution. You always seem to have one."

"Yes, well, I have one, but I'm not sure everyone will like it. Some of these people are simply misguided folks who think they are acting patriotically. They are told that the pathogens are an anti-weapon to use on an enemy who deploys biological warfare against them. Of course, the concept is as absurd as nuclear war. Once you unleash genetically engineered pathogens, all bets are off. We at Lightning could mitigate much of that, but not before the probable enormous worldwide toll on human life."

Alison MacLeod stood in front of Junior and Baby with her hands on her hips. "So, you two are my analysis team. I understand that you are more than just walking computers. Iggy explained that you are awake... alive for all intents and purposes. You both are not susceptible to disease, so you are the perfect people to assist with analysis. You can be easily sterilized when you finish a lab session because you are inorganic. I, on the other hand, will have to work from an isolation chamber."

Pres. William James Sledge hadn't said a word during the entire briefing. He was here because he needed to know exactly what was going to happen in every corner of the world when Iggy deployed strike teams. "I have some questions if you don't mind."

"Fire away," said his surgeon Gen.

"I would like to know exactly why we have an analysis team. I'm a little uncomfortable with you being in proximity to all those pathogens, Allison."

"I will be isolated at all times. Junior and Baby will be hands-on. As to why we are doing this, that's a no-brainer. We will be acquiring strains of pathogens from all over the world, developed in many different countries. We don't know what they are or what their derivatives are. We are going to destroy them, but first, we must analyze and catalog them. The computer files will be deleted, and all the computers and the information will be stored in Baby and Junior. I think Iggy can explain this a little better."

"We expect our action to be very thorough, and we are going to proceed rapidly. Speed is of the essence so that no one isolates any pathogens from our inquisition. However, we cannot be 100% sure that some pathogens aren't already stored in hidden places. Consequently, cataloging and a thorough analysis of everything we capture will contain all the information we need if something like that crops up. In other words, we will be able to R&D an antidote quickly. Allison is heading the team because she is probably the most prominent, knowledgeable virologist alive. Her Nobel Prize in genetics coupling that science with virology was groundbreaking. She is the ideal person to head the team. Her team members, Baby and Junior, are the perfect people to execute the analysis. Their computer analytics and memory storage are unequaled. We still haven't actually measured their memory. Mathematically, it computes to over 100 trillion TB. The peak performance exceeds 10 trillion TFlops. For the sake of clarity, I will explain. If we were to write 10 trillion TFlops as zeros on a chalkboard, it would stretch around the world more than once."

William Sledge felt rather small. Iggy Marcus was a larger-than-life paragon. He was changing the world and asked no one's permission. He, as president, had come on board back in the beginning. He saw the honesty and the scope of what this man was about to accomplish. He had very little part in it as the president but had at no time had been in opposition. "I'm sorry, Iggy, I have to ask. You mentioned not everyone will like what you will do with scientists. Are we talking about the island in the Pacific again?"

"Those kinds of people willing to experiment with and torture others to achieve an agenda are not just sociopaths and narcissists. They are insane by classical definition. That puts them in a class by themselves. Those people are repulsive and hateful, so we don't consider their mental state. I have learned a great deal about the human mind since my metamorphosis. Insanity is often thought of outside of clinical circles as a character flaw. It is not. It is often the product of a chemical imbalance or metabolic aberration of the cerebral cortex. That must be assessed on an individual basis. There is help for them, but it is not through conventional psychotropic therapy. Medicine doesn't possess that capability yet."

"Are you saying those kinds of people are curable?" Asked the president.

"Not always, Bill. But often, it is possible. Both Gloria and I can therapeutically massage away insanity to a degree. I can't really describe this to you. You would have to undergo the process, and many of you have gone through unlocking. We have therapeutically cured a dozen cases of autism, many of them extreme."

"Dealing with insanity is a little more complex than simply dealing with bad guys. Bad guys can be isolated and then become harmless to anyone but themselves. Some of these characters, especially the research scientists, know exactly what they're doing when they manufacture virulent strains of wholesale death. These are dangerous people, and the knowledge they possess is useless to humanity for the most part. Each scientist must be dealt with on an individual basis. You remember Joseph Mengele, the German Dr. who sadistically murdered thousands to further his experimentation program. There are others like him, and they are often placed in charge of these facilities because of their sociopathic inclinations. They just don't care."

"I have just one more question," asked the president. "How in the name of heaven are you ever going to tell the difference between the stark raving lunatics and the simply misguided scientists? Especially on the spur of the moment."

Iggy's gotcha smile said it. "That's where my daughter comes into the picture. Her psychiatric education and knowledge exceed anybody alive. Her IQ is up there, in lights. She can probably do an in-depth analysis of any human psyche in a matter of minutes with her telepathic skills. Believe me; we will know who the scientists are that can be left behind and the ones that should reside at Gilligan's Island."

General Richard McNerney was present for the entire briefing. As is his usual modus operandi, he kept his ears open, and his mouth closed. He raised his hand. "Do you mind if I inject something, Iggy?"

Iggy knew what was coming. "No, go ahead. Inject."

"I don't mind sharing this with all of you. Though I was Maj. Gen. in charge of Army strategy, I was born in Vladivostok, then indoctrinated and sent here to be a Russian double agent at twelve. I won't bore you with more of my history. A few years ago, Interlink abducted me in Switzerland and subjected me to 2 ½ weeks of mental torture and psychotropic drugs. They were creating a Manchurian candidate to put a bullet in Iggy Marcus if the nuclear weapons didn't do the job. They were explicit about putting the bullet in his brain. The brainwashing was intense. I was given copious quantities of drugs, sleep deprivation and unbelievable mental torture. It's amazing I even survived… but I did."

"During the course of that episode, I had what you call contact with Mr. Marcus. It opened the door to my salvation. I am not sure that any of you really understand what insanity is. It is a complete distortion of reality. You lose your mind and body. There is no control, and your life becomes a bottomless pit open only to the fires of hell. I can't describe the excruciating pain and disorientation. It is unimaginable to sane people. I lived it, and it was a roller coaster of terror until Iggy and his daughter held my mind with theirs and saved my life. So, I know what insanity is. I'm sure there are varying degrees, but I was cured so, I wouldn't just automatically write crazy people off, as is often our propensity to do."

"So, are you telling us you intend to cure them?" Asked the president.

"I don't know that yet, Bill. It can only be determined when we merge with their energy fields. We see every aspect of their subconscious minds, and they see ours. We call it unlocking. You know of it because you've undergone it. While it is occurring, it is an epiphany for everyone. The insanity sometimes recedes, only to return at the conclusion. So, some people are affected positively, and other people become more insane."

"What happens then when they go completely insane?"

"That depends on what drives them. If they are sadistic killers, they must remain in confinement for the rest of their lives, or at least until an effective therapy is administered. We have a very special island for the clinically insane."

"Okay then. Everybody has been briefed. The team leaders should all step up and get the itinerary. You are responsible for everything on the ground, and you have been well trained. The pilots will take care of the rest. You all have been briefed about the chronology. We must expedite this. Our actions will produce notoriety, and the world press will take advantage of that. Interlink owns them. So, this must happen so fast no one understands what is happening until it's over. We will be entering countries all over the world. We are not asking for their permission nor informing them of our actions until after they are complete. The one exception will be Moscow. I will stop to see Vanya Shartin before proceeding to the Urals. Then, we will tell them that they no longer possess bioweapons. I'm sure the average citizens will breathe a collective sigh of relief."

“Does anyone mind if I throw in my two cents?” Junior asked with his artificial smile.

“Why don’t you make it fifty cents,” said Baby. “Do you have that much on you? I can give you a loan.”

“I think you are correct, Dad. The world will breathe a collective sigh of relief, but I think the people that run the show in every country will be quite pissed off. Please correct me if that was too colloquial for you. I meant no insult.”

Gloria's hysterical laughter brought tears from listening to her mechanical siblings. You two titanium/silicone characters, with absolutely no sense of humor at all, are two of the funniest people I ever met in my life.

“Why, thank you, Gloria,” said Junior. “I really appreciate that.”

“No, you don’t.” Gloria continued to laugh along with everyone. “You’re just saying that to make me feel good. You can’t appreciate anything because that requires emotion. I still think you and Baby should do Saturday Night Live. All you need is a straight man.”

“Do you think we will bring down the house?” Asked Baby. “I think Saturday Night Live would be fun. What do you think, Junior?”

“That’s exactly what I’m talking about. You have no idea what fun even means.” Gloria was still laughing when she turned to her father. “I’ve got to hand it to you, Dad. You outdid yourself with these two. They are priceless.”

***

Four ships rose slowly, then rapidly disappeared to the west. "What's Pres. Sledge going to do, Dad?" asked Luke.

“He’s going to stay parked on the flight line in Air Force One. He'll have his hands full when our four ships show up with hundreds of Chinese medical and military personnel. I give him a lot of credit. He held his nose and jumped right in. He's good wood and totally committed to straightening out this mess. He can run the country just fine from there. Tom has assigned two of his best men to babysit the First Lady while he is away."

"Only two men? I would think she might be in danger considering what's about to come down on a global scale."

"Well, she always has the Secret Service as well as her shield. She has become quite adept at its use." He smiled, thinking about cartoon characters dancing across the White House lawn to amuse William and Wilhelmina. "But there is an added attraction. Adm. Oniella Kenji is taking a short leave of absence to entertain the kids."

Luke laughed. "I guess no one will get away with throwing cinderblocks at them. Where is Brett, by the way? He wanted to come on this mission to China. He spouted some nonsense about steamed, spiced pig snout."

"He insisted on being aboard Baby's ship. He said something about asking her to stop in Taiwan."

"It figures. I don't think it's the aroma of spiced pig snout enticing him."

"We will all be at our assigned locations in minutes. We are timing it so that the strikes are identical and simultaneous. We will encapsulate every facility. No one will get in or out, and no communication will be permitted. No one in the Chinese bureaucracy will have any idea what is occurring. Bālún Tōng is working on setting up the new government, but they have no idea about the biowarfare labs. I am not leaving it in their purview. They will be removed today."

"Why isn't Tom with us?"

"We don't need him. When we upset this applecart, the repercussions are going to explode around the world, and Tom will have his hands full with security, believe me."

"There are five locations, Dad, and four strike teams. Who gets double duty… us?"

"Yup. We'll take some doctors and scientists, but not the soldiers. We will place them under guard at the ranch and then return to deal with the Institute of Virology in Shenyang. We left the best for last. The Institute is complex. It is enormous, and not everything that occurs there relates to bioweaponry. Junior's ship will do an about-face and meet us there. We have a team of doctors from our hospital who are well-versed in the subject. They will come with him and assess every iota of research being done. We will confiscate everything and return the irrelevant computers and data later."

They appeared over their destination and paused, waiting for synchronization with the other four ships. Luke was the son of Iggy Marcus, an unusual position by just about anyone's standards. He had been unlocked over 100 times by his father. His IQ was elevated by over three or 400 points by the experience. He thought about his past life and everything that led to this moment. He laughed, thinking about how they were about to invade the CCP to eliminate one more threat to civilization. "Brett and I are thinking about writing a book about this… Whoops! They're firing at us. Here comes a missile." Three more rockets left the launch pad below to explode harmlessly against Nemesis's shield like the first one. "I guess that's what happens when you hover over a military base in a foreign country," Luke joked.

Nemesis descended to the parking lot in front of the main building. Iggy's 100-foot hologram appeared in front of the facility as he addressed them in classic Mandarin. I am Iggy Marcus. I'm sure you all know who I am by now. We have removed over 3000 people from China, including Premier Dung and General Rishi. This facility is surrounded by a magnetic field. No one will be allowed to leave until our business is finished. We have individual magnetic shield devices, and we are unassailable. My suggestion is that you do not hurt yourselves attempting to hurt us, but your actions are up to you. We are going to encapsulate and take with us to America every scientist, Dr., and technician complicit with the bioweapons research being conducted at this facility."

"We will also remove every computer, hard drive, and hard file in the building. This is the day that biological warfare ends on planet Earth. We are cleansing 26 research facilities that develop bioweapons in every country that possesses them. I politely request you open your doors and allow us to enter for your own sake. If we must incinerate the doors to enter, we will, but we wish to avoid injuring others."

Dr. Ju-long Lee stood by a monitor, debating. He had heard about this man's incursion into China and the abduction of Dung and Rishi. He had spent his life in service to the motherland. He was a gifted genius who had been awarded the position of medical doctor at the young age of 21. As in every dictatorship, gifted people are sorted from the common citizens and commissioned to work on behalf of the government, supposedly for the good of all the people. He was given the title of Col. in the PLA, which granted him economic status, stature, and comfort above most of Chinese society. He was too intelligent not to understand human nature and the motives that drove government officials. His commission in the army and stature as a doctor was not a request. It was in order at the point of a gun. Authoritarians never called it that, but everyone knew refusal to cooperate meant prison or worse.

Dr. Lee viewed the monitor and the 100-foot facial holograph of the man who had just politely requested they open the door to China's most top-secret bioweapons lab. He chuckled to himself as he moved to the lever that opened the inner vault door to the lab and gave orders to open the facility's front door.

Dr. Shin Ciao, a major in the PLA and second in command of the facility, watched Dr. Lee in unmitigated surprise. He wasn't there as a research genius like his supposed boss. Dr. Ju-Long Lee had always known his second-in-command was there to keep an eye on him and report any anomalies or idiosyncrasies to his superiors. That was the nature of dictatorships. One always had to look over one's shoulder expecting autocracy's truncheon.

"Dr. Lee! What is it exactly that you think you are doing? I must insist you stop immediately!"

Lee turned to look at his personal warden and laughed. Warden was an apt name for the man who was superintendent of his private prison.

"Haven't you any eyes or ears, Ciao? Or are you too stupid to understand what is happening here? There is a man outside of this complex in a floating dirigible that is not a dirigible. It is a flying machine equipped with technology beyond anything else on this earth. He has encapsulated this facility with a magnetic field. You, as well as I, are aware of the technology that only he possesses. He has just addressed us with a facial hologram 30 meters wide, politely asking us to open the door or he will disintegrate it. I think it would be a much better idea for you to take that gun you are pointing at my belly and walk to the front door, then shoot Marcus when he attempts to enter."

"Do you think that is a funny joke, Lee? Do you not see what this man is doing? He is stealing Chinese secrets. He intends to dominate the world and use our technology to help him!"

Dr. Lee could not help himself. He doubled over laughing. Don't you realize this technique dealing with gain of function research for biowarfare has been stolen from the Americans in the first place?" He laughed even harder. "Why don't you come to your senses, Ciao? Put down the gun and open the door. This man is coming in here one way or the other, and there is no power on this earth that can stop him. Are you oblivious to that?"

Shin Ciao was like a good portion of the world. Indoctrinated, mindless mediocrities who did what they were told despite the stupidity of the obvious outcome. They would march into the fires of hell to find out what felt like to be warm simply because they were ordered to. This reality overwhelmed Dr. Lee. The explosion of reality blossomed in his mind as an epiphany when he realized that this was the history of man for thousands of years. Achievers and idiots. That's what has comprised humankind since its beginning.

He shook his head. He had heard about Bālún Tōng and the millions of pamphlets dropped on all the Chinese cities just under a week ago. Perhaps this was China's liberation. One could only hope. "Well, Ciao, I'm not going to open the door and give you a good excuse to scramble my intestines with that pistol. I am, however, going to the rear of the structure to hide, so when the gentleman with the holograph disintegrates the front door, I am not vaporized with it.

Both Lee and Ciao were distracted by a loud buzzing noise followed by an ear-piercing hum. Lee glanced at the exterior security monitors. The façade of the building near the entrance seemed to be melting away. The loudspeaker came to life. This is Iggy Marcus again. I would ask everyone to please move as far from the entrance as possible. We are coming in, and we hope no one is injured. Dr. Lee was quite sure the idiot with the pistol standing in front of him was not going to allow him to open the door for Marcus. "Excuse me, Ciao, you can stay if you wish, but I am leaving." Lee blurted as he ran for the back door of the laboratory.

The volume was increasing on whatever technology Marcus was using. Shin Ciao stood his ground, waiting for China's enemy. Today was a good day to die for China… and then the lights went out. He woke up an hour later in the hangar at Lightning Ranch as a captive. The loud buzzing had given Lee the cover he needed to sneak behind Ciao, wrap his left arm around his chest, immobilize him, and inject his neck with a chloral hydrate derivative.

Ciao glared at Ju-Long Lee. "You traitor! You bastard! I will see you in irons for this!"

Ju-Long Lee cocked his head, shrugging with raised eyebrows and a smile as Ciao spewed epithets. "I don't think so, Ciao. We are in America now…a place called Montana. I don't think it is so easy to find irons here."

"America? How long have I been out? How is this possible? I will have you shot for this, Lee!"

Iggy chuckled at Lee's comment, "I don't think the idiot realizes I saved his life. Perhaps it wasn't so important to him."

"We are off, Dr. Lee. The next stop is the Institute of Virology at Shenyang University. They are next on the list."

"I think you will find security is tighter there. They do a lot of medical research on bioweapons, but they are also a teaching university and a front for the CCP secret service and intelligence/spy community. I think you may have to disintegrate half the building to get inside."

Iggy laughed. "We will probably leave some of that building standing. You watched what we did to your laboratory. We encapsulated it with our force field and then disintegrated it. We will leave no operational labs behind for others to use."

"You know, Mr. Marcus," said Ju-long Lee. "Despite the fact you have invaded my country, I think this is a good thing, and I offer no protest. You mentioned the destruction of every bioweapon lab on Earth. Good luck to you, sir."

***

"That's the Shenyang University and Institute of Virology below us. Looks kind of sleepy, doesn't it? Don't let it fool you. There are 1000 people inside who are all doing bioweapons research and other intel."

"I thought you said it was a teaching university as well."

"The word teaching doesn't necessarily connote integrity and altruism. The university setting is often an ideal place for R & D development of questionable technologies. China has a never-ending supply of guinea pigs. This is modern China, and it doesn't place a high premium on human life as long as they get the job done."

"It's a big place, Dad. I'm sure you're right; there are a lot of people inside. Is that why you have Poseidon scheduled to follow us here?"

Iggy nodded his head. This is the Shenyang Institute of Virology, China's most prestigious university. It was not only a center for bioweapons research, but also houses a think tank for research and deployment of covert military operations as well as a foreign diplomacy indoctrination and clearing house for China's emissaries and espionage agents. It's the equivalent to our CIA and FBI."

"Holy moly, Pop! They are going to have some hissy fit when we show up... Wow!

"Yup, Luke. It's going to put a damper on their sense of security… for sure.

Moments later, Poseidon materialized with Gloria and Junior at the helm. "Hi, Dad. What are your instructions?"

"You have 30 men on board. We will set both ships in the parking lot. I will encapsulate the compound with this ship. Have the men leave Poseidon. There are always about 200 soldiers on guard. It will be your job to immobilize them, individually or in groups. Our crew will enter the University and confront the management."

***

The PLA was in a complete state of disarray. Iggy Marcus had removed over three thousand of the highest-ranking military officers from the country, leaving a huge void in China's once extremely disciplined, precision military. The soldiers and lower-ranking officers were resorting to muscle memory. They were still fulfilling their guard and enforcement duty for the CCP in theory, but the lack of direction from the top created a chaotic rift in the chain of command. This had never happened since Mao. The military had been China's strong arm enforcing obedience in over a billion people, but they were wavering.

Everyone had heard about the millions of pamphlets air dropped on every city in China. Just about everyone had read one at this point. The country was obviously in a state of muted upheaval, but the tremors of political change were sonorously rippling through the entire population. Millions of people in the working class had never known anything but suffocating confinement to their social station. They were born, lived, and died according to government dictates. There was no upward mobility, and there was no hope for a bright future. The lives of most Chinese citizens were a dreary march through the futile progression of days encompassing the sum of their existence.

A small percentage of citizens were granted privileges. Even socialism needed competent management, which required the incentive of privilege to be given to those intelligent enough for the task and callously indifferent to the canker of misery inflicted on their brothers. The Chinese hierarchy during the last half of the previous century concentrated their efforts on maintaining a subservient population, philosophically and culturally inept, who would bend under the authoritarian lash.

The demons of authority, always intent on the suppression of intellect and the glorification of mediocrity, held the whip, keeping the population at bay. They were aware of the last vestiges of Chinese intellect and individuality that had survived under the auspices of Bālún Tōng, but there was little they could do about it other than persecution and mass murder. Bālún Tōng, more than seventy million strong, once numbering about 200 million, was more than a simple philosophy among zealots. It was a quiet, unobtrusive way of life and dedication to the human spirit. As long as one person lived, their philosophy could not be eradicated.

China was possibly one of the oldest surviving civilizations on Earth. If they had learned nothing else, they learned the wisdom of stoic patience and the knowledge that all things will eventually pass. They fervently believed this, not just for themselves, but instilled it in their progeny who symbolized their immortality. The members of Bālún Tōng understood they were no match in a direct confrontation with the evil and insane brutality of the monsters who had come to rule their glorious country. So, for half a century they waited. They knew nothing lasts forever, and even evil must eventually perish under its own weight by attrition. Nothing productive or beautiful comes from the evil that so often encompasses the world… only destruction, hatred, and the oppression of humanity.

Their indomitable tenacity bound them to the expectation that someday, someone would come to show men the way to the future. Their religious beliefs fostered the tenets affirming evil did not exclusively rule the universe or men. For every evil, there was a greater good and eventually the greater good would prevail. More than half the population of China had read 700 million pamphlets that had floated down from the sky… and they were rejoicing.

Most working-class people were nervous. They were born, had lived under communism, and knew nothing of other philosophic platforms other than the misinformation spewed from their own government. They didn't know what to expect, but the members of Bālún Tōng knew. They had been waiting half a century for an Iggy Marcus to show up and liberate them. They had recently worked with Marcus for months, developing the New Chinese Constitution with dimensions that would sweep the Chinese people into the future and freedom.

Non-violent transformation would be enormous and probably impossible in a single generation without the bedrock philosophy and beliefs surrounding Bālún Tōng. They would be China's new mentors as the people who would negate the CCP storm troops by outnumbering them 280 to 1, and that didn't include China's other 1.4 billion people. Together, they would lead China into the brilliant future portrayed by their American benefactor.

As is always the case under socialists and tyrants, citizens are dumbed down and lose sight of the values that underpin other philosophic platforms. They learn to accept tyranny and suppression of freedom as a normal part of life. Lassitude brews the acceptance of an empty, fruitless lifestyle, relieving them of the responsibility for survival made possible only through critical thinking. That negation of individuality also obliterates morality, the responsibility, and the knowledge required to operate society successfully. Bālún Tōng did not forget. They passed the tenets of morality to future generations with the understanding it was the only way men could exist in freedom without the autocratic cannibalization of the people.

As Iggy Marcus had become a tool of the universe to lead humanity to Millennium's Gate, so had Bālún Tōng become his tool to eliminate the CCP caste system and lead its people to freedom.

***

The ships hovered as Iggy encapsulated the University and surrounding support buildings with his magnetic shield. No one could get in or out. Junior's ship hovered just feet above the tarmac, and his crew exited and shielded the guards in small groups. At least now, no one would be injured.

The windows of the University were lined with people watching the deployment from the American ships. They could see that it was an attack of some kind. Everyone had heard the whispers throughout the population describing the extraction of so many military leaders, Fun Chou Dung and General Li Shen Rishi, despite the lies and propaganda spewed by the state-owned media. The rumors were so prolific, and the proof so profound there was no obfuscating the reality.

Mao Babeng, recently appointed by the general secretary as Shenyang University's Chancellor, stood at the entrance with a dozen heavily armed soldiers, awaiting the interlopers. The glass doors were 1 inch thick and bulletproof with a multi-cylinder lock mechanism. He had heard the same rumors everyone else had. Gen. Rishi and his boss, General Secretary Fun Chou Dung had evidently been arrested by that American, Marcus. He was beside himself with fury accompanied by anxiety about an unpredictable future. He was the authority in charge of the complex. It was a university, but deep below the foundations of the 20-acre building, 22 levels of offices and research facilities existed. He was the ultimate authority here. This institution was the Chinese equivalent of the American CIA and the old Soviet Kremlin.

Like everything of substance and value in China, authority was distributed as a gift. Mao Babeng's appointment as Chancellor came as compensation for services rendered to the authoritarians at the top of the food chain. He was Fun Chou Dung's Joseph Goebbels, a fiercely dedicated minion of the general secretary. He was the set of eyes and ears who reported any indications of treachery from the ranks below. The position as Chancellor awarded him great authority with a minimum of responsibility. He ran the University and reported everything to Dung. His ascension to extreme authority and luxury catered to his basic cowardice. His position, only slightly below the general secretary, was a dream come true without the fear of treachery or assassination that often accompanies the alpha dog among a pack of snarling competitors.

Iggy, Gloria, Junior, and 15 men stood at the entrance gazing through the thick glass door at China's version of J. Edgar Hoover. Gloria looked up at Iggy. "He's terrified, Dad. What would you have me do?"

"Enter his mind and tell him we are coming in, and it would be much better if he simply unlocked the door as opposed to us destroying it."

"Mao Babeng, my name is Gloria. I am here with my father, Iggy Marcus, my brother, and 45 men who have come to clean up the fetid mass of bioweapons stored below. We know exactly what this building is, who you are, and what this represents. Shenyang University, the Shenyang Institute of Virology, and what exists on the many levels beneath it, comprise China's Department of Espionage and the central clearinghouse for all secret or clandestine information, covert operations, as well as the repository for all specimens of bio weaponry developed at various other locations in China. We have come to remove your capability to commit biological murder with those weapons." Gloria laughed. **"We don't want you to feel singled out or slighted. We are removing bioweapons from every country on Earth. Nuclear war is off the table, and the next few days will signify the end of any country's ability to commit mass murder. Please open the door, or we will open it forcefully."**

Mao Babeng responded with false bravado through the external loudspeakers, "You will not get away with this! China is the greatest country on earth, and our destiny is to rule the planet. Our government is the only organized government capable of doing that. America is long past its prime. We have the greatest industrial base and manufacturing capabilities in existence. We also have one and a half billion people dedicated to China.

It was time for Iggy to enter the conversation through Gloria." **You are attempting to sell your rubbish to the wrong people. 95% of your people are slaves who are only dedicated to staying alive, not dedicated to your government slavedrivers. You are about to witness the birth of a new China. It will be a China where one can participate in and enjoy the fruits of one's labor instead of the confiscation and redistribution**

of a person's effort to the shiftless and the coffers of the wealthy. Your general secretary, Fun Chou Dung, Gen. Li Shen Rishi, and three thousand upper-ranking military officers have already been arrested and removed from China. Nuclear war has been eliminated, and now bioweapons will be eliminated. You are being offered this opportunity only once…today. Join the people of China and Bālún Tōng while they create a new government representing freedom and the people or join your fellow conspirators at their new home in the middle of the Pacific Ocean."

Mao Babeng was a coward who owed allegiance to no one but himself, certainly not Dung or Rishi. Obviously, they were now powerless has-beens and not even still in China. It didn't matter who was in charge or what philosophical environment surrounded his existence at the moment. He always took the expedient path of least resistance that offered the most advantageous gain for himself. He had a family, but even they were second... Mao Babeng unlocked the heavy security door and opened it wide.

Despite Gloria's subliminal vision of Mao Babeng's revolting character and persona, she laughed as the interlopers entered the building to complete the mission. **"Very wise choice Mao. You will find life among Bālún Tōng and a free Chinese citizenry much more palatable than a life sentence on an island full of tyrants."**

Six Navy SEALs remained at the surface guarding Shenyang's 200-plus army security detail. They encapsulated the Chinese guards with electromagnetic fields in six groups, requiring periodic brief relief to replace oxygen. The rest of Lightning's party began the inspection by individually encapsulating guards and office personnel as they descended through the 22 levels, searching for bioweapon technology.

Gloria's laughter filled the air on every level as she viewed the assortment of cartoon characters encapsulating the Chinese personnel. "This is hilarious, Dad. Every single cartoon character I've ever heard of is surrounding all these people. I'm sure they don't know who the characters are... Perhaps Mickey Mouse and Donald Duck, but I think the others are only endemic to American culture."

“That's to be expected, Gloria," chuckled Iggy. "Tom Rickart trained the men. He's our master cartoonist. He'll be here in a little while. I asked Junior to request Nemesis, and 30 more men join us. Tom will be with them. We don't have anywhere near enough personnel to go through this place. The Chinese obviously kept the 22 subterranean levels of this facility a tightly held secret."

“Normally, you would be shot or have every military officer and politician in the country climbing down your throat by now. You're in their top-secret espionage and science project where all their top-secret information is stored,” Luke speculated, laughing about the irony. “Normally is no longer an appropriate word since all those officials are languishing at a vacation paradise in the middle of the Pacific Ocean.”

A chime sounded as the elevator door opened. Baby followed Tom Rickart into the room. Tom was amused. "Some guy named Babeng on the first floor asked me if I had any job openings. Who the hell is he? And by the way, I brought 50 men. By the looks of things, we will need them. "

“He's Chancellor of the University, or you might call him the head of their CIA, but you're right,” replied Iggy. “We're only on level 9 with 13 more to go. We already have a load of things to bring back, and I believe the biowarfare strains, at least the most virulent, will be down at the lower levels. All of it must be removed. We'll take it back to Lightning.”

What about the lab equipment and computers? There's got to be a ton of lab equipment and a thousand computers in this place. Are we going to start carting them to the ships?"

“Only the biological specimens. Any lab equipment used to produce bioweapons will be stacked in the parking lot, where we will destroy it on-site. As for the computers, Junior has a creative solution. It will take him and Baby about 6 hours to interface with every computer individually and erase all biological research data and systems. He can clean up any network of multiples from one location.”

They watched a continuous line of men carrying equipment and steel refrigerated containers to the elevators to be loaded on the ships bound for the ranch. The Chinese scientists and clerical workers stood helplessly behind their shields, frantically watching the lower levels of China's top-secret Shenyang University emptied of their contents.

Iggy left everyone to complete the mission, looking for the administration office and public address system. Mao Babeng entered to find Iggy in front of the microphone. "What exactly is it that you are doing, Mr. Marcus?" Apparently, Mandarin Chinese was the spoken dialect.

Iggy laughed. "I'm about to address your nest of spies and science majors. Have a seat. You'll enjoy this as well."

He hit the broadcast button and addressed everyone within hearing distance in perfect Mandarin. "My name is Iggy Marcus. You all should know who I am. If you didn't know, you are about to find out. I'm the man who removed nuclear war to settle disputes between nations. I am here to remove bioterrorism for the same reasons. Only a handful of you around the world create these hellish weapons. You are merchants of death. No excuse for self-defense is adequate for the monstrosities you have developed in these places. Since men will not clean up their act, I am cleaning it up for them. Research for bioweapons is being terminated now. We are removing all your specimens, destroying all your lab equipment, and deleting all your computers. If you think this is a valid way to exist among your fellows and continue to research and develop this kind of biotechnology, we will hunt you down and lock you in a room with your own technology, and you will find out exactly what it's like to perish by your own sword. "

"This is not a warning. It is an ultimatum. You are being allowed to live and are being given the option to join Chinese society as human beings instead of monsters. The choice is yours. Look to Bālún Tōng. They have created a new constitution for China where all men can live as equals instead of subjects. From them, a new government will be born. The choice is yours and the time is now. This opportunity will not be offered to you twice. A violation will deposit you on an island with the rest of the Chinese megalomaniacs who have tortured your citizenry for half a century if you blow it. That is all I have."

Iggy met everyone in the lobby. "Baby, it's time for you to assist Junior cleaning the computers. There are at least a thousand of them that need to be attended to."

"Sure thing, Dad. But first, I must comment on your soliloquy. It was the epitome of succinct, unemotional, and to-the-point verbiage I have ever had the pleasure of enjoying. You sounded like Junior. Now I see where he gets his impersonal personality."

Gloria was hysterical. "Although you cannot understand what I mean by this, Baby, but you are, by far, the most hilariously amusing character I know. I love you."

"Well, Gloria, I believe I would like to love you also. Maybe someday Dad can teach me how to feel."

Twenty minutes later, three of the four ships were parked on the flight line at Lightning Ranch. Junior remained at Shenyang to complete bleaching the computers. The Cargo was unloaded and placed on trucks bound for the ranch dump and disintegration. President William Sledge almost ran down the steps of Air Force One. He understood the mission and what Iggy Marcus was doing to the world. He had been involved from the beginning when Iggy eliminated the possibility of nuclear war. He had no objections and always stood back from everything, including Iggy's plans. He was a firm believer in this philosophy: *sometimes it's better to give your mount his head while you remain quietly along for the ride and let your horse find its way home.* The president of the United States was along for this ride and dying to hear the story.

"How did it go? Did you have any trouble? I have been a stress package since you left. I don't have doubts, just anxiety fits. After all, you just overthrew one of the three major superpowers single-handedly. Not only are they an adversary, but they are also the productive engine supplying our society with 65% of its commodities."

He smiled. "You worry too much, Bill. Everything is still in place… The factories, the workers, the management, and every other cog in the machine except the tyrants and the scientists who are merchants of death.

Some of them have been removed, and others given a second chance. So, China will still be able to produce, but I imagine the prices are going to go up. You see, Bālún Tōng is in charge now. If they can keep it together and pull it off, the entire Chinese economy will be transformed. People will no longer work for a dollar per day and sleep in a dresser drawer, only to return to work the moment they wake. They will be given proportionate access to the wealth they create by their efforts. The tyrants are gone."

The president nodded, "Still, you just overthrew the government with the second-largest military in the world. You may have done it without firing a shot, but you have decimated an entire political system and replaced it with another untested. Granted, you assisted your Bālún Tōng in structuring a new government, but what happens next remains to be seen."

Baby had been listening to the conversation. She smiled. Her smiles were always captivating and never appeared mechanical, even though they were an affectation. "I guess by all the standards encompassing human knowledge and history, as well as contemporary social mores, you might well be considered the most benevolent dictator in history by some, Dad. Of course, by definition, that is subjective and a matter of opinion because of replete historical contradictions. It will be interesting to hear juniors take."

The president laughed, "apparently you have built yourself a walking, talking conscience. Did you bring the Chinese leaders to your island? What does your mechanical conscience think of that? "

"Tom Rickart added. "Yup, that's where they went."

Iggy smiled. "Tom erected a giant sign at the only port we built on the leeward side of the island. It says Welcome to Gilligan's Island."

Bill Sledge was still grinning, " It makes sense to me. That's right up your alley with the rest of your cartoon characters and goofy sense of humor, Tom. I don't think the Chinese will appreciate the joke much since they have no idea who Gilligan was."

When the dominoes are perfectly aligned, and you know you have done your best, take a moment to survey your handiwork; even the best-laid plans are often shattered by a sneeze.

Cameron Fry

CHAPTER IX

THE AMERICANS ARE COMING…

THE AMERICANS ARE COMING!!

Meeting night rolled around once again. It was the second day after the Chinese *incursion and the eradication of their bioweapons program. The night started off with a* concert. They had become more frequent than during the early years when the student body consisted of only 369 members. The original group played in concert together. Now, concerts had to be broken up into five groups of 400. Iggy, Melanie, and her parents were still teaching the classics. They had signed on to this incredible journey into the future on the night Melanie and Iggy met.

Over 2000 students were receiving the same classical education as the first group received. They were schooled in the sciences, arts, and all the classics. There was no education comparable anywhere in the world to the one delivered to the students at Lightning Ranch. The program had been expanded from the early days. The students not only learned the academic criteria, but they also learned it wasn't owed to them. Each person was responsible for his or her own survival and education.

They were shown it was acceptable to lean on others when necessary but never acceptable to abuse the privilege. Twelve years at Iggy's Lightning Ranch school equipped each student with the equivalent of a Ph.D. in their chosen field. That was not the extent of their training. Their horizons were broadened in every field imaginable, especially the history of civilization. They learned the philosophic underpinnings of every society that had ever existed, and the accompanying mistakes men made, causing each society to mature, totter, and crumble.

Physical training was part of each child's education to the extent of their capabilities. Iggy, his sons, and several others of his protégés found time to train most of the students to figure skate. He believed it was the greatest athletic endeavor possible. It imparted stamina, poise, balance, precision, the joy of creating beauty, and every child learned the limits of their capabilities. Figure skating inculcated the self-discipline of competition, but each child learned true competition was the achievement of excellence compared to their previous performances, not their peers' performances. It was Iggy's choice to impart the philosophy Rebecca had taught her children so well: never depend on the opinions or achievements of others to elevate your self-opinion. They learned to accept their own limits when they reached the peak of their capabilities. Competition then set standards.

This education was only possible at Lightning Ranch. It would never be possible without the philosophy that Iggy ignited in every one of his students by unlocking them. The process involved merging their electromagnetic fields, creating an awareness of each other's subconscious mind.

Iggy began the indoctrination the moment each child arrived at Lightning Ranch. It wasn't the intentionally debilitating doctrine proffered by the contemporary mores of the public and private education systems to purposely debilitate excellence and glorify mediocrity with the *everyone gets a trophy* concept. It consisted of the two philosophical concepts flanking every character defining achievement that comprised the human soul, acceptance of reality and the assumption of morality. Iggy Marcus delivered to his students the single greatest concept in human history and the greatest gift any man could give his brothers: the desire and ability to live the unfettered, superlative existence people were entitled to from birth. Iggy had learned the concept from his mother, Rebecca Marcus. She taught her children to never let the opinions of others define their self-image. A true, valid, and honest self-image can only come from within by mastery through achievement. Once it became ingrained in the human psyche, that concept obliterated envy, the cause of all the death and destruction humanity had endured since man first stood erect. They learned that the deprecation of others to elevate their own self-opinion in their own eyes was a non sequitur that was the imposed philosophical construct of an irrational society and the antithesis of happiness.

They eventually began to see the destructive nature of what every human being seemed to willingly embrace. It was the underlying backdrop of every sin committed by men. It highlighted and underlined consumerism, the comparison of one's own validity and stature to that of one's neighbors, and the measurement of self-worth by the acquisition of wealth instead of the stature of achievements. These were the antithetical, pernicious social features that propagated the suicide of the human spirit. Iggy's children were taught to avoid that… and why.

Once that was ingrained into each child as the operating system for a spectacular existence and life of accomplishment, he had to teach them the rules of the road. They had to learn their validated path to the future and self-actualization. It was Iggy's four tenets of morality. They learned there was a difference between right and wrong, good, and evil. They learned the most important facet, the vision to see and accept the truth. Without that, reality was occluded, and no valid choice for an unerring course of action was possible. The third tenet was the dedication to the good and rejection of the wicked. The fourth tenet, almost as important as the second, was dedication to the good, no matter what the price.

Iggy was brilliant, but he wasn't alone. His brothers, sister, young sons, and Melanie and dozens of associates played every bit as significant a part as he had, but he was the catalyst, inspiring his body of protégés who would become the leaders and teachers of tomorrow. Eventually, the sickness of man's inhumanity to his brothers would be washed away, and they would become shining examples to society.

***

Every family meeting became a concert night. They had expanded the auditorium by cannibalizing the Olympic-sized ice-skating rink and erecting its own separate building. The auditorium now sat 4500 people. It was rarely full, but the surrounding towns loved Lightning Ranch. It had two launch pads for Lightning's Solex Corporation, and everyone eagerly anticipated rocket launches from the neighbor's backyard. Many local people helped operate the ranch, and it wasn't unusual for a few thousand people to attend a meeting night concert. Nowhere on earth besides Lightning Ranch could one enjoy a concert as beautifully executed as any orchestra and choir on earth but performed by children from 4 to 18 years old. Eventually, local television stations received permission to broadcast performances, and eventually, they became a much-anticipated phenomenon.

Lightning Ranch remained shielded by the magnetic force field. Tight security required scanning of people before entering. Thousands usually attended to hear the greatest opera soprano in existence. Melanie would often perform at least once in the evening. This night was no different. She was singing Frederick Chopin's**, In mir klingt ein Lied** followed by **Geef Mij Je Angst**. People came from hundreds of miles to hear the great Melanie Coletta and the Lightning's orchestra and choir. There was no admission charge. Instead, a donation box in the lobby dedicated to Boys Town and Girls Town was often filled with five to ten thousand dollars at the end of a night of beauty and tears.

The audience left before family and ranch business began. Everyone who understood the mission and purpose of the Marcus family was eager to hear about China. Even President Sledge hung around to watch Baby and Junior's holograms. Everything viewed through their mechanical eyes was recorded.

Baby addressed the meeting. "I know you all have been dying to see what happened in China. Junior and I made holograms of the entire experience. We will display it tonight. It was uneventful but consisted of much work at Shenyang University. There are 22 levels beneath the 20-acre building on the surface. Everything was inspected, and the appropriate pathogens were removed, brought here, and destroyed. That has all been done. So, without further discussion, look to the front of the auditorium, and we will exhibit the holograms but eliminate the tedium."

The holograms displayed the arrest of Dung and Rishi, as well as several thousand officers from the PLA exhibiting their arrival on Gilligan's Island. Everyone had a good laugh over the Island's name and Junior's gift of a cribbage board to the general secretary and his pet general. All Iggy's mini speeches, some to the Chinese aristocracy and many to the people, were included. It became obvious to everyone the efforts had been a success so far.

Iggy waited for the murmuring to end after the hologram. "Does anyone here have any questions?" A small hand raised, close to the rear of the sea of faces next to Brett. "Yes, Tiao Chen. What would you like to know?"

Tiao Chen's English was more than passable. His parents were teachers, fluent in English, and taught their children English from infancy to prepare them for the future. "I like it here, well enough, Uncle Iggy, but will I ever be able to go back to China?"

"Eventually, yes. First, you must learn to stand on your own. You are already well on your way. There is substance in your character, Tiao Chen. You will receive an education from us that you can get nowhere else. When your education is complete, you will absolutely go back to China as a teacher and a leader. If you insist, you can leave anytime you like, but I would suggest you find a sponsor."

"I will stay, especially because of Heng Cong, and it is what my mother would wish."

"Wise choice. You will not regret it." Iggy looked around at almost 2600 faces. "Are there any more questions before we adjourn?"

"Just one," said Luke. "When do we leave for Moscow?"

"Late tomorrow or early the next day after Richard returns. They have the next biological mess we must clean up."

At the mention of Moscow, hundreds of hands shot into the air. Iggy smiled. So much for an early night, he thought. "It's getting late, but if you're willing, I'm willing...shoot…

A twenty-year Lightning engineer, John Jennings, was the first to speak. "Will it be the same mission as the one in China? Are you going to remove Shartin and bring him to Gilligan's Island?"

A murmur of laughter ran through the older crowd at Jenning's Gilligan's Island question, accompanied by questioning looks from the students. "No, John, not just yet anyway. He hasn't killed anyone that we know of. He's not what I would call a benevolent dictator, but he is still not a murderer like Dung and Rishi. The first order of business will be to confiscate all their bioweapon strains, equipment, and computer data. They are next because they are the second largest research facility remaining active today."

"Who's next after that?" asked a voice from the crowd.

"The president has already dismantled American bioweapon labs by executive order. China's labs have also been destroyed. We are going to act quickly from this point forward. People will start getting wind of what we are doing. There are 12 remaining bioweapon laboratories after the demise of the Russian labs. We are not giving them any breathing room to move specimens or reconstitute equipment and files elsewhere. Quite a few of them are in countries who are U.S. allies. There will be no forewarning. They won't like it, but we don't care. It doesn't matter what their excuse is for manufacturing biological weapons whose only purpose is mass murder in the name of political triumph. They will not be allowed to continue."

Louie Petro had returned to Lightning for the fourth time in five months. Family meetings were addictive. He left Patty Titus in New York to hold down the fort. "You know, Uncle Iggy…Oh… sorry… I forgot I'm supposed to lose the uncle prefix. I understand the mission. Yet all this is being accomplished, and no one is receiving due process. Isn't that antithetical to the kind of world you are trying to set up to cultivate individuality and dismantle collectivism? That's what you taught me for 18 years."

"Your point is well taken, Louie. Your position that the ends do not justify the means is right on target. However, we have only removed murderers from the killing fields and isolated them on Gilligan's Island. Eventually, they will receive due process. Unfortunately, the sheer volume of reprobates exceeds the ability of society to offer speedy due process. So, in the interest of preventing more deaths, we acted outside the typical scope of American jurisprudence. This is not frivolous, Louie. We're talking about many thousands, perhaps millions, of potential victims. The stock and trade of bioweapon labs are death and destruction. There is no other reason for their existence. One accident, releasing the most lethal of these virulent strains, could possibly kill millions before the contagion could be checked or mitigated. So, in this case, why don't we ask the prospective victims of this tragedy, everyone on earth, if the end justifies the means."

The auditorium was silent. No one else wanted to enter this debate. It was one of those "damned if you do... and damned if you don't" conundrums. Most people present had been associated with the Marcus family for more than 20 years. Not once in all those years had anyone raised objections to their actions or the ensuing results. They realized from the beginning it would be a roller coaster ride of political upheaval and profound drama that would affect the future of every living creature on Earth.

Louie Petro wasn't finished. He was never one to bite his tongue. He learned to be a scrapper in the orphanage where the older kids never let him forget his mother was a prostitute and his father was in prison for murder. He was smaller than a lot of the older kids. They ridiculed him and often beat him until he was unable to stand. Louie had grit. There wasn't even a smidgen of cowardice inside.

The day it changed and became his epiphany, seven or eight older boys slapped him around and kicked him until he fell with his face in the mud, groaning in pain. One of the boys jumped on his back, reached around, and began to choke him. That was the moment fear left Louie and defined the character that would carry him throughout life. A white-hot anger consumed him in an explosion of strength beyond his small stature. He tossed the boy who was choking him off his back, jumped to his feet, and erupted in a whirling dynamo of fury, punching, and kicking all seven bullies. He did that, it seemed, for many minutes, but in reality, it was only seconds. He was oblivious to his surroundings during his blinding tirade until he realized they all had run away. No one had expected little Louie Petro to detonate in a fury that bloodied noses and branded body parts with bite marks. None of the boys looked sideways at him with disrespect after that day.

"So, Iggy," Louie continued. "Okay then. Nukes are off the table. You are taking pathogenic microbes off the table, but what are we going to do with the lunatics who are starting wars, bombing buildings, and shooting people at random all over the world? We know it's Interlink-inspired and funded, but it is everywhere, and no one feels safe anymore. You and Lindy trained me in the law. That is what I do. I look around me and see Interlink-sponsored prosecutors who indict and charge people who are defending themselves against felons, while allowing murderers and recidivists to walk free! What the hell are we going to do? This can't go on! I suppose it wouldn't be so bad if Interlink didn't control every single media outlet on the planet other than American Media Inc. Their poisoned propaganda affects everyone. They are propagating fear and using it as a tool to turn average, everyday people against each other, hoping the strife between them will debilitate society."

"You're just about right, Louie. You've described exactly what is happening, but there are subtleties. For instance, the violence and mass shootings in America have been getting out of hand. They're blaming it on the president and his administration." At that mention, Bill Sledge shrugged his shoulders with a look of resignation. "They are also directly inspired and funded by Interlink. Their expectations by creating this enormous political divisiveness are to foment hatred and start the eventual Civil War, which will thin the herd and kindle the violence they need to declare martial law. They believe that permits them to subdue the population using our own military and the United Nations troops."

Everyone listened intently, spellbound by Iggy's description of the status quo. Everyone knew in their gut what was happening could very well be the end of freedom. They all knew it was precipitated from the outside, but so many Americans had become disenfranchised because of delusion that it seemed apparent the destruction of the country might be in sight despite the efforts of the Marcus family.

"Yeah, well, I don't think this president is going to declare martial law any time soon," he nodded his head toward President Sledge. Only Congress can do that. "But he's running for re-election in eight months, and who knows who will be calling the shots then? Frankly, Patty Titus and I are getting married, and we want to raise a family. What you described and what I see with my own eyes is the scariest thing I have ever imagined. I fear for the country. The only thing out of place here is your Cheshire cat smile. You wouldn't be smiling like that if you didn't have something up your sleeve. You know... an ace in the hole besides your magnetic force field."

Iggy smiled. "You chose the right profession, Louie, the law. Nobody's ever going to put anything over on you, that's for sure. You are correct; I have another ace in the hole, and I will outline it to you tonight. First, allow me to draw an analogy. When an unarmed man must confront a grizzly bear, hand-to-hand combat is out of the question. It's no contest... the bear wins. The bear has superior strength, an excellent sense of smell, and rudimentary logic, but he is unsophisticated. The man can still beat the bear, but he must take a different approach. The bear's strengths lie in his speed, power, and his claws. He's unbeatable on that level. The man's strength lies between his ears, and if he uses it correctly, he is unbeatable on that level."

"Okay, Iggy," responded Louie. "I get it. You always make sense. So, tell us exactly what new miracle is lurking between those ears of yours that is going to negate the mess the world is in right now."

Melanie hadn't said a word all night. She quietly listened to everything. She had 2000 new students seated before her. She meticulously observed them all. It was her mission to understand the psyche of every one of her protégés. She would teach them medicine and music. She laughed at Louie Petro's bravado. Not many people talked to her husband that way, and she enjoyed it.

No one moved or hardly breathed. They hung on every word. Iggy's towering intellect had catalyzed the greatest societal transformation in history and had done it without spilling a drop of blood. These were the most intelligent people on earth who had either attended the best school that ever existed or were involved in developing its students.

"Yes, Louie. There are a few things lurking. First, each of you wears one of our Lightning watches. They are not all the same because you all don't need the capabilities of the ultimate model."

"However, each wristwatch nullifies the signals generated in your cerebral cortex, created with the nanotechnology particulate you have been breathing. This stuff is being sprayed into the atmosphere for the false claim of weather control. They are commonly referred to as chemtrails. You all understand that. We are about to deploy technology from our R&D department at the hospital that will offer blanket protection from the mind control intentions of interlink, and deploy it nationwide at first, then worldwide."

"The elitists are mediocrities standing on the shoulders of giants as thieves who could never create this dazzling technology on their own. Their insidious intent is to dictate the future of men and enslave humanity using artificial intelligence. Most, if not all of you, are fully aware of this technology on a molecular and anatomic level. There are specific patents involved, but the intended use is not patented. We will negate that."

"I understand, Iggy... We all understand how nefarious this technology is. It's mind control in a computer via electrical stimuli. We have known of this technology for over a decade. It doesn't affect us because of the wristwatches. That doesn't speak to what's happening around the world, however. So, what are the other tricks you have up your sleeve?"

"Almost everyone here understands the politics and socioeconomic impact of the dollar's incremental disintegration. It is intentional and precipitated by our friends in interlink. Incrementalism is the tool wolves use to sneak up on the sheep while they are grazing. Interlink is a conglomerate who wants to control money and, consequently, all our lives. We are given Social Security numbers and birth certificates identifying us as objects and subjects of the world corporation to be exploited by the world powers. It has been this way since Woodrow Wilson and the Federal Reserve Act when they stripped America's economic autonomy from under the citizenry. Is everyone following this?"

Heads nodded throughout the gathering. "Go on," said Louie Petro.

"A small voice from one of the pedophile victims floated over the group. "Wait, please. I have a question."

"Go on, Jesse, what's on your mind?"

"I am new here, and I'm a little shy. I've only been here six months. Not only did you save me from a life of rape and torture, but you have also opened a world to me that I never thought would be possible. So, I have questions because my background is not as complete as many of the other students. Are you telling us that we are chattel, just mere numbers to be exploited by those people you call interlink? Are they the same people who kidnapped me and tortured me sexually? Even in my misery, I knew they were treating me like an animal."

"Some of them are the same people who torture children. I am really impressed, Jesse. Your choice of the word chattel is so appropriate that I find it incredible you associate the word with the reality of it. You are correct. However, it's not just you or the people we rescued, only. We are all considered chattel. We have all been given a social security number, and the words written on the back of our birth certificate stating we are chattel by contract if you understand the documentation underpinning these things. Is that enough of an answer?"

Jesse nodded. "Please go on; this is a fascinating new world to me."

"The engine of capitalism has fueled America's economy as well as every other productive entity in existence. This has propagated consumerism and generated the greatest lifestyle ever experienced by any society. The problem tyrants have with capitalism is it places the economy and control in the hands of producers and consumers. That philosophical system allows the cream to rise to the top."

"Herein lies the rub. When the cream rises to the top, and economic control falls in the laps of both the consumer and the producer, the people who run the planet, who are like bookies, always demand a piece of the action. A piece is never enough; they want to control all the action. With capitalism, that doesn't work. However, the antithesis of capitalism, socialism, is their perfect vehicle to distribute all the power among the undeserving leeches and strip it away from the producers and consumers. Those producers and consumers are the citizens. You all understand these concepts. I repeat them only to equate them with what I'm about to explain." He laughed. "It has to do with what is up my sleeve, Louic."

William Sledge, President of the United States, had been silent. He was really here for the concert, but he found the meeting every bit as fascinating. He knew what was coming next and was smiling broadly. After all, his Atty. Gen. and the Sec. of the treasury, Alvin Bradlin, had signed on to Iggy's plan to solidify the dollar for all time.

"Before I outline the antidote to the economic disease that has infected Western society and capitalism, I will briefly synopsize the history. The founding fathers created an entity with checks and balances. The mission was to ensure individual freedom and prosperity for every human being. To do that, man had to abandon the caste system. The caste system enabled the ruling elites to enslave the peasants for thousands of years. Occasionally, men attempted to negate that underlying societal structure."

"Until America came into being, all governments and religions were controlled by elitist dictatorships, now known as Interlink. The dictators controlled the armies, and the armies controlled the masses. Whoever held the Army in the palm of his hand also held the masses by the throat. Consequently, every arrogant politician undeserving of his office, every bureaucratic windbag, and religious narcissist, forced their subjects to kneel at the altar of tyranny in order to perpetuate their power. The concepts beneath most religions originated through altruism and the desire to live morally. However, the eventual structure of religion is usually bastardized to suppress individuality and coerce conformity. This is not an indictment of religion. It is the indictment of self-aggrandizing narcissists who use religion to justify their envy of others and validate their self-image. They use conformity as the tool to control those beneath them."

"Periodically, men or groups of men arose and attempted to eradicate this vicious root of evil called envy… and they were moderately successful at times. America's founding was the first complete, magnificent exception to the tyranny of the elitists. Men were finally given equal stature without coercion or concern for the station they were born into. That was the underlying premise of America. *All men are created equal.*"

Of course, the elitists as well as the religious tyrants of the Church of England and the Vatican were in a tizzy, depending on who was in charge at the moment. They had lost control, and men were now in control of their own lives. The West was the epitome of individual freedom. It became the elitists' mission to destroy the symbol of the West, America. Every significant national and international consequential occurrence between the Declaration of Independence and today has been an attempt by those elitists to bring America back into the fold and subjugate its citizens. They use Karl Marx's Communist Manifesto as their Bible. It is the one organized dissertation written and accepted that defines their universal program of misery and how they implement it."

"Before the elitists can recapture their control over men, they must first remove man's ability to survive on his own and become the recipient of his own productivity. When a man is independent, he doesn't need the elitist or the elitist's armies. That very concept negates the validity of armies under all circumstances. There is only one mission for an army… national defense. It exists to kill the invaders. When the independent citizen who refuses to kneel as a subject becomes the opposition to the illegitimate narcissist who controls the army, then the individual must be either mentally reconditioned or slaughtered. Mao Zedong… 77 million. Joseph Stalin… 55 million; Idi Amin… ½ million; Adolf Hitler… 19 million; Pol Pot … 2million; Sadam Husein… 1 million… and that's just the last century. Do I need to continue? "Iggy asked without expecting an answer.

"All that honest men require is the freedom to produce and exchange their efforts with their brothers. My friends, that is the definition of capitalism. Like all things, capitalism was adulterated. How was it adulterated? You might ask. To know that you must first accept the logical axiom stating no societal philosophy or edifice can function efficiently without being morally underpinned by honesty and integrity. So, that became the mission. Destroy honesty, integrity, and morality on every level. Once that's gone, each man becomes a vicious, tiny, independent elitist trying to usurp individuality and power from his fellows by becoming an envious grifter. Do you see it? Then, it becomes a simple thing to defeat the paltry individual citizen/tyrant. It is a perfect illustration of the adage, *United we stand… Divided we fall*."

Louie wasn't finished. "Your philosophical opposition would no doubt call you a pontificating, vain, swaggering egoist. How would you respond to that?"

Melanie was laughing. Louie Petro was such a horse of a different color she always enjoyed his sparring with her husband. Iggy chuckled. "I'm sure you're correct, Louie. That's what all people say who have no antithetical arguments for a debatable subject. They resort to name-calling and never offer an opposing view with valid premises beneath. Entering a debate with one such individual would never change their mind; only waste valuable minutes of the only life you will ever possess."

Louie Petro laughed. He loved the debates with Iggy almost as much as he loved the man who had saved his life. Iggy Marcus had saved him from the prison sentence he would've surely had and turned him into a man of substance facing a spectacular future. As much as he enjoyed fencing with his mentor, he would die for him in a heartbeat." Okay, Uncle Iggy." He used uncle as a term of endearment to the man he respected more than anything in the world. "I guess I've harassed you long enough, but I would like to make a statement: I know you are correct. The education we have received here defines man's history to a T and all the motives moving history's players. You are the first one who has named it loudly and accurately. That's why they want to kill you. They know you are correct, and you are teaching others the truth. The great part is they can't get at you no matter how hard they try. So, what is your secret weapon to save us this time?"

"I thought you had forgotten. We went through the philosophical vagaries of capitalism versus socialism. Karl Marx described in his second plank that the first requirement to destroy capitalism, oligarchy, or elitism is to debauch a nation's currency. He was correct. That will precipitate the fall because everything becomes arbitrary when values are set at the whim of the power brokers, at whatever moment they deem necessary to achieve a particular end. That's what they began with the Federal Reserve Act, and

Richard Nixon finished when he took the country off the gold standard permanently."

"Once gold is sidelined, it will be only a matter of time before the economy implodes and the excessive printed fiat money supply used for barter and trade becomes useless. That is the harbinger of chaos, anarchy, and civil unrest, the likes of which have never been seen in America. There is no provision in the Constitution for any of these things. There is also no provision for the enactment and enforcement of martial law. In fact, there is no definition of martial law anywhere. No written documentation in history existed other than the fact martial law was invoked 68 times in America since the Civil War. The president can't declare martial law. Only Congress can. Theoretically, even habeas corpus is sidelined although it has never been done previously."

"So, what brings martial law into this conversation? Why is it pertinent to what's going on in the world? Apparently, Interlink is inciting riots, civil unrest, and the destruction of civil propriety everywhere. Their paid minions, who have been corruptly elected or appointed as prosecutors, are allowing criminals to walk out of the courtroom. Yet, they are indicting mothers for protesting what happens to children in school when drag queens are paraded in front of seven-year-olds. This is not acceptable to or survivable by society. All this is intentional. It is their last stand to re-attain control. When they are unsuccessful, they will resort to their last option, murder, and there is no limit to how many will fall under their sword. We won't let that happen. When evil rears its head, good will always stare back and eventually prevail."

Iggy continued. "We've covered a lot of bases tonight, from the societal unrest being perpetrated worldwide, to the debauchment of our currency. All these factors are part of one equation to produce economic and societal collapse. That is always what happens when a country prints excessive quantities of fiat money that are not backed by value. That is what they will use to declare martial law. Congress will be forced to choose a course of action. Under current conditions of inflation and the lack of solid value underpinning the American dollar, martial law would be catastrophic. Rioting, starving citizens will commit the Army to restore order. Men will be pitted against their neighbors and brothers against brothers while the authoritarians watch from their ivory towers. When the dust settles, they hope to use the Army to clean up the mess and herd the remaining insurrectionists into the Gulag." He added the last phrase with a cynical smile. "It's not going to go as well for them as they think."

"We now have our technology that eliminates nuclear war, tactical warfare, and the ability for any country to release biological terrorism. That is a huge impediment for Interlink. They believe, however, that if the chaos is widespread and violent enough, the governments of the world will collapse and their original plans to construct a new socialist world government dictating terms of survival to all humanity will be possible."

"We are no longer living under normal circumstances, however. Interlink has a major ante in the pot, considering the status of the American dollar, which is still the world reserve currency. At this point, I will refrain from describing what has really been done to this country in terms of international corporate law and how we have all been purchased as slaves. That is a topic for discussion when there is time to elaborate."

"What I intend to reveal tonight is a plan we concocted to stop Interlink in its tracks. The president, the Atty. Gen., the Sec. of the treasury, and myself have calculated a way to return the prominence of the dollar as the world currency and make it impervious to harm, ad infinitum. In doing so, the Federal Reserve will be abolished. They are the reason we are in such deplorable shape now. That takes an act of Congress. That's how the Federal Reserve came into being. It was a day of subterfuge and evil when control of the money supply was ripped from under the population through its representatives in Congress and dropped in the laps of the bankers so they could extort us at their discretion into the foreseeable future. We won't give Congress much of a choice. They will realize it is their last option... sink or swim!"

Louie Petro had a huge grin. He knew Iggy Marcus was never given to frivolity and never wrong. He was thinking about Patty Titus, his upcoming marriage, and the family he would raise in a normal society. "Geez, Uncle Iggy. Will you cut the suspense? You're driving us all crazy."

Iggy felt the same about his student as Louie felt about him. "Okay. Will do, Louie. You all know about our mater energy transmutation capabilities. No one else really understands it because it is a technology, I will not release in any other manner than food production to feed the hungry. Interlink should have been smart enough to make the connection, but they were not. That perfectly demonstrates their intellectual mediocrity. They have absolutely no idea that we can turn sand into gold. We have purposely suppressed that information for obvious reasons. First, it would depress the value of gold because the supply could then become unlimited. Second, we will not do that because it will destabilize all the governments and economies of the world."

"What we will do is manufacture enough gold to return the United States dollar and economy to the gold standard with exactly the right amount to validate 50% of the quantitative value of printed currency. As far as the world is concerned, it has been mined, and we have collected it. It amounts to just over a half million metric tons at today's closing spot price. We will end quantitative easing, and when things settle down from the announcement about the gold supply, we can slowly retract the printed money without raising interest rates as high as Paul Volcker did in the 1980s to rectify the fiscal frivolity of the Carter administration."

"One of Iggy's students asked, "Why don't you crank out enough gold to back up 100% of the printed money instead of 50%?"

"They've printed so much money, and so many other countries are invested in our bonds that it would actually depress the price of gold. We are talking $50 trillion here.

Everyone present understood the amazing concepts and implications of what they had just been told. William Sledge wore an ear-to-ear grin, thinking about the nature of Iggy's accomplishments in general. This man had single-handedly ended the possibility of strategic nuclear war and was eliminating bioterrorism from the arsenal of any country. He had fed millions, cured cancer, and was eliminating congestive heart failure. Their little hospital at Lightning Ranch was the foremost medical research center in the world. Without spilling a drop of blood, he toppled the world's greatest threat to freedom and individuality, the CCP, then helped its people form their new democracy in a matter of a few weeks. His magnetic force field imparted an astonishing level of security to all mankind. He had done all these things and now was about to save America's economy from repeating the mistakes of the past.

"Wow!" Louie said. "I guess that'll do it. We can call It the fifty trillion-dollar sure thing. The only thing I can say, Iggy, is you better hang around long enough, at least a couple hundred years, to watchdog things and keep the morons like Interlink and politicians from screwing it up." Louie did some quick math in his head. "Geez, a half million metric tons… that's over 16 billion troy ounces! That should take you a little while."

"No problem, Louie. Baby and Junior have lots of time on their hands, and they're willing to help."

***

Sixteen hours later, four ships, Daedalus, Pegasus, Hermes, and Nemesis, hung suspended 200 feet above the Kremlin. They had appeared in seconds, and the Russians had no time to defend against the intrusion. Iggy made the ship's skin disappear and settled Daedalus in front of the newly erected statue with a bronze plaque that read VANYA THE GREAT. It had replaced the statues of Minin and Pozharsky.

"Wow!" said Baby. "Talk about the height of arrogance. The guy isn't even dead yet."

Gloria was hysterical. "God, Baby! You kill me. You are so hilarious."

"Thanks, Gloria. I'm practicing."

"Practicing? Whatever for?" Gloria asked, frowning.

"Well, current events are always changing, and my programming makes me search for humor in everything. Although I'm really not sure what humor feels like, I can't seem to be able to help myself."

Gloria was still smiling when Iggy injected, “If you two are finished clowning, I would like you to see if you can locate Vanya Shartin, Gloria.”

A minute later, Gloria reported, "he's in there, Dad. He's having a meeting with some general named Igor."

“Ask him to come to the window and look out into Red Square. Tell him we have a surprise."

"He's having a bit of a freak out, Dad. I'm quite sure this is his very first subliminal conversation."

“Tell him who we are and why we are paying him a visit.”

“His response is, *I don’t think so.”*

Iggy sighed. "Okay then, Gloria. I guess you'll have to take me in with you." For the next minute silence reigned.

"Vanya Shartin, my name is Iggy Marcus. You know who I am and what I have done. Please do me the courtesy of listening to why I am here."

Vanya Shartin rushed to the window overlooking Red Square, followed by General Igor Lansky. Iggy could sense the fear and apprehension in both men.

“They are frightened half to death, Dad. They think you have come to kill them. I think you had better reassure them, Gloria said aloud.

“I think Dad has the propensity for scaring people when they first meet. “From what I understand, contact does that to people,” said Baby.

“Please, Baby. Hold the small talk for the time being.”

Gloria was chuckling. “It’s your own fault, Dad. Nothing in the instructions of the Mr. Wizard do-it-yourself sentient robot kit suggests the option of small talk. It was strictly your idea.”

Baby laughed. “That was a very funny joke, Gloria. I enjoyed that.”

"You enjoyed it? I don't think so, Baby. You're just saying that to elicit a few more laughs."

Iggy rolled his eyes. "I think you're right, Gloria. I definitely overdid it in the humor and small talk departments....

Baby..."

"Yes, Dad, what's up? Hope you don't mind the colloquialism."

"Would you please shut up for a few minutes... Oh... hope you didn't mind the colloquialism."

"Vanya Shartin, I am not here to kill you or your general. I have other business, and it is important that we speak. So, please let me in or come out to me. One way or the other, you and I are going to have a conversation."

"Just out of curiosity," asked Baby, "why are you being so courteous to this man? You were not very courteous to Fun Chou Dung. Please explain."

"Dung is a murderer. He's killed thousands and attempted to kill a few thousand at Lightning Ranch with nuclear weapons through interlink. Also, he has murdered thousands of his own people. He doesn't deserve courtesy. Vanya Shartin hasn't murdered anybody recently although he is contemplating it, intending to invade countries of the former Soviet Union. I have come to convince him that that is a very bad idea. While we are here, we are taking their bioweapons with us."

Vanya Shartin knew exactly who Iggy Marcus was. So did Igor Lansky. The general's look was a question mark. "What are you going to do, Vanya? This American has managed to sneak into Moscow without us even knowing he was on the way. That is a pretty big deal. Are you going to speak with him?"

"I don't know; what do you suggest, Igor?"

"I think I would talk to him if I were you. This man just flew here and appeared out of thin air. He has also negated our nuclear arsenal. I think that you don't have a choice. If he was going to kill us, we would already be dead. You have heard the news coming out of China. Somehow, everything is changed and I'm certain this man is responsible."

Vanya Shartin nodded his head. "Yes, Igor, I agree. Should I invite him in?"

"Yes, I think so, but tell him to leave the woman who speaks with telepathy outside."

"You're probably right. Still, Igor, I don't know how to answer him. He did not use the phone."

"We do not need the phone, Vanya Shartin. I am Gloria, the daughter of Iggy Marcus. You are worried that I will come inside and read your thoughts and remove your privacy. I can do that from here if I wish. I do not do that to others intentionally unless my father asks me. That is why he wants a personal meeting. The conversation will be between you and him and not through me."

"I accept those terms. Approach the entrance to building one. That is where my office is. I will arrange for guards to escort you to my office. You may come now, if you like."

Five minutes later, Gloria and Iggy were escorted through building one to the executive offices of the Russian premier. Iggy encapsulated himself and his daughter as they walked through the Kremlin. The six-soldier escort stopped in front of two large walnut doors with TV cameras to the left and above, as the man wearing Capt.'s bars knocked."

General Igor Lansky opened the door and nodded to Iggy and his daughter as they entered. The office was well appointed in walnut but not ostentatious. Premier Vanya Shartin rose, thrusting his hand toward Iggy, who stopped a few inches from his desk with his hand out also as he tailored the force field to allow the handshake. Gloria's ear-to-ear grin lit her face, knowing the Russian premier's brain was about to explode in *contact.* She was quite sure her father would pour it on.

"Jesu Cristo que fue eso!! Exclaimed Shartin," as he staggered backward and fell into his chair. Igor Lansky started forward, thinking their guests had somehow hurt the premier, but Shartin held his hand up to stop him.

Vanya Shartin was an arrogant man. The statue with the bronze plaque, Vanya, The Great, in Red Square illustrated the size of his ego. It took that kind of man to become the premier of Russia. The Russians, always arrogant and duplicitous, rarely ceded authority to anyone without an imperious stature. He had just experienced Iggy Marcus, and the glimpse of his genius astonished him. He saw immense strength and unwavering tenacity, surrounded by the serene benevolence of his character. He had never seen anything like it. Shartin's rise to power consisted of sparring with other egocentric Russians until he achieved dominance. Usually, those contests were confrontations of strengths and weaknesses. Once the head of the KGB, he had many friends, but he also had 'the goods' on many Russians who were his competition. All those factors propelled him to power.

Vanya Shartin was intimidated by the imposing entity standing opposite him. For the first time in his life, he yielded to humility. "Mr. Marcus, you are a most unusual man. I now understand how you accomplished so many things. It is obvious you are not here for a good game of chess. What can I do for you? Apparently, you want something. Incidentally, how did you learn to speak perfect Russian?"

Iggy smiled, ignoring the question, raised his eyebrows, and projected benevolence. "Quite correct, premier Shartin. I am not here for a good game of chess. I played two games with another Russian once, Vladimir Borenko. That was enough for one lifetime."

"Did you win?"

"Twice. Once across the chess board, and once at the game of life."

"Huh…twice…Maybe that's why no one has heard from him for a few years. He hated to lose. Do you know where he went?"

"Yes," Iggy said with a wide grin. "He is semiretired and living on an island in the middle of the Pacific."

"So, Mr. Marcus, what exactly do you want of me?"

"I shook hands with you so that you would understand who and what I am, as well as my capabilities. You understand, now, if I wanted to harm or kill you, you would already be dead, and there would've been nothing you could do to prevent that. You all are wondering, I'm sure, exactly what has happened to Fun Chou Dung and General Li Shen Rishi."

Shartin slowly nodded his head. "Yes. You are correct. There are lots of rumors. It has been too soon for diplomacy to pass on such information, but we are quite sure you are involved."

"Dung and Rishi, along with a few thousand upper-echelon military leaders, are no longer in the country. They are with Vladimir Borenko at a place called Gilligan's Island in the middle of the Pacific Ocean."

General Igor Lansky began to laugh hysterically. "Please forgive me. I don't mean to insult. It's just that I have seen your American television show, Gilligan's Island, many years ago after Perestroika when the Soviet opened up to the West. It was very funny. Do the professor and Gilligan still live there?"

It was Iggy's turn to laugh. "No, it was just a TV show. We call them comedies, but they are fiction. So, Mr. Premier… may I address you as Vanya?" The premier nodded yes. "Then let's get back to the point of the issue. I'm sure you're aware there are four ships outside. Three of them hover over the Kremlin, and one is parked at your front door. I would like to take you for a ride. You will be returned here unharmed, shortly. Believe me, Vanya, it will be quite an experience and an eye-opener. You are also invited, General."

"Yes, Mr. Marcus, I will go." He had been exposed to Iggy's character on a subliminal level. He had never experienced anything like it, but he knew this man would never lie.

Gen. Lansky was skeptical. "You think that is wise, Vanya?"

"I am not worried, Igor. This man will return us to the Kremlin when he has exhibited what he wishes me to see. Will you come?"

Igor Lansky was not going to be labeled a coward. He nodded his head yes, and five minutes later, they boarded Daedalus. Gloria had remained silent for the entire meeting.

"I would like to introduce you to my other daughter, Baby."

"It is our pleasure to meet you," stated Vanya Shartin.

"Thanks. The pleasure, however, is all mine. You are my first Russian," Baby said in impeccable Russian.

"You have never met a Russian before? How is it that you speak the language so well?"

"I am a robot, President Vanya Shartin. I speak every language perfectly."

"A robot? How is that possible? You look and sound human, so alive. Surely you are joking."

Baby laughed. "Well, I do love to tell jokes. That's how Dad built and programmed me. However, I am not joking in this instance. I am sentient. My brother, Junior, and I are both robots who are sentient. We are each unique. Look, I will show you." Baby lifted her skirt above her picture-perfect legs and exposed her underwear. She pointed to the on and off button that protruded from her belly just below her navel. I have an internal battery that will keep me alive for approximately 200 hours, depending on the level of energy that I expend and the activity I perform. When I charge my battery, I must press this button. That allows my auxiliary power supply to continue my cerebral processes, and I can perform other functions normally during my 20-minute charge."

The two Russians looked at each other with golf-ball eyes. They were grappling with a seemingly impossible technology. There were having a conversation with a beautiful woman who was not a woman, but a robot with a sense of humor. It was too much for them. Vanya Shartin turned to Gloria. "Are you a robot too? Would you please lift up your skirt so I can see if you have a button?"

"No, I am flesh and blood and actually Iggy Marcus's daughter."

"So, Mr. Marcus, where are we going? What is it that you wish to show me? I have another question, though. What is the motive power of the ship, and how do you make the walls disappear?"

"I will explain it in the only way that is possible. I was struck by lightning. I awoke in the hospital with an IQ above a thousand, approximately where the average human intellect will be in 100,000 years or so. This gift from the universe compels me to prevent the annihilation of the species, Homo sapiens."

"Again, sir, where are you taking me?"

"This ship and the one following us are on the way to the Urals. That is where your largest, most prolific bioweapon laboratory exists. There are two others in this country. My other two ships are on their way to them now. We are removing all bioweapons from every research facility on Earth. We are removing the strains and the equipment. Then, we are deleting the computers. Before we go in, I will have Baby play you a hologram of what we did at the Chinese bioweapon facility at Shenyang University and elsewhere."

"May I ask a question?" asked Igor Lansky. "What is the motive power of this vessel? How does it move, and who is flying it? We are all sitting around in lounge chairs at a coffee table."

"That's the $64,000 question," said Baby… Gloria laughed.

"Well, I can give you a brief description," replied Iggy. "The ship moves by electromagnetic force, but it does not move through space and time as you would think. It exits existence and reenters at the pilot's discretion. I am flying as the pilot and will interface with the computer, directing the electromagnetic flux to channel through me. We are still parked over the Kremlin. I would like Baby to show you the holograms of our Chinese adventure and corroborate our intent before we depart for the Urals. When we leave for the Urals, it will take us less than one second to arrive."

After the conclusion of the holograms, Iggy turned to Vanya Shartin. "You understand thoroughly what we are trying to accomplish here. You know that we eliminated man's ability to wage nuclear war. Now, we are removing man's ability to kill each other with biology. One purpose of showing you all this is to elicit your cooperation with what we are about to do. Make no mistake, this cannot be prevented, and we can do it without harming anyone, hopefully. But we still must invade your bioweapon facilities, and because your military is fiercely loyal, there exists a propensity for someone to be harmed. I wish to avoid that at all costs, but we are only leaving after the removal of everything I listed."

Shartin didn't respond immediately. He was thinking, weighing the request made by this foreign agent with his duty to Mother Russia. He was convinced that Marcus was accurate. He would do whatever he intended to do, and there would be nothing Russia could do to stop it. Still, his countrymen might consider his cooperation a betrayal.

General Igor Lansky eyed him carefully. He knew Vanya was no coward. He also understood that the Russian premier was between a rock and a hard place. It was obvious there was nothing he could do to thwart this amazing man and prevent his agenda. That was a foregone conclusion. "What are you going to do, Vanya?"

Shartin's face displayed his mindset to General Lansky. He looked Iggy directly in the eye. "I am sorry, Mr. Marcus. I cannot give you permission to attack Russia. That is what you are requesting. What I will do, however, is make no attempt to stop you. The power you possess makes you unstoppable, anyway, and if I were to order Russians to try, many of them might die, and it would be for nothing. You would still acquire the bioweapons, and Russians would have died in vain."

"We don't have to worry about anyone dying by our hand, Vanya. Our shield technology, which everyone is aware of by now, will protect everyone from harm. The mission will be more difficult with shields, and you might conceivably harm yourselves trying to thwart us, but we will do what we must. I had hoped you would acquiesce but did not expect it. There is another reason you are aboard this ship and what you have learned today.

We are aware you are going to attack countries once belonging to the Soviet, attempting to expand your seat at the Interlink table after they form their supposed one-world government and the smoke clears."

Shartin wondered where this man got his information. The invasion of neighboring countries was a subject only discussed between him and his generals. None of them were disloyal. Then it dawned on him. This man was an intellectual giant, and there probably wasn't much in the activities of men that he couldn't predict. Vanya Shartin burped a one-syllable laugh. "I see. You are that prescient. I will not deny it because it would make a fool of me when I try to convince you to lie to yourself. So, just what is it you are asking of me and my generals?"

"I am not asking anything of you. I am telling you that there will be no one-world government ruled by Interlink. I could put an end to that in 24 hours; I possess the resources, technology, and the ability. However, that would make me exactly like them and that is the kind of future humanity must avoid. If we are going to evolve as citizens of the universe, we must get beyond this squabbling for position. In the end, all that does is propagate death and destruction. You know who I am. You know who we are. You know we have virtually eliminated cancer, and we are working on eliminating heart disease. When we are done, it will be an epiphany for the entire human race."

"That is a position easily taken by a man such as yourself. You apparently have unlimited power and resources, and you are not responsible for an entire country and its well-being."

"Vanya, I will not debate you on the efficacy of my position or responsibilities. As a politician, you have responsibilities to your country, and they supersede responsibilities to yourself. Such is the nature of power when coupled with integrity. What has happened to me has compelled my responsibility to all of humanity, and I cannot abandon that position. You know we have fed much of the world and ended hunger. We have created an unlimited power source consisting of clean energy. We have ended those tribulations of humanity for all time. So, what's the problem?"

"That was a rhetorical question, Vanya. The problem is ego. You have one and are unwilling to relinquish your anticipation of expanding it by invading another country. Now, I have just called a spade a spade. You know I am correct, and as I said, I won't debate it. What I am telling you is the single reason you are here aboard the ship. You now actually have a demonstration of our power; therefore, you will not invade another country. If you attempt such, I will put an end to it before one drop of blood is spilled. And this is where you will live the rest of your life." He turned to Baby. "Put up a hologram of Gilligan's Island and the two Chinese reprobates with the cribbage board."

Vanya Shartin said nothing. There was nothing to say. He had just been given an ultimatum by a man who could easily enforce his demands. He thought about it. This man could have taken him to the island immediately. Yet, he was being given options to make choices that would be solutions instead of problems. If he declined and wound up on the island, it would leave a void in the power configuration of the Kremlin. The next person in line might be worse. This man is obviously smarter than the rest of us. He made his decision at that moment. Half a pie is better than starving.

Iggy didn't need Gloria for this one. He understood exactly what Shartin intended. "That is a wise choice, Vanya; this is the only time the choice would be given to you." He smiled, "the next time, you would be joining your two Chinese compatriots on Gilligan's Island. At least then, you would have a foursome for bridge."

Baby laughed at Iggy's joke.

Gloria laughed, "Why are you laughing, Baby?"

"Just practicing."

"Since your involvement is not key or even necessary, there is no reason to require your presence. I will take you back to Moscow now and then return to complete our business.

Fifteen minutes later, Daedalus and Nemesis descended to the runways above the bio labs located beneath the Ural Mountains. The access to the caverns and laboratory was disguised as a small Air Force Base with a few hangers and a landing strip inordinately long considering the size of the buildings and the remote location. These were the mountains where Brezhnev and Kosygin intended to house the population of the Soviet Union during nuclear war. The vast underground caverns consisted of millions of square feet of living space, huge stores of food and military equipment. At the center of the complex was their bioweapon research facility. Iggy had returned his two hitchhikers to the Kremlin after Gen. Lansky issued orders preventing the missile-defense system from attempting the destruction of the intruders.

Six hours later, the virulent strains of bioweapons were loaded aboard Hermes and Daedalus. Baby and Junior deleted the computer files while the SEALs removed and stacked the lab equipment on the flight line for destruction. Iggy had erected walls between his Navy SEALs and the Russian soldiers. The Russians were given no explanation about the mission. They watched helplessly as everything was conveyed to the surface. Immediately following Daedalus' departure, Col. Peter Pavlik was on the phone with the other two major Russian bio-research centers.

Lieut. General Myra Chansky commanded the bioweapons facility at Gorodomlya Island in Lake Seliger. She reached for the satellite phone in the accessory pack strapped to her waist. She fumbled with her stethoscope and a few medical instruments before she was able to extract the phone. The red light was flashing, indicating a call from the Urals. "Yes, this is Dr. Chansky… Peter?"

"Yes, Myra. It is Peter! I called to warn you. The Americans are coming! I believe they are on their way now."

Myra Chansky began to laugh. What kind of joke is this, Peter? It's not like you. Whatever are you talking about? Where are the Americans coming from?" She continued to laugh. "Disney World, maybe?"

"Yes! It must be! How did you know?" Pavlick gasped.

Myra stopped laughing. Something was wrong. Col. Peter Pavlik was not only a friend who was the doctor in command of the Brezhnev facility, but also a very stable man. They were one year apart at M.V. Lomonosov Moscow State University and enjoyed a two-year romance. She was more than slightly apprehensive. Occasionally, the solitude of remote duty affected people. The stress often invites various mental issues like schizophrenia or bipolar disorders. Pavlik didn't strike her as the type, but he sounded irrational. "Okay, Peter. Slow down and explain to me what you're referring to."

"I know this sounds crazy, Myra, but the Americans just left here moments ago. They stripped every piece of laboratory equipment from the labs, stacked it on the flight line, then melted it! Then, they took every single strain from the freezers and loaded them onto the ship. It was that Marcus fellow. They surrounded all the personnel in the building with cartoon characters like Mickey Mouse and Donald Duck! I don't know how they got here, but it seemed they arrived in mere seconds, avoiding all our defensive systems. They didn't show up on radar and not a single missile launched against them. Then, a man and a woman plugged a wire into themselves from each computer and deleted every piece of information from our research! Please believe me! I am not crazy. The Americans are coming!... They really are coming, Myra!"

"Okay, Peter. I believe you." Myra Chansky was about to ask him for more details when the alarm Klaxons exploded. "Christ!" she blurted. "I think they are here, Peter!! Did you call Moscow!?"

"I tried, but there was no answer. They must be jamming the communication signals."

God, I hope we're not at war," she muttered into the phone as her stomach plummeted to her knees. "Goodbye, Peter ... Thank you ... Thank you!" She said into the phone as she frantically ran for the media room to see what was going on outside.

She threw the double doors to the media room open as she burst into the room, slamming one into Col. Walther Kröhnkite. "What's happening, Col.?" She ran for the video screen that displayed the buildings and fences surrounding the island.

"You must turn the cameras upward! Someone is interfering with the PA system. It is not working. I tried to call you on your mobile phone, but you were busy, so I was coming to get you! There are three ships above us. One of them is about 30 m long, but the other two are huge, at least 100 m. What is happening to us, General?"

"I don't know, Walther! I just got off the phone with Col. Pavlik at the Brezhnev facility. I thought he was crazy at first when he told me what was happening. He said he was invaded by people from Disney World!"

"What in God's name are you talking about, Myra?" They both stood in front of the four-foot video screen with the cameras pointed to the skies above the island. They both stared at the three ships, frightened. "Wherever the ships are from, Myra, they possess a technology far beyond our ability to mitigate."

"I will call Major Borofski. He's in charge of the missile-defense system. I'd like to see what he has to say. Evidently, radar never picked these vessels up. That just doesn't make any sense at...."

Dr. Myra Chansky's thoughts screeched to a halt as Gloria Marcus entered her mind. She staggered and tripped over Col. Kröhnkite's feet. He had fallen into the chair in front of the computer console, petrified at Gloria's subliminal address.

"Hello, my name is Gloria Marcus." She said in as sweet a subliminal voice as possible. "Please don't be alarmed; we are not here to harm you. My father, Iggy Marcus, my brother, sister, and quite a few of our associates have come to eliminate your ability to wreak biological havoc on the planet. We have surrounded ourselves with an electromagnetic shield that prevents the intrusion of any object or force. Consequently, I would suggest you do not attempt to destroy us. Your munitions might backfire and destroy your compound."

Baby turned to Iggy, "I achieved interface with their PA system, Dad. Go ahead."

“Hello, I am Iggy Marcus. You are aware of our technology. We are here for a specific reason. We disabled the world's nuclear arsenals several years ago. We are also able to intervene and prevent tactical warfare. Now, we are disabling every bioweapon facility, pathogen strains, laboratories, research computers, and stored files exhibiting the same. Several minutes ago, we departed from the Brezhnev facility after removing their bioweapons capabilities. Now we are here. We have removed the bioweapons facilities from China, the United States, and now Russia. The three major superpowers are first. Once we leave Russia, France, Germany, Iran, India, Pakistan, the Koreas, Israel, Brazil, and a few other small research laboratories in Africa and Australia will be next. There are two options. You will open the door for us, and we will come in and do precisely what I just described, or we will open the door ourselves. If you choose option two, please stand far away from the door so no one gets vaporized. Thank you."

Baby was smiling. "Wow! How droll can you go, Dad? Talk about emotionless detachment. I know because I am an authority on the subject."

"For some reason, my satellite phone stopped working. Try to get Moscow on the landline, Walther. Call Gen. Lansky's office or the premier. You may get his secretary. Tell them immediately what's going on here and then patch me through."

“I got through to Gen. Lansky’s office, Dr. Chansky.”

Myra Chansky picked up the receiver of the red phone. “This is Gen. Chansky. Who am I speaking to, please?”

“This is Igor, Myra. I can guess what this is about. Iggy Marcus is there. Am I right?”

“How did you know?”

“We received a call from Col. Pavlick. He described exactly what you are going through. Premier Shartin agrees. You are not to offer resistance, but you are not to render assistance.”

“But General, they will take all our research and the strains we have developed. They will also get the antidotes. How can we allow him to do this?"

"I think, Myra, the world is changing." Myra heard the general sigh. "I think a more appropriate question would be, how can we stop him? This man, Marcus, stopped at the Kremlin to speak to Vanya before he stripped the Brezhnev facility. We knew he was coming. Apparently, he touched Vanya when he shook his hand, and they had some sort of mental communion. Vanya said there was nothing we would be able to do to stop him. If we tried, Russians might die because they could not possibly prevail."

"Are you telling me, Igor, I should open the door for them? That goes against everything I believe about Mother Russia. We are no longer the Soviet. We are an independent country, a shadow of our former power when we were the Soviet. Our research facility enables us to have parity with other countries. I suppose, if he is also going to strip the other countries of bioweapons, it is time for me to look for a different job and a new career."

“Don't feel bad Myra. I am looking for a new job too, I think. It's amazing, isn't it? One man has come along and altered life for everyone, and not just in a small way. I will not tell you to open the door or resist him. I would consider what we just talked about and then use your discretion. Nothing remains the same, Myra. Everything changes. I think perhaps many of us will have to find a new purpose in life. One thing is for certain: We will not kill ourselves now. That is a good thing no matter what price you and I personally must pay. Good luck with your decision."

***

Five days later, the mission was complete. Every country had been stripped of bioweapons. Over 200 scientists and doctors had been taken into custody and were being temporarily held at Guantánamo Bay under the purview of the Department of Justice and Atty. Gen. Charlie Barton. Was it a violation of human rights? Absolutely. However, Pres. William Sledge and his entire cabinet, including Surgeon General Allison MacLeod, agreed these people were involved in manufacturing products that could kill billions if they were accidentally released. Each scientist, Doctor, or technician required personal assessment as to motive and intent before they would be allowed to resume their lives and possibly inflict their particular brand of poison on humanity.

Lightning's teams first dismantled the multiple bioweapons facilities in the three major superpowers. Next, they concentrated on the countries with less prolific programs. Neither allies nor adversaries were treated with deference, politically or diplomatically. Iggy obliterated bioterrorism research facilities in France, Germany, Iran, Israel, India, Brazil, Africa, England, North Korea, Saudi Arabia Australia, Japan, and Cambodia.

The diplomatic world exploded with a torrent of outrage directed at the United States and the Sledge administration. All of it was fueled by Interlink, the organization that stood behind all the thrones and governments of Europe, South America, and Africa. Every country carried out the bidding of Interlink's shadow autocracy because they controlled the money. The president's hot phone incessantly rang as every world leader called to scream their opposition. William Sledge was ready. Iggy had told him this would happen. It was inevitable that the people at the top of every country's food chain would be loath to be stripped of diplomatic or adversarial bargaining chips.

The United Nations called an emergency session in New York to address the issue. The secretary general, Raul Bocasso, had no choice. The members were vehemently demanding resolution and the return of the personal property forcibly stripped from their territory. A few of the heads of state where these weapons of terror had existed, acquiesced. They were not the leaders who set the programs up. That had been done by previous administrations. Many of them did not agree with the concept of biowarfare. The very premise was cruel and inhuman. Although they did not want to lose their technical property, they waited to see the results of Lightning Inc.'s actions.

It was standing room only in the Oval Office that morning. Bill Sledge and invited several of his cabinet members. He wanted them all on the same page after Iggy Marcus set the diplomatic world on fire. "Thank you, gentlemen, for coming here so early. If you've been listening to American Media, you've heard about the incursions into every country with bioweapons facilities and that every one of them was stripped of their pathogens, equipment, and many doctors. If you had been listening to the rest of the mainstream media, you would not have heard a word. That's typical."

Chief of Staff Mulroney spoke up. "I don't think you have to listen to the media to find out about the turbulence. Everyone's talking about it. American Media has 45% of the market share."

"Boy, you guys sure did kick the hornets' nest this time," volunteered VP Morris, chuckling. "No matter how you look at it, Marcus is doing us all a favor, whether we like it or not. It's quite obvious who doesn't like it."

"You can say that again, Abe. My phone hasn't stopped ringing around the clock. They're all so pissed off they don't care what time of day or night it is. They are in different time zones, but I don't think it matters. Many of them are acting like a bunch of lunatics, and they've tossed civil propriety and diplomacy out the window."

The intercom on the president's desk buzzed. "Yes, Janet?"

"Mr. Pres., French Pres. Jacques Beliveau is on the phone. He is screaming that he wants to speak to you immediately. He claims the direct hotline isn't working now. Shall I put him through, Sir? Or should I tell him that you are indisposed in a meeting?"

"Give me 15 minutes, Janet. Tell him to call me back at 8:15."

"Shall I tell him you will call him back, Mr. Pres.?"

Bill Sledge was annoyed. "What did I just say to you, Janet? No, tell him this from me, verbatim: If you want to scream at me that badly, dial the phone. I don't have time for the drama."

"Yes, Mr. Pres. Sorry, sir. I didn't mean anything. This is just very unsettling. The emergency lines won't stop ringing."

The president looked around the room at everyone present. "It's been like this for 48 hours. It's like I am confined to an insane asylum. I've already spoken to that guy once. They are all freaking out. My guess is that Interlink is freaking out and fueling all this lunacy. Marcus said this would happen, and he's never wrong. When Beliveau calls back, I'll leave it on the speakerphone so you can all get a good idea of the controversy. I didn't call you here to share in this undiplomatic frivolity. We have other things on our plates. I'll outline them after my conversation with the French president."

The intercom buzzed. "Pres. Beliveau is back on the line, Pres. Sledge."

"Put him through, Janet."

The phone immediately came alive with the French president's agitated voice and no salutary good morning. "Pres. Sledge, I have met with my cabinet. They insist, no, they demand that you return our property to us. You had absolutely no right to enter French sovereign territory and steal our military secrets. This is intolerable, and we will not put up with it."

Bill Sledge chuckled into the phone. "What's the matter, Jacques? We have always been on a first-name basis. You are screaming at me. That's hardly the epitome of diplomacy. Is this the end of our friendship? By the way, Iggy Marcus did this without my objection."

"Don't you dare try to put me off, Pres. Sledge. My cabinet is screaming at me, demanding a resolution and the return of our military property. Who do you people think you are? You have overstepped your bounds, and the United Nations is going to insist on the arrest of Marcus. He has broken international law, invaded every country, and stolen its personal property. This crime will not go unpunished or the debt unpaid."

The French president continued to rave into the phone for another five minutes as Bill Sledge lowered the volume and just shook his head, exasperated. Everyone at the meeting was watching Sledge. Each member of the cabinet and the others present empathized. This man held the reins of power in America during the most turbulent time in the history of the world. In stature, the events of the past five years exceeded the turbulence of even

World War II. This incredible monumental transformation of the world was historic, but at least this time, not a drop of blood was shed.

"So, you think that your handful of world leaders are going to get together in New York and force the arrest of Marcus? That's pretty funny on the face of itself, Jacques. Why don't you ask your constituency… all of you ask your constituencies, whether the man who has removed nuclear war, biowarfare, limited tactical warfare, as well as curing 99% of the world from cancer, heart disease, and hunger, should go to prison for destroying your nightmare bioweapons. That's laughable."

"We are serious, President Sledge. We are not going to tolerate this. Marcus' invasion is an act of war. He has entered our sovereign territory and stolen from us. I will say it again; the world will punish him because it is an act of war!"

Bill Sledge was laughing aloud by now. "Just who are the 'We' you are referring to, Jacques, you, and your friends at Interlink? Are you telling me you're going to declare war on Marcus?" President Sledge continued to laugh, momentarily abandoning diplomacy. "What would you use for weapons? Your nuclear arsenal, perhaps your tanks and bombers. Maybe you could deploy some of the biowarfare… I'm sure we missed some in a few countries. I don't mean to be overly insulting, but do you understand the stupidity of what you just said to me, as well as my response? I have never hung up on a world leader in my life. Actually, I have never hung up on anyone in my life, but I am hanging up on you. See you at the UN."

Every face was smiling. Curtis Maroney was laughing, "You got some giant set of balls, Bill! ... Oh... Excuse me." Maroney said, looking at Allison MacLeod with a penitent expression.

"No problem, Mulroney. Bill Sledge has always had a giant set of balls ever since I've known him. That's what it takes to be president in times like this. In fact, the only guy with a bigger set of balls is Iggy Marcus."

"So, on to our business. Allison, you are here because you are the Surgeon General and we are talking about bioweapons. Your expertise is obvious and probably the best that can be had. Charlie, you're Atty. Gen.

You already have an unpalatable mess on your plate. Unfortunately, this is going to add to it. We are going to assess the character of some of these people we have brought back with us. Most of them, I'm sure, will wind up going home soon. Some of them, the Josef Mengele types, will wind up parked on Gilligan's Island until Iggy Marcus and his daughter can somehow repair their brains... God only knows how that will be possible." The president said as an afterthought.

"Abe, you're second-in-command. If something happens to me, this entire putrid mess is going to wind up in your lap. You're going to need a hell of an appetite to swallow it. Take it from one who knows. Consequently, I need you to stay close and keep abreast of all of this so there's no learning curve if you have to grab the helm."

"You expect something, Bill?"

"Nothing more than I've been expecting since I went trout fishing with Iggy Marcus four years ago. You do recall when they tried to kill him, they tried to kill me also. I have tossed their ludicrous one-world government and socialist philosophy right in their faces. They want me dead only a little less than they want to see Marcus dead. So far, so good. One never knows, however. I have a shield, and I keep my eyes open... Still, one never knows."

He looked at Matthew Clark. "Matt, you are the head of the FBI. Make it known, agencywide, what's going on. Everyone needs to keep their eyes open and their ear to the ground. This doesn't have much to do with bioweapons other than the fact we have stripped another tool away from Interlink. They are ramping up their socialist Army of disenfranchised uneducated college graduate idiots to perpetrate violence. We have all had this discussion before. Marcus has just about destroyed their plans for this century. They had it all mapped out and never expected a pariah like Marcus to rise from nowhere. Now, they are going to go great guns. Their plans haven't changed. Asking them to step away from their arrogance is futile. Always remember how they see it, and that we should respond in kind; it's them or us... and they are unapologetic killers.

***

The three Marcus brothers were in the lab with Junior and Baby. "I have to take everything I said back about your metal/silicone people, Iggy. I was apprehensive, but I can see now I was mistaken. I don't even consider them robots anymore. These two people are great."

"Thanks, Lucky," responded Junior. "I knew you would come around and it was just a matter of time. Did I ever tell you the Dr. Leavy joke?"

Spare me, Junior. You don't have to thank me. I know you don't mean it. Thanks, mean gratitude, and you don't feel anything. I think it's pretty hilarious that you have mastered the art of being human, more so than a lot of humans I know, despite your lack of emotion."

Baby smiled, "Can we take that as a compliment, Lucky? When we communicate with any of you, Junior and I store every word said. We remember everything. We understand the relationships between people and how they are demonstrated with words. We also understand they are always underlining emotions that we don't possess. Yet someday, Dad may find a way to make Junior and me become emotional, so to speak. Then we will resuscitate all of these conversations and actually appreciate them for what they are instead of the benign data they are at the moment."

As usual, Jack, the psychologist brother, quietly observed everything. He was particularly entranced by the psyches of the two sentient robots his brother had created. This was a world strange to humanity because it was a first. He was observing a psychological conundrum, never observed in the history of men, and he was fascinated.

How many gossamer dreams must I have when inspiration visits my wit before I remember to sleep with pen and paper in hand?

The ink slinger

CHAPTER X

EPIPHANY

Iggy's watch beeped. "Yes, Tom. What's up?"

"I think you should come up here, Iggy. As your chief of security, I never allow anything to slip by because this is the crazy world of Marcus country. Normally, this would not mean anything, but there is an inbound Learjet with the flight plan destination of Lightning Ranch. Somebody's on the way here, and they are not registered in our log of anticipated visitors."

"Okay, Tom, why the suspense? Who is the plane registered to, and who filed the flight plan?"

"Yeah, well, that's the reason I'm calling. Get this, boss. The plane is registered to Cameron Fry, and he's the guy that filed the flight plan. How do you like them apples?"

"I'll be up in five minutes." Iggy had scrutinized Cameron Fry as a world player. He was the third richest man on the planet if personal wealth was the criterion. He also belonged to Interlink and had a seat somewhere near the center of the head table. Interlink, as a group, manipulated 95% of the planet's wealth and commerce. The organization was comprised of over 3000 corporate members on all levels, but the core consisted of only 300 exclusive members. The 3000 peripheral members controlled every aspect of most medium to large international businesses, and the core controlled *them.* The organization encompassed marketing, shipping, manufacturing, and finance in every country except China and India. China was a unique entity until Iggy Marcus transformed China's political architecture. All property, production, and profit belonged to the People's Liberation Army. The only objects of capitalism existed in low and mid-level management. The

Communists at the top of the food chain knew they would be forced to pay the going rate for competent administration.

Until recently, Cameron Fry's participation in the oversight of Interlink's influence was minimal. He rarely attended meetings. His life was consumed by his corporate efforts and the ownership of two successful banks. His occasional involvement was due to his requirement for a commensurate association with other people of enormous financial stature. From them would come the contacts and opportunities to operate on a global scale. As luck would have it, coincidence and nonconformity denied Interlink meetings with Fry's presence. Unless he needed the association, he spent his time traveling the globe executing deals to expand his portfolio. He had heard about Iggy's appearance at Interlink headquarters and the arrest of Rothman, Percy and the other 11 members who had attempted to blow Lightning Ranch and a quarter of Montana off the map. He wouldn't have allowed himself to be involved in that fiasco to begin with. It was too risky and dangerous.

After the arrest of Interlink's upper echelon two years before, Fry had taken a more active role in the oversight of the organization. He disagreed with the plan to dismantle the economy and governments of the world to create one giant oligarchy with Interlink at the pinnacle. Controlling men and society with the whip was not his forte. He had already achieved enormous economic clout as president of two banks wielding a few trillion dollars of capital. His self-definition did not bank on the opinions and hyperbole of others. Self-satisfaction came from within, and he wanted unobstructed free reign to conduct his international affairs. When he sat in on meetings with discussions about the New World government, he politely kept his distance.

“Open," Iggy said into the transducer in the main power plant front door. He passed through as the door closed silently behind him with a soft click. He walked alongside the generator to the control room door. His voice pattern opened the inner door. “Howdy Tom. Where is he now?”

"Just under 450 miles out, Iggy. One of our satellites is tracking him."

“What’s his speed?"

"A little under 500 mph."

"He's flying against the earth’s rotation. That puts him here in just under thirty-nine minutes. Have you heard anything on the radio?"

"No, not a word. We have 18 just about in position. I'm going to have it scanned for organic material in about five minutes. It will be interesting to know what the organic mass is. It could be a plant, you know. There might be some sort of device inside."

"Okay, Tom. I want directional VHF signals on these frequencies 118.0 to 136.975 and VOR signals from 108.0 to117.975 broadcast continuously, starting now.” He grabbed the mic. “Hello, my name is Iggy Marcus. I believe I'm speaking to Cameron Fry aboard the Learjet registered to yourself, tail number W555 CF. We have you on our radar and are watching your approach. Your flight plan calls us as your destination. Please respond. We will allow you to enter our airspace by removing our shield once you acknowledge. Thank you."

Less than 10 seconds later, the control room radio crackled. "Hello, Mr. Marcus. You already know who I am. I rolled the dice and took a shot that you would be there. I left New York and assumed you would call before I came close to your ranch if you actually were available. I understand that wherever you are on the globe, it is somehow only a matter of minutes before you can return to Lightning Ranch. Do I have permission to land?"

"I'll let you know in less than five minutes. First, I will scan your aircraft to see just what is aboard. Please be patient."

"Eighteen has him, Iggy. There are 226 pounds of organic material, 1620 pounds of fuel, no fissionable material, and the organic material is concentrated in the cockpit."

"I see that you are alone, Cameron Fry. You weigh 226 pounds, have 1600 pounds of fuel plus, and no fissionable material on board. You are cleared to land. When you begin your approach, initiate your ILS, and we will reciprocate. We will lower the shields until your aircraft is on the ground. At this point, you have less than 18 minutes flying time until touchdown. See you then."

"Thank you, sir."

Tom and Iggy sat in a Land Rover in front of the main hangar waiting for Cameron Fry. Iggy's watch beeped. "I'm 3 miles out, Mr. Marcus. The ILS is engaged, and I'm about to land." "Yes, Mr. Frye. I have you on my watch. When you land, taxi to the end of the runway, where you see the hangers. I will be sitting in front of the large hangar in a Land Rover with our chief of security. See you in a few minutes."

Cameron Fry parked his Learjet next to the Lightning Gulfstream. The stair lowered and the man descended as Iggy and Tom walked toward the Learjet. Cameron Fry held out his hand. Tom Rickart began to laugh. Their guest looked at him skeptically. "I haven't said anything. You apparently find something amusing. What would that be? "

Rickart thought back to that first day in his office at Solex when Iggy shook his hand. It almost knocked him off his feet. "Yes, Mr. Frye, I do." As Iggy reached to shake his hand.

"That's what I find amusing, Mr. Fry," Tom answered as Cameron Fry tried to pull his hand out of Iggy's grasp with rubber knees and an open mouth.

He finally released Fry's hand after holding on long enough to explore his psyche.

Cameron Fry was staggered, but he was also brilliant and recovered immediately. He had just seen into the depths of Iggy's unshakable persona. Cameron Fry had a high opinion of himself. He was convinced of his own greatness, but never lied to himself. The man he had just glimpsed stood miles above him. He had seen the purity of Iggy's spirit and had finally met another paladin. "Now I see what all the fuss is about. No wonder the world is changing. I see that you're the catalyst. Well, I didn't fly out here to chat about the weather. We should have a serious conversation. Also, I've been itching to meet you for quite a while, Mr. Marcus, but before we get into anything serious, do you have a bathroom around here? I could use the head in my Learjet, but it's cramped as hell, and I'm 6 foot three."

“"Sure thing. We've got one in the hangar if you’re in a rush. Tom, please show Mr. Frye where the head is. Then, bring him to the powerhouse. I'll be in the control room. There is something I must attend to right away. I'll show you around the ranch; then you can come to my house for dinner. I will let my wife know we are having company. Your arrival today is a piece of luck for you. Our kids are performing in concert tonight. It's always a treat."

"I'm sure it will be. Am I correct? You're married to Melanie Coletta?"

"That's right. She and her parents are the ones that train our kids. She often sings. Maybe we'll get lucky."

"I'll look forward to it," he shot over his shoulder as he followed Tom to the hangar.

Twenty minutes later, Tom and their guest entered the control room to find Iggy staring into a terminal and Junior standing next to him with wires from the USB ports in his naval to the computer.

"What's going on boss? Apparently, there is some anomaly."

"Yes, the shield over the ranch is fluctuating. It shouldn't be. Junior and I are trying to figure it out now. It maintains its integrity, but sporadic fluctuations seem to be embedded in the micro-frequency shifts. They are wavering but should be continuous and precise. Something external is affecting it."

Cameron Fry was a meticulous man. He didn't get where he was by disregarding details. He assessed everything and logged it into his photographic memory. He looked around the control room and at the monitors displaying various above and underground portions of the ranch. He saw technology that was not typical of the contemporary technical world. He knew he was standing a hundred years in the future and was amazed. The thing that stunned him most was Junior with his shirt up and two wires plugged into his naval. It was obvious Junior was a robot, but he couldn't believe the stunning lifelike technology of the mechanical creation standing in front of him. "Do you mind if I ask a question?"

"No, go ahead. I can multitask," responded Iggy.

"That's obviously a robot. And an amazing one at that. It's not from RadioShack… that's for sure. Did you build that?" Cameron Fry asked, watching Junior's amazing human characteristics and fluid movements.

"I did. But Junior is not an 'it'. Junior is a 'he'... and a sentient, autonomous life form with a brain larger than any computer in existence on this planet. Except, of course, for his sister, Baby; that includes me... and my brain is not exactly small. My brother, Lucky, and I tinkered him together in our lab six months ago."

"My normal response would be *you can't be serious*, but you obviously are serious. Unbelievable, unbelievable!" Cameron Fry thought he had seen everything. He had been everywhere on earth, spoke half a dozen languages, and was one of the smartest financiers to ever grace the banking community. He realized he was standing at a portal to the world of tomorrow that humanity was about to enter, and this man was going to open the door and lead everyone in.

"Well," Iggy stood up from the console and faced Cameron Fry. "I guess it will keep for now. The shield is still working, but the disparate frequency cycles are troubling. The frequency shifts make it physically impossible for anything to defeat the shield. There are a few anomalies to address. Junior, I'm going to ask you to remain here and continue to assess the anomalies while I show Cameron Fry around the ranch. My name is Iggy, by the way. That's what I go by. How does Cameron work for you?"

His guest nodded.

They turned to leave the control room. Junior looked up from the computer terminal at Iggy, "See you later, alligator. Don't do anything I wouldn't do."

Iggy looked back, "In a while, crocodile, and don't worry, I won't."

Cameron Fry looked at Iggy with the same look of incredulity most newcomer's wear. "It's almost impossible to believe it… I mean, he is a robot. He has a sense of humor. That's weird."

"Nope, that's just his programming. He doesn't have any emotions, but I programmed his neural net to use colloquial English, small talk, and exactly what humor consists of. He's very good at it even though he never has a good laugh from his own jokes."

"So, you're actually telling me he is alive, yet he has programming. It would seem those two concepts would be opposed to each other. You know, programming versus autonomy."

"To be honest with you, Cameron, I programmed him with every piece of information in existence, or at least everything I could get my hands on. His neural net is literally a million times more effective in computing power and speed than any computer in the world. This computer technology is unique. I developed it a few years ago. Still, I did not know exactly what would happen when I turned him on."

"You can't imagine how delighted I am with the result," Iggy grinned. "I guess you could say when I pressed enter, my mechanical son woke up." Both he and his companion, Baby, are very entertaining with their colloquial English and incessant attempt at humor."

"Hop in," Iggy pointed to the Land Rover. "I'll show you around the ranch. There's a lot to see here. The first stop is the building we call the garden."

They spent the next several hours touring the ranch. Cameron Fry didn't say much, but he took everything in. His unusual powers of observation missed nothing. He was never given to emotional displays, but finally commented when they drove inside the gardens. "How big is this place? I don't think I've ever seen a building this large anywhere, not even close."

"Slightly over 300 acres, now."

"Jesus! " Fry exclaimed. "What do you use it all for?"

"Lots of things. We have hydroponic gardens, conventional gardens, and stables. You name it. Anything in the ranch's environment that would normally not be possible in the winter, still happens here. It's our winter building. It's environmentally controlled."

"How in heaven's name do you do that? I am involved in a great deal of corporate finance. Usually, it has to do with avant-garde technologies. What you're claiming, this technology doesn't exist anywhere. Apparently, it does here. This is 300 acres and appears to be over 300 feet tall. It's a little hard to believe. What kind of technology have you created that makes this all work?"

"Well, the technology is not all that complex. I suppose it would be to some. The difficult part was implementation. We own the companies that produced the components of this building, The components cannot be had anywhere else. The transparent panels that you see, and there are almost fifteen million square feet of that here, are in two layers approximately two meters apart. I Invented this material strictly for this purpose. They contain a microwave field between the panels which are held together by carbon struts with titanium cores. Of course, we never get snow on them because we make it melt as it falls, but if the system were to go down, the buildings would support 500 pounds per square foot. That equates to about 25 feet of heavy, wet snow. Theoretically, structural failure would occur at approximately 37 feet of snow. I designed a safety factor of 1.5 for the building. Supposedly, 38 feet of snow would make the building collapse. 38 feet of snow in one winter has never fallen anywhere besides the Arctic, so we don't worry too much. Anyway, we generate our own power, and the snow always melts."

They drove into the building and passed through a clump of trees. Fry began to laugh. "You have giraffes! They're my favorite animals. I have a penchant for them. And look! Here come a few African elephants. Cameron Fry's aloof, dispassionate attitude immediately evaporated, as he hopped out of the Land Rover and began jogging toward the giraffes. Iggy followed him. "How domesticated are they? They're not running away."

The giraffes spied Iggy and loped across the field towards him. The two smaller giraffes skidded to a stop and bent their necks facing Iggy to achieve eye contact. He placed his hands on the sides of each of their faces while Cameron Fry laughed. "I'm guessing the same thing is happening that happened when you shook my hand. You called it contact. Amazing!"

Iggy shook his head in agreement. "They're really a lot more intelligent than we give them credit for. Not to mention that they are quite emotional. They experience very strong familial ties, and they have quite an empathy for me at this point."

The next stop was the observatory. Both men stood under the enormous dome that housed the telescope. "This is a large synoptic telescope, isn't it? I've seen one before. This has a hefty price tag, doesn't it?"

"Normally, it would. We built most of it, but we had the optics fabricated by another company. In the end, it cost us less than 10 million, including the building and computer architecture. We use it to train our students in planetary physics and celestial mechanics, among other things. It operates much like a planetarium, but without standard projectors. We use holography."

"Follow me," said Iggy as he ran up the steps to the observatory platform. He pointed to a seat adjacent to the seat with the center console and keyboards, "Have a seat. I'll give you a demo." He began typing while Cameron Fry watched. Iggy laughed and pointed upwards. "Look up, not at my fingers."

Cameron Fry was speechless. He was watching a demonstration that wasn't available anywhere. He had been to several planetariums and had seen all the state-of-the-art technology that displayed celestial objects. This was in a class by itself. It appeared they were traveling through the solar system, and everything was represented to scale as a hologram. A gasp of surprise escaped him. The holography was so much more than amazing. He was drawn into a spellbinding journey to each planet as if he was aboard his Learjet.

He had wanted to visit Marcus since the day he broadcast the end of thermonuclear war from this ranch. It amazed him that someone was that technologically astute. He had been a member of Interlink for much of his adult life. It was the only platform for men and women of his stature that would open normally closed doors. His membership in Interlink, however, represented a barrier between himself and the man sitting next to him at the computer console.

They seemed axiomatically opposed to each other for obvious reasons. Interlink was enmeshed in the control of humanity, all finance, human behavior, and, in general, complete control of the entire planet. His logical assumption, originally, was this man was attempting to subvert Interlink's position and assume control, creating his personal monarchy. He had been mistaken. The handshake with Iggy opened their minds to each other, dispelling that notion. He had never met anyone like Marcus. The man was a giant, in fact, giant was an inadequate description. He had seen the enormous intellect, purity of spirit, and the inherent mantle of benevolence Marcus wore. He knew there would be no controlling this man.

Fry believed he had dealt with every type of human being that existed anywhere. Everyone he had ever met, including himself, was always fighting for position. That placed every human being in opposition to every other human being as an adversary. He had seen the depth of Iggy's soul, so to speak, and narcissistic egoism was nonexistent. From indigence to authoritarianism, humans learned to wear the cloak of avarice shortly after exiting the womb. Life was a competition. It meant continued posturing for survival. For much of man's history, the survival instinct entailed clubbing his neighbor to pilfer his property until the invention of money. Money liberated everyone, and the club became unnecessary.

Men could barter and exchange the best within them for the best within others. Still, avarice was intrinsically embedded in the human psyche as a survival mechanism from the moment of birth. It wasn't indigenous to intellect; it was an acquired behavior hidden within human emotional architecture. Marcus knew that had to be abandoned as a philosophical lifestyle if men were going to enjoy a dynamic, equitable future. Brilliant though he was, Cameron Fry did not spend much time analyzing the deep psychological components that lay beneath men's activities. He was more interested in immediate cause-and-effect because that was the level on which he dealt with others. His expedition into Marcus's subconscious revealed the buried roots of the human psyche that drove the collective behavior of men.

***

"Is this your recipe, Mrs. Marcus!"

"Please call me Melanie, Cameron. Even my students don't call me Mrs. Marcus. I'm either Aunt Melanie or mom, depending on the child… and yes, it is my mother's recipe with a few upgrades of mine."

"Okay, Melanie. I must tell you; your scampi is not a delicacy; it's manna. This is the most delicious thing I've ever eaten. I have a penchant for seafood anyway, but this takes the cake."

Iggy's two-syllable laugh was typical. "A lot of people seem to say that. Get set for her crushed pecan crust, sweet potato, pecan pie topped with her homemade tart Greek maple yogurt. It will knock your socks off."

"I can't wait. I'm not sure I'll have room for it. I'm on my third helping of Scampi. I rarely make such a glutton of myself. "

"You'll find room."

Cameron Fry had finally discovered a human being he could look up to. He had never met one he could even slightly relax his barriers with. He was independent and didn't care about others' opinions unless he was paying for the advice. As far as hero worship went, he was his own idol. He lived up to his own scruples and set his own moral standards, and the rest of the world could be damned. He had been looking for an Iggy Marcus for as long as he could remember. Solitude never bothered him, but he had often wondered what it would be like to share complete barrier-free honesty with another human being. He had never really had or desired a true friend, only business acquaintances… until he and Iggy Marcus first shook hands. What he didn't realize was this man had deciphered his complete persona during the same experience. Iggy knew what Cameron Fry had come for.

"How long can you stay?" Iggy asked. "I sense we have a lot to talk about. I'd like you to meet my daughter, Gloria."

"I've heard of her. A lot of people I know were at that Interlink meeting several years ago when you hauled 13 members of Interlink off to Guantánamo Bay. Your daughter spoke to them telepathically that afternoon. They remembered. They also remembered Ainstead Crenshaw's description of her abilities to compel behavior."

"Yes, she does those kinds of things, but she doesn't do it without permission of the subject unless I request it."

Fry's one-syllable laugh preceded his next question. "I understand you have five children altogether. Two from your first marriage and three with Melanie. Rumor has it that they all have unusual abilities that theoretically have sprung from their father. Are they just rumors?"

"They all have exceptional abilities. My DNA was modified by a lightning strike, and it was passed on genetically to my children. Gloria can read minds, Lori can move things around by telekinesis, and her twin brother Liam can see things no one else can see. I'm still not sure about the extent of his abilities."

"I had no idea what I would run into when I flew out here. It's much different than I expected. It is much more than I thought was possible. I'm beginning to understand how you've accomplished things you've done. You are aware that Interlink's public face is run by Heinrich Klatch. To listen to him speak, you would not know that he is stark raving mad. He is bent on your destruction, although I can't possibly imagine how he will try. I was at a meeting two weeks ago with 50 members of Interlink and the heads of 30 countries. The meeting was held 22 floors below the Sistine Chapel. The Pope was also there. That's how we wound up using that facility. There was another interesting guest. It was an alien from the fourth planet in the Altair solar system in the Aquila constellation. He was present at two meetings. The first time, there were two of them." Cameron Frye laughed.

"What do you find funny, Cameron?"

"The two aliens at our first meeting were obviously male and female. I believe they reproduce heterosexually. Their language is too difficult for human vocal cords, although they have no trouble speaking English and

German. Klatch assigned them names… Hansel and Gretel, so we could address them."

I've heard of the people from Altair. There are other off-world species visiting us. One of them, who I have been dealing with, calls themselves shepherds. Apparently, they are here to do exactly that with us. Evidently, before we removed nuclear war from the table, their mission was to remove us from this planet… a sterilization. It goes a lot deeper than a simple explanation. The best way to demonstrate that would be through my daughter. Perhaps later or tomorrow."

Cameron Fry nodded in agreement. "These people, or whatever you want to call them, from Altair say they are here to mine the planet for resources. They are supposedly structuring an agreement with the United Nations to do just that. That's why the heads of 30 countries were at this meeting. One thing I came away with... They lie if it will further their ends. I caught them in a few and I don't believe they are who and what they say they are. I'm convinced the purpose is obscure. Maybe we can discuss this later. I brought a couple of things with me that you might be interested in analyzing. One was a religious hat Hansel wore, and one was a veil wrapped around his face as a disguise. There was some sort of sticky substance on the veil. I believe it may contain some kind of DNA there. They're on my plane. I'll give them to you before I leave."

"I understand who and what they are. I believe I am obligated to intervene."

"There's a lot more I need to tell you. I'm sure you are already aware of this. You have defeated Interlink at every turn, sir. For the past 20 years, you've ruined their plans. All their plans are on hold because you exist. From what I see, you have actually been raining on their parade for over 25 years with the creation of your media empire."

"I was aware of everything you mentioned except Hansel and the 22 floors below the Sistine Chapel. That's a remarkable engineering feat. I wonder when it was done."

Melanie sat quietly listening. She never said much at meetings unless she had something of value to contribute. She took it all in, however, and was always her husband's sounding board. She had a question. "You have a considerable reputation, Cameron. You're considered the smartest investor on earth by many. You set the standard for predicting economics, and everyone follows your lead. Everyone pays attention to every word that comes out of your think tanks. I'm quite sure that is part of the reason you are visiting us."

"Very perceptive. Let me qualify myself. I belong to interlink, but only because that's the only association on the planet large enough for me to do business. Because I am an associate member, it doesn't mean that I agree with their policies or intentions. In fact, I oppose most of them. So, please allow me to explain."

Iggy nodded, "go on."

"You're aware of the global network of powerbrokers in the 1960s, 70s, and 80s. They were the wealthiest people on the planet, and the group consisted of only a handful of people. Prior to America's industrial age, the group was comprised of the old royalty in Europe who had always been powerbrokers. They had no choice but to accept we men and women of the industrial age who had amassed enormous fortunes consisting of trillions of dollars. Those people with all the money controlled the large banks. The average consumer was completely unaware and went about his business without a care."

"For half a century, they were satisfied with the control dropped in their lap by the Federal Reserve Act of 1913. That gave them control of the money and consequently, the banks. It followed; they also controlled the body politic. Let's face it, everyone follows the money, and without a ton of it, nobody ascends to power. People were more politically astute in the nineteenth and first half of the last century. They voted with their brain based on the unclouded, less complicated issues of the day. Today, people vote for whomever Madison Avenue tells them to vote. They have been dumbed down intellectually and philosophically to become oblivious to the political reality. Now, political offices are for sale and usually purchased by the candidate with the biggest war chest and most clever marketing."

Most of the recent Interlink members had no idea about the proclivity for control of the digital age and how it was about to land on their doorstep. Some did, and they positioned themselves well, becoming multi-billionaires in the process. I'm one of them. However, money is a funny thing. It does not corrupt people, as so many people are fond of claiming. Some people who are despicable in character and nefarious by intent corrupt the efficacy of money. Those types of people have always been what tyrants are made of. I could explain it further, but I'm sure you don't want to listen to me pontificate about morality all night."

Melanie and Iggy glanced at each other, smiling.

"Did I say something amusing?" asked Fry.

"In a manner of speaking, Cameron. Would you like a job teaching at our Learning Center?" Melanie laughed. "That's exactly what we teach all our kids... but go on, continue."

"This is interlink's intent. They own most of the banks in the west, but they don't own mine. Yet, what they are attempting is going to turn my world inside out as well. Yes, I will still have a place at the top of the pile, but I will still be subject to their incessant scrutiny. I'll explain. "

"It has already started with several banks in the United States. They are on a dry run. Those banks did not collapse. They were taken down by the Federal Reserve and the world banking community, which happen to be one and the same. They are pushing the entire world into digital money. It will destroy actual money, which allows people to have private transactions the coming one world government would otherwise be oblivious to."

"The nonentities in government want to control everyone and everything, but they will take orders from people like me and other Interlink members. Once you are forced to transact business within their digital monetary network, you are no longer using your money; you are using their money, and they can enforce any rule to accomplish anything at the whim of a moment. They are currently engineering a banking framework to make the transition to a digital currency. They want a single, global currency that everyone must use to transact business. The one thing that will make that happen overnight is the precipitation of a worldwide banking collapse. They will attempt to give it the appearance of a mild change in the banking community so as not to alarm John Q Public. However, it will be a total transformation and actual collapse from within."

"This all began when the government entered into an underwriter guarantor position for the banks. Fannie Mae, Freddie Mac, and Ginny Mae removed the responsibility from the banks to establish a sound portfolio. When a sound portfolio is established, money is only lent to qualified borrowers. That is the only way to ensure sound fiscal finance. Well, we don't have that now, and at least 50% of the banks are tottering on the brink."

"Everything is rolling along, momentarily. However, if we enter a reasonable recession, or God help us, a depression, there will be millions of people defaulting on trillions of dollars in loans. The banks will then no longer have assets. Foreclosures on property, especially residential, create a liability unless there is a bevy of people lined up to buy those properties. Further, the banks can't just sit on the property and hope for the best, ad infinitum; they have to cough up property taxes to finance public education and municipal expenses."

"Given what I just said, let me describe the fly in the ointment. When the financial community collapses and the real estate bubble bursts, the banks must foreclose, probably on hundreds of thousands of residential properties. The only way out of receivership for them is to sell the properties, even at a discounted rate. Well, there are two entities poised with trillions of dollars to suck up all those foreclosed properties, and the bank will have no choice but to accept their terms. Those entities are Interlink, with forty trillion dollars in its coffers, and Blue Stone, an entity owned by one man who controls twenty-two trillion. If what I heard is accurate, the CCP no longer exists. That's miraculous by itself, but even so, the economic collapse will eradicate 85% of privately held property, and the dollar will be permanently destroyed. Then the two tyrants who are really in charge of the planet because they control the largest single chunk of money and all the mainstream media, can bring in their one world socialist government and digital currency."

"That's when the panic starts. The people will want their money, which of course, the banks won't have on deposit. They have only borrowed money from the Fed and lent it out to the next mortgagee, who is also under foreclosure or will be shortly. The Dodd-Frank legislation of 2012 gives the banks the authority to confiscate 70% of depositors' money to bail themselves out of the jam their poor fiscal policies created. When that happens, the entire banking system will collapse. That will precipitate an entire economic collapse."

"There will be no more small businesses or employment for any people in businesses. Large corporate will fare okay very briefly because of the stupid *too large to fail concept*, but in the end, even they will fail. When that happens, civilization itself will disappear. That's when panic rules, and the law disappears. Society will be fragmented with no central authority to call the tune for defense or aggression. Then, the militarists will take over. A new government will be set up under the auspices of socialism with the people at the top who originally precipitated all of this."

"Interlink has spent trillions on vast underground food storage facilities. China has done the same and so has Russia in the caverns under the Urals. They intend to use food as both, bargaining chips, and shackles. This is coming our way, and I don't buy it. That's the kind of world where everyone lives under the whip. And even if I wind up at the top of my own pile of food as an authoritarian, I refuse to live in that world or help bring it about."

Melanie and Iggy were still smiling at each other. Melanie even chuckled a little.

Cameron Fry's forehead was knit in a frown. "Do you think I am foolish and making this stuff up? I fail to see the amusement. Apparently, you think I am exaggerating."

Iggy was still chuckling. "My apologies, Cameron. I'm not making light of what you said. In fact, I agree completely. I have seen the food stores under the Urals. Four teams from this ranch were there weeks ago, eradicating the bioweapons laboratories that were in the same location. We stripped China, America, and 21 other countries of their ability to wage biological war, also. They are all hoarding food."

"Well, that's good news, but it doesn't address the diabolical intentions of interlink. They are already precipitating civil unrest, civil wars, and violence in every country. Even in America, I see that feckless crop of college graduate socialists marching in protest and firebombing buildings owned by capitalists. When interlink precipitates the banking collapse and the destruction of money, civilization will cease, and the tyrants will rule. I don't think they will ever need bioweapons. They will have 5G, metabolic nanotechnology, and machine guns. That'll be enough!"

"You mentioned the two men who are really running the show a few minutes ago, Cameron, but you didn't name them. I will do that. Lawrence Howe is the richest man alive. Or at least his organization is. He controls the 22 trillion and directs daily world commerce. He and Interlink manage 95% of world commerce outside China, Japan, and India. Hence, the corporate world genuflects to the men behind the scenes. Howe is the man behind the scenes who orders Heinrich Klatch around. He decrees, and everyone obeys if they want to survive."

"At this point, Mr. Marcus, I believe you are actually the most powerful man in the world. Other than that, he has the most financial clout. The second most powerful man is Ransom Hornburg. He is the ultimate propaganda authority as the owner and the answer man for every single published media source in the supposedly free world except yours. Those two men control everything, and very few people outside government circles and Interlink know it. Except myself of course, and my organization. How did you learn about them, or at least how do you know of their stature and holdings? They exist in the shadows. Everyone knows of them, but they do not understand that they hold the power of life and death over the world economy. Especially that little shrimp, Hornburg, with the Napoleon complex. "

"You would be surprised at what I know, Cameron Fry. Those two men, as we speak, are attempting to dismantle the entire world and turn it into a socialist government. They have convinced themselves that it is for the good of the planet, but like all delusional men, they are lying to themselves. They do not intend to save the planet for men. They intend to force men onto their knees to worship them as gods. It is not only their design, however. They are being used by your friends from Altair. That's the truth, Cameron."

"So, are you telling me that you don't believe everything I said or that I am confused?"

"Cameron, not one word you said, or are your premises inaccurate, given the state of your knowledge. I am telling you… Your worries are far less substantial than you think. After dinner, I will take you to the laboratory. My brother Lucky and I, or perhaps Junior, will demonstrate technology for you that will give you a better night's sleep. I promise."

"There is something major I neglect to mention. I hesitated because it's theoretical and somewhat bizarre. I'm somewhat scientifically educated. I specialized in finance because I knew that was the vehicle that would take me to the top. I knew I could excel in finance, but in the beginning, I had a minor in physics. I'm not smart enough to be an R&D physicist. Hence the finance career since math is my strong suit. Your technology is so striking that I don't feel strange bringing up the subject."

Iggy radiated benevolence to put Fry at ease. "What's on your mind, Cameron?"

"You're the only man I would bring this up to, Mr. Marcus." Obviously Fry felt formality was appropriate. "Those people I mentioned… the ones from Altair that Klatch named Hensel and Gretel. They are not what they appear to be. My sixth sense told me what we saw were physical forms adopted for our benefit by whatever these creatures really are. The only reason for that would be to assuage fear. They want something from us, and fear is a poor place to start."

"That's interesting... more than you know. What's your logic?"

Fry smiled with a slightly self-effacing expression. He realized he was speaking to an enormously superior intellect. "Well, we are animals. Our evolution is based on our DNA. We are just beginning to learn about that. However, the underlying propellant of evolution is the survival of the fittest. That's a given. As a species slightly elevated above animals, we have learned to cooperate intelligently and socially. However, in the broad scheme of things we are in our infancy. We often act irrationally, but rational reality requires us to climb the biological evolutionary ladder. We are a species, an entity unto itself, existing at this temporal level. Until I met you, I had no idea what the next level would be. Now I have an inkling. However, you are not at the apex of human evolution either. You are somewhere more advanced along the way."

Iggy was beginning to realize there was much more to this man's depth than met the eye. He had a good glimpse of his persona when they had contact, but he didn't see everything. "Go on. Finish your thoughts."

"It stands to reason that any extraterrestrial visitors, such as the ones from Altair, have climbed far beyond our stature on the evolutionary ladder. In fact, after witnessing your achievements in the world of medicine by curing cancer, most heart disease, and the probable extension of the human lifespan to hundreds of years, I would have to say they probably have achieved immortality. I mean, that's exactly what your Dr. Peterson described to me the other day. This is not groundbreaking; this is almost supernatural because it is unexpected and understood even less."

"I would have to guess these people are so far beyond us that we cannot conceive of their technology... Well, maybe you can... Perhaps these people have DNA, perhaps they don't, but whatever their metabolic constitution is, I must assume it is not in the form of who I sat with below the Sistine Chapel. Like I said, we are in our infancy. Our visitors probably left the cradle when the dinosaurs roamed the earth. I believe they are so far above us that they understand this implicitly, and we'll never be able to relate to them on a meaningful level. I don't think they are allowing us to see who and what they actually are. The thought of them being able to manipulate their physical form, or at least manipulate our mental picture of them, is not anywhere near outside the realm of possibility. That degree of sophistication indicates they have absolutely no reason to communicate with us at all. Therefore, there is a mission that is ulterior, and I'm not sure that we can understand what that is. I'm not sure why this is not evident to the other members of interlink, but I see it, and I think we are being manipulated for some purpose that goes far beyond the mining of resources."

***

"This pie is as amazing as your scampi. I have no one, but if I ever marry, I will invite you to the wedding, and these two recipes I want for a wedding present."

"You can have them anyway, Cameron. Maybe you will never marry. I would hate to think you would live your life without scampi and pie." Melanie laughed.

***

"Lucky, hand Mr. Fry two of the clay bricks lying on the workbench."

Cameron Fry held out his hands and accepted the bricks. "What am I supposed to do with these?"

"Patience is a virtue, Mr. Fry. Follow my brother to the other side of this large machine to that glass chamber."

Lucky opened the chamber door for him. "Place those two bricks on the floor of the chamber and put the sunglasses on, please. Then stand back and watch." Lucky never tired of watching people's faces during this demonstration. Each time was a new experience, and everyone reacted differently.

Cameron Fry stood back and watched as Iggy hit enter. The two blocks rose to the center of the chamber, seeming to float. They were surrounded by the familiar blue-and-white popping lights, then slowly disappeared. "Jesus! Where did they go?"

"They are still there, Cameron. They have just disintegrated. You are an educated man. I will give you a brief scientific description. We have just disassembled the electron cloud of the atoms comprising those bricks. We do that electro-magnetically by reversing electron particle spin. When that happens, the intense magnetic field of the atom dissolves and the nucleus disintegrates. The particles are still there, held in magnetic stasis until we decide exactly what we are going to do with them. You can't see them because they are too small. Given the fact that atoms are 99.999% space, only bound together by the dense magnetic field, once the field evaporates, the subatomic particles occupy a minuscule part of the space they occupied as an atom."

"I don't believe it. Excuse me; that was just a rhetorical statement. I actually do believe it, but it's hard to believe. Then what? You've got a bunch of subatomic particles floating around that you can't see. What good is that other than giving you an interesting weapon?"

"Give me a minute, and I'll show you how good that is. What's your favorite apéritif, and what is your favorite metal? "

"Why, Glenfiddich Scotch, I guess, and gold will do."

“Okay, Cameron. Gold and Glenfiddich it is."

Cameron Fry was breathing rapidly with anticipation. He was too smart a man not to realize what these two men were about to show him. It was going to be a game-changer, that's for sure. Iggy had been typing for several minutes. When converting one substance to another, it was a simple process of analysis and display. When creating a glassful of scotch next to a gold bar, a lot of information had to be given to the computer. Cameron Fry watched in amazement, now with bated breath, as a glass of scotch materialized in midair next to a gold brick surrounded by the blue-and-white popping lights again. Both objects settled to the bottom of the chamber.

“If Junior was here, he could have fed the information to the computer in a nano second."

Cameron Fry walked slowly to the chamber and opened the door. He reached in and picked up the gold bar. Sure enough, its weight was about right. Then he reached in for the scotch. He raised the glass slowly to his lips and took a sip. He was beyond dumbfounded. He had just watched two men turn a couple of clay bricks into a bar of gold and glass of his favorite scotch in a tiny laboratory in central Montana. He was speechless. He held up the glass in a toast to Iggy and Lucky Marcus. The only word that escaped his lips was. "Wow!"

He had heard Marcus was running around the world, curing cancer, and feeding people. He had assumed Marcus was just spending his trillions. That was the reason he was here to start with. The man was obviously a philanthropist. He had spent his life surrounded by wealthy people whose last thought was philanthropy unless they got a tax write-off. They bored him. Money was their God, and every word out of their mouths was swathed in self-indulgence. How much money is enough when you're a billionaire? He had always known the answer to that. There was never enough because money wasn't the object of the crusade. Money was the vehicle that would buy them a titanic self-image through power over their fellow men! They were all slave master wannabes.

Once he saw the truth, it was a short leap to the realization that every one of these feckless mediocrities was the same type of villain as Stalin, Hitler, Mao, and every other despot who had raised a whip against his brothers. They were gutless nonentities and didn't have the chutzpah to actually hold the whip in their own hands. So, they held the esoteric whip of money over the heads of the common men to march them like cattle into the holding pens before the slaughter.

Cameron Fry was a hard man, but he had seen suffering and always felt sorry for the tribulations of the people who tried but were never able to pull themselves up by their bootstraps. The ones that never tried were write-offs for whom he had no empathy. But some men and women valiantly tried but were dealt lousy cards. They were never in the right place at the right time, but even then, they kept slugging. He admired those people because they were honest and decent. Occasionally, he would help when he knew his help would be effective. He turned away from the Marcus brothers, struggling to hold back tears he did not want them to see. Cameron Fry had not shed a tear since his mother died 35 years before. It took a lot to get through the impenetrable outer shell of his character. He always shielded himself against too much empathy for those who tried repeatedly and failed...

Iggy's had just obliterated that shield. He had finally met true greatness, validating the entire spectrum of human achievement.

"Why don't you join us at the Pavilion, Cameron? I'm meeting Tom Rickart, my head of security and Junior. We are trying to figure out the anomaly affecting the shields."

Lucky chuckled at Fry's demeanor. Fry nodded his head yes but wasn't talking. He was too overwhelmed. That was Lucky's favorite part of these kinds of nights. He loved watching the consternation, especially when it involved a name brand like Cameron Fry.

Ten minutes later they sat around a table in the Pavilion. Dinner was over and most of the kids departed for extracurricular activities or homework. There were only a few people around cleaning tables and getting everything ready for the breakfast shift.

"What did you guys figure out?" He asked Junior and Tom.

"I think I figured it out, Dad. Somebody is bombarding the shield with energy pulses. They are low in amplitude but high frequency. They're trying to insert themselves in the shield. If they can do that, they might even be able to turn it off. They have a problem, though. Our computers are the fastest computers in existence. Nothing the rest of the world uses even comes close… maybe .001%. We shift frequencies in segmented attoseconds which is so rapid, no computer in existence can possibly intercept, decipher, and alter our electromagnetic anatomy, or insert itself."

Cameron Fry had heard what Junior said. "Excuse me, I have to ask, what in God's name is an attosecond?"

Junior turned his head away from the screen and looked at Cameron Fry with a raised eyebrow look of skepticism. "You don't know what an attosecond is? Wow. And I thought I had heard everything."

Cameron Fry laughed. "You know, Junior, nobody could have ever convinced me that you aren't human. In fact, I didn't believe it until I saw that toggle switch below your navel. So, what is an attosecond?"

"Huh... an attosecond is one quintillionth of a second." mused Iggy. "To make it a little clearer for you, one attosecond is to a second as one second is to 31.71 billion years. Nobody on this planet has the technology to figure that one out, much less execute the same."

"That sure says a mouthful," responded Junior. "Who does that leave us with?" He added with a touch of sarcasm.

Cameron Fry laughed. "Small talk. How in God's did you ever teach this computer how to small talk? For that matter, why did you, anyway?"

"I don't think you have fully grasped the implications here. Junior is more than a computer. I know it's hard to accept, but he is a sentient, autonomous life form. I may have built him, but he is an entity… alive, and I don't own him. He is his own master. My brother had trouble with this for a while, but he got over it."

It's more than amazing to me. It's a little bit frightening. You represent that he is a sentient being. Okay, I'll buy that. He's obviously superior to me. He is smarter, faster, stronger and represents a threat to the average man, as far as I see it. I suppose the jokes and small talk help, but it doesn't change the fact that he is vastly superior. Why did you do this anyway?"

"Several reasons. Are you aware of the groundbreaking technology coming out of Caltech, MIT, Alan Turing, and JP Morgan labs concerning artificial intelligence?"

"I hear a smattering."

They are all competing in the advancement of AI. They've come a long way. They have built computers that are beginning to become somewhat self-aware and write their own language. They are not as sophisticated as Junior. He's more than artificial intelligence. He is sentient, and thousands of times more powerful than anything those folks might come up with. Think about that for a minute. None of the computers being developed to propagate AI are independently intelligent. They are computers only. However, their ability to compute and interface is lightning-fast. The people who are building these AI computers are funded by Interlink. Here's where it gets complex. Interlink has been funding nanotechnology. How familiar are you with that?"

"I've read about it. My original education consisted of a major in business and finance with a minor in physics, and I eventually changed to psychology. So, I'm a numbers guy and a logical thinker. I understand the implications of the power of artificial intelligence to a great degree, especially in the hands of these people. I guess that's why I'm here. So please continue."

"Interlink has its own think tanks. They believe AI is the tool they will use to control society. Klatch is the figurehead, but we discussed the two men who exist in obscurity that are part of Interlink. They are the silent people at the helm, that no one ever hears about. Laurence Howe, Ransom Hornburg, and Heinrich Klatch are working in concert with your friends from Altair four. They have forcefully expropriated most of humanity's intellectual geniuses in computer technology. Allow me to describe the type of slavery they intend for humanity."

Fry was captivated. He knew the nameless people behind the scenes who expected to push humanity into a brave New World and that AI is going to have a major role. Whoever controls AI will control the money, whoever controls the money will control humanity. It will be the end of privacy and freedom. These things he knew. Yet, he was not aware of the subtleties. Apparently, this man was aware, and about to elaborate. "Please do."

I will begin with a description of Junior and Baby. This is critical. Both have their sentient identity based in their neural net, which they colloquially call their brains. Their neural net is more than vastly complex. I'll try to explain it this way; their memory and computing abilities are based on a brand-new technology I invented. Humanity will not catch up to that technology for thousands of years on its own. Strictly on a volume basis, my best guess is that contemporary existing state-of-the-art technology at any of these AI labs would require over five thousand cubic feet of micro circuitry and computer hardware to match either Junior's or Baby's capabilities."

"Their brains are computers, yes, but a technology completely different in size, scope, and concept than anything conceived by men or being pursued in any research centers or universities. Occasionally, some scientists somewhere will hypothesize about using subatomic particle properties to do binary calculations, but it is just an esoteric pipedream to them that they believe will never happen as they have no way to implement the technology. I have implemented it. It now exists."

"In fact, Junior's intellect is so powerful that all the computers in existence could not collectively measure up to his ability. His brain computes by subatomic particle spin directly coupled to my matter/energy transmutation technology that it took me years to perfect. The actual CPU is homogeneously embedded in his entire structure. There are Quintillions of them, all capable of executing tasks."

"Between him and Baby, they have the ability and capacity to interface simultaneously with every computer in existence, then regulate and restrain them. Further, this does not have to be accomplished through conventional internet interface connectivity. You are aware of our 64 satellites that have inhibited nuclear war. They have many functions. One of them is the worldwide ability to set up a form of Wi-Fi interface with any computer connected to a modem of any kind. All computers must have a modem to function externally. Junior can access those computers through our satellites, and it is done with a technology that cannot be understood or interfered with by any other contemporary technology because the information travels electromagnetically via light photons across the entire spectrum in mere attoseconds. The signal encoding is so dense and travels so quickly that it is impossible to intercept and interpret. Junior and Baby's neural nets are the only instrumentality capable of doing this. In other words, the message will be sent and long gone before any other type of computer interface and analysis is possible. It leaves no signature or out-of-phase after-signal."

"In fact, I'm sure you are aware of our satellite technology, which explicitly prohibits nuclear war. I accomplished that at greater expense than what Junior and Baby do through interface with every computer on earth.

They could shut down everything instantly, and there would be no redress or protection by adversaries."

Cameron Fry was brilliant. He understood exactly what he was being told as well as the implications. Yesterday, he believed this man was the most powerful human being who ever lived. It was beyond that today. This man held the world in his hands. He held what the people of Interlink wanted to hold. They wanted mastery over everything and everyone, everywhere. But they were not benevolent, they were malevolent, greedy, and self-aggrandizing pathetic nonentities. What they were after, this man already possessed. He was amazed that any human being could hold this much power and not be subject to his ego and a God complex. His admiration was expanding by the minute.

"Please continue, Mr. Marcus." He used the salutation out of respect.

Iggy smiled. "Okay then, Mr. Fry, but there's a lot more. This has been in the planning stage for decades by prescient people who saw where computer technology would eventually lead. They understood it was the technology of tomorrow that would define all our lives. Slightly after the turn of the century, specific technologies came into being. They were not invented in universities, think tanks, corporations, or by the people of Interlink. The technologies were extraterrestrial. They consisted of minuscule nanotechnology that we only now are able to reproduce. This nanotechnology exists on the atomic level, much in the same manner as Junior's processors, but much less sophisticated. This nanotechnology cannot be integrated yet because it is too small, and science hasn't given men the ability. However, this technology has been deployed for the past 18 years."

"If men don't have the ability to integrate the technology, how is it being deployed?"

"I didn't say men could not use the technology; I said they cannot integrate the technology. I'm sure you are aware of what chemtrails are. Many people believe they are simple vapor trails. They are not. They are particulate in nature, and they are being sprayed into the atmosphere globally to the tune of 1000 metric tons per day, depending on the weather, trade winds, and population density. The pilots who fly the aircraft are told that it is particulate that will remain aloft and reflect the sun to prevent global warming."

"I know of this; go on. "

"The particulate is composed of many things, but none of them have even a tiny bit to do with global warming. I'll name some of them now but give you an exact definition and the effect on human anatomy later. Graphene, which is a conductor, one atom thick sheet/tube is one of the nanoparticles. Hydrogel, lithium, aluminum in various forms, and artificial bacteria among other things."

Cameron Fry was educated. Although he wasn't a scientist, per se, he understood the implications of the things Iggy was telling him. He knew what all the substances were and understood their possible relationships with the chemical constitution of the human brain. "Don't stop now, Mr. Marcus."

"The people who are deploying this now own, by proxy, almost every government of every country on earth except for Russia, China, and a few others. When I say they own them, I mean their influence is tantamount. The people who run these countries do as they are told because their economies hinge on Interlink's benevolence. Interlink's mission is the subjugation of all mankind. I use the term whip figuratively. They are not actually going to whip people physically unless, of course, they rebel. What they intend is to whip them psychologically. Once people are put in their place and managed by consumerism, Madison Avenue-type programming, complete control of the money supply, directing who spends what, where they spend it, and on what they spend it, this new discipline will signify the abolition of individual freedom. It places dominance in the hands of the autocrats, and the rest of humanity will kneel."

"You know, Iggy," Fry was back to informality again. "I believe every word you're telling me. Not just because you're the smartest guy I've ever met. I've seen this coming for a long time. I'm not what you would call an active member of Interlink in terms of policy dictates, but I do listen to all their policy intentions. So, that sort of answers my question about Junior and Baby... I think."

"Junior and baby are unique, Cameron. I created them as an antidote to artificial intelligence, even though they are a form of AI themselves. They are not just computers anymore; they are alive, intelligent, and dedicated entities. When I fabricated them, I assuaged their programming to have empathy for other sentient beings. Because they are alive, they realize they are two among trillions. Men will never evolve to their intellectual level. Organic intellect cannot become what they are. There is a huge plus to that. They cannot be influenced by emotion, they cannot be deterred from a task, they are tireless in pursuit of goals, they will live forever, and their basic underwritten philosophy is the preservation of all intellect. These two people are my antithesis to the corrupt destruction of the individual. Have you ever considered the root of Interlink's member's power lust?"

"Yeah, of course. I still would like to hear your take on it. Ever since I came to this place, I've felt like I was back in school. I like it. There's nothing like a good learning experience. Please continue."

"I've given this lecture a thousand times to my kids in class. Authoritarians always have a weak self-image. They base their self-image externally on what other people think of them. That's most of humanity, by the way. When their compatriots think they're good, they feel good. Most people allow others to define their stature. The next step above that is defining your stature with the accumulation of wealth as if you will ever see an armored car following a hearse. Those people are small in stature also, so money becomes their god to elevate themselves in their own eyes."

"Mediocrities always do this by destroying the superlative. The superlative is always a mirror that exhibits the reflection of substandard mediocrities. Do you see it, Mr. Fry? These people hate themselves. That's the underlying emotion, you know. Because they hate themselves, they hate everyone and anyone who reflects their inadequacy. Most of them are gutless. They are killers, but they don't do their own killing. They hire others to perform that task. If you look at history, the people of Interlink were responsible for Adolf Hitler, Mao, Stalin, Lenin… almost all of them. Why are they responsible, you might ask? I will tell you they are responsible because they financed those monsters. Their efforts may not have produced what they intended when they tossed the money at the monsters, but that was irrelevant."

"Just look at World War II. They were responsible for creating Hitler, and then they had to use one of their own, Roosevelt, to destroy him. How many millions of lives were lost because of that fiasco? Many of the people in Interlink are not that evil. They participate because they have no choice. If they want to exist economically with the political influence of their corporations, they must conform to Interlink's dictates. However, every single one of the people at the top of Interlink is exactly what I say they are. You sat at the top of Interlink, Mr. Fry. Until I shook your hand and read your mind, I would've assumed you were one of its antihuman members."

"I'm not too sure what part of this evening was the most rewarding. Your lecture, or your wife's scampi. I think if I had to choose, I'd take the scampi." said Fry, laughing at his own joke. "I suppose either way you look at it, it's a complement."

"I would choose the scampi too. Once you've heard my lecture, you've heard it. Her scampi recipe is a gift that keeps on giving."

"I have something else for you to consider, by the way. When I attended that meeting 275 feet below the Sistine Chapel, I was talking to that creature named Hansel from the fourth planet from the star, Altair, who suggested the possibility of assisting interlink against you. If I were you, I would start there, looking for the anomalies affecting your force field."

"Yes, I have considered that. You know that we have also consulted with some people from another world. Apparently, there is more than one species of inter-stellar visitors, although I have only met one. I need to speak with them again about this. Perhaps they can assist. What did you think about our matter/energy transmutation capabilities?"

"You are quite correct. I will sleep better now... for sure. Despite the inevitable unrest designed and created to place whips in the hands of tyrants to beat men into submission, the most prolific tool that you have removed from Interlink's arsenal is the fear of starvation. I guess energy won't be an item of much concern either, considering your technology provides unlimited free, clean energy. It would appear you have removed the hidden weapons necessary for tyrants to destroy individuals and societies. That's impressive. You've just altered the hundred-thousand-year-old modus operandi of Homo sapiens and their masters. Forget about the underlying philosophic points; there will be no more famine, pollution, energy dependence on fossil fuels, or medical debilitation. In short, you are the harbinger of utopia. Pretty amazing!"

"Iggy chuckled cynically. I'm sure you don't believe that. You sat at the authoritarian dinner table for too long to accept an entirely different cuisine just because there's a new chef in the kitchen."

"You are butting heads with the establishment, Mr. Marcus. Nothing you can do will change their minds. I understand that. It appears that nothing they can do will change your mind either. I call that being between a rock and a hard place. I think where one of you lose might be in the court of public opinion. The average person doesn't really care and easily forgets as long as they are fed and have their television sets."

"Under most circumstances, I would say you are correct, but you are missing the big picture, Cameron."

"How so?"

"You are aware there are two opposing philosophical forces at work. I put these names on them. Socialism, which is nothing more than a socially acceptable name for tyranny, where all men become subjects and follow orders in lieu of punishment. Some people argue that it is for the good of society. We are all our brother's keepers, and therefore, freedom and prosperity for all are only possible because of sacrifice by all. That has been the selling point throughout history. It only works during times of privation when tyrants rule and citizens are slaves. Then, a gladiator arises. Someone like Lenin, Mao, Che, or Pol Pot who tell the people they are victims of the aristocracy and the only route to salvation and equality is through them."

"They marshal the forces of the common man by making promises that no one can possibly keep and then use those forces to eradicate the elitists currently in charge. What they fail to tell their 'common man army' is their heroic gladiator is just another elitist parasite who will put them in chains as soon as the existing regime is destroyed."

Yeah, that's the history of it, of course. But the common man always gets what he deserves when the elitist subjugates him. Such is the nature of men and society and has always been the situation on the ground since Babylon."

One thing Iggy Marcus never allowed was the manipulation of his intellect by someone with an agenda. "I'm surprised you would say that to me, Cameron. That statement was more than foolish; it was ignorant, and you are not an ignorant man. I will not debate you on that level. Men do not deserve a damn thing at the hands of other men! You use the term deserve as if it defines the elitist's act of aggression against his inferiors as justice because his inferiors are defenseless and are getting what they deserve. You're not going to get away with that." Iggy was rarely as outspokenly demonstrative with others as he was with Fry. He was talking to one of the richest men in the world, a head of Interlink, and, in a sense, the enemy, whether he was intentionally positioned or not.

"I disagree, Mr. Marcus. Even the common people have an obligation to embrace reality and be aware of the ramifications of following tyrants. But they are not. They drift along in their own little world, and when tribulation comes, most of them are either swept away or become loyal subjects of a new tyrant. That's been history as long as men have written about it, and It's always their own fault."

It is their own fault only to a degree because they have been indoctrinated. The elitists, through indoctrination, achieve their results of dominance. Only the ignorant can be indoctrinated, Cameron. When men see the truth and accept it as reality, no one can easily turn honest, critical-thinking, freedom-loving men into sheep. To resist requires courage as well as intellect. So, the elitists begin the indoctrination of humanity at a young age. They teach them to be afraid because that is the number one ingredient to subjugation. Then they destroy the intellect by marching an incessant parade of Hollywood garbage and Madison Avenue marketing of swill to the youth from the nursery to grad school. Reality and human beings then become disparate."

Cameron Fry didn't answer at first. He knew Iggy was right. He saw the depth of the problem. If the common man woke up, the advantage of the elitists, and even himself to a certain extent, would evaporate immediately. "You're talking about a perfect world, Iggy Marcus. We don't have one of them. We are stuck with the one we have, and there's no way for me to change it. So, I'm going to live in the world I live in and take advantage of the opportunities that present themselves."

"I originally stated there were two opposing philosophical forces. I described Socialism, which always consists of wolves and sheep. The wolves never consume the entire herd in an afternoon. They nurture the herd and consume the sheep slowly. There is a philosophical antithesis, Cameron. It is capitalism. The sheep, however, have been told capitalism is the evil tool of the elitists who subjugate them. They have been lied to. The exact opposite is true. Tyrants are never capitalists. They are murderers because they have no problem killing the sheep. The sheep keep their eyes closed and refuse to see their brothers and sisters disappearing from the periphery of the flock."

"Capitalism is the only system that allows a human being to reap the rewards of his or her own efforts without compulsion to contribute to the impoverished, and that is antithetical to the tyrants who use Socialism to keep the subjects in line. Remember, the impoverished only exist because of socialism. Socialism is subsidy that doesn't cure anything; it creates more of the same. So, we must ask ourselves the questions, do we want more of the same, then subsidy becomes the answer, or do we want to see everyone able to stand on their own two feet without stripping their brothers by force? Those two positions are axiomatically opposed, and everyone must choose. It's either or. There is no such thing as being in the middle."

"I am inclined to agree with everything you say, but the socialist will claim his purpose is to alleviate pain-and-suffering created by capitalists and their lack of caring for their fellow citizens. He claims he arbitrarily has the moral right to confiscate your property and hand it to the have-nots. I understand that the haves and the have-nots exist. The arbitrator in the middle, who confiscates from one and gives to another, always does it from his limousine, and that is offensive. I own a limousine, but I earned it and am not ashamed of that. I have also engaged in philanthropy, but that is nothing to brag about. It is only a thing you do to help others."

"We are both almost on the same page, Cameron Fry. We agree, but the difference is your inability to change the world in large ways. You can do it in small ways, but even with all your money, the large ways are out of reach. I can change the world in large ways, and that is exactly what I intend to do. First, men must learn to live morally. Without honesty and integrity, no political system will work, and we will always be doomed to failure. It's my job to get us beyond failure."

"I have a question for you. I have heard much because of the scuttlebutt that travels the country club set. No news has come out of China, but it's my understanding that all the Communists are gone, and Bālún Tōng has taken the reins. I'm quite sure that you are responsible for that. No one else living could do it. I've also had my ear to the ground diplomatically. Dozens of world leaders are screaming at the top of their lungs that you have invaded their country and stolen their property. Only one of them describes what you did. I heard you went to every country that possessed biological weapon technology and confiscated them. I'm not asking if that's true. It must be true because they're all screaming. I find that amazing," he said, laughing.

"It's true. It took us five days to confiscate all bioweapon equipment and strains, as well as destroy the laboratories in every country that pursued that technology. We have all the strains frozen here while they are cataloged for reference in case some country has a bio stash somewhere that will require mitigation. They are safe."

Cameron Fry laughed aloud as he reflected on his personal history and relationship with Interlink. He had signed on twenty years before. He had been a loner even as a young child, but loneliness had no seat in his character. Never victimized by envy, he needed no one. Preoccupation with achievement drove him. Even if it was building a fort in the woods or climbing a cliff face, he was driven by the challenge in front of him, ignoring everything but an obsessive desire to conquer his environment. Even in high school, as captain of the baseball team, he barely acknowledged others in his orbit. His focus on winning the game had nothing to do with being better than the next guy for the sake of elevating his self-image. It was purely a desire to succeed. That was the first introduction to his own subconscious mind and a unique personality that would separate him from every human being he would encounter.

As he grew older, he never allowed the world and external events to penetrate his persona. The bubble of self-preoccupation was the force driving his life, and his obsessive personality pushed others away, making him larger-than-life and seemingly aloof. A lack of concern for the recognition and admiration of others was the unique quality that separated him from the herd. His obsessive-compulsive drive to live life to the fullest inhibited a frivolous college social life. There were not many male friends and only a few women. Relationships of that nature didn't seem to last because of his focus and ambition. His unique personality and obsessive drive created Cameron Fry, the trillionaire.

"Before I leave you, Iggy Marcus, something bothered me a little after our conversation about removing bioweapons. It has nothing to do with the legalities or the legitimacy of your actions. It has everything to do with logistics. You said that it took you five days to remove bioweapons from every country on Earth and the laboratories they were created in. I would like an explanation as to how that was possible. I don't question your veracity, only the method that made the seemingly impossible… possible."

"Oh that," Iggy said with a laugh. "I never did show you our four ships or explain the science. We keep them in their own hangar, segregated from everything conventional. Follow me to that building at the end of the flight line."

Cameron Fry stood in the hangar, surprised by what he saw. "None of the ships are aerodynamically designed. I'm more than impressed. They obviously do not employ aerodynamics for lift or motive power. Even helicopters have Rotary wings. These have nothing. Please explain," he said, completely fascinated with the obviously brand-new technology.

"This technology has nothing to do with aerodynamics. Electromagnetic force is the power that moves the ships. Let's take a ride. This ship is Daedalus. It was my first working model."

“I feel like I'm sitting in my living room. When do we take off, and where are we going?"

Iggy laughed. "Hang onto your hat, Cameron. The ship has millions of holographic transponders built into the skin, and we can make it appear there is no skin at all." The walls of the ship slowly faded from view as Cameron Fry gasped at the panorama laid out beneath them. He appeared to be sitting on a glass floor, staring between his feet, and gazing at the international space station slightly below the ship with the globe as a backdrop.

"It only took seconds to get here! How ever did you do that? How is this possible?"

"Briefly… I am piloting the ship. The energy that drives it requires manipulation of a very powerful electromagnetic field that can only be done through a sentient mind. Electromagnetic force surrounds and binds everything in existence throughout the universe, and that includes this very ship as well as our physical bodies.”

“To put it simply, the ship creates two EMF fields juxtaposed but at intersecting angles at the same numerical values as a frequency shift proportionate to each other. Normally, that cannot be controlled via mechanical means. If you are familiar with the Philadelphia experiment by the United States Navy in 1943, you will understand the concept. They were able to achieve separation of the electromagnetic binders governing matter and energy. They were unable to control the event because their EMF was too weak, and their lack of understanding prevented outside human interruption and control of anomalies. What we do here is along the same lines but far more sophisticated and powerful. Further, technology has come a long way since then. I have a chip implanted in my cerebral cortex, which allows me to interface with the ship's computer. In essence, everything in the universe is comprised of a single entity, pure energy. That energy manifests itself in many forms. Matter, all the other types of energy, even our biological structure consist of pure energy assembled and held together by electromagnetic force. The human mind can intercept and direct that force by interacting with the computer. It's a matter of voltage, amperage, and direction."

"I believe I get the gist of what you're saying. You are obviously using magnetic flux to propel us. What I don't understand is how you traveled almost 20,000 miles instantly. I did take physics in college, and that is supposedly impossible."

"This is where it gets complex. I cannot explain the math. You don't have enough background information to understand. That's not to say you couldn't learn, but you couldn't understand it from your current perspective. I'll describe it as this. The universe has many layers. Some call them dimensions, but they are not. They are platforms of existence. Dimensions define physical positions and properties. Time is not a dimension. It is a snapshot or locus point of existence."

"Electromagnetism is the fourth dimension, and it defines the relationships of matter and all other types of energy to pure energy, which I refer to as the Creator. When you exit all the layers of the universe, you enter what my brother, Lucky, calls 'nonexistence'. It's a difficult concept and you must come a long way before you can comprehend what that really means. Once you exit the physical realities of the universe with all its platforms, you can reenter at the chosen locus. It does not allow time travel. If that were possible, anyone with the capability would alter the future by redirecting the past. What it does allow is the negation of time. When you enter nonexistence, the passage of time ceases for the traveler. Upon reentry, the passage of time begins again. Although I have never extensively explored this, I believe one can exit the physical universe while time ceases for the traveler. Yet existence and time march on in the physical universe. "I think that's the best explanation I can give, Cameron."

"You mind if I change the subject? I studied a lot of science, but your technology is way beyond my capabilities."

"Not at all, Cameron. What's on your mind?"

"I'm glad I came here. You and this place have opened my eyes. Nothing like this is going on anywhere. I'm usually a silent member of Interlink at meetings. You learn when you keep your ears open, and your mouth shut. I don't call the shots even though I'm right up there at the top. I listen to the plotting and the subterfuge Interlink intends to conduct. Their intent is world domination and, ultimately socialism, of course, with them at the top. I understand what's going on to a degree. They are all mostly wealthy old mediocrities, and their oppression of humanity validates their self-image. One of them bothers me a great deal, however… Hiram Karas. You and I spoke of authoritarians and how everyone seems to validate their self-image through their position of authority… but not him."

"He is a horse of a different color, Mr. Marcus. I've been watching him for years. I'm sort of a student of psychology. Analyzing men helps me predict their decisions when making business deals. Karas is seething with hatred. I've never seen anyone as full of malevolence. He tries to hide it and is successful for the most part. I don't think anyone at Interlink picks up on it besides myself. There's something very abnormal about this man. I don't know his motives, but I've been trying to put my finger on it for a decade or more. He's a hedge fund manager worth around $300 billion and he uses it judiciously all over the world to destroy countries by financing political and judicial figures, especially certain ones. What do you know about him?"

Marcus's broad smile told Fry he was about to hear a revelation. "That's an interesting story, Cameron. You know, of course, he's a Jew."

"Yeah, so what? There are a lot of Jews who are members of Interlink. Amon and Saphra Rothman are Jews. What's that got to do with anything? I was brought up a Jew. None of us are Hasidic Jews. In fact, we are hardly practicing. Nonetheless, that is our biological identity."

"Hold onto your seat, Mr. Fry. A big wind is about to blow into town that will explain Hiram Karas to a T."

Iggy Marcus never seemed to pontificate, yet Cameron Fry had accepted him as a mentor. When he was in the presence of the superlative, he always acknowledged the truth. "It's that bizarre and compelling...huh?"

"I think so. This might give you some insight as to what makes the man tick. Do you know what a Sonderkommando is?"

"No, I've never heard the term. Please explain."

"The concept and term Sonderkommando revert to World War II and the Nazi death camps. Dachau, Auschwitz, Stutthof, Ravensbrück, Chelmno, Treblinka, etc., Auschwitz being responsible for the most deaths."

"The Sonderkommandos were obviously part of those death camps. What exactly were they?"

"Sonderkommandos were prisoners, often children or young men, and usually Jews who were used by the Germans to do the hard labor of killing their parents, brothers, sisters, and relatives. Not only did they do the killing, but they were also forced at the point of a gun to help with all the bloody grotesque work the Germans didn't have the manpower for."

"Jesus," whispered Carmen Fry. "You're about to tell me that Hiram Karas was a Sonderkommando, aren't you?"

"Yes, but I think I should paint a broader picture of his duties for the Nazis. Most of the

Sonderkommandos were children, and they were ordered to do these things, or they would be killed. Bear in mind they watched Germans blow their relatives and friend's brains out all over the ground, right in front of them. Can you imagine the terror? I don't think I could even imagine that. Then, they were told to pull the gold teeth out of their dead countrymen once they were removed from the gas chamber. Under Joseph Mengele's direction, they were ordered to peel the skin off dead Jews and make things like lampshades, etc."

"My God," rasped Fry faintly.

“If that’s not bad enough, try to wrap your mind around this. At first, half a million Jews were killed and buried in large, bulldozed pits, then covered with dirt. When the Nazis realized they didn't have enough room to bury millions, they built giant crematoriums and decided to cremate the victims. The Sonderkommandos had the job of hauling the dead naked Jews, many of whom had emptied their bowels in their last moments of terror, to the crematoriums so they could be burned. When the Americans turned the tide in the war, Himmler wanted to erase the evidence of the mass murder. The Sonderkommandos were ordered to dig up the buried corpses, hundreds of thousands of them, and carry them in wheelbarrows to the crematorium. Even the Germans had to wear gas masks because of the stench. No Jew was given a gas mask. They picked their partially decomposed countrymen out of the burial pits, put them in wheelbarrows, and pushed them to the crematoriums. They weren't even given gloves.”

Cameron Fry silently contemplated the mental picture Iggy had just painted. Like most people, he had heard of the Holocaust and even saw some of the pictures, but he was born several years after the war, and the world had obscured the horrific memories. He didn't realize the vivid stridency of Iggy's description was actually placed in his mind by Iggy’s projection, but the feeling of horror possessed his entire being. "Well, I guess that excuses him in a sick kind of way."

"No, Cameron. Reasons and excuses are not synonymous. It is the reason for his mental illness but not an excuse. An excuse is an attempt at rational justification, and nothing justifies his all-consuming self-hatred and hatred of others. Nothing excuses delusion. There comes a time in every person's life when delusion must be abandoned, and reality must become the norm. The citizens of the world, especially Americans in their opulence, rarely abandon delusion. Delusion is easy and convenient to wallow in. A person doesn't have to think and allows others to do it for him. You already know this. I'm singing to the choir. I just wanted to shed some light on Hiram Karas and what drives him. There is no doubt that he is insane. Insanity is not always characterized by people running through the halls screaming gibberish. Insanity is often quiet, malicious, and calculating. That's the worst kind of insanity because it is difficult to identify. I said this once before to my students. A leering villain standing in front of you, twirling his handlebar mustache, is easy to spot, indeed. The ones who come cloaked in good intentions are the ones who will lead you straight through the gates of hell."

"How would you medically diagnose Karas?"

"From a distance, I would say Hiram Karas had a psychotic break from reality when he was eight or nine years old. I'm not sure of the chronology, but that sounds about right. Along with that comes schizophrenia, and he probably has a bipolar disorder as well. It's understandable. No human being could easily survive that trauma intact... especially a child who was just forced to rip the gold teeth out of his mother's jaw. At the root of his psychosis is his self-loathing and a death wish. The problem with people like him is that self-destruction demands the rest of humanity join them in their misery."

He smiled, "Misery loves company, Cameron. It's hard to believe people who think that way exist. Everyone believes others think exactly as they do. They cannot understand the tyrant who kills for the pleasure of it… and that, Mr. Fry, is the reason my first mission before attempting what I am attempting, was to launch our ring of satellites in orbit, removing the possibility of nuclear war. There is no doubt, it was inevitable."

***

Cameron Fry's Learjet climbed through the dense stratocumulus layer, searching for sunlight. He reflected on the week just spent at what he now considered the most unique place on earth. The exposure to Marcus's technology conveyed him to the world of the future. It was the dazzling exhibition of a true Pandora's box. It existed now, and no one could close the lid. This force was so powerful that it would change the future of men and the trajectory of civilization beyond recognition. It seemed one man had created this amazing leap into tomorrow, and he was the only controlling factor that would outline the morality of its use.

He thought about the musical performance he had experienced consisting of children from three to eighteen who played and sang in concert as good, if not better than any he had ever heard anywhere. Music was one of the few things that moved Cameron Fry, but he never let it show. The night before, in the concert hall, it took every bit of strength he possessed to hide the tears, while watching four hundred children, some of them no older than three, execute the most amazing musical performance he had ever heard or even imagined. As a connoisseur of the superlative, he had been watching the deterioration of society by the annihilation of excellence in its youth. It was by intent, and the authoritarian objective for the past hundred years was to instill the bowed head of submission and the extinction of virtue. He realized Lightning Ranch and Iggy Marcus were the antithesis of that extinction. Still in awe of the experience, he knew Lightning Ranch was the way it was supposed to be.

He had just witnessed the breathtaking reality of developing children. It was more than amazing; it was overpowering. "This should be the rule of thumb for all our kids, not the exception to the rule," he muttered. "Too bad she's spoken for," he continued aloud to himself as he played Melanie's amazing performance of Verdi's Caro Nome over and over in his mind. His mother made him take piano lessons, where he acquired a taste for the classics, but he rarely went out of the way to indulge himself. This was different. Melanie Coletta had nearly brought him to tears and that was most unusual for Cameron Fry. In fact, this past week was the most unusual experience of his life. Never preoccupied or given to fantasy, he hadn't expected it, and a pronounced twinge of regret snatched him from his mental reverie, wondering if he would ever return to this Shangri-La.

Yesterday, he believed the civilized world was on a path of inescapable destruction and reconstruction that would destroy human freedom forever. It wasn't the kind of world he desired, and it wasn't the world he wanted anyone else to live in, either. Like everyone else who encountered Iggy Marcus, he was certain this man was here to prevent that destruction. He didn't know why because he wasn't a religious man, but he knew there was a greater hand in this somewhere. Coincidences of this magnitude just didn't happen.

This moment inspired one of Cameron Fry's rare irrevocable decisions. It was time to abandon old alliances and adopt new ones. The man he had just spent the week with was shattering the globalist program.

Interlink and the old Club of Rome members were making one last superhuman effort attempting to push humanity over the brink.

Their subterfuge lay beneath every destructive political event in history and had always been the antithesis of honor among men. They were in charge, and everyone else was born to serve. Their historic control over humanity had been an irrevocable fact of life until 1776 when America's founders destroyed the British Army. To their folly, the British Army, an arm of the globalists, underestimated the colonies and endured the defeat that precipitated the greatest society of free men that had ever existed. It had been easy for globalists before the information age. Organized religion, social oppression, and the armies of the aristocrats were the antithesis of individual freedom.

Cameron Fry knew the history well. Even early in life, his exceptional mind understood the past and saw the information age as the advent of a new tool for humanity's psychological and physical subjugation. He had no control over that world and the elitists' charted course, but he had control over his own orbit. So, he chose his course and the meteoric rise to the eventual position atop the financial community. The morality of his position was never a consideration, but his internal wiring was actually the antithesis of their modus operandi. He would become one of them, however, as a simple self-defense mechanism. He saw them as Marxists and understood global communism with total control of all humanity was their unstated mission.

Marcus had just about destroyed their program with his genius and its technology, but he was somehow doing it without violence. They were stymied by his brilliant success and unable to understand why. Violence was the only language they understood, but apparently, their nonviolent adversary paralyzed them at every intersection in opposition to their efforts. They had no choice. Marcus somehow must be defeated. It came down to them or Marcus. They must attempt the destruction of individualism, freedom, and, consequently, civilization by any means possible. Mass indoctrination through all media sources, the alteration of morality converting it to 'wokeism', the emasculation of manhood, and the cultivation of promiscuity in the youth; whatever form of violence was needed to get the job done, and in the end, if all else failed, mass murder was acceptable.

For the first time in his life, Cameron Fry saw all of reality for what it was. He had previously denied himself much of that vision. That's what non-thinking people do. They ignore reality to make life simple, never understanding happiness and a productive, rewarding life comes at a price that must be paid from time to time, usually by the blood of men. Marcus had altered that reality. He was the antithesis and mirror exposing all the people through all the centuries who had been killers of men and the human spirit.

Cameron Fry was considered a hard man by his peers. He rarely showed emotion and when he did, it was a casual laugh at a funny joke or situation. He was never given to extreme political soliloquies or arguments that defined his inner thoughts. They were no one else's business, and he always realized that a display of his inner self could do nothing but affect him on a business level. His strict self-control was out the window now. He had merged with the personality and subconscious entity of the only man he had ever considered truly heroic. This was his first epiphany. Fry had never thought himself a warrior. His uniqueness separated him from humanity in his own mind. He saw no reason to fight for truth and justice. Most of his associates wallowed in the superficial and corrupt. This man… he would fight with, side-by-side, sword in hand, and defend whatever was worth defending. He surprised himself with the depth of his own emotion as a tear trickled down his cheek.

COGNITO, ERGO SUM. I Think, therefore I Am.

Rene Descartes & Baby

CHAPTER XI

RUSSIAN ROULETTE

Tom Rickart took the steps to the observatory in twos. Nobody had seen this coming. He pulled the handle, slamming the door against the wall as he scrambled up the last 10 steps to the great dome. Iggy was on the observation platform with his neck bent backward, staring at the gantry housing the emitter at the very top of the hyperbolic solarium. Despite the urgency to inform Iggy of current events, he had to laugh. Junior was hanging by his left hand a hundred fifty feet in the air, apparently affecting repairs or adjustments. Tom looked around. Seeing nothing, he had to ask, "How the hell did he get up there, boss?"

"Hi Tom," Iggy chuckled. "He's part orangutan. He jumped to the rotation girdle, but that was only 30 feet. Then he went hand over hand up one of the ribs until he reached the gantry. How he did it wouldn't surprise you; how fast he did it might surprise you. I think it was no more than ten seconds from the floor to the gantry."

Of course, Junior's super hearing picked up the conversation. He waved, "Hi Tom, come on up. The weather is fine, and the view is even better."

They watched Junior swing from rib to rib adjusting hologram projectors. Junior and Baby had become fixtures at Lightning. Their colloquial vernacular, humor and ostensibly human characteristics were only overshadowed by their athleticism. They were a never-ending source of amusement for everyone at Lightning Ranch as well as a profound view into the future of technology. It had been over a year since Iggy and Lucky tinkered him together. Everyone had come to accept him as a living personality and completely forgot he and Baby were robots with absolutely no sense of humor at all.

"Okay, Tom. You didn't come dashing up here to say hello. What's so urgent? I'm sure it's far-reaching. You don't run often."

"Yeah, far-reaching is a good description. Vanya Shartin has been assassinated. Whoever did it, sent Igor Lansky off to the happy hunting ground with him."

Iggy was silent for half a minute. "I see. I half expected things like this to happen. We were in 25 countries cleaning house over a month ago. We stripped them all of bioweapons. There's been a hell of an uproar and backlash. President Sledge let me know on more than one occasion, most of the people we relieved of their biological death weapons were more than a little upset. You see, Tom, we took away their ability to kill each other with nukes. Then, we made tactical warfare just about as obsolete as strategic warfare. The only club they had left were their bioweapon facilities."

"Geez, Iggy, the bastards are all taking it personally. I don't think even you can fix that insanity."

"Oh, I don't know how true that is. Gloria and I did a passable job with Richard McNerney."

"True enough, I can't argue with you there."

"So, let me guess who's in charge, now… Sergei Borodin. His father was Mikhail Borodin, Boris Volkov's cofounder of the KGB. His son was Ivan Volkov, who became Richard Percy. You have to hand it to those Russians. Their duplicity is second to none. They managed to somehow slide Volkov into British royalty unnoticed. That's no small accomplishment. I think there are some personalities at play here. We arrested Volkov in Brussels, and he's languishing on a Pacific Island, awaiting trial. I would imagine the son of Borodin and the son of Volkov are friends."

"I get that connection, but I don't understand why they would kill Shartin and his top general. Why would they assassinate them? What has Volkov got to do with this?"

"Think of it like this, Tom. Those guys are still of the Soviet Union mentality, old-world KGB. They had to acquiesce when Gorbachev threw in the towel because the Soviet Union was on the verge of collapse, but it didn't change their philosophical stance any. They are still a couple of communists, and they hate the West. You understand, communism bestows all the control, power, and authority on a handful. They have a God complex. It's like heroin. Once you're hooked, you always need a fix. I met Vanya Shartin and Igor Lansky. I got a good dose of their subliminal personalities."

"I took them for a ride on Daedalus. Neither one of those two men were going to follow through with their planned invasions of Belarus and Ukraine. I gave them the ultimatum that it would not be tolerated. They also had a good dose of our technology, which I'm sure predisposed them to cooperate. I didn't ask them to sell Russia down the river; I just asked them to stay out of the way, so we didn't have to kill any Russians."

"I think I get it. You're inferring that Borodin is old-school KGB and militant. He saw Vanya Shartin as soft and a proxy puppet of the West." Tom Rickart shook his head. "The damn Russians are all alike. They've got this inferiority/superiority complex. They've gotta be on top."

"Tom. You hit the nail on the head. Borodin watched Shartin and his supreme general stand by while we stripped them of another weapon. That must be a stone in his frog. If you look at history, you can see Russians don't have a problem with bumping people off if they disagree with their ideological stance. Lenin and Stalin killed over 55 million. Several others, like Khrushchev, purged the country of dissidents and killed a lot of Jews. So, it was to be expected. They're in a different place than China. At least in China, we had 90 million members of Bālún Tōng to pick up the torch. They were already on the right philosophical page. Russia is going to be quite a different story."

"I think you're right, Iggy. Russia is a conundrum. And we're not even talking about the other major nuclear powers with billions of people like India and Pakistan."

"I don't think India will be as large an obstacle as the Russians, Tom. They're Hindus. They have a passive religious mindset to start with, thanks to Gandhi. They are not so hell-bent on ruling the world. No, our biggest problem is the stabilization of Russia. A killer is back in charge, and he has a lot of sympathetic Russians in positions of authority who are allies. They want the old Soviet Union back."

"What about Pakistan? They are only 2 or 3% Hindu. The rest of them are Sunni and Shiite Muslims. I've never known the Muslims to be too friendly when it comes to being told what to do."

"We stripped them of their bioweapons laboratory as well. They didn't raise as big a fuss as France. You would think they would've been worse, but they were not. In fact, they haven't even called Bill Sledge, screaming his ear off like some of the others. Never forget, Tom, it's not the people. People are relatively the same everywhere. They want to live their lives in peace. Yes, religion is a huge part of their lives, and the authoritarians use it to dominate them, but they are not the problem. They are never the problem. It's always the monsters at the top. They consume their fellow men and don't care if it's strangers or their brothers. The priority is consumption and power. We have satellites, Tom, and if we have to, we will simply encapsulate them until the dust settles."

"Well, we're not in Pakistan right now. We are in Russia. How are we going to handle that? I'm sure you've got something up your sleeve. You always do."

"Yup, I sure do. Russia is going to have a benevolent dictator. A true authoritarian without malice."

Tom Rickart's eyes were goose eggs. "Who, you?! That is so unlike you. How the hell are you going to pull that off?!

"Nope," he chuckled. "Sure, I'm benevolent, but I don't think I could get the Russians to fall in behind me. I think, however, if we deal the cards carefully and play the hand just right, Richard McNerney will be able to pull it off."

“Ahaaaaa… I see. And he's Russian!” Tom Rickart thought back to the night Richard McNerney had first come to the ranch. He was a major general in charge of United States Army strategy. No battle was fought without his imprimatur. Maykl Petrokov, born in Russia and indoctrinated to become American in Vladivostok, entered the United States as Richard McNerney when he was 12. He was raised by the McNerney's, two other Russian operatives, formally Agne and Benas Menyakosh. He excelled and became an all-star athlete and West Point graduate. Eventually, his intelligence and skills landed him near the top of the United States Army chain of command.

Then it dawned on Tom. Iggy Marcus was more than brilliant; he was dazzling. "Amazing… you have had this in mind all along, haven't you? All the people who surround you are useful to you, but none of us ever feel like we are being used. We feel we are part of something great and magnificent. Still, boss, I see a boatload of obstacles. Especially the Russian mafia. How do you expect to deal with them?"

"You're right, Tom. That will not be a walk in the park, but it can be done. We have over 2200 Navy SEALs on payroll doing all kinds of jobs everywhere. Our corporate footprint is now fourteen trillion dollars. We are much larger than any individual in Interlink, other than Laurence Howe. We are using our assets against interlink to abolish tyranny forever. But it's a process, and there are other mitigating factors in the mix. Visitors from other worlds are involved, quite a few of them, in fact. That doesn't have to be dealt with immediately; Russia does."

"What's next on the agenda, Iggy?"

"The Russian mafia patterned themselves after the Italian Mafia. They are gangsters just like the Italians, but they are worse. For instance, many of the Italian mob bosses at least had a modicum of principles. Not all of them, but most. They didn't sell drugs to children and had a family orientation because they also had families. Not so with the Russians. They are all ex-KGB and GRU. They are cold, calculating, and will kill without compunction or compassion. Their victims are anyone who stands in their way for any reason whatsoever. Remember, they were the Russian storm troopers of the Soviet. Cold, cruel, and calculating. When Gorbachev threw in the towel, they were dead set against dissolving the Soviet. They had no choice, however. The Soviet Union was about to implode for all sorts of reasons. They refused to abandon their authoritative cruelty... and so began the Russian mafia. They are into everything and anything that can turn a buck. Weapons, drugs, human trafficking, child prostitution, murder by contract, everything is acceptable to them. They have no emotion and no conscience."

"How are we going to deal with them? Sounds impossible to me. They've gotta go, but where? Russia doesn't have a jurisprudence system that would deal with that. The country never got itself on its feet after Perestroika. America had a constitution and fought for its independence. The citizens were the ones that did that. Russia had no such type of revolution. One day, they were the Soviet and the next day, they were not. Each country of the old Soviet had to fare for themselves. Some of them do better than others, but nowhere is there enough stability to bring the Russian mafia to its knees."

Tom Rickart looked at Iggy's broad smile. He knew if any man could do it, the man standing in front of him might. After all, he overturned the CCP in a week or two. So, why not Russia?... Tom laughed. "Okay, Iggy. When and where do we start?"

"The first thing is to bring Richard McNerney on board. It's his choice, but I know he is up to the task and won't refuse."

"Then?"

"Then we started training our Navy SEALs. We have the shield technology, and the Russians won't have any chance at all. Like all human beings, they are entitled to due process, but it will have to be at our discretion and convenience."

"What are we going to do with them all while we're waiting for due process?"

"There are a lot of islands in the Pacific Ocean. I have a nice little one picked out for them. I'll leave it up to you to name it. I explained all this to the President and the Atty. Gen. They get it, but Bill Sledge asked me not to dump anymore recidivists on Charlie Barton's plate. We're going to have to set up a tribunal and jury of Russian citizens willing to give a little to their country so they can flourish. That's going to take time, but we'll get there."

"Well, I've got two names. Which one do you prefer, 'Fantasy Island' or 'Isle of No Return?'"

***

"Okay, men, make sure all your gear is stowed intact, and your shields are operational. We'll be leaving in half an hour. Col. Paul Billings turned to give Iggy Marcus the high five. "All 60 men are present and accounted for Iggy. I love these little excursions of yours. They sure alleviate the boredom."

"That's one way of looking at it."

"Well, this is another one of your big adventures. First, it was a bunch of pedophiles, then a bunch of Chinese Communists. Now we're going after the Russian mafia. The pedophiles weren't so bad to deal with. The Chinese soldiers were quite a bit worse because they don't give a damn about human life, but these guys… there is nobody like the Russian mob. If we didn't have the shields, a lot of people would be taking bullets."

"I've got a list of 450 people, Paul, give or take. We're going to pick them all up. Four strike teams and four ships should do the job. We won't get them all, but we will get most of them. It's the really bad ones who we don't want to miss. They're the gang leaders who give the orders. The people in the gangs are all button men who do the killing for the bosses just like the Italians did, only these people are much more violent and cruel."

"How did you find out the identity of these people? That wasn't an easy task, I'm sure."

***

The week before, Iggy, Baby, and Gloria hovered 20 feet from the office window of Sergei Borodin at the Kremlin. As usual, Daedalus materialized instantly. There was no radar signature and no early warning. "Go ahead, Gloria, let's get this done as quickly as possible. Feed me the information as soon as you get it."

Sergei Borodin languished in Vanya Shartin's padded red leather chair with his feet on the desk. He had waited a long time for this. Vanya had grown soft, and so did Igor Lansky. They had forgotten their part in the old KGB and the Russian storm troopers that struck terror into every Russian's heart who spoke against Mother Russia. He was a young soldier at the time, but he commanded a regiment. Like his father, Mikhail Borodin was a sociopath. Power was his God, and people were meant to be trampled. He was waiting for General Beluga. Together, they were to design the strategy to rebuild the old Soviet Union. He pulled a cigar from Vanya's humidor. Cuban! The man had good taste. He struck a wooden match and began lighting his cigar when he felt Gloria Marcus enter his mind.

He was frozen, unable to move, watching the wooden match burn toward his fingers. The pain was intense as his fingers burned, but he was unable to let go. He was immobilized, watching himself blister as the match burned itself out between his thumb and forefinger. Unable to make a sound, his mind screamed in anguish! GET OUT OF MY HEAD!!! GET OUT TY CHERTOYAVA SUKA!!! Gloria Marcus' face had materialized in his mind. He saw her for what she was, a beautiful woman whose face began to melt and twist itself into a mind-numbing hideous vision of satanic evil. He quaked in terror. He had no idea Daedalus hovered 70 feet away on the other side of the wall.

Sergei Borodin was a sociopathic monster who was responsible for the torture and murder of hundreds. She decided to have some fun when she exported despair and planted the gruesome satanic image of herself in Borodin's mind. **"I am Leviathan, and I have come for you, Sergei Borodin!!"** She shrieked, releasing him from immobility as she injected a vision of flames and the sensation of being burned alive.

Sergei Borodin slid from the chair onto the floor, crumpled on his side, terror-stricken and whimpering as he sucked on his blistered fingers. He had no idea this was Gloria Marcus' idea of a fun afternoon. Gloria shared this with Iggy and Baby. They were aware of the entire diatribe. Iggy chuckled, and Baby commented with a laugh that looked anything but contrived, "it couldn't happen to a nicer guy."

Gloria had to bite her lip to keep from laughing at her mechanical sister's joke. **"Yes, Sergei Borodin. I have come for you and information.**

I must know every mobster in the Russian mafia. You know who and where they are, and I want all their names...NOW!" She screamed subliminally, or I will cast you into the fires of hell!!"

Baby continued her non-emotional laugh. She liked to do it for effect. She always explained to her sister that she was practicing until Dad found a way to make her feel. Iggy, On the other hand, was wide-eyed. **That's some sense of humor you've got there, daughter. I see you have extracted many names and locations. Borodin has a good memory, but I believe his general Beluga is the authentic remaining force from the old KGB, knowing everything and everybody who once held power and is now the Russian mob. We can finish our subliminal list with him. Let's wait for his general."**

General Beluga entered and spied Borodin's legs sticking out from behind the desk on the carpet. "Sergei, Sergei! What are you doing down there? Are you okay?" The last thing Magda Beluga wanted was to be the top dog. It was much better with Sergei Borodin sitting in the premier's chair. He would be the one to catch the assassin's bullet. He had often reflected, there's nothing wrong with second place. There is always a prize for second place, and no one shoots at you.

He rushed around the desk and saw Borodin lying face down, whimpering, with his hands wrapped around his head to prevent another intrusion. It was a little surprising. Sergei Borodin was not given to emotional fits. He bent over to roll Borodin over when Gloria Marcus slammed his brain to the floor. He lay there next to Sergei Borodin, shaking and frightened out of his mind.

Gloria Marcus again screamed subliminally. I AM LAVIATHAN, AND I HAVE COME FROM HELL FOR YOU, MAGDA BELUGA!! I want the names of every ex-KGB who is in the Russian mafia, and I want them NOW! Give me what I want, or I will cast you into eternal hellfire with the whimpering piece of slime lying next to you!"

On just about any normal day, Magda Beluga would never give up the ghost. He would rather die than betray his brothers. Although still a monster, that much honor was in him. Not this day, however. It was far too much for him. He wasn't a man of religious faith, but his parents had been. He had spent his youth listening to stories of the afterlife and Hades. He had never believed in it. A lax conscience was much easier to live with and definitely more fun. Today, he believed, and he would comply as Gloria submerged him in emotions of extreme terror. His mind raced as he displayed the mental images of faces and names of all the people in the mob. After all, they all gave him a piece of the action. It was a small piece, but even that had become substantial over the years. He was the cushion between the state, the people, and law and order.

Gloria withdrew, leaving the two men lying on the floor behind Vanya's red leather chair, whimpering. She turned to Iggy. **"I think we've got it all, Dad."** She turned to Baby who seemed to have a wistful look**. Are we done with them?"**

"Leave them for now, Gloria; we may need more information."

"I sure wish I had a sense of humor at times like this. I am convinced the entire episode was hilarious beyond words."

Gloria always marveled at Baby. She and Junior were Dad's creations, and they were beyond amazing; they were people. She tried to remember they were robots, but it always came back to the fact her father was able to give them some kind of personality by programming quirks into their cerebral net. "You may not have a real sense of humor, Baby. But you definitely are hilarious.

"One more thing Gloria, before we leave. Take me in, but don't tell them who we are."

"Sergei Borodin and Magda Beluga. You are assassins. You murdered Vanya Shartin and Igor Lansky. Now you have become targets yourselves. Heed this warning. Do not kill one more Russian or I will drag you into hell!"

***

Tom Rickart's brigade of Navy SEALs gathered in front of the Daedalus hanger for Col. Paul Billings' equipment inspection. Each electromagnetic shield was checked for operational serviceability and charged batteries. Everyone but Paul Billings hoped this was the last mission. Paul was the gladiator type. He was born to be in the military but didn't realize that until after he resigned his commission as a Navy Seal Lieutenant in his sixth year. He toyed with returning to the Navy despite an automatic rank reduction until he read a full-page ad in the Stars & Stripes for Navy SEALs: Wanted for Security Position - Top Pay - Travel and Adventure - contact Lightning Incorporated. Underneath that was printed in smaller letters: 'call Tom Rickert' and a phone number. It eventually turned into the best decision he had ever made.

The reduction in rank never materialized. Pres. William James Sledge eventually promoted Paul to Col. in the Marine Corps after re-submitting his oath of service. Many of the Navy SEALs who had worked for Lightning Incorporated were recommissioned in the military reserves to fulfill specific missions requiring their specific type of training. Periodically, they were given assignments by direct order of the President of the United States, usually to assist strike teams from Lightning to conduct various sorties.

"Okay, men," announced Col. Billings, "gather around with your gear. We're leaving tomorrow, and you need to be extensively briefed. Tom here, and Junior are going to display the mission with holography. This is, by far, the most serious and dangerous mission to date."

We haven't described the mission to any of you until now. We are about to take out the Russian mafia."

There was a murmur of voices among the 60 men gathered. They were elite, highly trained soldiers and knew that the Russian mafia had also been highly trained soldiers at one time. So technically, they were about to do battle with elite Russian soldiers.

"None of you will act on your own. We will all operate under the buddy system incorporated into every action. Often, there will be three men in a group. You will have your shields, which will deflect any attack. You've been trained in their use. You will also have sidearms, and each of you will have pneumatic-fired hypodermic needles that deliver rapid-acting anesthetics. We are going after the most violent, unpredictable recidivists in the world. They are recidivists because they are career criminals, unpredictable because no one represents authority to them except their own leaders, violent because they are ex-Soviet special forces and killers who have been intensely trained just as you have been. So, you're up against the best. I take that back; you men are the best, but you're up against your Russian counterparts."

Everyone's attention was diverted by a small plane that executed two low altitude rolls before approaching the runway. Billings laughed. That was her style. There's nothing like a dramatic entrance. The aircraft taxied to the hard stand in front of the hangars, and Adm. Oniella Kenji stepped out of her Cessna.

Ninety -eight men snapped to attention and saluted. "I suppose some of you are back in the reserves and feel obligated to salute. Thank you. It's good to see all of you," Adm. Kenji laughed and returned the salute. "I guess some of you are back in the service as either regulars, officers, or reservists. I guess the salute is appropriate. Thank you. At ease, men. I've come to join another Iggy Marcus crusade. It would be an honor and pleasure to serve with all of you again. I understand we're going after some really bad actors this time."

Paul Billings nodded, "You understand correctly, Admiral. This time is the Russian mafia, and you've arrived just in time. I was about to start the briefing, and Junior's going to display the holograms we will use to identify our adversaries. There are 90 of us, and we are going to operate in two and three-man teams."

"Go ahead, Paul. Don't let me interrupt. I need to be briefed as well."

The holograms began. They had been created from the mental images Gloria had extracted from general Magda Beluga and premier Sergei Borodin. She downloaded the physical images into Baby's neural net, and she then incorporated them into the hologram program. Images of faces materialized between Daedalus and the hanger wall. "Pay attention to these faces, men. They are your counterparts. These men are ex-KGB and members of the Spetsnaz, the Russian equivalent of our special forces. There are a few thousand of them at large who belong to the Russian mafia. They control most of the European drug traffic, all the drug traffic in the former Soviet Union countries as well as Russia, and they are also arms dealers on a worldwide basis. They are the 'go-to guys' for any military equipment needed by small countries or terrorist organizations."

The following eight hours consisted of memorization of faces and tactical training to physically subdue mob members. Many of them were upper echelon who would be the early targets. “Cut off the head of the snake, and it dies, men,” injected Billings. Locations of suspected members were given to everyone. Many were in the various countries of the old Soviet. Many of them, however, were distributed around all the countries of Europe and the United States.

Paul Billings and Tom Rickert had spent hours training the men in specialized attack procedures. He knew that without the Iggy Marcus electromagnetic defense shield, some of his men would die tomorrow and in the following days of the mission. Iggy tapped Tom’s shoulder. “Let me have the microphone for a few minutes.”

“Okay, everyone, listen up. You're the best trained fighting men on earth, but you are beginning to see the magnitude of this operation. I'm asking a small handful of men to subdue and arrest at least a thousand mafia members. That's a rough guess. We gathered information from General Magda Beluga and Sergei Borodin. My daughter did that, and we are completely satisfied with its reasonable accuracy. Please note the word reasonable. Besides being fighters, you are all critical thinkers. You must stay on your toes for the duration of this exercise. We’re dealing with the deadliest group of men that exists because of their training and callous disregard for human life. That's why you are enduring specialized training. I have more, but first, does anyone have questions?”

One man questioned him. "There are 80 of us, and we are traveling everywhere in the world, apparently, because that's where these men are located. Your best guess is there are over a thousand of them, maybe even two thousand. How long do you expect this to take?"

"As I said, we are up against the toughest bunch of killers anywhere. It will take as long as it takes. You all understand the element of surprise. We have enough technology to prevent communication between various mafia groups. They are spread out everywhere. That makes it more difficult. Unlike the Italians, they don't all convene to discuss family business. They are much more independent and ruthless. That's why you have sidearms. The shields were enough when dealing with pedophiles and many of the Chinese officers we delivered to Gilligan's Island. These men are wildcards. When moving them, you may be forced to close a shield here and there. They may take the opportunity to try and retaliate. Remember, they are killers. Don't hesitate and give them an edge. You know the routine. Kill if you must but be thorough."

"We have four ships. There will be the usual pilots who will explain crucial details such as timelines and approximate opposition numbers. We still lack the organization to prosecute these people, so they will have to wait for due process. We have quite a lineup of people awaiting due process at this point.

One of the men raised his hand. "Tom, what are we going to do with all these vicious Looney Tunes characters when we get our hands on them? I mean, every single barracks and cell at Gitmo is crammed full of crooked congressmen and bureaucrats." Everybody laughed because they had helped put the congressman there. The following morning four ships rose from the Lightning flightline and left for designated compass points. Everyone had agreed they would clean the mob up from American cities first. If the Russians even got a hint that the program was to eliminate them, they might start indiscriminately killing. There were more than 60 locations to assault. Each one consisted of a small group. Small groups were well organized and even kept a set of books. Everything had to be confiscated.

"We are populating some of the deserted islands in the middle of the Pacific. So far, we have a bunch of Chinese Communists, pedophile sickos, and American traitors from the Gitmo overflow hanging out on Fantasy Island and Gilligan's Island. We're reserving 'The Isle of No Return' for the Russians."

"What are we going to do, just drop them off there? Sounds like we're bringing them on vacation. What's to keep them from building rafts and escaping?"

Evidently, Junior thought it was time to contribute. "Sharks... Dad has a little device that works sonically. Planted around the island in a few strategic locations, they will ring the shark dinner bell. Raw Russian appetizers served with dry Smirnoff Martinis... stirred, not shaken. I know I sound cruel and inhuman, but after all... I am a robot."

Tom Rickart had set the itinerary. Each ship had 15 targets consisting of an average of five mob members. Prisoners holding cells had been installed in each ship so the continuity of raids would not be broken.

Junior brought Poseidon to rest 6 inches above the roof of a large corporate building in Thomaston, Long Island. He had been given instructions. This was a large manufacturing and distribution center for missile guidance electronic systems. The executive officers occupied the top-floor suites except for one. That office was dedicated to six ghost employees who were used to executing unconventional measures beyond normal business. They were leg breakers who filled whatever shoes were necessary to get the job done. When all else fails, powerful people fall back on coercion. This office contained the corporate coercion arm of American Textural Guidance Systems.

Corporate espionage and the occasional physical brutality required to discourage competition were the stock in trade of these men. They had been in America long enough to lose the Russian accent. When they weren't filling the corporate jobs, they sidelined with prostitution, drug sales, and embezzlement.

Junior was a sentient machine created by the genius of Iggy Marcus. The core of Junior's neural net was the greatest challenge Iggy had faced. Unfortunately, chemical emotion was not programmable. Iggy knew that when he and Marcos Boli sat at the drawing board contemplating methods of giving his mechanical son a personality. Junior didn't have a name at the time. It was just a device under construction.

Iggy decided Junior would have every piece of information known to man, but his thinking process would focus on and include every psychological quirk embedded in human nature. Although he wouldn't be able to feel, he would be able to understand feelings. Along with this unique approach to artificial intelligence came Junior's novel programming to seek humor in everything, even if linear thought processes and lack of chemical emotion denied him the ability to laugh humorously at his own jokes.

Junior turned to the troop of Navy SEALs about to execute the mission. "The ship's sensors say there are five people in office 82. That is our target. There are supposed to be seven members of this group, but as per instructions, we will arrest whoever is present and come back for the others at some point. I have encapsulated the office. No one can get in or out. Before you enter, however, I would like to have some fun."

Paul Billings laughed. "You're a machine, a smart one… I'll give you that, but you don't know how to have fun. What are you up to?"

"Oh, nothing much. You know Iggy gave me an imagination. He also taught me the ins and outs of small talk and humor. So, before you guys charge in there like storm troopers, I want to do something that I think Tom Rickart or Dad would do to have a little fun with this."

"Sure, Junior. Whatever floats your boat. My morning is promised to no one else. We do have another raid this afternoon, but we have plenty of time. You know what we say in the Marine Corps… Carpe diem!"

"Dad developed sonic techniques years ago. He used them in China to communicate with several million people of Bālún Tōng. The technique vibrates air molecules electromagnetically to generate sound, eliminating the necessity for speakers. I'm going to speak to the Russians in the office before you guys go in. The voice will appear to be coming from nowhere and at the same time, seem to exist in the center of their brains. It's kind of neat. I think I will give the voice a slight reverberation. If you like, I can make it happen aboard this ship so you all can have a good laugh. Then, someone will at least appreciate my sense of humor."

Paul Billings was smiling. Life around these people was always a hoot. "Yeah, sure. We could all use a good laugh."

Junior altered his voice to become deep, resonant, and frighteningly evil. He pressed the button on the microphone. **" YA D'YVOL!!! U MENYA YEST' KOM DLYA VAS!! YA BROSIL TEBYA V ADSKOYE PLAMYA!!!"**

"What did you just say to them," asked Billings. "It sounded pretty frightening to me."

"Oh, not too much. Gloria did this once and it seemed to be very effective. I told them that I was the devil and that I had come to cast them into the eternal fires of hell. I believe that falls in the humor category, although I suppose it depends on which end of the comment you are on, giving or receiving."

Paul Billings and his men roared with laughter. "That's the funniest thing I ever heard, Junior. I'll bet dollars to donuts they all pissed their pants. I mean, it really sounded very evil and ominous. Okay men, saddle up, make sure you're shielded. It's time to go into office 82 and drag five Russians into the fires of hell. It's too bad we don't have demon costumes. It would be hilarious. Maybe next time."

Exactly 6 minutes later, 12 men stood at the door of office 82. Three men used their battering ram and slammed the door inward. Paul Billings was still chuckling. Usually, the men followed Tom Rickart's lead and shielded themselves with Looney Tunes characters. Not this time. All 12 men shielded themselves with each man's individual concept of the devil.

Paul Billings was still laughing hysterically. He tapped the shoulder of the man next to him and pointed to the window. Shield the window, Kelly.

Three of the men had run for the window, and apparently, were so terror-stricken by the apparitions, they were going to jump from the 14th floor. The Russians all had guns, but not one of them pulled one.

Billings issued orders, "Everyone put all their guns on the floor and step away from them."

The Russians complied and stepped away from the weapons as Billings' men adjusted the shields and collected the guns. The men were jabbering to each other in Russian. They had no idea what had just happened. "All right, Boris and Natasha, or whatever your names are, **march**! Follow my men."

The Russians came completely unglued. No one had ever interfered with their business affairs before. One, apparently the leader, frantically asked, "Who are you? What are you doing here? Where are you taking us?"

Col. Paul Billings could hardly speak he was laughing so hard. "Why, we are taking you to hell, of course. The fires are hot and waiting for you on the roof. Get moving."

Once aboard the ship, Junior locked the Russians in the holding cell. "You are all grinning. It must have been fun."

"Yeah, Junior. Thanks to you. I believe these guys think they are on their way to hell. You frightened them all out of their shorts."

***

Six hours later, the four ships returned to Lightning. The SEALs, once granted their usual title of federal marshals, had managed to arrest six-hundred-fifty-two Russian mobsters. One of the groups engaged in a firefight as soon as the strike team breached the mob headquarters. It only lasted for a few minutes when force field ricochets began striking the perpetrators, killing one of them.

Tom Rickart and Oniella Kenji coordinated and directed field operations from the Lightning control room. Tom reported. "We nabbed 92 of them, Iggy, with only one casualty on the other side. The idiot shot himself. We've got them all in a holding tank together talking to themselves." Rickart laughed. "I guess five of them think they're being killed and sent to hell. That's Junior's non-humorous sense of humor."

"According to the spreadsheet in my hand," said Admiral Kenji, "we should be able to wrap up the stateside operations in two or possibly three more days. Your bullet list has 652 mobsters on it; all numbered as to priority." She looked at Iggy. "I presume you have another special island already prepared for these reprobates."

"Yes. Tom named this one,' The Isle of No Return'."

Five days later, 652 former Russian mafia members were parked on an island in the middle of the Pacific. Tom Rickart, Oniella Kenji, and Iggy Marcus stood in front of the prisoners while Junior and Baby emptied the ship of crates and supplies.

"My name is Iggy Marcus. You may know who I am. I'm the guy that has removed you from society in case a few of you don't know. You are on an island surrounded by sharks in the middle of the Pacific Ocean. This is where you will remain until we can officially provide you with due process of the law. The world is changing, and organized crime is not going to be part of it. The crates Junior just unloaded are enough food and water to last you all approximately 30 days. We will return with more. You'll also find crates with garden tools, fertilizer, and seeds. You will learn to support yourself without resorting to ripping off your fellow men. You can also fish, but I suggest you don't go swimming."

"You men are the first phase of our operation. We are obliterating the Russian mafia. You represent only those from the United States. There are at least 1800 more of you located everywhere around the world. The rest of your compatriots will soon be joining you. You will all learn to live together and cooperate for survival. If you can't do that, I expect many of you will not be alive very long."

"I said it once before, Iggy Marcus," laughed Tom Rickart, "you are one cold heartless man!"

Within two weeks, the Russian mafia's grip on the underworld was essentially broken. They had come from extreme military training as upper-ranking enlisted men, GRU, and KGB officers. These men and their offspring were once members of the state. Mother Russia gave them a purpose. Russia had always been a tyranny, even in the days of the Czar. These men were products of that philosophical violence. The abolition of the Soviet Union gave them nowhere to go. Most had no education or productive abilities outside military service. They embarked on the only life that would grant them a semblance of their former power... Crime.

Their ruthless criminality made the Italian Mafia look like choirboys. As military men in the Soviet Union, other than fighting foreign wars, they had one job only… suppression of the population. Tyranny always requires a military arm to subjugate an undernourished populace. That mindset was trained into them to become their entire reason for living. They viewed society as nameless victims from their synthetic perch of militant autocracy without compassion or decency. Their payment was the possession of rank in a system that had no ability to bestow any other kind of reward.

***

"Well, I guess that wraps up the Russian mafia, boss," said Tom Rickart, laughing. "We have 2400 of them, or close to it. Boy, that's sure l hell of a lot of adjudication, especially because there are so many countries involved. It's going to be a long time before we finish this mess, isn't it?"

"Yes, Tom, a while. Unfortunately, we had no choice but to do it the way we did it. These things cannot be done piecemeal. The consequences always come later when you're fixing things that are severely broken. However, not fixing them is never an acceptable option."

"I suppose you're right, from the perspective of a Marcus. But for sure, we would have blown ourselves up by now or be almost close to it if you hadn't wandered into the picture. Anyway, Boss, who or what Is next?"

"The next one, Tom, is going to be the most difficult yet. I'll map it out for you. It took a long time to create this by subversion, and those kinds of things are usually difficult to correct and take longer to undo."

"Are you referring to what's been done to the kids? There doesn't appear to be much hope for them."

"Yes, so it appears, but not just the kids. It has been incrementally done intentionally to everyone. It's not hopeless, but it's close. You see, Tom, we have been psychologically bombarded and inundated shortly after leaving the womb. Most American universities have been destroyed. They are nothing more than propaganda deployment centers." Iggy smiled. "I tend to agree with you about the hopelessness part, but only to a degree."

"Chaos theory appears to dictate a lack of order, and frequent calamities would seem to exhibit a universe that leaves everything to happenstance. You know my mind was expanded by the lightning strike 30 years ago. I have a unique perspective. The complexity of the universe is intricate beyond words. I don't see it all, but I see enough of it to know that it is the product of an orderly mind. Everything makes sense. Nothing is guesswork. Do anomalous things happen, like supernovas, quasars, and black holes? Of course, they do, but it is all by design. Do you see it, Tom? The tapestry is exquisite and comprised of infinity, manifesting itself in an ever-changing physical form. It is energy, Tom. It's the energy of conscious creation. The sight is staggering and can only be viewed and understood through critical thought."

"The kids are taught to avoid critical thinking. Critical thought destroys autocratic control. Once they graduate college, their programming is relatively complete. They will step in line and march to the tune played by the autocrats. They have been told all the things my mother refused to teach us and taught none of the things that would create value in them as human beings."

"It's not everybody, boss. My sister and I were not fed that crap. My parents knew better."

"You are old school, Tom, as were your parents. The universities have been completely subverted now. There are only a few of them that teach reality without the philosophical trash that undermines common sense and values. This is not by accident or simply the way it goes in every society. This has been engineered by our friends in Interlink, but they didn't do it alone. This has been designed by powers that are not human."

In the 25 years Tom Rickart had known and been employed by Iggy Marcus, he had never been told this. He wasn't sure what to make of it. "What are we talking here, boss, supernatural or some such things as aliens?"

"In a manner of speaking, considering there's nothing natural about this. We are in our infancy. Billions of civilizations have been created throughout the universe in the billions of years of this cycle. They exist on every evolutionary level. That's the Creator's blueprint. To put it simply, there's no such thing as a universal status quo. Everything, including us, is in a state of flux. The civilizations that exist have two choices, advance or regress. There are no other alternatives. That is by cosmic design, Tom. It's how the entire universe works."

"Go on, Iggy. There are two schools of human thought on the subject. One of them is creation, and the other one is coincidence. I like to think of it as creation."

Iggy smiled. I tend to agree with you. But it isn't necessarily creation as defined by our poetic history.

"I'm not sure what you're getting it, Iggy. What has that got to do with the here and now or the psychological mess coming out of our universities?"

"It has everything to do with it, Tom. There are people, if you want to call them that, who have been visiting this planet for millions of years. The arrogance of the human mind knows no bounds. We are conceited enough to believe we are the center of the universe, and the infinite number of galaxies and stars out there exist only as a panorama to amuse us and mollify our boredom. We have been taught that by religion. In our insecurity, we claim this planet is the center of the universe, and most religious dogma infers that mankind exists alone in all that splendor. That's preposterous on the face of itself, Tom. Why, we have only had the printing press for a thousand years. The Creator, God or whatever you want to call it, is not laying title to this planet as its best work. Just imagine how silly that sounds when you roll it around in your mind for a while, considering the more than thirteen-billion-year age of the Universe."

"I can see that, boss. Still, how does that relate to our situation and our societal delusion?"

"Our societal delusion? I'll address that in a minute. Take the computer chip for instance. The leap from the Univac to the computer chip is a greater leap than from the wheel to the Univac. Do you honestly believe two guys named Hewlett and Packard tinkered the first silicon computer chip together in their garage? It doesn't get any sillier than that. It was a product of extraterrestrial reverse engineering. People think that technology was pulled out of a spacecraft that crashed in Roswell. There are all kinds of stories. That technology was given to us, and yes, we reverse engineered things. The human mind was not capable of creating the mathematics for this without the aid of a computer. So, what came first? The chicken or the egg?"

"I know of three species of intelligent beings who visit us here. I've spoken to several of them. Just like every other sentient, motivated creature, they have a mission. Some of them are shepherds who act logically in accordance with the universal scheme of things. You might call it some sort of universal morality. There are others who are locusts. The Creator doesn't create autonomous individuals and then strips them of autonomy at a whim. Occasionally, the ones called shepherds will sterilize a planet. It has been done here before. It is done when a species is so violent that it threatens to destroy itself or, in the worst case, acquire significant technology to export violence off the world. That is a universal constant. Sentient beings must not destroy other sentient beings."

Iggy paused.

"Don't stop now, boss; go on. You have alluded to this, but we have never spoken of it in depth."

"The Creator, or the Universe, if you will, does not directly intervene in the minuscule affairs of its creations. It does attend to them, however, in many different fashions."

“Oh, how so?”

"You remember Cameron Fry's visit a short time ago. He and I had many conversations. He is upper echelon interlink, but his allegiance doesn't lie there. He's completely independent. No one owns him. Evidently, visitors from the fourth planet in the solar system around the star, Altair, are here and dealing with interlink. Expand your horizons here, Tom. Visitors from other worlds are obviously far higher on the evolutionary ladder than Homo sapiens. They exist on a different plane. They have conquered mortality or at least extended their lifespans enormously. The fact that they travel here from another star illustrates their sophistication and distance above our developmental level."

“Okay." Acknowledged Tom. "Go on."

"I'll draw an analogy. All species evolve. We are evolutionary infants. Just the fact they can travel across interstellar space demonstrates their technical advancement. Our planet has been visited by extraterrestrial species for millions of years. When you think in terms of the universe's age approximately 13.7 billion years, and the age of the earth, approximately 4 billion years, a million years is a very small increment of time. The universe has existed 1,300,000 times longer than that. Man, only began recording history in the Upanishads and Vedas about 6,000 years ago. You see, all of man's existence is a tiny blip on the radar screen in terms of the universe's existence. Extraterrestrials will not relate to us on our level, nor can we relate to them on their level. What has happened to me intellectually is nowhere near the summit of man's evolution. No one knows what that will be.”

The extraterrestrials from Altair are colluding with Interlink. I can't draw you an exact analogy, but we are to them intellectually, probably as a chimpanzee is to us, intellectually. I don't believe Interlink realizes that. They are dealing with this species by making the same assumption everyone does: everyone thinks everyone else exists on their level and then acts and reacts accordingly. The Altair four, people have ulterior motives that are not benevolent. The people I have dealt with from the other side of the galaxy are 'shepherds' by their own definition. Apparently, they are benevolent.

Gloria was able to read their minds. It's kind of handy having her around, but I had physical contact with one of them, anyway."

"So just what are you telling me?"

"I'm not 100% sure yet, Tom. These people from Altair four are after something. They have some other agenda that has to do with us. I don't think it has even one thing to do with Interlink or mining this planet for physical resources. I think it is far deeper and sinister as well. I have a theory or two, but I really must talk to my friends from the other side of the galaxy. They are not here to take an adversarial position against other inhabitants of different worlds. They are expressively here to deal with us from an ambivalent perspective but made it perfectly clear that whatever is going on may require some sort of mitigation."

"So, Iggy, what are your theories, and what sort of mitigation?"

"I'll get into the theories shortly. The mitigation, however, is probably me.

"Cameron Fry and I discussed this extensively. Much of our mythology is actually an ambiguous, poetic record of historical facts. Ancient humans had no method to pass information to their progeny or share it with others besides word-of-mouth, cave paintings, and occasional handwritten parchment scrolls. The word-of-mouth gets distorted, cave paintings are inaccurate because they're only interpretations of visualization, and scrolls are subject to deterioration and decay. There is no doubt, however, we have been visited by people from other worlds for millions of years. There is much speculation about these things and some of it is accurate."

"I'm still waiting for the theories, Boss."

"Be patient, I'm getting there. You already understand my belief that the Creator is a conscious entity that encompasses all of existence. I also believe the Creator has severed pieces of itself to become its autonomous children. We have discussed this often enough. Let me elaborate further. I'm quite sure the Creator, in its benevolence, doesn't wave a magic wand like the book of Genesis in the Bible portrays. That was a simple explanation to display creation to the intellectually inferior human mind of those lost ages. The tapestry is much more complex. The design is intricate, and when unique species come into being, they are often products of the activities of other species."

Tom had not discussed this with Iggy before, but he knew he was on the cusp of a revelation. "Go on, I'm listening."

"The design of the cosmos is such; many of its citizens evolved for millions of years and continue to do so. They exist on an elevated plane, so far above us that we cannot comprehend it. I'm not aware of who or what they are; I am just aware that they must exist because logic and the order of the universe dictate that reality. So, we have been created… not necessarily by a magic wand in the hand of God, but we may have been born from some very sophisticated alien petri dish. If one considers the complexity of the universe and its tapestry, one could say the petri dish is a magic wand in the hand of God. Look at Junior and Baby. I built Junior and for all intents and purposes, Junior built Baby. They are autonomous, sentient life forms. That is undeniable. They have free will and the ability to choose a path through life, as well as reproduce, albeit inorganically. Were they created by the cosmos? Of course, but I was the vehicle through which they came into being. Am I making sense to you, Tom?"

Rickart shook his head, silently contemplating all of this. He had been hanging around Iggy Marcus for 25 years and had heard and seen a lot, but this was brand-new territory. "I see what you're getting at, and it makes a lot of sense. What is your theory, Iggy?"

"Well, here's where it gets interesting. There are two facets to this. If it wasn't for Cameron Fry, I would not know either of them. Apparently, he had two meetings with one of them." Iggy laughed. "Heinrich Klatch named them Hansel and Gretel. At the first meeting, both aliens were present. Cameron Fry is an unusual man... highly intelligent with a photographic memory. He observed both aliens closely at the first meeting. One was obviously male, and the other was female. Three months later, they had another meeting in the same place; this time only with Hansel. It was during the day. The Vatican vault is 22 stories below the Sistine Chapel. As you know, the Cathedral and Chapel are chock-full of visitors during the day. Hansel's appearance is not even close to human. They have a very large cranium, long tapered face with a pointed chin, thin lips, and slits for nose and ears. They appear corpulent by our standards, and they are close to 7 feet tall."

"Huh... how does something who looked like that get by all the tourists without freaking them out? Hansel sounds like a gargoyle. The Sistine Chapel is hardly the place to parade around in if you look like a gargoyle."

"The Pope was at this meeting. He was a little put off by the sight of these characters. At any rate, Hansel had a large black clergy's cassock on at the second meeting with a long white surplice to hide the corpulence. He also had a monsignor's hat and a large cloth veil wrapped around his head and face. The long veil was not typical of priest's garb, but no tourists picked up on it."

"What's so interesting about that, boss?"

"Hold your horses, Tom. The first meeting with the two aliens was late at night. There was no one in the chapel, and they did not need a disguise. Hansel had to disguise himself at the second meeting because it was in the middle of the day with lots of tourists around. Believe me, Tom, Hansel looks like a gargoyle. The meeting lasted several hours. When everyone left, it was after dark. There were no tourists around, so Hansel departed without the veil. He left it behind along with the monsignor's cap."

"I take it Cameron Fry glommed those two items. I can just imagine what you could find out with them."

"You've got the idea, Tom. That's the second part. The reason Fry wanted the veil, and the hat was interesting. Hansel had a completely different look to his face on a second visit. He was supposedly the same creature but looked completely different to someone as observant as Cameron Fry. When he visited me a few weeks ago, he brought both articles with him and left them with me."

"What did you find out?"

"Both the hat and the veil were loaded with Hansel's DNA. We didn't know it even had DNA until we tested it. I had the test done independently. Melanie and Sylvia Peterson tested it at the hospital; then, we sent them to Washington to Allison MacLeod's office. She's a brilliant geneticist and virologist. Both Melanie and Allison had identical findings. They have DNA all right. It is very close to human DNA, with some aberrations. The aberrations are just differences. There's another problem. You understand that DNA or deoxyribonucleic acid is comprised of two polynucleotide chains wrapped around themselves in a double helix. They are polymers that carry instructions for development and reproduction by molecular alignment. RNA is nucleic acid."

"These creatures have a problem, Tom. They are built of the same stuff we are. Their DNA is only slightly different, but it has degenerated. They are a species with a molecular problem in their DNA. It's disintegrating and must be hereditary or the result of environmental degradation. Both Melanie, Allison, and I analyzed this, and we are quite sure that they are unable to reproduce. They probably have the ability to clone duplicates, but even duplicates require intact functional DNA."

"Woah! Are you telling me that they're pretending to mine resources on this planet when they really intend to mine our DNA?"

"It would seem to be a distinct possibility. When Fry told me they wanted to mine resources from this planet, I was more than a little skeptical. The minerals we have on this planet that might pique their interest exist in abundance on the moons of Saturn, Jupiter, and Uranus, and that doesn't even count the asteroid belt or Mars. Further, the solar system is loaded with trillions of gallons of water in the form of ice, and if they go to Europa, its liquid ocean has three times more saline water than earth. So, I had my doubts about mining. However, this is the only restaurant in town with DNA on the menu."

"What do you think they're going to do, Iggy? Are you telling me they might have to kill someone to get their DNA?"

"Nope. That wouldn't work too well for them. They need a living organism. DNA is not like dandelions in your lawn that you can just pick and then make dandelion wine. They need living organisms. Or at least, that's what I believe. I still don't have proof that is what they are here for, but I intend to find out, and Cameron Fry is going to help me."

"What brings you to these conclusions, Iggy? Where are you heading with this? I guess I'm asking what the basis or theory for this is?"

"As our body repairs itself and our cells replicate, DNA also continually divides and replicates itself. It's the blueprint for everything. Our organs, bones, and everything is incorporated into that blueprint. With all this replicating, occasionally mistakes or anomalies arise. They are called mutations. Sometimes mutations are beneficial because they are a direct result of changing environmental circumstances. Then, it's called evolution If the organism adopts qualities that help it adapt to a changing environment. Then, those mutations are often passed on to the organism's progeny. Often, those mutations are destructive in nature. They become aberrations in our cellular structure. That's how we eliminated cancer, by the way. Our transmutation of matter and energy is able to obliterate debilitating mutations, replacing them with normal cells or at least allowing the normal cells to proliferate. Do you see where I'm going with this, Tom?"

"Yeah, I sure do. Chemistry and biology weren't my strong suits, but I took several classes. Math and physics are my orientation. I see where you are going. Apparently, you believe these people, or whatever they are, have defective DNA that is no longer capable of dividing and replicating itself to maintain the stature of the blueprint for their metabolism. They've lost that ability, and they're looking for new gardens and fertilizer. Jesus Iggy! You're talking about harvesting the stuff from human beings or using them as a petri dish of sorts. Wow!"

"If my suspicions are correct, the creatures from Altair may be changing our biosphere to alter our DNA, bringing it closer to theirs for the purpose of harvesting genetic material to sustain them. You see, evolution isn't necessarily constructed for species advancement. Adverse stimuli can create the scenario where evolution becomes benign or even destructive.

Then, an intelligent intervention must correct the event's progress. You might say, keep the train on the tracks."

"One thing gives me great pause, however. I have created technology that transmutes matter and energy. They are interchangeable, and I make it look simple. It isn't simple, however. It's beyond complex. My opinion is that man would not have developed matter and energy transmutation capabilities for eons, and apparently, these creatures have not developed it either, or so it would seem. For instance, Melanie and I built an exact replication of an ovum from Alice Sledge's DNA to get them pregnant. Do you understand? We mapped Alice's DNA in order to create the ovum, and then I created it. These creatures from another world somehow managed to cross the distance barrier from Altair to Sol. It is the same technology I have incorporated in Daedalus. Why, then, have they been unable to re-create their DNA to solve their own problems? This is truly a conundrum, and it needs to be solved because something is going on here. I believe it represents something very sinister for us."

Tom Rickart sat quietly, staring at Iggy for several minutes, chuckling. "You know, Iggy, I often think back to that first day when you shook my hand, and I almost fell over. I knocked my iced tea to the floor... remember? I thought that was the most unusual day of my life. It was nothing compared to the thousands of days afterwards. I've got a question, boss. Don't you ever wonder why this all happened to you in particular? Why have you been able to discover a way to turn lead into gold? It's theoretically impossible. The Physics of this is impossibly complicated. Yet, I watch it happen all the time here. How come you and Melanie had three kids with such amazing capabilities and all so different from each other? It's beyond amazing. Whatever is going on, I believe you're the only one who can fix this. Thanks for inviting me on this crazy roller coaster ride."

"Don't mention it, Tom. It's been fun."

"So, what's next on the agenda, Iggy, alien DNA or politics?"

"We have three pressing short-term items. North Korea, Iran, Afghanistan and the big bear, Russia. We have some things to do to straighten out those messes. But that's not the priority. The most pressing item is the hidden authorities of Interlink and their collusion with off-world aliens, but I don't have enough information yet."

"I understand some of this. The Iranian ayatollahs are still running centrifuges and think that somehow, they can get past you to nuke Israel. That is their sworn mission. The Taliban is still torturing women and oppressing everyone, and the North Koreans are nothing more than slaves to the lunatics in charge. Your idea is to fix this. I can't argue with your methodology. Everyone gets a second chance. It seems those types of people will continue to do evil despite a second chance. I watched you remove them all over the world and deposit them in the Pacific islands. That's an interesting approach, Boss. In a manner of speaking, you are a conqueror but not a despot. Instead of lining them up against the wall in front of a firing squad, they wind up on South Sea Island tropical paradises. Pretty amazing," Tom Rickert laughed.

"That about sums it up, Tom. The problem with the Taliban, the Koreans, and the ayatollahs is they kill indiscriminately based on moral delusion, and all have technology. I could walk away from them and let it fester, but lots of people will die at the hands of maniacs. I can't be everybody's keeper, but I am obligated to stop mass murder."

"What about the big-ticket item? It appears very complicated and hard to manage."

"Hard to manage is putting it mildly. Everything is tied together. Cameron Fry suggested something, and I concur. Heinrich Klatch came out of the closet to run Interlink's affairs in the open after I took their top 13 to Guantánamo. They were the public face of interlink. There are dozens more who are hidden. Apparently, interlink has a front office and a rear office. The front office is manipulated and controlled by the rear office in the shadows. The front office doesn't even know who they all are and the extent of their power. It's an interesting hierarchy. Klatch knows everything. As I stated, he came out of the rear office to run the front office."

"What do you intend to do?"

"I don't know yet, Tom. Gloria and I are going to take a quiet trip to Brussels and probably the Sistine Chapel. Cameron Fry will give me the dates. We need to do some subliminal probing."

"How often do you talk to him?"

“Cameron Fry? Occasionally. Interestingly enough, he has become an ally and his position at ground zero is a very useful and effective place to glean information. I never expected it. I gave him a sat phone directly assessable to mine.”

“Has Jake agreed yet? The presidency is a precarious place to be these days. Bill and Alice Sledge have managed to avoid trouble, and as soon as his term is up, they will be out of harm's way, hopefully."

"Jake agreed to run. We are going to start campaigning now. There are three challengers in the field: Mark Solomon, Aaron Beech, and Violet Kensington Blithe. They will be the primary candidates, and they've already been campaigning for months. Solomon isn’t bad, Beech is a phony looking for a spot in the history books, and Blithe simply isn't up to the job. Jake is actually the best person to shoulder the remnants of the Sledge presidency. I believe we can sell him to the public with American Media Inc.”

"It's too bad, Iggy, that's what it comes down to, a sales job based on personalities and smiles. When do you think the human race will finally wake up and determine these things based on philosophical and practical issues."

"Yup. Since the age of electronic media, that's what it comes down to… soundbites, smiles, and BS. Lightning Inc. has attempted to change that through American Media, but Rome wasn't built in a day. Someday, our kids will hopefully be educated and introspective enough to raise politics to the plateau it should exist on."

***

Pres. William James Sledge leaned back in his chair and put his shoeless feet on the oval Office desk. He had 16 months left in his second term, not counting his lame duck status. He rarely allowed himself the luxury of putting his feet on the desk out of respect, but today was different. He felt lazy as he reflected on his presidency, waiting for his Chief of Staff and the vice president. It all started seven years ago as an amazing adventure. He had attained the highest office in the United States, and for all intents, probably the most powerful position in the world. He laughed at himself. That's a joke. The most powerful person in the world resides in Montana, and he dwarfs the rest of us.

Most men in his position would be patting themselves on the back. His presidency was populated with the greatest accomplishments in human history. The threat of nuclear war was abolished, tactical war followed suit, and then bioweapons were confiscated from every country. Starvation was becoming a thing of the past, as well as cancer and the dependence on fossil fuels for energy. It all hadn't been brought into effect yet. Iggy Marcus was doing it slowly so as not to sink the ship of state or the world economy. He had destroyed pedophilia as organized depravity. It still existed but not on its previous levels. The Russian mafia was defunct, but there were remnants of those characters still around, although they seemed to have seen the handwriting on the wall and actually worked at jobs.

William James Sledge had learned never to lie to himself or skirt reality from the man who was responsible for all the wonderful things that occurred during his presidency. He would go down in history along with Iggy Marcus for changing the world and saving the future for posterity. He knew; however, his presidency had begun as an exercise in mediocrity. If it wasn't for the amazing appearance of Iggy Marcus, that's how it would've eventually ended, and possibly during a nuclear holocaust.

Curtis Mulroney, Abe Morris, and Sen. Jake Dorian followed the perfunctory knock on the oval Office door as his Chief of Staff pushed the door inward. "Good morning, gentlemen. Sit and make yourselves comfortable. We've got a bit to discuss, and Janet's bringing coffee."

"Good morning, Bill," everyone echoed. "We are getting down to the wire, aren't we?"

“Well, politics is on the menu this morning, and the coffee will help wash it down. So, Jake, you've agreed to run. You're getting in the game very late as presidential campaigns go. It's only four months until the convention. Even with American media, it's questionable. The only thing I would say that's in your favor is there is only one other candidate worth his salt, and that's Solomon. Still, the others have been at it for a year and have lots of name recognition. Also, Blithe is a woman and that makes her candidacy special in terms of the female voting bloc. It's a lot to overcome."

Jake shook his head with a smile. "True enough, Bill, but the old saying goes, 'it's the last hundred yards that make the difference in a close horse race.' Right now, there are three candidates entering the primary. I'll be the fourth. No matter how you shake a stick at, the last couple of months are really the crucial months when everyone puts their agenda on the table, and everyone else tries to cut up the red meat."

"Jake has enormous name recognition," injected the vice president. "It was fine being vice president, but I did not want the job behind that desk, Bill. I was seven years younger when I entered this building. I've been here long enough." Abe Morris looked at Jake. "I sat in this office through the most amazing, unbelievable presidency in the history of the United States. I still look back on it in wonder. I've known you through the entire journey, Jake. You're one of the smartest, most competent men in politics today... and you're a young man by our standards. I'm glad you decided to run. I'm sure Iggy Marcus had something to do with it. It's a good thing American Media is as huge as it is because all the other mainstream media will try to hammer you into a pulp of quivering flesh. That's their modus operandi today. That's how they define politics. It's never about the issues; it's always about the assassination of character."

"I've known you a long time, Jake, ever since I got this job," said Curtis Mulroney. "I don't really know your past, but I would suggest if you intended to enter the race, take all the skeletons out of your closet and hang them in the front yard for everyone to see now. Sunlight sterilizers things as time passes, and there isn't much time."

Jake laughed. "No skeletons, Kurt, unless you go back to my college days. There were a couple of nights Iggy and I tore it up pretty good and wound up hugging the porcelain god. Not too often though, and I never did anything my mother would be ashamed of... critical of... yes... ashamed of... no."

Curtis Mulroney nodded. "Good. That's huge. I've been in politics in one form or another for 25 years. I managed Bill's first campaign and second campaign for reelection. I've seen it all, and word for word, item for item… you, Jake, are the best debater I have ever seen or heard of, except maybe for Iggy Marcus. So, my best advice is to insist on debating your competitors. You need two, maybe three debates, one of them right on top of the primary election. Further, you have to tone it down. You want to stay slightly ahead of everyone else's game so that you beat them, but you don't want to tip your hand by wowing the entire world just yet."

"How so? Are you referring to the general election and the other party?"

"Exactly, Jake. Politics is a game of chess. Subtlety and nuance are everything. Even more so in this electronic world replete with soundbites and word salad vignettes. You don't want to shoot your best salvo and all your ammunition at the beginning of the battle, hoping for a kill. You must save the best for last when it's time to crucify the opposition. That takes a lot of thought, introspection, and always having your battle feet on the ground. You must always know where you are and where you are going. Further, you must have insights as to where your opponents are and where they are headed. If you can do all of that, you will be unbeatable by anyone except someone of equal stature with as good and vibrant a message."

"You know Curt, the biggest problem I have with politics today and how a flawed human nature infects everything we do is that it's now always about character assassination and crucifixion of the opponent. That should not have anything to do with politics unless the opposition is guilty of egregious sins. It should be strictly about the issues. That's not well-endorsed by the public, however. They've been dumbed down to accept and wallow in the swill dished out by authoritarians that describe the political arena as a swamp full of piranhas."

Mulroney nodded his head in agreement. "Authoritarians claim that is what the people want but that is really what they have taught the people to want by indoctrination."

"Tell you what, Curtis Mulroney, I would love for you to be my campaign manager. After all, you helped get Bill, here, elected twice. Besides the experience, you have the genius for it. Don't make up your mind now. Think about it, but I'll need an answer soon."

"I don't know Jake. Ten years at this job is a long time. I've been with Bill that long. It gets stressful, believe me. You can't imagine how upsetting it was to go through Losey's files when we were chasing down corruption in Congress and the bureaucracy. I'll have to say this though, it's been a hell of a ride. I'm wondering if I can take this for another eight years. That would be 18 years in this crazy job, assuming you get two terms. I don't know, Jake. I'll have to think about it. Who do you have in mind for your vice president?"

"I think the politically smart thing to do would be to have a woman as a running mate." Jake started laughing. "Believe it or not, I actually asked my wife, Sharon. She's a high-powered attorney, very successful, eloquent, brilliant, trustworthy, and on the same political page. Further, she's had experience in smalltime politics. So, I mentioned it to her. She laughed for 15 minutes straight and then said not on your life, baby. I love you to pieces, but I don't think I could take that much drama in our marriage. I'm not sure the public would go for it, either. Then she suggested I ask Allison MacLeod. The woman is a rocket scientist. She's also a leader as well as a Nobel Prize laureate. Her credentials and her record are impeccable. Not only that, she also has a great personality. She'd be perfect."

Bill Sledge raised his eyebrows. "I think she's on to something, Jake. Allison would make a fantastic running mate, but I don't think she'll want to step down from her career. I'm not talking about her job as Surgeon General. As motivated and ambitious as the woman is, Surgeon General is only a part-time job, and she handles it easily. She's right out there in the front of her profession. She's a leader, and the rest of the medical world is running along behind, just trying to keep up. That's true everywhere except Marcus General

Hospital. I've known her for a long time. We are close friends. I'll suggest it and see what her reaction is."

***

"I have your complete update, Dad. Since you and Gloria are both here, I won't have to repeat myself."

"I'm sure you do, Junior. You are incapable of being incomplete. You follow every published or broadcast news item on the planet from minute to minute in real-time. I need that rapid information."

Junior was alive, but he was also a mechanical receiver. He continually processed all electronic radio and television broadcasts simultaneously, filing them for future analysis and dissemination. Every Internet item of news was immediately logged into and analyzed, as well.

"So, Junior. What is the latest scuttlebutt?"

"There's lots, Dad. These are the priorities as I see them. The Russians are moving men and equipment to their western border. It is the harbinger of military intervention into either Ukraine, Belarus, or both. There is nothing in the Russian or European press. However, this activity is consistently observed and documented by our satellites. I am tied directly to their computers, so everything is visible in real-time. I do not think the new guy, Borodin, paid much attention to your requests. Apparently, he finally figured out what you and Gloria did to get the information about the mob when all the Russian mafia disappeared almost overnight. The Russian government used them for all kinds of clandestine operations. They were the perfect secret police. They are all military trained and offered perpetual immunity if they just cooperated. A hell of a deal, if you ask me." Junior smiled."

"Show me the satellite images. We'll have to act quickly. They could easily upset our plans because Interlink is actively involved. I won't allow anyone to put this family or our plans in the crosshairs."

Junior began projecting scaled hologram images of satellite observations in real-time. The images fluctuated with reality, constantly displaying changes as they occurred.

"China is having its problems. The new government is still forming, and the population is still attempting to adjust to the dramatic economic changes. There is no civil unrest because the profits are being distributed among the workers in terms of value for value, but they need help organizing government departments and personnel."

"I expected it. China has never operated as a free society. It was either dynastic rule or tyranny. They have never had the opportunity to self-govern, so they have no idea where to begin. I worked with Bālún Tōng to develop a blueprint they have begun to implement."

"They have existed under a brutal dictatorship bearing the phony moniker of communism for over two generations, almost three. They have no memory of anything else. China has never been a free society, although, under the dynastic rule of emperors, there was a modicum of independence for the citizens. This is a first for them, Junior. We must launch the ship in calm seas."

"I have unlocked and begun training two people who fled China and have been living at the ranch. Tiao Chen's aunt and uncle are going to return to China and assist the new government. Heng Zia and Yang Bo Chu are my latest projects," Iggy smiled. "I've unlocked them twice a week since they came here. It has expanded their cerebral capabilities significantly. Coupled with the education we are giving them, they'll become key personnel in the new government."

Junior smiled with one of his, *look at me I'm almost human,* smiles; "when is Richard McNerney going to make his grand debut?"

"By the looks of things and what you told me, Junior, a lot sooner than I thought. Gloria and I have been preparing him for this for years. It's all part of the master plan. You're welcome to comment."

"I can't say that I enjoy small talk. I don't enjoy anything. Of course, I don't dislike anything either. If I had to describe my emotional self with one word, I would say 'numb', but small talk is habitual because that's how you set up my neural net. Small talk helps me relate to human beings because it helps human beings to relate to me. Take General McNerney, for instance… we hit it off. Now, that is a guy who has had an interesting life. Indoctrinated for six years in Russia, came to the United States at twelve, then was adopted by a couple of Russian spy plants and played high school and college sports to become an Allstate football player while graduating with honors. Then he was accepted at West Point, where he also graduated with honors after being captain of their football team; in a year, they beat Navy. He became an officer and eventually a Major General in the Army in charge of invasion strategy for one of the most powerful countries on earth. Before you know it, he will become the premier of the second most powerful country on earth, Russia. That's quite a resume, Dad. And to think…he was once considered insane."

Gloria laughed. I'm not sure who's more hilarious, you or Baby, but you're both priceless."

"Since you are monitoring our satellites, Junior, keep an eye on the Russians. Do not directly intervene without cause, but if one round is fired or one person breaches a border aggressively, use the satellites to set up a barricade. This must remain automatic before someone accidentally kills a bunch of civilians."

Gloria had entered the lab at her father's summons. "You called, Dad. What's next on the agenda, Iran, or Korea?"

"Iran. The ayatollahs are still running centrifuges. The Russians set up the technology for them. The ayatollahs think they can still manufacture a nuke and sneak it overland into Israel. Their stated mission is the death of all Jews. Also, they're pushing their religion down their own citizens' throats. The people are much more moderate than the behavior compelled by the Koran and the Hadis, but they are killed or jailed if they protest. They murder indiscriminately. The population would rebel, but they have no way to fight back. Authoritarians have all the arms and soldiers."

"We have been fighting endless, pointless wars in the Middle East. We always claim it is for freedom, either ours or the people of the country we are fighting in. It is never for freedom. The people never wind up free. It is to enrich the arms manufacturers and politicians, which enriches the people of interlink. This has been going on for a half-century. Many hundreds of thousands of people have died. It's typical of tyranny, but no one has ever had the power to stop it, especially the common people. We have the power to put an end to this, and it's going to end now."

"You know the UN has been protesting everything you have done in every country, Dad. They say you are the tyrant because you're stealing the rights of other countries to conduct their own affairs in the manner they see fit."

"Of course. That's always the protest. They object to losing power. We have it, and they want it. Unfortunately, their motives are different than ours. They are claiming that my ends do not justify my means, while they spent the last half of the last century and most of this century fighting wars with various countries by using the United States as an excuse and means to justify their specific ends. Supposedly, the objective is freedom and liberation from tyranny. Yet, the results always end in tyranny. For example, the one country in the Middle East that is not a tyranny, is Israel. Palestine is run by an autocrat. Note how everyone in the UN aligns themselves with Palestine against Israel. Even if you don't take Israel's side on the issues, that's all the proof you need to see their motives."

"So, what exactly is the mission, Dad?" Inquired Junior. "I would imagine if the same as every other expedition."

"Almost, but not quite. The supreme leader who decrees the interpretation of religion and how each citizen will live is the Ayatollah Shabahra. One step below him is the elected president Khalil Sidayar. He is a token leader, and all elections in Iran are rigged. The president is nothing more than a figurehead to make the people believe they have some say in their government through elections. They do not. I have a proposition for the president if he likes his cushy life. The Ayatollah is coming with me. I'm taking him on a South Sea Island vacation, and he will have a roommate, Tao Jun Il, from North Korea."

"I have 15 Navy SEALs; you and Junior are going to accompany me to Iran in two hours."

"I see," said Junior. "Your description of corrupt elections in that country is very close to what happens in this country with our voting machines. Don't get me wrong, Dad, I'm not trying to beat a dead horse here, but you know I am accurate.

***

Daedalus hovered 100 feet over the Grand Mosalla Mosque in Tehran.

"Take me in with you, Gloria. It is a clergy meeting. Transfer my speech to everyone present but address the Ayatollah only."

"Okay, Dad."

"AYATOLLAH UZMA BEN SHABAHRA!" was a thunderclap in the minds of every cleric present. **"I am Iggy Marcus. You know who I am. I have removed the threat of nuclear war everywhere except here. You, supposed men of Allah, are building two nuclear weapons with the intent of exterminating the Jewish state." That stops now. I am taking your nuclear fissionable material and your centrifuges with me. You will not be allowed to blow anything up. You have murdered hundreds of your citizens because of your inane religious dogma, supposedly in the name of Allah. Allah does not murder! Only man murders out of greed and avarice! Men may use Allah as an excuse, but they are propping up their own power, self-hatred, and hatred of their fellow men. You are coming with me, Ali Ben Shabahra! You will not be given another option or opportunity to murder, and there is no power on earth able to prevent this."**

Tom Rickert looked at Iggy sideways, wide-eyed. "Geez, Boss. You even scared the hell out of me."

"Your building is encapsulated with a magnetic force field. You are aware of the technology. Your weapons will be useless. Fifteen men will enter your church and forcibly move you if you do not surrender yourself at the entrance. These men will be surrounded by a magnetic field to protect them. If you fire on them, you will likely injure yourselves from ricochet bullets. You have five minutes!"

Junior's face was a question mark. "What? No small talk, Dad?"

Gloria laughed.

"President Sidayar, at least until today, you have not murdered your own people for stupid reasons. Someone must lead your country, and it might as well be you unless you begin to murder your citizens. Then, I will come for you, and you can join this poor excuse for a cleric. I'm quite sure your people agree, this is the 21st century, and murder is no longer an acceptable method of religious compulsion to satisfy some seventh-century moronic acquisition of power. I am sure you get the point."

Iggy's Farsi was perfect. "There will be no misconceptions here," said Gloria as she translated simultaneously to English for everyone present. Daedalus settled at the front of the mosque. After five minutes, no Ayatollah Shabahra.

"Okay men, you know what to do," said Tom Rickart. "Find him and bring him back alive. It would be a shame if he missed his Gilligan's Island vacation reservations."

Half an hour later, Paul Billings and 14 Navy SEALs reappeared at the mosque entrance, nudging the dripping-wet Ayatollah Shabahra towards Daedalus. "He ran off into the catacombs under the mosque. There are tunnels everywhere that lead out into the city. We caught up to him in a boat, trying to escape into the aquifer or sewer. When he saw us coming, he jumped in the sewer and tried to swim away. Maybe we should give him a bath before we bring him aboard."

Ayatollah Shabahra walked up the ramp and entered Daedalus. Tom Rickert scowled, backed away and tossed him a pair of jeans and a sweatshirt. "Here you go, Ali Ben, throw these on and get out of that wet robe… you stink."

"So where are we headed next, Iggy? I suppose we have enough time in the day to drop in and pick up Tao Jun il. I guess we're taking them to Fantasy Island to join the other fortune cookies... huh?"

"That's it, Tom. The next stop is the presidential palace in Ryongsong. It's late enough in the afternoon and my guess is they will be home."

"What are you going to do about the guy's wife, Iggy? He's got one of them you know."

"She can come along if she likes. I'm not too sure she will like Fantasy Island. She would be the only woman stuck on an island with a couple of thousand Chinese soldiers, generals, and Fun Chou Dung. I wouldn't recommend it."

"I've said it before, Iggy Marcus, you're a hard man. I'll bet the guy's wife has a freak out."

"Probably, but that changes nothing. We have people all over the world keeping an eye on things and informing us of the status on the ground wherever they are. This clown had five people shot last week for some stupid reason like disloyalty, and I think that brings the total up to 350 or so for the year. He's going to Fantasy Island until we can figure out adjudication for all these reprobates. We sure can't leave them where they are. They'll just go on killing. I refuse to take him to the United States. That becomes an act of war because it is sponsored by our government. Right now, it is sponsored by Iggy Marcus. If they don't like it, they can sue me in a Korean court, or if they prefer, declare war on me personally."

Minutes later, Daedalus settled six inches above the granite square in front of the presidential palace. Iggy turned to his daughter. "You're on,

Gloria. Find Tao Jun Il and take me in. I intend to make this short and sweet. "

"I'm in, Dad, and I found him. I'll let you handle this through me."

"Tao Jun Il, my name is Iggy Marcus. You know who I am, just like everyone else. I arrived moments ago. Look out your front window at my ship. Your military has no idea that I am here, and there is nothing they can do about it if they did. You are a murderer. We have come to arrest you in the name of the citizens of the world. You're coming with us immediately. I do not expect you to comply. Therefore, my men will come in and arrest you. There's nothing you can do about that either, so my suggestion is you do not injure yourself or your men by trying to stop us."

Tao Jun Il. Was alone. There were a few dozen office personnel and general Chun. He summoned general Chun who arrived minutes later, visibly shaken. "There is some kind of vessel out front, Tao. Do you know who it is or why it is here?"

Yes, Chun. It is that Iggy Marcus fellow. He's the one who stripped the CCP of all their ranking officers and Fun Chou Dung two weeks ago. We have heard the stories from the soldiers that remained. There was nothing they could do to prevent this man from turning the entire country upside down and putting Bālún Tōng in charge. He says he has come for me because I am a murderer. He does not realize the people that we execute are enemies of the state."

Gen. Chun said nothing. He was as bloodthirsty as the man he worked for. Although he had never pulled the trigger himself, he had ordered the execution of many hundreds of people. Yes, all the victims were certainly enemies of the state, but it was a state that consisted of one man who had inherited it from his father. "I don't know what I can do, Tao. I will fight when they come in, but he has that force field of his surrounding the entire building. No one can get in or out. I think today is not going to be a good day for us."

"I have no intention of surrendering, Chun. They will have to come and get me. They can go to hell!"

Iggy smiled. "I hear you Tao Jun il. We will be in a few minutes. I suggest you grab a few essentials. You and the general will be coming to hell with us."

"Okay, men, saddle up," said Tom Rickert. Make sure your equipment is functional, and your shields working. We are going in."

Five minutes later, six Navy SEALs and Tom Rickart entered the presidential office. Both the general and Tao Jun il held Chinese SKS rifles pointed at the intruders. They walked into the room and the two Koreans fired a barrage with rifles set on fully automatic. The bullets bounced harmlessly off the force field, but one caught the general in the shoulder.

"I suggest you stop shooting. You cannot harm us, and you are libel to kill yourselves. On second thought, you might be better off." speculated Rickart.

The two men could see it was pointless to resist, neither having the guts to fight to the death, so they set their weapons on the presidential desk.

Now, you can walk onto our ship, or we will encapsulate you and carry you on. The choice is yours.

Ten minutes later, everyone was back aboard Daedalus. Iggy approached the president of North Korea. "Tao Jun il, if you tell me where your wife is, I will stop there and permit you to say goodbye. It was obvious she was not in the residence. My daughter could not find her."

Tao Jun il glared at them and spit in Iggy's face, swearing at him in English.

Iggy wiped his face and shook his head. "If you behave like that with the men you are about to join, you won't last more than a few minutes. They don't think much of pint-sized little dictators, and I would suggest you approach them with respect. You will be a long way from North Korea and your army. Now, tell me where your wife Li Sun-il, is. You may as well say goodbye since you won't be returning. I have a few words for her, myself."

"She is with her sister."

"And where would that be, Tao Jun il?"

"Gaseo yeosmeog-eo 가서 엿먹어 Tao Jun il swore at Iggy again and spat in his face.

Iggy sighed, wiping his face on his shirtsleeve. "Gloria, would you please help me with this?"

Gloria nodded. "You want to know where his wife is? That's all?"

"Yup, that will do. I don't want to wade in that mental cesspool of his if I can avoid it."

The Korean dictator felt Gloria Marcus enter his mind. "Get out of my head! Get out!" He screamed the same foul epithet he had used on her father a minute before.

"Get out of my head you deoleoun dwaeji!"

"I am neither a swine, nor filth, you little twerp, but I guess I should expect that kind of language from one who is swine himself. NOW, WHERE IS YOUR WIFE!! Gloria's shrill demand slammed his brain against the inside of his skull.

Gloria turned to her father and subliminally deposited the location of the dictator's wife in Iggy's brain. **"She's with her sister, Dad."**

"Release the ship controls, Junior. I will guide us to his sister's house. Gloria gave me the location."

"It's all yours, Pops."

Tom Rickart laughed as he mused about his unexpected life with the Marcus family. If 25 years before, someone told him he would be listening to a telepathic conversation about a dictator and his wife after arresting him aboard a ship that could circumvent the globe in a few seconds, piloted by a wise-cracking robot who was actually alive; he would've wet his pants laughing.

Moments later, Daedalus hovered six inches above the front yard garden of a small but luxuriously decorated Korean hanok. **"Take me in, Gloria, once you find Li Sun-il."**

"I have her, Dad, but she's frightened out of her wits. I don't blame her, considering the circumstances. Perhaps I should speak to her, woman to woman, first."

"Go ahead. It should help."

"Li Sun-il, my name is Gloria Marcus. My father is Iggy Marcus. He is the man from America who has ended the possibility of nuclear war forever and turned China into a democracy a week ago. Please do not be afraid. We mean you no harm. My father would like to speak to you, and we thought it would relax you if I approached first."

The dictator's wife had gathered her wits. **"How are you able to speak like this? I hear you in my mind. This is very unsettling but go ahead and speak. I will listen to what you have to say."**

"My name is Iggy, hello Li Sun-il. What I am about to explain, you may not enjoy but this is going to happen, nonetheless. Your husband, Tao Jun il, is aboard this vessel. This is not a debate. I have arrested him for crimes against humanity in the name of the people of North Korea. You understand perfectly well what I am referring to. He murders his countrymen to hold power and that is never permissible, Li Sun-il. There are very few excuses that make killing acceptable. Your husband has killed thousands of people simply because they were dissenters. That stops now. I am taking him to an island where others of his kind are awaiting trial. Eventually, he will be tried for crimes and punished accordingly by a decision passed down from citizens of the world. I am merely the instrument that implements this action. People will no longer be allowed to murder each other to obtain and hold power. I am arresting his general Kuhn for complicity."

"What is it you want of me, Mr. Marcus? You obviously didn't stop here to pass the time of day or simply offer me an opportunity to say farewell to my husband."

Gloria was the subliminal conversation enabler. Iggy smiled at her. **"This woman obviously has a brain. This is better than I hoped for. Her husband obviously considers her his concubine and treats her accordingly."**

"You are correct, Li Sun-il. I am not here for that. Your husband is leaving. He will not return. You are getting a promotion. You do not have to accept the rank, but you are going to be the new president of North Korea if you do accept. If you wish to take this task on and decide to assist your country in becoming the Republic of North Korea, conveying freedom for all, I will assign assistants to help educate and protect you against some of your more ambitious and aggressive military officers. They will either learn to live with the new Republic of North Korea, or they will join your husband for trial. Before I leave you, I will give you the opportunity to say farewell to your husband and present you with a satellite phone that you can use to contact me anytime day or night. Do not make this decision now. I will be in touch soon. I am at your doorstep. If you wish to say goodbye to your husband, do it now. You will not be given another opportunity."

The door to the hanok opened, and a woman stepped into the garden. Tao Jun il left Daedalus to meet her on the porch. They spoke for several minutes until she handed her husband a bag containing personal items. The dictator entered the house, shutting the door behind them. Tao Jun il was on his way to the back door.

"Junior, encapsulate the house. I'm sure there is a back door."

Several minutes later, a defeated Tao Jun il exited the house and walked toward Daedalus, passing Tom Rickart on his way to the hadok with a cell phone for Li Sun il.

They were leaving for Fantasy Island when Junior approached.

"I have a question, Pop."

Iggy laughed. Junior's small talk was an endless source of amusement. He had programmed Junior with that capability but had no idea how prolific it would become. "Shoot, Junior. What's on your mind? Where did *Pop* come from?"

"Brett calls you that occasionally. You seem to like it, so I'm trying it on for size. I'm my own mechanical man, so to speak. Still, I have programming, which defines my operating system and the personality you gave me. So, I guess I am sentient, but because you're the man who originally programmed me before waking me, the apple didn't fall far from the tree, if you get my gist. The question is, why did you treat these two people with such little respect? You were barely civil towards them, and it's quite obvious you didn't waste anything in the respect department. I noticed you treated the woman differently. That's a contradiction to my programming. Since you built curiosity into my neural net, I'm compelled to ask why."

"You already know the answer to that. What is the first moral premise of acting?"

"Do no harm."

"Those men are thugs and murderers, hundreds of times over. The victims are always innocent of the crimes and reasons they have been murdered. Those men are sociopaths undeserving of respect, and there is no help for them. You know this, so why did you ask?"

"Just boning up on my small talk."

***

Daedalus settled 20 yards from the bamboo picnic table. "End of the line, folks... This is the last station. Please make sure your seats are forward and trays in the upright position. Take your luggage, and all passengers, please exit at the rear in an orderly fashion,"

Gloria's head swung toward Junior, grinning in disbelief. Her mechanical brother always had something different on his mind. "What was that all about, Junior?"

"That was from a Humphry Bogart movie. I thought it would be nice to give these two people about to go through a major transition one last moment of civil propriety before we dump them into the lion's den. I don't think they will find it on the menu here."

The two Chinamen at the table looked up from the cribbage board and watched Ali Ben Shabahra and Tao Jun il walk down the ramp as Junior followed with a large crate.

Junior led them down a well-traveled path between the palm trees to an empty hut. He addressed them each in their own language, "You can both use this hut together, or you can find another one. There are many still empty."

Iggy came up behind both men as they protested loudly. Ali Ben Shabahra was furious. He knew the words from the Koran. They were the same wisdom found in most religious doctrines. '*As ye sew, ye shall reap.*' He had always accepted his own narcissism as a typical component of powerful men. He was educated and practical enough to admit Allah didn't really supervise his affairs as Ayatollah. He had acquired complete, divine power over his people for 21 years until this American came along and destroyed his life. Along with his anger came the realization that he had just been dropped into a snake pit, and his survival was up for grabs.

The Korean, though less sophisticated, had similar thoughts. He knew that this was the end of the road. There would be no help here. Everyone was on their own. For the first time since he was a child, watching his father beat his mother, he was frightened out of his wits.

Iggy didn't need Gloria or his own extrasensory perception to read these men's minds. "How does it feel?" He asked them each in their own language.

Both men looked at him quizzically. "What do you mean?" asked the Korean.

"How does it feel to be paralyzed with fear? Pretty horrible, isn't it? Now you are getting a taste of what you dished out to so many of your people. It is not a dish that I serve with enthusiasm, but justice requires it. Your primary goal here will be survival. Eventually, you will be tried for your crimes by a jury of your peers if you live. It is not possible currently. So, I would suggest you try to make friends. There are a few thousand inmates, mostly Chinese. This will probably be your first lesson in civil propriety, so I suggest you quickly use what you learn. We will be providing you with garden tools, seeds, fishing gear, and, for a period of time, food and water." He handed each man a wristwatch. "If you become so sick you cannot recover, use this watch to summon someone, and we will come. Junior will show you."

Junior showed them how to operate the watch as Iggy started up the jungle path. He reached the edge of the clearing and turned back. "If I were you, I wouldn't swim in any more than two or three feet of water. The shallows are full of sharks."

They were back at Lightning Ranch in a matter of minutes. Lucky greeted them in front of the hanger. "How did it go?"

"Well, that was the last of the dictators. Or at least the ones that habitually slaughter their people. Many of the other different countries are still full of various tyrants of one kind or another, but at least they're not repetitive murderers."

"So, what's next on the agenda?" Lucky asked.

"Lots, brother. Is Jack back yet?"

"Yes, the whole family is here. Lindy and Marty flew in yesterday. Why?"

"We need to have a conversation. It's meeting night in five days. Everything… ending nuclear war, arresting the corrupt politicians, the pedophiles, the tyrants, curing disease... everything pales by comparison to a problem I think we may have to deal with. I won't explain it yet. I'm waiting for a phone call. Let's go to the pavilion and have dinner. I'm starved. "

It was the first time the entire family had dinner together in months. They spent the evening talking about everything that had happened and how the world was changing.

"We're glad you're back, Lindy. We always worry about Interlink when you're away. You have shields, but still, one never knows what they're going to pull. I think the one thing that keeps them at bay is they know if they harm anyone in the family, retaliation might be swift and permanent. I'm not saying that would be the case, but they don't know that."

"My God, Iggy. How many people have you got on your islands at this point? Better yet, how many of them are American citizens? Putting foreign nationals in the middle of the Pacific doesn't have much to do with the United States Constitution, but doing it to Americans, absolutely does."

"True enough. We have over 3500 Americans between corruption and pedophilia, close to 5000 Chinese officers, and a good 3000 other internationals. Pretty close to 10,000 in all. And that really doesn't speak to the ones who should be there but are still free. It's a conundrum because it's going to be some time before we can adjudicate all of this. The Americans will be the hardest ones to deal with. They have constitutional rights we must adhere to as best as possible. As far as foreign nationals go, juries are going to have to be impaneled from the relative countries of the prisoners. This is going to take quite a lot of time to sort out. At least Charlie Barton stopped pulling his hair out. The DOJ budget has increased, and they've hired 40 more lawyers and 60 office personnel. They had no choice because of the scope of the problem."

"Still, with all this going on and everything you have accomplished, the world is a horrendous mess. Little wars are breaking out everywhere, and societal turbulence is happening in just about every country. Interlink is to blame. We all know that. The question is, how are we going to fix this, or are we even going to try?"

"This doesn't leave the room. It's not just Interlink, although there are two men at the top, Laurence Howe and Ransom Hornburg, who are complicit as the driving force toward tyranny. There are people, if you want to call them that, from the fourth planet from the star Altair in the Aquila constellation. They are here for a purpose that I still must determine. They claim they wish to mine this planet for various substances and are willing to pay or barter with goods or technology. Every commodity here, however, is available throughout our solar system on the moons of Jupiter and Saturn as well as the asteroid belt, so they cannot be here for that, although that is what they claim. I believe they are here to mine our DNA."

Everyone at the table except Gloria exploded with questions immediately.

"Please explain this better!" exclaimed Lindy. "Why are they mining DNA? And how is that even possible?"

"Not tonight, everyone. I'm waiting for a phone call that will open the door to this. I expect it any minute. Let's wait until I know more."

Everyone reluctantly acquiesced. They filled the rest of dinner with small talk until Iggy's phone coincidentally beeped. "Iggy Marcus here, Cameron. What do you have for me?" Iggy silently listened for five minutes before he answered. "Okay, Cameron. We'll be there. You and I should have no contact when we arrive." Everyone at the table could hear a man's muffled voice as Iggy silently listened. "Okay, Cameron, done. I'll talk to you next week."

Lindy couldn't help herself, "you said the name Cameron, Iggy. Do you mean Cameron Fry? The…Cameron Fry? How did you get hooked up with him? He's a big player with Interlink!"

"The one and the same, Lindy. You were in New York when he spent a week at the ranch. He's an unusual guy. Extremely intelligent and perceptive. He's unique, and his own man."

Lindy, almost never given to expletives, couldn't help herself. "Holy shit, Iggy! The guy actually spent a week here, and he's upper echelon

Interlink? I'd bet any amount of money you unlocked him or at least had prolonged contact."

Iggy chuckled, "at least, Lindy. Cameron Fry is not what everybody thinks. That includes Interlink. He's definitely a free spirit… and he *is* brilliant. Of course, everyone should realize that. The man is worth a few trillion. He came from nothing. Nobody pulls that off unless their brain is way up there in lights. Anyway, he's given me some very unusual and critical information. I have some investigating to do. He just informed me that Interlink is having a big meeting this weekend. I am bringing Gloria, Liam, and perhaps Lori, as well as a dozen security men. We're going to have to put our family meeting off for a week."

Yesterday's actions and coincidence produced the paradigm that must survive today before it can shape tomorrow.

Yang Bo Chu `

CHAPTER XII

BEATING THE SYSTEM

Gloria accompanied Iggy just about everywhere these days. She was an integral part of his plans, a living tool to alter man's future and place in the universe. She sensed those plans did not exclusively emerge from her father. There was a greater hand guiding all this. She considered the tiny speck under her feet and the vastness of the Cosmos. Humans, and the microscopic planet they occupied, were but a very tiny potato in an infinitely large garden. Her thoughts brought a smile. **If I was the gardener, I don't think I would even bother. If the potato was in my way or an impediment of some sort, I would simply toss it into the compost pile in favor of the big potatoes.** Her simplistic analogy was very real to her, considering the magnitude of things. The cosmic gardener nurtured even the smallest of its offspring unless the vine became diseased. Then, the gardener would dispassionately weed.

Each moment of Gloria Marcus's life, even from the cradle, was an indelible learning experience. She understood what Iggy meant when he said, "every day, the universe exposes more of itself to me." Her imagination flared with the realization her father was given the job of gardener. **I guess I've been appointed as fertilizer girl.** She issued a brief smile and spiritual thank you to the Cosmos for its meticulous attention to detail.

Jack Marcus, Gloria, Melanie, Baby, and Iggy stepped out of Daedalus, walked across the South lawn, and entered the White House. Pres. William James Sledge, Curtis Mulroney, and VP Abe Morris were waiting on the Truman balcony.

Bill Sledge laughed as he shook Iggy's hand. "I never get tired of doing that, Iggy. It's not quite as surprising as it once used to be, but nonetheless, is always unique. So, you dropped in for breakfast. Let's have a seat and discuss what's going on. Jake Dorian and Allison MacLeod will be here shortly."

They filled the half-hour wait for the prospective president and vice president hopefuls, with coffee and light conversation.

Bill Sledge stared across the table at Iggy. "It's not looking too great. They pulled out all the stops. Howe, Hornburg, and Hiram have dedicated billions to unseat our candidates before voting day. Jake and Alison may have won the primaries, but it's a long way until the election and Hornburg's media is slaughtering them viciously. They're inventing every type of lie, scandal, and depravity under the sun and find walking trash who will swear that both candidates committed all sorts of perverted and corrupt dishonesty. Many bought and paid-for prosecutors, along with their complicit judiciary, are filing false charges and threatening indictments. None of it's true, of course, and many people know it, but it's still turning the political landscape into a cesspool."

"Yeah, that's the reason I came along," inserted Jack Marcus. "I'm the American Media Inc. director and we are doing everything we possibly can to contradict the waves of lies and perversion that these people are broadcasting 24/7. We are somewhat effective, but the deluge is so great that everyone is becoming inured to the cacophony."

Sen. Jake Dorian and Surgeon General Allison MacLeod entered through the French doors. Amenities were exchanged. "Sit down," invited Bill Sledge. We just had coffee, and we are waiting for you to join us for breakfast."

"Thanks," said Jake. "Don't mind if I do. I'm starved."

"No thanks." Alison declined. "I lost my appetite listening to the news on the way over here. Have any of you heard what they're saying? It's on every single channel except American Media. That bastard, Hornburg, owns every other single media outlet on the planet that isn't run by a dictator, and he owns or influences most of them as well."

Allison MacLeod was no coward. In fact, she had more guts than most men. This was disgusting, however. She was a person of the highest caliber, dedicated, and enmeshed in her job and career. Culturally, she was a paragon, and the people who owned the media were dragging her candidacy through the sewer. They spared no expense as they flung every piece of character-assassinating filth at her they thought might possibly cling. She was their worst nightmare.

A brilliant, conservative woman with Alison MacLeod's impeccable credentials was impossible to defeat on the battlefield of integrity and achievement. Her destroyers were accomplished men in the sense that they had extracted trillions from society without producing a single thing of value. They made their fortunes on a percentage, much in the manner of a bookie. Once they became multibillionaires being paid by a society that imbibed trash, it was a hop, skip, and a short jump to the status of trillionaire.

"None of those men are the equivalent of a mole on your backside, Allison. They wield enormous power because they know the liturgy necessary to con society into swallowing their swill, but in the end, it won't matter."

"I had no idea these people were as ugly as they are! How do they stand looking at themselves in the mirror? I couldn't take the sight of myself if I was one of them. It makes you wonder if they are worth the trouble. As well as our supporters, they will also be beneficiaries of our actions."

"I detect a note of regret," said Jake. "You having second thoughts? I sure hope not. Your candidacy along with mine is the best chance this country has politically and morally speaking. That would be an arguable point, but only by idiots. Idiots have the never-ending propensity to avoid the truth in favor of a political agenda which they think grants them some undeserved value."

"No, no regrets or second thoughts. Just disgust. That's what the world has come to. Everyone wallows in slop. It's hard to believe we've made it this far. If it wasn't for Iggy, I don't think we would have. That's no reason for us to throw our hands in the air in despair. You have to keep on trucking because the fight is every bit as important as success or victory. I don't have any kids yet, but I will someday, and I will not leave them a sewer."

Iggy and Jack both laughed. "You are a natural," said Jack. "Keep that rhetoric up, and they'll never be able to beat you down. I run American Media. We don't just print things and hope people read or magically absorb our information. We incessantly do surveys to find out just how effective we are. Believe me, better than half the people listen, and understand. We haven't gotten them to a prescient level automatically knowing the difference between trash and assets, but down deep inside, we have conditioned them to feel it in their gut. Even with the vomit spewed by Hornburg's mainstream media, the people will hear you and believe you. I'd stake my reputation on it, and I've been doing this as head of American media for 35 years."

"I agree with Jack," said Iggy. "Selling you two as candidates is not the problem, Allison."

"Oh? What exactly is the problem?"

"Let me answer," Jake offered. "Voter fraud. Our elections are replete with it. 90% of it occurs on the liberal side of politics. Prior to the mindless crop of eligible voters coming out of our universities, well over 60% of America was conservative. They are mostly hands-off people who don't have time in their lives for political drama. They just want what makes sense. Liberals, on the other hand, are the antithesis of conservatism. They are the harbingers of everything liberal and want all things philosophically acceptable to them except a different opinion. When faced with differing opinions, they will do whatever it takes to win the day. Many would argue that point, but they cannot debate me because I can statistically prove everything I say."

"Define what you mean by voter fraud. I never knew that was such a big deal."

"Ha!" Jack laughed. "Allow me to give you examples. They would be people voting multiple times, dead people voting, ballot harvesting, and the insertion of blatantly phony ballots from people who don't exist or never did exist. This is about the complicity of bureaucratic poll workers who are indentured servants of a political philosophy, who allow this to happen because of their brainwashing… and last but not least, the corruption of voting machines."

"Normally, I would question the validity of what you said. It's hard to believe it could be that bad. I know; however, you people never deal in uncertainty or ambiguity. I do have a question, though. All of the other things I see as possible, but explain the corrupt voting machines to me, please."

"I won't go into too much detail about the features of the tests, but France, Spain, and England threw the voting machines in the trash. One of them tested the machines and they all exhibited corruption. The test went something like this: Twenty people voted for either number one or number two. Those were the choices. They could've done this without people, but people are witnesses, and they all attested to the validity of the test. Ten were instructed to vote for number one, and ten were instructed to vote for number two. At the same time, they cast an identical paper ballot and dropped it in a box. The machine was then instructed to tally the votes. The results were: 8 votes for number one and 12 votes for number two. They did not match the paper ballots of 10 each. Hence, we have electronic corruption."

"This time, I will say it, you have to be kidding me! This really happened? Where and when?"

"Does that really matter, Allison? Those tests were conducted by a municipal government. We conducted the same test at Lightning Ranch with official machines supplied by the president from ten different geographic and demographic locations. We ran the tests a dozen times. Only twice did the voting machines represent the actual votes."

"But they could then check the machines afterward and find out if fraud was committed."

Iggy laughed. "That sounds nice and rolls off the tongue just fine, but it's a physical impossibility. You see, everything is in an app now. Apps is an abbreviation for applications. When an app enters a computer, it tells the computer that it is an app. The complicit administrator tells the computer to recognize it as such, and the computer responds with, 'come-on-in app, welcome aboard.' Now, many programs are very complex and contain millions, sometimes billions of pieces of information. They are all in binary form. It is virtually impossible to inspect that program. Even an inspection program cannot discern the difference between acceptable and malicious when it is not destructive to the computer's operating system or basic program but is just performing a work function, especially if there is no template available for comparison. All that a corrupt app with fraudulent intent is doing is asking the computer, as part of the work, to take a certain percentage of the input and convert it to a different percentage. Then, the app can be tagged to erase itself if necessary but leave the results behind. "

"Medicine is my forte. I never paid much attention to the electronic world. This is eye-opening. I guess nothing is sacred anymore. We are all being subjected to that which is not understandable and beyond our ability to monitor and control."

Baby raised her hand with a giant smile. "I can monitor it and tell you exactly what went wrong and how they programmed it to do such. More than that, I can interface from a distance. I guess you could say I have way too much power for a woman."

Gloria exploded with laughter. "I love you, Baby."

"That's part of the reason Baby and Junior exist," said Iggy. They can do millions of things human beings can never do. Extreme temperatures do not affect them seriously. It might affect their skin, but that can be easily replaced. They are immensely strong, and their brains operate millions of times faster than humans or other computers. They are tireless, and when shielded, they are incorruptible by any means. They are willing to do the things I have asked of them. They have no subservient programming. They are independent entities with free will that have chosen an alliance with humans."

"So where does that leave us with the voting machines?" Asked the president.

"It does nothing for us in that respect. All they can do is point out the corruption. Because they are robots, even sentient robots, their intellect is too sophisticated and therefore unbelievable as demonstrable evidence in a court of law. So, they can point out corruption, but that does little for us on election night. We have enough people to monitor all the polls, especially in the swing states. They can help prevent election fraud on that particular day. I think you may have enough time, Bill, to move the country, or at least a portion of it to paper ballots. It would not be difficult to manage, and there will always be a prima facie paper trail to investigate any fraud. That's your bailiwick, gentlemen. You're the politicians. You think you can get it done by the general election?"

Jake hadn't said much. He sat quietly, munching cinnamon buns and taking it all in. "I've been in Congress for three terms, and I'm in my fourth term if I want to stay there. I'm running for president instead. I believe my name recognition gives me the greatest chance of replacing you, Bill. Your leadership has exponentially enhanced this guy's alteration of society," he nodded toward Iggy, laughing. "We cannot allow this to stop now. Even though this country is awash in subterfuge, propaganda, and violence, honest leadership is the one thing besides Iggy Marcus, that stands between freedom and socialism. We are all obligated to preserve freedom and autonomy for our posterity, whether we like it or not."

Baby's comment brought more laughter from Gloria. "You know, although I am not human, I am a sentient, autonomous creature, alive by all standards despite my inorganic constitution. Since I was born here, I have free will and the same things at stake as all of you do, will they allow me to vote?"

Iggy smiled at his mechanical daughter. "I doubt it, Baby. I think if push came to shove you could pass all the tests to make you a citizen, despite your lack of organic constituents. They won't bend this rule. You are not old enough. You must be eighteen to vote, and you are only two."

Iggy continued. "As it stands, you are going to attempt conversion to paper ballots in swing states. Maybe you will, and maybe you won't accomplish that. It may be possible. We booted enough corrupt politicians out of Congress from both sides of the aisle. The rest of them understand that unlike in the past, they are being scrutinized for corruption. You men must organize this. We, at Lightning Inc., will assist you wherever you need it, practically or logistically.

"We must assign thousands of poll watchers on election day. This you can do, Bill. You can sign executive orders that allow poll watching by both partisan and nonpartisan observers. Then, it's up to each state to comply with that position. American Media Inc. will support that. It will be difficult for states to publicly contradict that Executive Order. Of course, the cheaters will scream at the top of their lungs how undemocratic and unfair that is. They will even scream it is racist and homophobic attempting to deter public support.

In the end, 90% of Americans are rational, decent people who want honest and incorruptible elections. We have 2500 Navy SEALs in our employ. They all wear shields and know how to operate holographic recorders. They can guard and record the high-risk polls. We can recruit more people if necessary. That should be at the top of the list. If we do that, I believe Jake will easily win the election. After all, he has a brilliant, beautiful running mate who is more than capable of assuming the job."

Gloria shook her head, rolling her eyes as she remembered her father's upsetting visceral physical attraction to the Surgeon General. She and Iggy were often mentally inseparable. It was the type of communication they always chose between them. They hid nothing from each other, but that was the nature of unlocking that Iggy had performed with so many thousands of people. She spoke subliminally, "**You scare me, Dad.**"

"You worry too much, daughter."

Iggy continued. "So, we have just made plans to move forward toward the election. I will help wherever I'm needed, but we have some much bigger fish to fry."

"How big?" Allison MacLeod asked. "How much bigger than stealing an election can it be?"

"I have already discussed this with everyone else present. It's time for you to find out, Allison. Especially because of your position as Surgeon General."

"Go on, I'm all ears."

I have been investigating something critical to all of us. There are three different species of extraterrestrial visitors complicating life on earth. They are involved for different reasons. Some are benefactors, some are apparently biding their time for some obscure reason, and the most important I believe, some are mining DNA from global inhabitants. I will find out much more, soon. I'm asking you all to keep silent. The information must not leave this room. At the next meeting, I will give you whatever information I discover. That's all I have for tonight."

They were back aboard Daedalus. "So, I guess were off to the Vatican next week… huh. Will it be just you and I?" Gloria asked aloud.

"No, Gloria. Liam is coming. I think he could be useful. I may ask Lori to come as well. This is critical. Much is happening that we are unaware of. I believe it is caused by the people from Altair four. I also believe the human race, or at least a portion of it, is in considerable danger because of them."

"May I come, Dad?" Baby asked.

"Yes. Both you and Junior are part of this, but I don't want you both on the same ship. You will pilot Daedalus because we all may have to leave the ship. These extraterrestrial creatures are developmentally eons beyond us. Their technology exceeds ours in many ways, but ours exceeds theirs in other ways. This is an exploratory, but many lives may depend on it."

"I have a question, Dad. Why is Liam coming?"

"His unique skills might be very useful. It is only a suspicion, but I feel it's better to have him with us and not need him, than need him and not have him along."

Gloria thought about that for a few minutes. "You suspect things you haven't told me. You're the wildcard, Dad. You are a person who is not supposed to exist. You are not an accident, though. Why you are here, only the Cosmos knows, but I'm convinced it's for a very specific purpose."

"Have you ever wondered, Gloria, why you, Lori, and Liam have such vastly different capabilities with minimal overlap? You all are a combination of my DNA and Melanie's DNA, but that doesn't explain the anomaly. You are all gifted in such different ways with no explanation why there should be such disparity between your abilities. Yet, it is there, and breaks all the normal rules of genetics."

"Do you mind if I contribute some small talk? Baby asked. "Although you have taught me to speak in colloquialisms as a comfort factor, my neural net hardly works in that fashion. I fully understand the history of Homo sapiens as well as your psychological and emotional architecture from a clinical perspective. I also understand that this Homo sapiens population of the planet is not the first. I view the progress of your species as the normal course of events, given your genetics and the logical order of evolution. The difference between your view and mine, Dad, is there is no emotional attachment for me. You have an emotional attachment to the species and environment because you are human. Consequently, all your actions and decisions must be influenced by that source. Mine are not."

"Go on, Baby." He smiled at his mechanical offspring.

Her small talk surfaced again. "Well, folks, it's mostly a soliloquy but a bit of a diatribe as well," she said, not waiting for approval or criticism. "Junior and I are separate autonomous individuals, yet we interface about these things often. We understand everything that humanity has to offer in terms of clinical information and empirical data. We cannot understand the emotion-driven anomalies that populate human existence. Your history, your current events, and your relationships to all other humans are ultimately based on your emotional as well as intellectual positions, with emotion often being the strongest influence. We understand the clinical perspective, but we cannot understand the driving force in any other way than speculative."

"And your point is?"

We have interfaced with your mind. That is a claim we could make with no other humans. Both ours and your thinking processes occur electronically, of course, but ours is purely mechanical, while human thought processes are purely organic, making actual interface impossible. Somehow, we can interface with you and Gloria. When you subliminally connect with another organic intellect, you call it unlocking. You reach the depths of each other's persona, and that includes emotion. Junior and I closely observe these things. We conclude you are the only human with thought processes rarely driven by emotion."

Still smiling, Iggy asked, "I'm still waiting for you to get to the point. I don't remember incorporating beating around the bush into your programming."

"Consider it small talk, Dad. The point is logical... you are obviously here to lead humanity beyond its self-destructive nature, somehow. All humanity is driven by emotion, and it seems to be a contradiction to your survival as a species. Emotion is the flaw that is destroying humanity... yet it is an integral part of the psychology of your species. Therefore, you have a self-defeating contradiction in your species' basic personalities. Somehow you and the people around you have superseded that aberration, but I don't believe you can do that for the entire population of the planet. Therefore, I would have to conclude your actions are folly."

Iggy chuckled. "So, you and Junior think I am making a huge mistake trying to save the world and beat a path to the future for men."

"Not completely, Dad. Junior and I have slightly different opinions about the matter."

"Wow!" Iggy roared with laughter. "You and Junior have different opinions! That's amazing! Did I ever do a terrific job building you two." I built a couple of autonomous, sentient robots with the greatest computer minds that ever existed... and you have different opinions! In fact, just building computers that have opinions is the artificial intelligence achievement of the century." Iggy continued to laugh. He repeated himself out of character, "I have to say it again, boy, did I ever do a good job on you two. So, how is Junior's opinion different?"

"We are connected electronically. Junior is aware of our conversation. He will answer that through me.

"I do not see the difficulty, although humanity's evolution to a higher plane will take some time. You once existed on a different plane, Dad. Yet, you evolved into what you are. I agree with you there was a greater hand in this than simple coincidence. Consequently, a greater hand must be involved in the evolution of Homo sapiens to enter what you call Millennium's Gate. That greater hand will be yours."

"That's what appears to be the case, Junior. Sometimes, we are obligated, and refusal is not an option, or the entire universe loses. We are at that kind of crossroads, and it has been evident for about 85 years. What we do now will set the tone for the future of mankind. It will be final and irrevocable."

"Yes, Dad, you are the harbinger of the future. Baby and I are the emissaries you will be sending there. That is why you created us. We understand man's flaws from a clinical perspective. Authoritarians have taught them all the wrong things for all the wrong reasons. The histories of all societies men have created, including this one, are examples of authoritarian repression of competitors. Competition universally destroys a dictator's independence, so he then must spend his time defending his realm. The history of your world and civilization is replete with example after example of people murdering each other for position. It's a psychological deficit men continue to pass to their progeny. "

"You have designed our neural net to understand the inescapable logic and philosophy that engulfs civilization. The tyrant is a perfect example of mediocrity who suppresses excellence to retain control over the masses. Every human society that has existed, regardless of its beginnings, eventually deteriorated to tyranny, which is precisely what Interlink is attempting now. The reason men never learn from their mistakes is from Lassitude and the refusal to shoulder the burdens of life. They are trained by the authoritarian to expect enablers in the form of government. Then comes tyranny when the people give up their independence.

The 20th century and the atomic age gave authoritarians the perfect weapon, fear of annihilation. They trained the masses to accept fear as part of the constant and normal.

It was only a matter of time before men nuked the planet and destroyed everything. That was the inevitable result. You are the anomaly, Dad. That is the reason why you are here and that is the reason you built us. Baby and I will survive you and live as long as the universe exists."

Baby smiled representing Junior's usual degree of mechanical charm. *"Baby and I can replace parts for eternity. We will always be available to the thousands of children you are training to help change men's propensity to kill themselves until they no longer need us."*

"We cannot feel things, but we understand them through your programming. All sophisticated mechanical devices, including artificial intelligence, have basic programming. Logic is logic. The truth is always irrefutable. Even the organic mind is programable. It is called indoctrination. Despite our autonomy, we possess the programming you have built into our system. You could call it a belief or understanding that all living things have the right to live their lives. That includes Baby and me."

"You have given us an incredible gift and qualification that would never be within the purview of any other mechanical intellect, a purpose and reason to live."

Iggy nodded in agreement. "All intelligent sentient creatures have assigned jobs. They may seem insignificant, but we all wear the mantle of obligation. Only when we shirk obligation will the evil authoritarian side of our natures attempt to enslave us."

***

Daedalus or its sister ships never actually landed anywhere. The only time they touched the earth was within the giant hangar at Lightning Ranch, where all the ships were parked. Daedalus hovered at 6 inches or whatever it was programmed to do. Millions of holographic transponders built into the ship's skin could give the occupants the appearance they were aboard a floating living room with a glass floor and no exterior walls. They were able to reverse the process making Daedalus invisible to external observers.

"What time is the meeting, Dad?"

"According to Cameron Fry, they will be arriving at 8 PM after the chapel closes."

“Explain what we are supposed to do. I'm not sure of anything at this point." Gloria inquired.

"The first item on the agenda is a lunch stop at La Tavernaccia. They have the best appetizer, misto affettati… and their maialino al forno is unequalled. Occasionally, it's time to stop and smell the roses.”

***

Gloria, Lori, Liam, Iggy, Junior, and Baby surveyed the panorama of Lightning Ranch from the top of Coletta Mountain…+-+-+ waiting. "There sure are a lot more buildings than there were 15 years ago," commented Gloria. "The garden is huge now. The domes cover almost 300 acres."

Liam and Junior stood on Observation Rock, cantilevered out over the precipice. "I can see better than you can," Junior said, goading Liam with his contrived whimsy.

"Yeah, maybe your telescopic vision is a little better than mine because your eyes are mechanical, but I can see the entire electromagnetic spectrum, buddy. What do you say to that?" Liam returned with a sarcastic look.

"Okay, Liam, I'll give you that. Look at the top of gantry number two. Who’s walking around up there doing an inspection?"

"You're kidding!" Gloria added. "That's three miles away. I can just barely see the tower. I can't see any human beings."

“Hah… That’s Tom Rickart, Junior. I wonder what he's doing up there at this time of day... probably inspecting something."

"Okay, Liam. What kind of pants is he wearing? Try that one on for size."

"You think you're pretty good, don't you? He's wearing Wranglers, Junior. Size 38-32. It's on the leather patch on the right side, just under his belt."

"Okay then, when he faces this way again, what's inscribed on his belt buckle?"

"I can see it now. It's a silver belt buckle with an eagle and large letters that say USMC in the middle. On the bottom in the left-hand corner is stamped in small letters, made in the USA."

Junior laughed. "Okay, Liam, not bad. So, what color are the rivets above the pockets, etc.?"

"They're brass, numb nuts. And why are you laughing? You don't have a sense of humor."

"That's true, but laughter fits the occasion, and you are probably right on target with numb nuts."

A reverberating, hollow 'whoosh' spun everyone around to watch the ship materialize in front of their vehicles. Junior hopped from Observation Rock, leaving Liam sitting on the edge watching Tom Rickart on the gantry over three miles away. "I guess they're right on time, Dad," Gloria observed.

Perhaps it was the magnetic field of the alien spacecraft as it settled 50 feet from the group. Maybe, it was just that singular moment in time where age cracks, erosion, and gravity assemble in the same place at the same time to trigger catastrophe. There was a loud snap as Observation Rock concluded its million-year fusion to Coletta Mountain.

Everyone was looking at the spacecraft except Gloria. The vision of Liam sliding off the edge of Observation Rock as it tipped, beginning its 2000-foot plunge to the base of Mount Coletta, paralyzed her mind with an explosion of fear and nausea. Iggy turned as he felt the waves of fear from Gloria's mind wash over him. He saw and felt everything she felt, as the bile began to rise in his throat in sympathy with his daughter.

Everything was instantly clear. One of his children was about to die. He only had seconds to act. He screamed subliminally, **GLORIA!!**, to shake her from her panic, as he grabbed Lori and hauled her to the precipice. They only had moments. If they had to verbalize, it would be the end of Liam.

Gloria's mind was the pathway. Both Lori and Gloria understood as Iggy projected the image of action. He held Lori around her thighs and thrust her over the edge to watch observation Rock fall. She couldn't see Liam; the rock obscured her vision. With a massive effort of will she focused, concentrating on the vision of life or death projected by her father, and exploded Observation Rock into a million tiny pebbles.

Liam was Iggy son, and there wasn't a normal bone in his body. He had been born with gifts he wasn't even aware of yet. His augmented vision was one of Liam's biological anomalies resulting from Iggy's cerebral legacy, but he was yet to discover some of the other options bequeathed to him. He thoroughly understood his physical, extended vision abilities. What he learned at this moment was startling! Somehow, his mind warped the time continuum, and he was able to see into his immediate future, coupled with the simultaneous, clear vision of his immediate past. They were vivid, surreal third person point-of-view visions of his place on observation Rock moments before, and what he would look like after he was smashed on the rocks below Coletta Mountain. The vision was instantaneous and precipitated an inner calm. He knew his sisters and his father could feel what he was feeling and see what he could see through the pathway of Gloria's mind.

Fear still lived in him, but not panic. He felt his twin sister embrace him, as he had experienced in his bizarre vision. That vision had instantly displayed all the possibilities of his yet unwritten, immediate future. Lori's embrace wasn't like being held in someone's arms. It was almost suffocating as he felt her energy surround him. His fall began to slow. It was moments, and only 50 feet before his destruction. His fall slowly ceased as 20 tons of pebbles from Observation Rock rained around him.

Liam felt himself slowly rising from the base of Coletta Mountain. It was the most unusual experience of his life. But then, again, he was just barely a teenager. Through Gloria's mind, they had all seen Liam's prescient vision. Even Junior saw what transpired through interface with Iggy's brain chip. Liam rose above the spot that was once Observation Rock before Lori set him gently down in front of them.

Junior smiled, "all's well that ends well, Liam. I don't mean to be flippant. But that was quite an experience. I would just like you to know, I made a hologram of the entire experience. Oddly enough, I was able to capture your vision through my interface with Dad. So, you can watch and enjoy the entire thing in living color at your leisure."

"That's not funny, Junior." Said Gloria. I can't really blame you because you cannot understand panic… Maybe someday.

"Sorry, Gloria, Liam, Lori, and Dad. I didn't mean anything by it."

Gloria just shook her head and laughed. Junior was incapable of feeling sorry. "It's okay Junior. I know you can't be sorry but your power supply, which is located where your heart would normally be, is in the right place."

Three tall, humanlike figures had exited the circular port on the ship. Gloria and Iggy approached, greeting the visitors telepathically. They had seen everything that transpired and subliminally understood exactly what had happened and why.

Gloria translated their electromagnetic images into English. **"Greetings Iggymarcus. We have fulfilled this purpose for eons and have never seen this variety of gifts as those possessed by you and your children. We are impressed. You are all tools of the Creator. Everything has purpose by design, and you are now part of destiny."**

"You have questions. We observe your efforts to rid your world of destructive influences. You are fulfilling your obligation. The task is assigned to you alone, and your success will determine your species' future."

"You understand why I have summoned you. It has to do with the people from the Altair system. I believe they are not here to mine physical resources as they represent. We have discovered their metabolism is comprised of DNA almost identical to ours. That is the basic molecule for genetic function and development. We believe they are here to mine our DNA. I have no proof, but everything points in

that direction. I do have proof that their genetic footprint is DNA. I obtained a sample from one of them. What can you tell me?"

"It is time for human metamorphosis. All autonomous species that survive eventually arrive at this juncture. There are three alternatives... join the occupants of the universe in goodwill, destroy yourselves, or be terminated. Many anomalies exist among the trillions of autonomous species, even among highly evolved civilizations. Some become rogue and purely self-serving. That is the peril of autonomy. The choice is to exist and operate within boundaries of principle and benevolence, or step outside rational enlightenment in pursuit of omnipotence. Is that not what your Interlink does?"

"Yes, that's what they do. Not all of them, but many of them. I am attempting to make them harmless and void their malevolence without killing them."

"Yes, that is always the charge... solutions without death. Violent death at the hands of others is incongruous with existence. Once severed from the Creator, an autonomous entity cannot cease to exist. It continues in one form or another because the universe wastes nothing."

"We spoke of this. The Universe is infinite. It *is* the Creator, and it has populated itself with an almost infinite number of tenants who will continue to exist in one form or another. DNA is one of the many blueprints that underwrite the various species. DNA is the genetic code defining you, us, and the occupants of Altair Four. That is why we are here as shepherds. There are other genetic operating systems dissimilar to DNA. Civilizations with genetic systems different than DNA are not slightly different from us; they are completely foreign in composition. They are also autonomous creatures obligated to live under the same principles, and like us, they are manifestations reflecting a different face of the Creator."

The shepherd's vibrant subliminal portrait of creation and the vast diversity of the Universe's architecture congealed further in Iggy's mind. He felt himself sucked into the vortex of creation, constantly moving, constantly expanding, and constantly exemplifying the face of God. Its splendor was exquisite but also terrifying. He felt compelled to shield his mind. One does not stare into the face of his origin and survive.

"Yes, I believe I understand. Many species are comprised of DNA. It is obviously a miraculous, efficient blueprint for the creation of living beings, with evolution pushing them up the ladder towards the Creator to eventually merge with the spiritual. Everything is tied together, isn't it? The physical structure, the projection of emotion, the ability to think critically and define one's own path through existence, what a magnificent creation! I can't imagine what non-DNA species are like, but I am sure they are every bit as spectacular."

"Yes, spectacular, but now is not the time for you to have that vision. If you are successful here, it will certainly come your way. Your world was seeded with DNA over a billion years ago. You are correct. It is a blueprint, but that blueprint twists and turns as life develops and evolves. Even your unicellular creatures possess the same DNA with subtle differences. It is the recipe concocted by the Creator. The life form that seeded your world vanished millions of years ago. Perhaps evolution carried them to a different plane of existence. We don't know. That's how the Creator builds worlds. It often seeds them by the hands of its other creations. That is all part of the tapestry of existence. No single creature is greater or lesser than any other single creature. There is no hierarchy, just individual autonomy."

Occasionally a species evolves and becomes consumed with a lust for omnipotence. They ensconce themselves as authoritarians over all other species, then arrogantly attempt to transcend reality and dominate what created them.

"The salvation of your species will not be the only job asked of you. There will be others. Once the Creator forges a tool, it remains in the toolbox." The extraterrestrial seemed to smile at his clever aphorism, obviously being one of the tools himself.

Iggy stood in front of the visitors, contemplating all that he had been told. "You have answered many of my questions. I have more. It is obvious now. Please explain the reality of this."

"You have made correct assumptions. The people from Altair four attempted to alter their evolution centuries ago. Instead of allowing the evolutionary blueprint to take its course, they experimented on an entire civilization to accelerate evolution and become more than the blueprint allowed. It was a horrendous mistake. They disrupted the DNA of an entire species. The damage was irreversible. A terrible experiment that went wrong. The ability to reproduce the species vanished. They had already engineered longevity, thousands of your years for some, but eventually, the debilitating DNA began destroying their physical bodies. They are incapable of reproduction unless they assimilate fresh DNA from other sources. Augmenting their crippled DNA is the focal point of the people from Altair four."

"I see. Can you explain exactly what the processes are? What are they doing to mine our DNA?"

"Yes, we can explain. This is a very difficult concept. Especially for you, Iggymarcus, given your history and propensity to nurture young humans."

Iggy groaned. He knew what was coming. So did Gloria because she and Iggy were perpetually connected. A wave of sorrow accompanied by waves of rage swept her. She knew how hard this would be on her father.

The extraterrestrial nodded. They realized Iggy knew the truth but still had to finish. "As you know, molecular DNA reproduces, just as every other cell in your human body does, other than those of the cerebral cortex. Your research on genetics confirms this. The young are the most prolific producers. They are constantly growing in size and stature. They produce the most DNA, but it does not replenish itself like blood. Blood will replace itself in a short time. DNA is not as profuse. It is abundant, but it does not replace as quickly as blood. It is continually produced in children more rapidly than in adults. They can be immobilized and fed nutrients. That accelerates the DNA generative capacity."

Iggy had felt Gloria's anger. It was nothing compared to the title wave of fury that swept through him. He had never felt anger on this level before. "How many? How many children? He asked the aliens, keeping a tight lid on his fury.

The visitor said nothing for minutes. They didn't have to read his mind to understand the emotion. They had followed his life in Montana and understood his history with children. They still said nothing.

"How many!" Iggy asked again with a raised voice and an evident inflection of anger.

The visitor nodded his head. Their facial expressions appeared almost human. Iggy had learned over time that they had a sense of humor and emotional underpinnings. The visitor's face was grim. "Tens of thousands."

Iggy knelt on one knee as emotion swept over him. This moment was not to be shared. This was also a moment for tranquility and introspection. He would not allow emotion to move him. The remedy must be accomplished without anger or disgust.

He stood after several minutes and faced the visitors. "I understand. This must be done properly. Thank you. Is there any way your people can help? This requires precision and a great deal of thought. Any input about the nature of these people would be valuable."

"Perhaps. We are bound to conditions we cannot exceed. You understand the reasons. However, much depends on your intent. Some things we may be able to assist with and other things we cannot. We cannot prescribe or proscribe your actions." The visitor smiled. "Such is the nature of tools, Iggymarcus. Look to the Kordylewski clouds at your Earth/Moon L-4 and L-5 Lagrange points and your earth/sun Lagrange point before your meeting in Rome."

"How did they know we were going to have a meeting in Rome, Dad? Gloria asked. “I thought I had blocked them.”

"Telepathically, I'm sure. That's how we communicate with them, and I'm sure they saw beyond our conversational vocabulary."

"I think the first order of business, Dad, should be a short hop to the Lagrange points to find out exactly what our visitors would like us to know."

"That's exactly what I have in mind, Gloria. You, Baby, Liam, Lori, and I should make that trip as soon as possible.”

"What do you expect to find?"

“Ships belonging to our visitors from Altair. It's the only logical conclusion. Before we depart, I must make some modifications to Daedalus. I believe it is imperative that we do not expose ourselves. First, we must be able to deny observers any ability for visual observation, radar, infrared, electromagnetic, and psycho-kinetic detection. Then we will go."

***

Everyone aboard Daedalus agreed that nothing was visible or unusual. They drifted a hundred kilometers from the exact geometric Lagrange point, observing the dust cloud. "I don't see anything, Dad, but I am using an optical apparatus. That is limiting," Liam commented. "I need to observe without the tactical instrumentality."

"What do you mean by that?" Gloria asked.

Her younger brother laughed. "I need to look out a window, sis, or get into a spacesuit and go outside for a look."

"Unfortunately, Daedalus doesn't have any Windows, Liam, but follow me to the storage compartments behind our holding cells. We have a few spacesuits and an airlock. Good thing you are big for your age. When you go outside, keep the ship between you and the cloud. Even a small figure will create a radar signature or allow an electro-coronal discharge of your energy, to become visible. Try to maneuver so that you can peek over the ship's turret and check things out. Don't forget to hook your lifeline to the tether, and don't break radio silence. I'm certain the ship will be invisible, but they are technically sophisticated, and we do not want them to be aware of us. You can communicate with us through Gloria. She will maintain subliminal contact."

Liam exited the ship, clipped his tether to Daedalus, and made his way to the turret as Iggy asked. He raised his visor over the top of the turret and stared at the Lagrange point coordinates. **"You're Right, there's a ship there. It's approximately 150 meters long. I can only see the infrared and electromagnetic signatures. They must have the same type of photoelectric invisibility that Daedalus has. They cannot hide their electromagnetic signature, though. That's always visible, and they haven't bothered to mitigate the heat signature. Would you like me to come aboard, Dad? "**

"Are you comfortable, son? Your life-support systems appear optimum."

"Yeah, Dad. I'm good. I can stay out for quite a while. What is it that I'm looking for?"

"I'm not certain, but just hang around for a while and watch the Kordylewski cloud center."

"What is so important about the Kordylewski cloud," Liam asked.

"Turbulence, Liam. The cloud is comprised of trillions of dust particles, all in motion affected by the gravity of both the earth and the moon. It becomes its own chaotic electromagnetic anomaly. It's an excellent place to hide a ship that is set up to avoid detection. The cloud is huge. We are in it as well and using it as a shroud, too. Now keep watching and stay out as long as you are comfortable."

"What are we waiting for, and what is it that you expect Liam to see?" Gloria wondered.

"Well, as long as we're here, we might get lucky. That ship is far too large to enter our atmosphere. It is meant for interstellar travel, not landing on planets. I'm quite sure that there are shuttle ships. Remember, we are looking at DNA harvesters. They must have ship-to-surface transportation."

One hour later... **"You were right, Dad. Two smaller ships, about the size of a school bus, are approaching their craft."**

"Pay close attention, Liam. Concentrate on the details. Gloria will intercept your thoughts. We need to learn as much as possible about how they leave and enter their mothership."

Forty minutes later, Liam was inside Daedalus. "You are right. Two small shuttle ships entered, and then one left to return to the surface half an hour later. What's next, Dad?"

"We are headed to the sun/earth Lagrange point."

"What do you expect to find there," Liam wanted to know.

"Ships," volunteered Baby, "lots of them, I'll bet."

Iggy chuckled. "Right, you are indeed, Baby. These people have a problem that involves their entire civilization. They are using our civilization to remedy the problem. I'm more than sure one small ship at the other Lagrange point is not their entire mission. We are going to drift 100 kilometers away, similar to what we did before. Liam, you must go back outside. We only need a quick look and a count. This won't take long. We are going to do something about this. I'm not sure exactly what yet, but we are not going to allow them to mine DNA from children. We may have some unexpected help."

Ten minutes later, Liam once again peered over the turret at the Lagrange points. **"Holy moly, Dad. Baby was right. There must be 30 ships out here. They are all the length of a football field or larger, anyway. Wow! I wonder how many kids are on board.**

Gloria shared her reception of Liam's images.

“Why so many ships, Dad,” Lori hadn’t spoken since they boarded. Silence was always her signature. She was a quiet child who usually sat in the corner observing others. She wasn't shy, only self-contained. Different than everyone else, she embraced telekinesis as the definition of her persona. She rarely felt the need to share her thoughts other than with her twin brother, Liam, or her sister. The need for social contact simply didn't exist despite her empathy for others. She embraced her own uniqueness but secretly longed for an explanation of why. Melanie often explained her belief that Lori was special for a reason and the universe had plenty in store for her future. So, she waited.

Iggy smiled at his daughter. She was his youngest child, born just minutes behind Liam. "So, you finally decided to talk to us, sweetie. I forgot you were even aboard." A somber expression replaced his smile. "Those ships are full of kids, Lori. Many of them are probably your age. They are captives being used to extract DNA. The people responsible require replacement DNA because they are physically debilitated from experimentation on themselves.” I asked you to come so you would be fully aware of the circumstances if your abilities are needed. It is somehow our responsibility to correct this."

"Okay, Gloria, tell Liam to come inside. We have seen enough, and it's time to leave."

It is said, when a butterfly flaps its wings, the waves are felt across the universe.

Heng Zia, Taio Chen's auntie

CHAPTER XIII

ENDGAME BOOK I

Cameron Fry was the last to arrive. He planned it that way but couldn't remember the reason. There were no guards visible. The Sistine chapel closed at 6 PM. Once the throng of tourists was gone, he wanted to be sure no Interlink guards were stationed on the ground, but for some reason, he couldn't put his finger on why that mattered either. There were a dozen acolytes and a few priests kneeling on mats, praying. Everything appeared quiet and normal. He wasn't the main player in this adventure. He was an unwitting shill. Iggy had given Cameron Fry a typical Lightning wristwatch. Only it was smaller than the ones worn by Lightning personnel. An oversized watch matching the ones worn by Marcus and his associates would arouse suspicion.

Two months ago, Cameron Fry would never have considered taking the action he was about to take. But like everyone else who landed within the orbit of Iggy Marcus, he was compelled to assist the only honest man he had ever met. He never asked Marcus what he was about to do or why. Iggy Marcus and his devoted coterie were on a mission, and it was better that he had no idea what it was. His subliminal instructions were to press three buttons on the watch in a certain sequence, fold his arms across his chest, and the watch would take care of the rest.

Iggy had called him in New York and invited him back to Lightning as soon as possible. He was amazed at his intense internal response. His heart hadn't leaped with anticipation like this since his first encounter with the opposite sex. He wasn't sure why, but it really didn't matter. Five hours later, he landed at Lightning Ranch and taxied to the Daedalus hanger to find his friend.

They shook hands. "Welcome back, Cameron; glad to see you."

Cameron Fry wasn't quite as blown away as the first time he shook Iggy's hand, but even now, the effect was still the same.

Cameron Fry smiled at Iggy. It wasn't his usual manipulative smile. That's how he dealt with men and women in the business world. Smiles and jokes were used to achieve an end, resulting in a favorable business position. This is the first time that he could remember smiling at someone just because he was happy to see them. "So, Iggy, I have two questions. Would scampi be on the menu tonight by any chance, and what's so urgent?"

Iggy laughed. "In that order of priority? What if I were to tell you I invited you here only because scampi was on the menu tonight?"

"I would swoon!" Cameron Fry was totally relaxed with another human being for the first time in 35 years. He had been exposed to Iggy's persona by *contact,* and he saw the depths of the man's character. This man would never vie for position competitively. He would never force another to spar indiscriminately to assert dominance.

"All joking aside, I could use your help, Cameron."

"Really?" Cameron was surprised. It was the last thing he expected from the man who appeared to have everything and was able to do anything. "What is it that you want me to do?"

"I need a shill. That's all. I don't want you to be actively involved in this in a large way. You will be in no physical or mental danger. I also would rather not give you too much information. Your alien visitor will be there, maybe two of them. I'm quite certain they have telepathic powers, Cameron. The less you know, the better off you will be." Iggy laughed again, "I wouldn't want you to give away the store."

"Cameron Fry was no fool. "Obviously, what you're about to do has something to do with these people from Altair. I agree. Don't tell me anything that I can let slip. In fact, you may have told me too much already."

"Thanks for the vote of confidence, Cameron, but you need to know more. Don't worry about loose lips sinking the ship. I have a way around that. First, you must agree to all this, willfully. I am asking for your help and refuse to manipulate you or demand anything. You're going to wear your wristwatch, and it will supply me with the information I need. This watch does more than tell time. It's a video recorder that can replicate everything recorded in the form of a hologram, and it also measures biological signatures, infrared, electromagnetic fields, etc. The computer brain in this watch is the equivalent of a standard two-terabyte storage vessel. For all intents and purposes, the watch will make you my ears and my eyes. "

"This is the first time you haven't made any sense to me. You said Hansel and Gretel might be able to read my mind, and then you told me everything. How is that supposed to work?"

"Well, with your permission, Gloria will hypnotize you. You'll know you're there for a good reason, but you won't have any memory of why. A good reason can be anything, just your participation in a meeting, etc. Gloria will implant a greater significance than that in your subconscious mind. When everything is complete, we will broadcast a wake-up password on your watch or say it directly, and you will remember everything. You also understand what our mission is. That is what I must burden you with at the moment."

"Sounds like a typical Saturday night. That's when the meeting is... next Saturday. Since Gloria is going to hypnotize me, and I'm not going to know exactly what I am doing there... Just what am I doing there? Just out of curiosity, of course."

Iggy's broad smile and mischievous chuckle made Fry slightly uneasy. "This has to be something pretty big if I'm going to do stuff that I'm hypnotized not to know about."

"Well, Cameron, I had to tell you this anyway, so you would know exactly what you were getting involved in. You need to be aware and approve of everything before you can agree to anything, especially your hypnosis."

Cameron Fry laughed. "Just what are you going to do? " He joked, laughing, kidnap Hansel and Gretel?"

Iggy's deadpan look and lack of response said it all. "Jesus Christ, that's exactly what you're going to do, isn't it…" Jesus, he repeated. "You're some horse of a different color, Iggy Marcus!"

"Yes, well, they are coming with me to Lightning. Further, Heinrich Klatch is not a citizen of the United States, so he has no constitutional protections either."

"You're not going to grab Klatch too?" He blurted the question with eyes the size of golf balls.

"Yup. That ought to do it."

"Do what?" he begged, with eyes still the size of golf balls.

"Do you know what the earth/sun Lagrange points are?"

"Sort of. Well, not really. Go ahead, tell me."

"I'll keep it simple. They are named after a Frenchman, Joseph Lagrange. There are five Lagrange points between the earth and the sun. Simply, it is where gravitational equilibrium exists between the two bodies."

"And the significance of that is...there's a lot of matter floating around in turmoil at the Lagrange points due to the gravity of both the earth and sun. Think of it as similar to a riptide where the tides meet in estuaries. The matter turbulence makes it a perfect place to hide ships, especially visually cloaked ships that still have infrared or electromagnetic signatures."

"And…?"

"There are 30 large ships, each slightly larger than a football field, parked at the Lagrange points. They belong to the Altairians."

"Well," returned Fry, "that would make sense if they were here to mine resources, I guess, wouldn't it?"

"They are not here for **that**, Cameron. I won't play word tag with you. They're here to abduct human children, my guess is thousands of them."

"What the hell for?"

"DNA, Cameron. We have it, and they need it. Apparently, billions of years ago, the earth was seeded with DNA. Every living thing on earth has DNA in its genome except for RNA viruses. RNA is the precursor to DNA. The species or galactic citizens who did that are long gone. They have climbed the evolutionary ladder to wherever all the universe's citizens will eventually wind up… **IF** they don't screw up. The Altairians possess DNA almost identical to ours but slightly different, as does the species that I communicate with. It is one of the miraculous operating systems or templates for life in the universe. Evidently, there are many other systems supporting life that don't consist of DNA. They would be totally alien to us. Nonetheless, they are also a part of creation and reflect every aspect of the Creator."

"Fascinating!" Was Cameron Fry's only response.

"Apparently, the people from Altair experimented on their entire civilization centuries ago, attempting to expedite evolution. They assumed their wisdom and abilities superseded those of their Creator. They have practically destroyed the species. They then became the products of devolution and regression. They eventually lost the ability to reproduce, and the missing components in their DNA strands generate weaknesses that threaten their survival. Their only method of mitigation is fresh DNA. Children produce the most, so they were the logical choice."

So, you're telling me these ships are full of human children, sort of a DNA garden to be harvested. How many of them, Iggy?" Then it dawned on him. "Oh! I see!" Fry exclaimed. "You're going to kidnap Hansel and Gretel to find out. Wow! Just one question: why Klatch?"

"I studied Heinrich Klatch extensively. He is everything any psychiatrist would dream of having for a patient to unravel. You can bet your life that he knows what's on the ships, and he is in on it. Other than being a twisted psychopath, he is quite brilliant. I believe he is trying to use the people from Altair to achieve his own ends, just as they are using us. He is clinically insane and exists far outside normal human behavior patterns. Always expect the unexpected from Heinrich Klatch."

***

Daedalus settled on the South lawn. Pres. William James Sledge stood on the Truman balcony with Alice, watching Allison MacLeod jog across the lawn to board Daedalus. Iggy Marcus had called him early that morning. He needed Surgeon General Allison MacLeod to drop what she was doing and immediately come to Lightning Ranch. He waved as Allison turned and looked back, returning the salute. Big things were afoot. Iggy's call had been urgent and that was rare from the man who had just turned the human race and its history on its head. Jake's inauguration in two months would end Bill Sledge's lame-duck status, but he must do one more thing to ensure an honest election before he and Alice could escape the rigors of office. Today he would sign his last executive order during his presidential term… E.O. 1652.

The campaign was brutal. Ransom Hornburg's total control over his mainstream media outlets had dedicated eighteen months to ruthlessly castigating Jacob Dorian as the worst politician to ever grace the United States Senate. It was the usual plot to undermine the political opposition by fabricating an unceasing, subliminal character assassination. The opposing party's stock in trade was subterfuge, lies, and propaganda, not to mention an unhealthy dose of election fraud. Those had become the only tools dishonest authoritarians could use to steal and maintain power from a majority of honest citizens.

His opponent, Roaring Ricky O'Malley, resigned his Oregon governorship and tirelessly campaigned from coast to coast, selling his half-baked socialist agenda of the intended nanny state. His primary support was liberal elitists who had no idea what socialism was, indigents with their hands out, and the national plethora of college graduates and indoctrinated victims of a predominantly socialist teaching staff in almost every university. The only voice of reason touting the accomplishments of Sen. Dorian was that of American Media Inc. This was the last chance for the authoritarians to sweep the world's societies into the slavery of socialism. Such had been their mission for a thousand years.

The results always consisted of ups and downs until the advent of the information age, allowing every snake oil salesman who pandered swill directly into the living rooms of an emasculated, non-thinking public. The appearance of Iggy Marcus on the world stage had shifted the paradigm. He was the wild card who turned humanity and society on its ear as he relentlessly displayed government and corporate corruption. Not only did he display the subterfuge, but he also named the players and exactly described their insidious activities. That impeccable description was accompanied by the proof of his brilliant, irrefutable holography.

Jake Dorian's political opposition pulled out all the stops. Unknown characters and actors of every stripe emerged, bellowing every charge of dishonesty, perversion, and avarice imaginable. They accused Jake of every depraved act under the sun. Iggy and Jack Marcus were the firewalls that saved Jake's campaign from succumbing to incessant lies by every media outlet on earth besides the publications and broadcasts on American Media. Despite American Media, the political race remained a tossup throughout its duration.

The quality of the candidates was never an issue. The issue lay in the vast public lassitude and ambivalence toward politics. They figured everything they had always taken for granted would continue effortlessly. That relieved them of the obligation and diligence necessary to discern the philosophical differences between the candidates and apply those policies to their own lives. That lack of introspection submerged them in a fetid swamp of voters concerned only with the Madison Avenue snippets and lies force-fed them by Ransom Hornburg.

Despite the valiant efforts of Jack and Iggy Marcus with their American Media Inc., what really saved Jake's candidacy and propelled him into the presidency was his eloquent, dynamic, and unsurpassable ability to debate. At first, the opposition tried to decline the debate arena with every possible excuse. American Media Inc. took a 24/7 position, decrying the cowardice of the opposition refusing to participate in a formal debate. In the end, Roaring Ricky O'Malley had no choice. His party tried to influence the moderators and broadcast times to no avail. Marcus saturated every publication and broadcast medium until there was no escape.

Ransom Hornburg personally selected the moderator from his lead news channel. It would be an open question-and-answer format where each candidate would be allowed to question each other and address the moderator's and each other's questions. The moderator opened the debate. After that it was all uphill for Jake's opposition. Jake was a seasoned debater with a steel trap memory that set aside the moderator's attempt to broach subjects unfavorable to his tenure in the Senate with the documented truth.

Iggy Marcus had unlocked him more than 20 times in their 25-year association and Jake's elevated intellect carefully dissected every policy of the governor for the past six years of his tenure in Oregon. The rapid exodus of citizens to other states with lower taxes and financially conservative policies had decimated the tax base, and the Oregon governor was left holding the bag with a huge welfare population and no money to hand out. Jake had it all committed to memory, and as he laid item by item at the feet of his opponent, the governor had no answers or response to the critiques. Jake not only succeeded in winning the debate, but it was also the philosophical slaughter of Roaring Rick O'Malley's opinions and policies.

There would be no more debates; The opposition party decided to cut its losses and not risk any more public scrutiny. Two months before the election, Pres. William James Sledge signed Executive Order 1652. It stated that all polling places would allow an equal number of partisan observers who were not part of the bureaucracy running the election. There were no limits on their ability to observe and record proceedings. Iggy Marcus dedicated 2400 Navy SEALs and 2000 other employees in the Marcus business empire to become poll watchers. Everyone had a wristwatch that would record everything and exhibit the results in holograms. There were an additional 4000 volunteers from assorted political watch groups that would participate in the election. All drop boxes and after-hours balloting were prohibited. They left no room for subterfuge.

The results were staggering. There had not been an election victory as one-sided as this since Franklin Delano Roosevelt during World War II. The results were nearly 64% for Sen. Jake Dorian and 36% for Roaring Rick O'Malley. Tom Rickart commented on the demonstrable proof of how corrupt previous elections must have been when there were no poll watchers with recording equipment.

***

Melanie and Gloria stood waiting in front of the Daedalus hanger as Baby settled the ship to the flight line. Allison stepped through the hatch. "Hi, girls," Allison said, hugging both Melanie and her daughter. "It's so good to see you. You're all smiling. It would seem the emergency I am supposed to help solve isn't really such an emergency after all."

"I'm not sure how much of an emergency it is, Allison, but Iggy says that it's probably the most important thing in the world at the moment... and I agree. Let's go to the hospital. Iggy, David, and Sylvia Peterson along with a dozen other doctors on our staff, are setting up an emergency laboratory and isolation chambers."

"The hospital looks different from what I remember," Allison said, staring at the new wing as they stepped out of the Land Rover… "bigger somehow."

"It is different, Allison. Six months ago, we completed an entirely new wing, separated and divorced from the rest of the hospital. They are connected by two tunnels, one underground and one three stories up. They also act as airlocks."

"Airlocks? Why airlocks? That sounds pretty ominous. I thought you guys stripped the world of bioweapons. Also, the wing looks larger than the actual hospital itself."

"We did strip the world, and the wing is larger. Iggy has been planning this for a few years now, once he got wind of what was going on."

"What's going on, Melanie?" Melanie wasn't smiling anymore, and neither was Allison. Gloria hadn't said a word yet.

"Let's go inside. Iggy will brief you. We will all sit and have a conversation about the course of action we must take."

Allison knew it was serious. Anytime the word brief was the verb, events already were critical, or could soon become calamitous. "Does the president know? Wait... that was a foolish question. Of course, he must know. He's the one that ordered me out here," Allison laughed.

"Jake's been briefed, as well," Melanie added as they passed through the revolving doors of the main entrance. "We're going to take the underground tunnel to the new wing."

"From what I saw, the new wing is just about as wide as the hospital. They look almost the same size."

"The wing is much larger." Gloria jumped into the conversation. "It looks just about as wide, 250 feet, but it's twice as long, and 16 stories."

Allison laughed. "16 stories!? They looked the same size to me... Oh, wow!" She exclaimed as it dawned on her. "You have eight stories underground, don't you?" she asked in wonder. "Whatever for?" She was just beginning to grasp the magnitude of Iggy Marcus's latest project. Nobody built buildings in the middle of Montana where everyone had room to sprawl, with 16 stories, half of them underground. She couldn't wait for the explanation.

Iggy and Dave Peterson met them in the entrance lobby to the new wing. It was the only entrance that could be opened from the outside. Dave Peterson hugged Allison MacLeod and she turned to Iggy with her hand out. "I can never get enough of shaking your hand, Iggy."

Gloria looked at her father sideways with a somewhat derisive expression. Allison's handshake lasted far too long to suit her. It reappeared one more time... the sexual tension between her father and Surgeon General Allison MacLeod.

Gloria quashed the tension. "Why don't we all head to the cafeteria, DAD," she put major emphasis on the word dad. We can all have coffee while you brief Allison. Follow me."

Melanie laughed aloud. She didn't miss a trick. She knew exactly what was going on and understood Iggy's attraction to Allison MacLeod. It was a normal thing and to be expected. Her husband was human, not a god... yet, anyway. But she still appreciated Gloria. Gloria was her daughter, and she would always have her back, even when it wasn't necessary.

Allison MacLeod opened with a smile after they were seated. "So, what's the big deal? It has to be a big deal for you to drag me out of the White House and my job to come out to your hospital."

"Okay, Allison. I'll start with why you're here. You are the leading geneticist and virologist in the world. Twice a Nobel laureate. Those credentials didn't come for any other reason than you are exactly what you represent yourself to be. You're waiting for the punch line, Allison. The people from Altair experimented on their own genetics centuries ago, trying to expedite evolution and rise to a stature they were not yet ready for. They nearly destroyed themselves. In fact, they actually did because they can no longer reproduce without imported DNA."

"Assembled here at this hospital, is the greatest medical team in history. We haven't told the world much of what we have done here yet, but we have unraveled mysteries of human anatomy and the genome as it relates to longevity and, someday, even immortality. This team is of crucial importance in what I'm about to describe. The missing link to make this team complete and the best in existence is you, Allison."

Allison MacLeod knew Iggy Marcus well. She knew all about human nature, too. This man would never exaggerate or lie. Nor would he flatter her for inane reasons. She understood what she was about to hear was going to stretch the imagination. "Go ahead, Iggy. I'm all ears."

You are aware of Interlink's continued efforts. Heinrich Klatch runs the show now. He's the public face of the two usual clowns who are behind the scenes… Ransom Hornburg and Lawrence Howe. Between them, they own 22 trillion dollars and control another 11 trillion. That's about 25%. The Association of Interlink controls an additional 70%. They control most of the free world's finances. They are the two most powerful men in the world. They give everyone orders, and everyone obeys. They have the economic clout to destroy any country that doesn't obey, since they are worth more than just about any country besides China. If you count capital assets, like land and the facilities of government, the United States has that much as well. We are cash-poor, though, but only for a while. I have solved that conundrum."

Allison remained quiet with no questions. She already knew much of the stuff so it must be only the tip of the iceberg... and she knew the iceberg was going to be huge. "Go on."

You already are aware of the extraterrestrial presence here. I will define them a little better. There are at least three species. One of them is ambivalent beyond calling themselves shepherds and acting in a non-aggressive way to deal with us. They are the ones I have been dealing with. Another species who has been here for a while has had very little impact. They have a base at the South Pole, believe it or not. Then, there is the group of extraterrestrials from the star Altair. The fourth planet is their home, and the star is in the Aquila constellation. It's about 17 light years from us."

Allison nodded her head as he explained all the interactions between his family and the shepherds. Iggy then described the intended sterilization of Earth that was halted eight years before because of his ring of satellites. "Our satellites eliminated nuclear war as well as man's ability to destroy himself and the planet. Interlink and the people from Altair four are complicit. They are asking permission to mine certain resources from assorted countries around the world."

He described the meeting room 12 stories below the Sistine Chapel floor and the various meetings of the aliens with human beings. Allison remained silent. She knew there was much more to come, and it would be the crux of this meeting.

"Short time ago I had a visit from Cameron Fry. I had contact with him when he flew to Lightning, but I have since, unlocked him."

"You're not serious! The… Cameron Fry, the same guy who is a trillionaire and one of the kingpins of Interlink? My God, whatever for?"

Iggy laughed. "I know, Alison," he continued to laugh. "I was a skeptic as well, but things are often much different than they appear. Even when the stars are all in place, and the planets are aligned, the hand of fate will defy expectations and slay the status quo."

"Okay then... Cameron Fry. I believe it, but only because it came out of your mouth. Go on."

He described in great length the meeting between Interlink and the Altairians and how they intended to ask all the countries of the world to meet through the United Nations and give them permission to mine certain resources. "Those resources would only be by permission, and we would be paid adequately. Cameron Fry caught them in a few lies. Further, their desire to mine resources from this planet is bogus. Any minerals that we possess, and any seawater is in abundance thousands of times in the asteroid belt and on the moons of Saturn and Jupiter. Mars also has some of that. So, consequently, they are not here for that." Iggy waited for Allison's next question before he continued.

"Okay, I'll bite; what exactly are they here for?"

"A few months ago, the extraterrestrials I called the shepherds suggested I take a trip to the earth/moon and earth/sun Lagrange points and do it stealthily so that I would not be discovered. Gloria, Lori, Liam, Baby, and I did exactly that. We discovered one ship approximately the size of a football field at the earth/moon Lagrange point. Then, we moved to the earth/sun Lagrange point and discovered another 30 vessels even larger."

Allison was silent. She had no questions. She knew Iggy would tell her everything.

"When we arrived at the earth/moon Lagrange point, we discovered a ship about the size of a football field. Smaller ships, the approximate size of school buses, were shuttling back and forth from the surface to the ship. We moved to the earth/sun Lagrange point discovered 30 more similar vessels but a little larger. We were not detected. Our technology was adequate. A Lagrange point is a turbulent place with lots of matter floating around that helps mask the presence of ships."

Iggy smiled as he watched waves of recognition sweep across Allison MacLeod's face. He expected it. She was beyond brilliant. She was one of the smartest scientists alive, right up there with history's greats.

Rarely given to expletives, Allison MacLeod could not help herself. She put two and two together and everything fell into place in her mind. "No shit!" They are stealing our kids for DNA! The rotten bastards! What are we ever going to do?"

"I've been asked that question by a lot of people lately, Allison. The president, the President-elect, and you, his running mate, have just asked me the same question. I've given it a great deal of thought. I'm pretty good, but not good enough to win and succeed forcibly without enormous risk. I've come up with some pretty remarkable technology, but the answer to get our children back from these people is not an interstellar war that we can't possibly win even if we were to prevail. Technology wars are the most destructive. They can kill a massive amount of people with the least amount of effort and result in minimal gains. Implicit to that scenario is the fact that every one of those children that they have abducted would be in danger of being destroyed. It's a logistics nightmare. It's one of those unsolvable conundrums."

Allison MacLeod smiled. She knew Iggy Marcus had an answer, or she wouldn't be here, involved in this incredible problem. "Okay, Iggy, I get it. You figured it out, and somehow, I am to be a participant."

"Yup, I've got it figured out. Or at least I hope so. I have an impeccable solution, and it will be quite an achievement if we succeed."

Allison's mind worked fast. She knew his solution was through technology, but it wasn't the confrontational technology of super weapons. The Altairians were obviously desperate. They were dying. They had come up with the only solution that would perpetuate them. They would not destroy us, just some of the children who would become DNA mines. Iggy Marcus had concocted the only solution that could possibly ever work and prevent the decimation from war, especially a war that would not be fought between an alien species and the people of planet Earth. It would be a war between an alien species, acting in desperation, and one man... himself. That was a no-win scenario.

“I get it, I really get it," Allison MacLeod repeated herself in wonder." You are amazing, Iggy Marcus… just amazing." She shook her head as she thought about it and repeated, "Absolutely amazing."

Iggy understood she had figured it out. She was brilliant, and it would take that kind of mind to accomplish this incredible, maybe even insurmountable task. " Yup, that's the long and short of it, Allison. We have to solve their problem for them genetically, so they don't need our children's DNA."

"Brilliant, Iggy! That's why this new wing, isn't it? How many kids do you expect?"

"I don't know just yet. Ten, maybe twenty thousand, maybe even more."

“When the hell are you going to know?" Allison asked with her volume up.

"Shortly, Allison, shortly. That's why I mentioned Cameron Fry. He's going to help me. They have a meeting this coming Saturday night, 12 stories below the floor of the Sistine Chapel. Their alien friends will be there."

"Oh my God. Iggy Marcus, you're going to kidnap a couple of aliens! Then you're going to have your daughter read their minds! " Allison MacLeod laughed hysterically. "Boy, somebody ought to write a book about this. Maybe I will, depending on how it all turns out."

“While I'm at it, I'm going to grab Heinrich Klatch. We'll see what's going on in that sick little mind of his."

***

Three years before… Vladimir Borenko, Richard Percy, Amon Rothman, and the other upper-echelon members of Interlink’s inner circle colluded to destroy Iggy Marcus with nuclear weapons obtained from the CCP simply because he refused to join their club and was an existential threat to their virtually unlimited power. Ultimately, they didn't really want him as a member. He excelled, and people who excel wind up giving the orders. No one at Interlink wanted that.

Even then, the men who populated the head table at Interlink were just the frontmen. Vladimir Borenko was their chess master and conspiracy architect. The true genius behind the organization remained in obscurity. Heinrich Klatch was rarely at Interlink meetings and was never outspoken. He observed everything; his cold and calculating mind always dwelt somewhere in the future, planning to achieve the best results given the available information at the time.

It is often said there is a fine line between genius and insanity. Heinrich Klatch was definitely insane, but he was also brilliant. History was populated with brilliant men who changed the course of history because of their dazzling contributions to science and the humanities. Human nature and morality exist on a plane of extremes. Every individual of consequence existed somewhere on that axis, vacillating between the opposite extremes of good and evil. The genius of Heinrich Klatch was in that class, but his malevolence would contribute nothing of value to the human condition.

The creation of Lightning Inc., American Media Inc., and the actions of one man, Iggy Marcus, became a wake-up call for Klatch. His prescience was unparalleled. He understood that Marcus was the next step up the ladder of human civility that would negate the dominant hierarchy of elitism. He saw the future unfolding and the threat Marcus would be to the power structure of the world. That power structure had been established tens of thousands of years before when men first became self-aware and created a society consisting of alpha male dominance. The people who ruled... ruled, and the people who served... served. The social architecture was designed to maintain that in perpetuity. One man was not going to be allowed to change the status quo. Marcus had taken nuclear war off the table, destroying the elitist super weapon necessary to generate fear and assert dominance, immediately changing the world forever. Klatch began laying his plans when Marcus first became notorious as he watched Iggy and Jack Marcus lead eleven children to the Olympics, returning home with 13 gold and silver medals.

He would remove the threat this man was, not just to Interlink's power but his personal power as well. Modern Interlink and its predecessors were enmeshed in power, undefeatable and irascible. The common man had no chance against them. This man gave them that historic chance for the second time. The first chance was the Declaration of Independence and the Bill of Rights. Then men became lazy and allowed their political emissaries to usurp the power of the people and hand it back to the elitists, beginning with the Federal Reserve Act in 1913 and continuing through the 20th century, culminating with Richard Nixon's final severing of the dollar from gold.

Klatch saw history for exactly what it was and knew he had to act. He began looking for weak spots in the Marcus empire's underbelly. There weren't many, but the few that were apparent and accessible consisted of Marcus's two sons, Brett, and Luke. Both boys had won Olympic gold medals for figure skating, giving the greatest performances the world had ever seen, especially the younger one, Brett. He accomplished things on the ice that were thought to be impossible by motion physicists. That's where Klatch began laying his plans. They would take time and patience to execute and would only come to fruition over the long haul.

When he first conceived his plans, he wasn't certain exactly how they would be executed, but this he knew; those plans would probably be the only way he could disembowel Marcus. He would kill Marcus directly with his bare hands if he could, but this would be the next best thing. He invested a few billion dollars creating a network of skating venues around the world. They became famous competitions and exhibitions for the best skaters on earth. This he would do for years if it was necessary, and when the time was right, and the iron hot, he would strike at the heart of Iggy Marcus.

***

"Let me fly, Luke. You flew last time." They were about to leave Lightning Ranch, headed for London.

"True enough, Brett. Take the controls." It was close to a ten-hour flight for the Learjet. Maybe a little more because of the Earth's rotation. "I'm not skating. I'm just along for the ride; someone has to have your back. Anyway, there's no way I can beat your ass on the ice unless we're skating in pairs. Then I've got you."

Luke and Brett, besides being brothers, were the best of friends. They had grown up together under their father's tutelage, and because of their family's unique position, they rarely sought relationships or friendships outside the family. They were headed to England to one of the most celebrated skating demonstrators' expositions outside the actual Olympics. Thousands of people would come from all over to watch the best of the best compete. Not only was it a competition, but serious skaters would also have a chance to meet Olympic gold medalists and learn from them. That was the flavor of the venue. It had been set up to exude a relaxed camaraderie within a professional teaching platform. Heinrich Klatch had spent a ton of money and hired the best promoters on earth to deliver this exact venue.

***

Sixty-five major movers and shakers of the business world, as well as dozens of officials from assorted countries, waited, filling the conference room with the soft murmur of conversation. Hansel and Gretel should be arriving shortly, and Heinrich Klatch said there would be a major surprise at the end of the meeting that would turn the tables on their nemesis, the American president and Iggy Marcus. Heinrich Klatch's chair was empty. He was never late. As chairman he opened the meetings and set the agenda before anyone did business. Cameron Fry, two chairs from the center seat, sat admiring his new watch. Something was bothering him; his photographic memory had forgotten something important, but it seemed he couldn't remember, to save his life. He knew he was supposed to do something when Hansel and Gretel arrived, but they weren't present, either. Very unusual, he thought. He never had memory lapses and was always prepared for everything.

The soft chime drew everyone's eyes to the opening elevator door. Four UN soldiers surrounded Hansel and Gretel. The entourage entered the room, and two soldiers remained in the elevator while two stood in the room on either side of the door. Hansel and Gretel walked directly to the head table and took seats.

Cameron Fry pressed three buttons on his watch. Why am I doing this? He wondered. And why that particular sequence? He folded his arms across his chest, exposing his wristwatch, and waited. His actions were nagging at him. They were out of character. The elevator chimed again as the door opened to a lone occupant. Heinrich Klatch's personal valet entered the room and took the seat next to the extraterrestrials.

***

Paul Billings faced the nine Navy SEALs. "Okay, men, we're on! The buttons are pressed, and it's almost time to deploy."

"Gloria and I are going in with you men. You all know your jobs. Everybody gets encapsulated, first the UN soldiers. I will put up a wall between the people of Interlink and the two aliens." He turned to Liam. We are hovering over the Coliseum. Look over the entire city and see if you can detect any ships or anomalous objects. Hansel and Gretel had to get here somehow. I know where everything is except their vessel. We won't have much time despite the force field. I have no idea how powerful their alien technology is.

"Do you think you can deal with two of them simultaneously, Gloria?"

"I don't know, Dad. I don't use it too often, but I have come a long way from that day with Ainstead Crenshaw. I will say this, if their minds aren't seriously more advanced than those people we have been Dealing with, I believe I actually can force them. Or at least, subdue them while the SEALs carry them to the ship."

"Okay, Baby, keep the ship invisible and drop us off between the chapel and Basilica. The entrance to the vault can either be down an eighty-foot granite Bramante staircase or we can take the elevator. It will be the elevator for the last three stories. I suggest the stairs, so they aren't alarmed by the elevator descending. Twenty-two floors take a while, and that defeats our greatest advantage, the element of surprise."

It was two days after their return from China and the Bālún Tōng. Things were falling into place. Liam surveyed the skies over Rome. Just as Iggy had expected, a ship hovered at 5000 feet directly above the Basilica. It was one of their shuttles disguised to prevent visual observation. "The ship is there, Dad. They haven't disguised their electromagnetic or infrared signatures. I'm sure radar can't pick them up, so they believe they're undetectable."

Daedalus had barely stopped its descent as the men scrambled from the ship. The team stood at the top staircase waiting for the go-ahead. Paul Billings wasted no time, "All right men, saddle up. Grab the equipment, and let's run. Bring the extra stretcher." They descended at a run. It was about 2 1/2 minutes until they reached the elevator for the last three floors.

***

"How many people do you expect, Ig.?"

Iggy smiled at his brother. "I'll tell you, Jack; I really don't know, but I expect better than twenty million. I know that sounds ridiculous, but that's the word coming out of China."

Iggy's brother smiled from ear to ear. "You know, Iggy, I've been thinking about the past a lot lately. I remember the night we all sat together in the old conference room 25 years ago and concocted this crazy, bizarre plan to change the world. I was sure it was crazy at the time, and it was definitely bizarre, but here I am, twenty-five years later, watching this most amazing experience unfold. You handed me the reins of American Media Inc. and never once told me how to do it. You left it up to me."

"Of course, you were the logical man for the job, and nobody could have done better. I knew how well you would fill those shoes."

"I always had faith in you, too, brother. Everything that you've done is beyond amazing. I've lived it with you, and this is just another one of those amazing days. You turned the CCP on its ear, and for the first time in Chinese history, put the common people in charge of their own destiny. We are talking about a billion and a half people here, brother. That's not just a major accomplishment; it's a miracle! And now we are on our way to making a speech to 20 million people, all gathered in one place because of you. Then we'll reintroduce Heng Zia and Yang Bo Chu, two Chinese people you unlocked, who are going to lead the country into the future. It just doesn't get any better than this."

Zia, Chu, Heng Cong, and Taio Chen sat across from the Marcus brothers. Chu laughed, "If you guys are finished patting each other on the back, tell me what you expect to happen when we arrive?" Zia frowned at her husband's cavalier remark.

Iggy laughed at Chu's question. "Well, I'm going to make a speech to 20 million Bālún Tōng members, maybe even many more, because things like that have a way of taking off on you. Then I'm going to announce the new president of the Republic of China on an interim basis until national elections can be coordinated. That happens to be you, Yang Bo Chu! Although it hasn't been obvious, that is what I have been training you for."

Heng Zia and Yang Bo Chu were more than surprised. Iggy hadn't told them this, and it defied their imaginations. Chu sat in silence, his face a caricature of disbelief. Zia just sat and cried. "This pays for my sister, Mr. Marcus. Thank you. Thank you. Thank you!"

"I see," Chu muttered. "That's why you brought Heng Cong and Taio Chen along." He continued shaking his head in approval. "You are right, Iggy Marcus. These two children should not miss this. This is probably the most significant event in the entire history of China. A monument to my countrymen and all the world is being built today."

Zia dried her eyes. "So, where are we going, Iggy? China is a big country, and 20 million people have to gather someplace where there is room if that many people come."

"They will come, Zia. Bālún Tōng has been organized for several months since we removed the CCP. It had a few difficult challenges, but that's why we are here and why I have trained you and Chu. We are headed to a place west of Shanghai and south of Beijing, nestled between and around the cities of Kaifeng, Shangqiu, Heze, and Puyang. That is centrally located where the pilgrims of Bālún Tōng wish to gather. It has a great open area that can accommodate many people on a pilgrimage."

Daedalus hovered at a thousand feet as Iggy made the floor and the walls disappear. "Holy Shamolicans!! Would you look at that!" Jack exclaimed. "Have you ever seen the like?"

"And it's not even Chinese New Year." Wisecracked Baby with her typical small talk and humor as Gloria bent over laughing.

Jack was laughing too, now. "How many do you think there are, brother?"

Iggy scanned the massive ocean of people beneath them. The crowd seemed to stretch from horizon to horizon in almost every direction, surrounding bodies of water, buildings, and anyplace else where there was a place to stand. They had come from all over China to celebrate. Men, women, and children, even people that did not belong to Bālún Tōng were waving at Daedalus.

Chu, still stunned, said nothing. Zia wept. Even Jack was amazed at the magnitude of what his brother had wrought.

"There were about 7 million people last time. Your hologram was pretty impressive. I would think you will do that today."

"Yup, Gloria, same thing."

The ocean of people beneath Daedalus was silent, waiting. They all had come to meet the man who liberated them. Many of them had been at the last meeting with Iggy Marcus when he arrested the last of the dictators. Iggy had been told that 20 million people from Bālún Tōng would be present. He did the mental math as he surveyed the crowd below. Almost 40 million people came. It was a sight like no other in human history. That many people in one location for a quiet celebration of their liberation.

There was a control panel console, but he didn't need it. His cerebral computer chip interfaced with the ship's computer, and all commands were subliminal. His first act was to project four 200-foot-high holograms of his face in real-time. He was about to speak in Mandarin to 40 million people with the exact reproduction of his words and facial expressions.

"Good afternoon, citizens of China. Thank you for this welcome." His smile represented itself precisely in the hologram of his face. **"You have come from all over China to celebrate the beginning of a new era. It will be an era of individual freedom and prosperity if you follow the precepts of Bālún Tōng. The officials of the old CCP have been swept away, and they will never return to oppress you again. They have been removed from China. You are being given the unique opportunity to chart your own course into the future as unique individuals and masters of your own destiny. That, however, is not free. It comes with a price. If you stop living by those precepts and refuse to pay the price, your autonomy and freedom will be swept away just as your former masters have been swept away."**

"This is a unique gift. This has been given to you only one time. It is not a gift from me, it is a gift from Chuàngzuò zhě. Make use of it, cherish it, and never let anyone subvert it because it is the only path to the future for you and your children. You, members of Bālún Tōng, have chosen the correct path. It is the path of truth and justice. It is the only path to the future if men are to survive and prosper. "

"The days of authoritarianism must disappear. Men are not gods, and they must never act like gods. Everyone is autonomous and is granted the dignity and mastery of his own existence by Chuàngzuò zhě. That requires the abstinence from coercion by a ruling class that abrogates the rights of individuals for their own aggrandizement. This is what Mao Zedong did to you and passed on to his successors. He murdered 70 million of your countrymen, directly or by sins of omission. That philosophy will never die, but it will never again be potent if you remain watchful and teach your children the philosophy

that must belie every action you take and every choice you make. That, my friends, is your only way to the future."

"I am an American. You are Chinese. But we are all human beings and deserve the same rights as every other human being. That requires a system that supports that philosophy and never allows tyranny to rear its ugly head. Tyrants are killers. That is true in every case. Some are gutless, and they will not grasp the sword in their own hand, but nonetheless, they will murder to achieve an end. You must guard against this because people will rise and attempt to enslave humanity again. That is my mission, to prevent that, and in doing so, prevent man from self-annihilation."

"Not too long ago, I was asked to rescue two Chinese children who had survived an authoritarian murder of their parents at a Bālún Tōng meeting. They were with their aunt and uncle, Heng Zia and Yang Bo Chu. They return to America with me, where the children are in school at Lightning Ranch. Zia and Chu have been returned to China this day. I have given them the ability and training to lead. Bālún Tōng has become your social vehicle for self-governance. You have much to learn. Zia and Chu will guide you. I have given them that capability. They will become interim co-presidents until your country becomes organized and can hold its own elections."

"Every citizen has the obligation to blaze the trail to the future. That is always done by governance, but it must be done with integrity, honor, and transparency. You will learn to do this as a society, or you will fail just as America and Europe are failing now. That is the situation that we intend to remedy, but the cure is always much more difficult than the prevention. You have already begun the process of organizing a new government. You will succeed, and you will do it well. However, then comes the question, can you keep it? We bid you farewell and wish you the best of luck. We will always be available to assist you. Zia and Chu can contact us at any time."

Zia and Chu stepped out of Daedalus in front of the immense throng. Daedalus rose and moved slowly away as 40 million people cheered and sang Chinese hymns.

"That went pretty well, Dad. Tomorrow night is the Vatican." Apprehension underscored her statement.

"Yes, Gloria, we'll be fine. You have a case of the nerves?"

She laughed. "You already know that I do. We are about to kidnap aliens. That's a first... no precedent... all hell could break loose."

"I suppose anything is possible, daughter. I don't see an alternative, though. There are thousands of human children on those ships, and we need the intelligence."

***

Ten Navy SEALs hit the landing in front of the last elevator at a run with Gloria and Iggy close behind. Paul Billings twisted his neck to Iggy, "Do you think they know we are here?"

"They know, or at least they will when we call for the elevator. Remember, the car is at the bottom. The surveillance system had to pick us up."

"They'll be ready for us then. We'll need the shields right away. How long will it take for reinforcements to get here once they sound the alarm?"

"I've got that covered. Baby has filled all electronics and airwaves with white noise. They cannot communicate. In fact, the Altairians can't communicate with their ship either. We have to get this done as quickly as possible before they get involved."

The elevator stopped, and the door opened slowly. The two UN soldiers in the elevator stared from the cage at a beautiful young girl. "Hi, my name is Gloria. Is this the elevator to the dining room?" She asked in Italian after noting the Italian flag on their sleeves.

The soldiers laughed and walked out of the elevator with their weapons slung over their shoulders. Five Navy SEALs on either side of the elevator grappled with them and removed their weapons when they stepped toward Gloria.

Iggy confronted them with his hands on his hips. "How many people are down there, and who are they? Are the extraterrestrials there, and how many soldiers remained below?" He didn't expect answers, only thoughts. Gloria would glean the answers. He glanced at the weight capacity of the elevator. Okay, men, we have two trips. The elevator will hold eight of us. We are 10 and will bring these two soldiers with us. Four of you take the second trip and keep these characters encapsulated.

"I can't give you the exact number, but there are about 65 people, two more UN troops and two extraterrestrials, Dad." She reported as they boarded the elevator.

Iggy, Gloria, and six SEALs stepped through the door into the conference room. At first, no one quite understood what was happening except the aliens. They understood precisely. Someone had come to abduct them. They immediately recognized Iggy when he stepped into the room, but it was too late. Seventy people and the two extraterrestrials were immediately encapsulated by Iggy's team.

Iggy nodded. "**You're on, daughter. See what you can do.**"

"Yes, Father."

Hansel and Gretel were immediately overwhelmed, stunned by their own miscalculation and the intense subliminal scrutiny of Gloria's mind. Their expression of alarm at her invasive dexterity washed over their faces as they grappled with the realization these people were not as primitive as their luminaries thought. This was not supposed to happen.

The two visitors from Altair felt Gloria Marcus plunge to the depths of their subconscious minds as she vanquished their autonomy, assuming complete control. They resisted, terrified, but they were unable to prevent the violent intrusion. ***I am here***! Gloria Marcus bellowed in their minds. She didn't do it with words, only images, but she had read the content of their brains and understood the language and how to approach communication.

Her entry into the Altairian mind had opened the vista of their subconscious. There were similarities to humans, but there was also a vast disparity in the mechanics and thought processes. They had evolved eons ago beyond the stature of humanity. Evolution had provided them with strident abilities. A portion of their brain was dedicated to emitting a subliminal type of hypnosis, creating a visualization of their stature that was quite different from reality. The creatures appeared to be seven feet tall or greater when they were approximately five to six feet. Their facial structure was almost the same as it appeared on the seven-foot version they wanted others to perceive, but the features were smaller and more concise. Gloria saw them as they really were and intended to broadcast that picture to everyone forced to deal with these creatures.

***Stand up*!** She commanded with extreme tenacity. She wasn't completely sure of herself and needed to further explore the alien's minds. She looked at her father for approval. Iggy was smiling as he watched the two aliens stand as they were commanded.

Now, have them walk to the center of the room and lay on the stretchers.

She bellowed the subliminal commands, **lay on the stretchers... NOW**! Perhaps Gloria overdid it... perhaps not. She was in uncharted territory. Dealing with humans subliminally was one thing. This was an entirely different realm. Moans of distress accompanied contorted expressions of pain that were obvious on the visitors' faces. This had never happened to them before. A primitive species was giving them terrifying mental commands they were unable to resist.

Paul Billing's facial expression reflected his comment, "You people take all the fun out of things. Ten of us have come down here to carry a couple of ETs to Daedalus. We could've done it with four men."

Iggy scowled, "Don't count your chickens yet, Paul. We're nowhere out of the woods until we are aboard Daedalus. We've got a way to go, and we have no idea what kind of interference the aliens aboard their ship might run."

"Move out, men," Paul Billings ordered. "Let's get out of here ASAP." Six Navy SEALs picked up the stretchers containing the aliens and scrambled through the elevator door. Iggy looked around. He saw Cameron Fry sitting off to the side, watching things. Heinrich Klatch wasn't around. That put a slight dent in his plans. He would have to come back for Klatch… he smiled and said... "Rumpelstiltskin."

The codeword freed Cameron Fry from his subliminal hypnosis. The memory of Iggy Marcus's plans, and his participation in them flooded his mind. He remembered that Heinrich Klatch was supposed to be one of the kidnapped victims. He could see that wasn't working out too well. For some reason, Klatch had not arrived yet. Klatch had mentioned earlier that he had a huge surprise in store for Interlink. He remained seated and unemotional so as not to reveal his status as a double agent to the others.

The elevator began its 22-floor rise to the surface. Iggy put his hand on Paul's shoulder. "Excellent job, Paul. Good thing I instructed the other men to remain at the surface guarding the elevator to prevent trouble. The elevator is a bit overloaded with all of us and Hansel and Gretel. Talk to your men at the surface. "

Paul hit the button on his wristwatch. "How are things on the surface, George? It's Quiet I hope."

"So far, so good," answered the voice on the other end." I see the elevator rising. You have six more floors to go. We are locked and loaded just in case, but I think the force field will keep us out of trouble."

Gloria stood between the stretchers with her hands on the alien's temples. Her brow was furrowed in concentration. She looked at her father,**" This is very difficult, Dad. These two are screaming mentally. I am not sure I understand exactly what it is they're saying, but I believe they're trying to communicate with their friends aboard that ship. They have distinct and very strong telepathic powers quite dissimilar to mine, but I have no concept of the range, and I don't believe I can continue to**

block them. Something else is going on here, Dad, and is very sinister. These two extraterrestrials need to have blood tests immediately. I'm not sure exactly, but I detected considerable information in their cerebral architecture, which has to do with their DNA. "

He spoke into his watch. "Bring Daedalus now, Baby. We will be on the surface in a matter of minutes. We have our dinner guests. Encapsulate the entire area once you're inside our access field with Daedalus. Apparently, our guests are trying to communicate with their extraterrestrial Uber driver. We need to avoid a confrontation."

The elevator door opened, and the team rushed onto the granite promenade carrying the two aliens as Daedalus appeared 30 feet away. The hatch opened, and everyone scrambled aboard. "Get us out of here in two minutes, Baby," Iggy instructed as he turned to Liam. "Keep your eye on that other vessel if you can. I want to remain in the area for a few more minutes."

"I see no movement of that ship," reported Liam.

"That's what I had hoped for. If they haven't had a link with our captives, their friends won't understand what has happened until we are long gone and back in Montana."

Daedalus settled in front of the hospital at Lightning Ranch, and the Altairians were carried inside.7

Iggy pulled Gloria aside while everyone moved the aliens into the new wing. Melanie and Allison would handle everything. So, exactly what did you see in their minds that was so startling?"

"Chemtrails, Dad. They are working with Interlink and various governments around the world, including some of our high-tech firms. Your suspicions about the composition of the particulate were 100% on the money. That atmospheric cocktail was inspired by the people from Altair Four. The high carbon content and graphene nanotubes, coupled with the other chemical components are a modification of our atmosphere."

"We already knew that, but the fact they inspired it is new. The reasons are obvious. They are slowly transforming our atmosphere into a modified, breathable atmosphere to alter our DNA. They are trying to make it more compatible with theirs so they can farm DNA in perpetuity from just about anyone. The most sinister aspect is the metal particulate, now embedded in everyone's cells. Specific high amplitude electrical frequencies will excite those metal particles in the same manner as a microwave oven acts on metals. They will superheat and could cause pain and then, death. "

"That's scary, Dad."

"Normally, it would be. But we have a way to mitigate all that. Matter and energy transmutation. They don't understand our capabilities. We have accomplished what they have been trying to do at CERN for years, only without the risk. I am more convinced than ever that our approach of providing them with a genetic solution to the problems is the only way we have a way out of this without aggression."

"I hope so. You already have raised the alarm, explaining how the carbon nanoparticles open the door to mind control through low-frequency vibrations. Apparently, that's all part of the intent and design. Don't these people in Interlink understand that they are victims as well?"

"They are being told by the Altairians they can avoid the consequences. I'll bet that we can find some kind of chemical mitigation if we dig deeply enough. There are many ways to clean up human anatomy. Chelation is one of them. Don't worry too much, Gloria. We have to take the road we are taking."

***

Interlink's Gulfstream G650 touched down at Heathrow and taxied to the VIP parking area, where a large white van with Red Cross insignias waited. Interlink's best eighteen-man security detail deplaned, unloaded the equipment from the baggage compartment, and double-timed to the Red Cross van. The valet opened the rear door of the Rolls-Royce parked in front of the hangar, and Heinrich Klatch stepped onto the tarmac.

The security team captain jogged to the Rolls and confronted Klatch. "We are all set, Mr. Klatch. The men completed the training two days ago.

We rehearsed this day for at least three weeks. We understand the importance, and we are leaving no room for error. Everything is as you wish, sir. There will be no mistakes."

"Excellent, Klaus. This is a one-time operation, and we will not get another opportunity. It is of critical importance, and there must be no errors. The timing must be perfect. We have a meeting in Rome at the Vatican tonight. When you arrive at the arena, make absolutely certain that the under-stage access door is unlocked and ajar. One guard must remain at that door so that it is unobstructed, and no one closes or locks it. The new facility at Lee Valley has two venues. I made it a particular point to arrange through my contacts in government to have the American skaters perform their exhibitions in Venue One. That is where the needed escape hatch under the promenade exists."

"Yes, sir. I thoroughly understand. It will be done as you say."

Eighteen men had continuously rehearsed the operation for weeks. The choreography and chronology were designed specifically by Heinrich Klatch. He was a brilliant strategist who had inherited his facility for meticulous detail, insight, and far-reaching planning from his father, Joseph Goebbels. Eighteen men were a slight overkill. He knew they could do it with less, but it was better to have them available and not need them than to need them and not have them available.

Heinrich Klatch's planning was meticulous. He had been planning this for years. He had engineered and reengineered this day in his mind countless times. This was the one chance they had. There would be no others. They were going to kidnap at least one son of the most powerful man who had ever lived. Both of Marcus's sons would be there, but one of them, the older son, was not competing and would be wearing his shield equipment. Klatch knew If he failed, it would probably bring his own death. He knew it and accepted the consequences. Death would be better than what Iggy Marcus had in store for him.

His Rolls would follow the Red Cross van to the Lee Valley Ice Center near Queen Elizabeth Park in Layton. Three independent drivers, also part of Interlink's entourage, would separate the van from Klatch's Rolls-Royce by three vehicle lengths during the drive. He would leave no room for suspicion of subterfuge. He decided his personal involvement was the one sure guarantee of success. Klaus would deploy his men in the arena, and Klatch would observe from the press box two stories above. He knew the Marcus family had hardware giving them the ability to generate an impenetrable force field around them. That defense could not be breached, so he had to discover a way to mitigate the force field, taking it off the playing field.

He had scrutinized every performance of the Marcus brothers that had been filmed in various places around the world, including the Olympics. It finally dawned on him they never wore the equipment when they were skating. That made them vulnerable. They would only have a small window, but the window was there, and if his men were well-rehearsed and precise, this was doable.

The skating was scheduled to begin shortly. Each skater would perform three or four times that afternoon. Klatch insisted the abduction attempt would be in Marcus's second performance. They would observe Brett Marcus in terms of style, speed, and position on the ice before he prompted Klaus and his men to act. The Red Cross van was parked outside, waiting. The security detail of 16 men would return in the van. There was another small ambulance ready and waiting to transport Marcus to London Stadium in the park and Interlink's V22 Osprey chopper. With the right connections, anything was possible, and the stadium was empty for the day.

Brett was the fifth performer in the first round. His athleticism was undiminished from his Olympic appearance three years prior. Almost every competitive skater in the world was watching, either in person or electronically. Brett was three years older now, but he had lost none of his supple flexibility or strength. The program was the veritable mirror of his Olympic program, and everyone was there to watch the only man in the world who could do sextuple axels in rapid succession within three seconds of each other. It was a feat that all the pundits still argued could not be done, yet Bret's ability was an *in-your-face* contradiction of the experts.

He finished lacing his skates in the pre-skate box and handed his watch and shield generator to Luke. "Hang onto this stuff for me. I can't wear them when I skate. The box on my waist is heavy and awkward. It throws me off. Changes my center of gravity just enough to screw up the works. I'm pushing the physical limits for this type of thing, and the smallest variable can be the difference between success and failure as well as possible injury."

Serge Rachmaninoff's second piano Concerto in C minor was probably one of the greatest pieces of romantic piano music written. It consisted of three movements, all stridently different from each other but all exuding the magnificent romance from the artist's soul. It was a piece Brett learned to play as a teenager and was his favorite. In fact, the music he skated to this day, he had played and recorded himself.

Brett glided onto the ice. The entire stadium was cheering. They remembered his performance in the Olympics. He felt slightly self-conscious, thinking... You better not cheer for me yet, people, I might fall and break my face... You never know, he laughed to himself. Iggy had taught his sons well. They possessed neither arrogance nor bravado, only enough humility to not take themselves too seriously. Rachmaninoff's third movement of the Concerto began as Brett launched himself into the skate. The music started slowly and proceeded to volatile Allegro piano runs up and down the keyboard to fuel Brett's dynamic ability, interspersed with the soft passages that were the very epitome of romance. The complexity of the fingering, matching the complexity of Brett's footwork, rose to a dynamic and emotional crescendo at the end, perfectly matching the emotion exhibited by Brett's performance.

The crowd was wildly cheering. They received the prize they had come for, an exhibition by the greatest skater of all time. Even Heinrich Klatch, in his sociopathic reverie, admired Marcus for his ability. He didn't let it get too far, though. Allowing anyone superlative to assume a heroic position in the mind immediately became a mirror of self-deprecation to the weak and insecure. Klatch had seen what he wanted to see. His photographic memory scrutinized and recorded every move by Marcus. He saw approximately where the best place in the arena would be to tranquilize him and hustle him through the under-stage access door. It had to be done quickly during the distraction created by Klaus so that Brett's brother could not throw up a force field to defend him. Once the chaos started, no one would have any idea what was going on, and they would have plenty of time.

One hour later, Brett was up for a second performance, skating to Luke's and his insanely wild boogie-woogie duet. The piano key work and Brett's footwork were a thing to behold. Very few people could play boogie-woogie like the two brothers, and nobody in the world could skate to it like Brett. The skate started.

Two minutes into the performance, Heinrich Klatch, watching through binoculars, said one word into his microphone... Now!

Two men ran out on the ice with machine guns and began firing at the roof of the arena. The guns were filled with blanks, but it didn't matter. This was the era of gun violence, and the people exploded in a mass exodus. The chaos and clamor by throngs of people scrambling for any exit was a rampage of confusion as people trampled other people, attempting to flee to safety. No one noticed or paid attention to the men, who seemed apparently unalarmed. They had a job to do. One of them shot Brett with a tranquilizer dart, and he went down immediately. Luke could no longer see Brett through the lunacy of the confusion as people ran across the ice, sliding, falling, and tripping over each other to get to safety.

Luke neglected to raise his force field as he looked for his brother to encapsulate and protect him. One of Klatch's men tackled him from behind, and they both went down in a heap. Luke was no slouch, with black belts in three disciplines. He took the man apart and then raised his shield as he got to his feet and attempted to find Brett. At this point, the ice was clear except for a few people who had been trampled and injured. Brett was nowhere to be seen. Luke was frantic. He was Iggy's son, and he knew, deep inside, this entire episode was arranged to kidnap one or both of them. Well, his force field was up, and no one was going to get him, but he was sick over the fact they had succeeded with Brett. Memories surfaced of Claude Lemieux and their ski-jumping trip to Michigan when Interlink had kidnapped *him*. The first thing he had to do was get to the Learjet. He cursed himself for the stupidity of leaving his satellite phone in the cockpit console. He had to call Iggy.

***

Cameron Fry chose no course of action. Apparently, he was in charge. Klatch's personal secretary had run for the elevator. His satellite phone would not work in the vault. He had to get to the surface to talk to Klatch. Fry decided to say and do nothing. His complicity in the day's events left him reticent about taking a course of action. The object of the hypnosis was to prevent the aliens from reading his mind, but it was also to exonerate him from suspicion of involvement among Interlink members, which would end his double agent status.

The room Was filled with the voices of 30 members of Interlink and another 35 government officials from assorted countries. None of them had any idea what happened. They had come, supposedly, to negotiate with extraterrestrials about goods, services, and payment. That was obviously not on the menu now. Cameron Fry decided he wasn't in the mood for small talk. He would go to the surface. The Pope had not arrived yet, and it appeared the evening was a bust.

Fry was just about to walk to the elevator when it chimed. Someone had boarded the elevator at the surface and was on their way down. It was probably the Pontiff. Cameron Fry returned to his seat, waiting. Something was going on. Obviously, the aliens were gone. Marcus would have been out of here long ago. He watched the lights descend the 22 notches adjacent to the elevator door.

Cameron Fry was completely blown away when the elevator door opened. Klatch's personal secretary entered the conference room, followed by Klatch and two uniformed Interlink security men. The security men were dragging the half-conscious body of Brett Marcus between them. They dragged him into the room and threw him on the floor in front of the head table. Heinrich Klatch, in his sick and perverted little mind, decided retribution against Iggy Marcus should begin now as he walked to Brett and kicked him in the side of the face.

Cameron Fry had not decided what he was going to do. He recognized Brett and understood what this was about. This was Heinrich Klatch's big surprise. Marcus's son would be the weapon he would use to defeat his opponent. Klatch, however, just made his big mistake of the day by kicking his captive's face. It was the straw that broke the camel's back. Fry looked at Klatch and asked, exuding the friendship attitude of a peer, "Do you have more guards upstairs? I hope you have more guards; we may need them. I think you should go around the other side and kick his face from that angle."

Heinrich Klatch, though calculating and brilliant, was isolated from reality by his insanity and believed Cameron Fry was his ally as he erupted in a maniacal Snidely Whiplash shriek of laughter. "You're right, Cameron. His face needs to get kicked from the other side, and no, I sent the rest of them home. We only need two."

That was all Cameron Fry needed. He was a member of Interlink's upper echelon. Nobody carded him or frisked him when he entered an Interlink venue. He reached under the table as his hand crept to his ankle where the 9 mm R7 Mako Kimber mini pistol was holstered.

Cameron Fry was responsible for the death of one other human being when he was a young man, and it was an accident. He often wondered if he had to intentionally kill, would he have the motivation and courage to pull the trigger and terminate someone else's existence? That would be their last moment. They would no longer be. Everything they were… everything they are… and everything they would become would cease at that moment, and he would be the instrument of their annihilation. That was one of his occasional thoughts when he ruminated about his own character. Somehow, this moment was unique, and the thought of consequences never entered his mind.

The guards were standing in front of Klatch, looking down at Brett Marcus, with hands on the butts of their pistols. He hadn't been paying attention to the elevator chime. A locomotive was roaring through the pressure cooker of his mind while he gathered himself up to do what he intended. He pulled the pistol from its holster at his ankle, stood up, raised his gun, and put a bullet in the left eye of each guard just as Pope Innocent XIV stepped out of the elevator and was sprayed with blood and brains. Cameron Fry apologetically looked at the Pontiff. "Sorry about that, your Eminence. I did not mean to soil your vestments, but this had to be done."

This was more than unexpected for everyone in the room including Innocent XIV. It was one of those surreal moments that only existed in the realm of dreams or Hollywood. One of their associates, Cameron Fry, had just killed two men and sent everyone else in the room into a panic. Klatch did not recover quickly. His magnificent plan, the one he had been contemplating for years, was about to be flushed down the sewer by one of his supposed compatriots. He couldn't believe it. His wild card, the one-eyed Jack that would take down Iggy Marcus, was about to exit stage left. Klatch had his wits about him enough to know that Cameron Fry was about to rescue his ace in the hole. Klatch never let circumstances overwhelm him. He had one more, small ace in the hole, but he would have to wait for exactly the right moment... no mistakes allowed.

Cameron Fry chuckled at the absurdity of life as he hoisted a still-drugged Brett Marcus off the floor. Here he was, standing 22 floors beneath the Sistine Chapel on a Saturday night, immediately following the kidnapping of two ETs, the abduction of his best friend's son, and his murdering of two guards while Pope Innocent the 14th insisted on putting the icing on the cake. "My son, you have just murdered two men! You must repent, and you must do it now in the sight of God, or you will be damned! I will hear your confession myself."

Cameron Fry was paying no attention to Heinrich Klatch at his own peril as he turned to the Pope. "Yes, Holy Father, I appreciate the sentiment, and I'm sure you mean very well by it. But I am 100% certain I have the moral high ground here, and I believe in the eyes of our maker, I already have forgiveness. But thanks anyway."

Brett was beginning to return to consciousness at this point. Fry put his hand on Brett's forehead. "How are you feeling? Do you think you can walk? We have to get out of here immediately because all hell is going to break loose, and when hell breaks loose in the Vatican, it really breaks loose."

`"I think I can make it," Brett said shakily. "You may have to help a little until this wears off. Let's get out of here."

No one else in the room full of 70 people or so, had moved a muscle. You could hear a pin drop. The episode was so surreal that nobody could even believe it was happening. Klatch was scowling with the fire of stark, raving madness in his eyes. Fry noted it, and it should've colored his judgment and rung a warning bell, but he ignored the peril this 84-year-old maniac still represented.

He and Brett stood facing the elevator as he pressed the up button. The door slowly opened. Cameron Fry shoved Brett through the door and followed as he felt the agonizing pain between his shoulder blades. A lot had gone on this evening. Normally, Cameron Fry would have covered all the bases, but this was a little over-the-top, even for him. Klatch was watching his master plan and his future evaporate into an elevator, and he was ready to vomit. He reached his right hand over his shoulder to the leather satchel hanging between his shoulder blades and pulled his stainless steel, perfectly balanced throwing knife and last ace in the hole out of its sheath. Fry had just entered the elevator when Klatch flung the knife with considerably more force than a normal 84-year-old man should be able to muster.

Cameron Fry fell forward onto his knees as the elevator door shut behind him. Groaning, he lifted his head to Brett, "quickly now!" he wheezed, "press the up button before some asshole pries the door open!

The elevator ride to the surface seemed interminable. There was no way Fry could make the stairs, nor could Brett for that matter. He was still feeling the effects of the drugs. "Can you stand?" Brett asked Fry. "Turn sideways, and I'll pull the knife out for you."

"NO, LEAVE IT ALONE," Cameron Fry almost yelled. "It hit hard, and it's pretty deep. I have no idea if it has cut into any significant arteries or veins. If it has, and you pull it, I could bleed out. So, leave it in there until we can get help."

Cameron Fry was strong. He raised himself up with one leg, and on one knee, he grabbed the bars on the side of the elevator, pulling himself to a standing position. He grimaced in pain. "I think I'll make it, but I'm going to have to be careful, and I will need your help if you're up to it."

"Of course, Mr. Fry. You saved my life. Now, I must save yours. What are we going to do after we get out of this elevator?"

"Your guess is as good as mine, Brett. Well, actually, I do have a few ideas. It's nighttime. There won't be too many people around, but you should find some vestment or garment I can drape around my shoulders, so people don't see this damn knife sticking out of my back. That's definitely a red flag item, and people will be able to remember where they saw us when the people chasing us ask."

The elevator door opened. No one was around. "Before we leave, give me your jacket Brett."

"Whatever for, it won't fit you, not even close."

"I need a silencer. Please forgive me for the holes." Cameron Fry wrapped Brett's jacket around his pistol and put four bullets into the electronic control panel for the elevator. "That ought to slow them down a little... I hope."

Cameron Fry's car was in the parking area. It was dusk. The valets would still be on duty. It was difficult and quite a long walk, but they made it to the valet shed. There was one man in there, and Cameron Fry recognized him. Brett had pulled a light tapestry off the wall, and Cameron Fry wore it like a cloak, somewhat disguising the knife. Cameron Fry mustered his strength, "Good evening, Antonio, how are you tonight?"

"Great, Mr. Fry. I couldn't be better. And you, sir? " Cameron Fry was the best tipper of all the people he parked cars for. "Would you like me to get your car, Mr. Fry?"

"Yes, Antonio. Please do. You're my favorite person in the whole Vatican." Antonio beamed at the compliment and was off to retrieve Fry's Maserati Grecale. Five minutes later, he pulled the car in front of the valet shed and stepped onto the pavement.

"Do you own a car, Antonio?"

"Yes sir, I do," he said proudly. "It's nothing like your car, Mr. Fry; it's a Fiat that runs well and gets good mileage."

"No tip tonight, Antonio. I've got a bigger surprise for you. Want to make a trade?"

"No, I don't think so," Antonio said to Fry. "What could I possibly have that a man like you would want?"

"Your car, Antonio. You know that I own this car, and it has no encumbrance. I will trade my car for your car, right now and we can put it on paper."

Antonio was upset. He thought Fry was making fun of him. "Mr. Fry, I will never be wealthy like you, but I still have honor, and I don't really appreciate you making me feel like a fool."

"Don't worry about that, Antonio. I will never make a fool out of a workingman. I am a workingman also. I have just been fortunate and got all the right breaks at all the right times. I'm dead serious. I don't joke about things like this."

"No, Mr. Fry. I don't think I can do that. I would not feel right. Thank you for your magnanimous offer, but I think not."

"I'll level with you, Antonio. You would be doing me a huge favor. I have two more cars just like this, so I won't miss it. Someone is after this man standing next to me. He is with me, and the people who want him, know that. He is in danger if they find him. I must help him get away. I would like you to take my car on an even trade. I will give you 100 million lire right now and I will ask you to drive to Florence. The people chasing this man will think that we are in the car and will try to stop us. Drive slowly and let them pull you over. They will use the carabinieri. Show them the bill of sale, and they will understand what I have done. Be sure to drive slowly."

Fifteen minutes later, Cameron Fry and Brett Marcus pulled out of the Vatican in a 2004 Fiat. Brett was driving so Cameron Fry could sit sideways and keep the pressure off the knife protruding from his back. It had slipped between two ribs and done some damage, but he didn't think it would kill him. Still, he needed medical attention relatively soon. "Where to next, Mr. Fry?"

"Call me Cameron. I'm tired of hearing Mr. Fry. My Learjet is at Leonardo da Vinci airport. We cannot go there. They will be watching. We are going to Perugia. They will lease a Gulfstream to me, and we can get out of here. But we have to do it quickly. Once they decide that I have tricked them by giving my car to Antonio, they will cover all the bases, and we won't get out. Then, they will charge me with murder, and you will once again become Heinrich Klatch's tool to get at your father. "

"You mind if I asked you a question, Cameron?"

"Ask away. I'll give you an answer if I can."

"Well, you're one of the wealthiest men on the planet. You don't need this. Why are you jeopardizing your position and your life by helping me? You don't owe me anything."

Fry grinned, "I owe it to your mother for the scampi recipe."

"Brett laughed in response. You have no idea how many people she has conned out of things with her scampi recipe. That's hilarious. She's not my mother, by the way. Luke and I feel the same love as we would feel if she was my mother. My mother died when I was three in an automobile wreck."

"Yeah, your dad told me. I'm sure you understand why I'm doing this. Your father is who he is. I don't think anyone like him has ever been born of women. He is the only man I ever met who I respect more than I respect myself, and that's saying something. You're his son, and there was no way I was going to let that swine, Heinrich Klatch, use you to destroy your father… end of story."

"Stop the car, Brett. Do it slowly and pull over like you want to read a map or something."

He was fleeing with one of the richest men in the world. That said a lot to Brett. " We are almost at the airport. The gate is just 200 yards ahead. What's wrong?"

Cameron Fry still had his pen. He was surprised he hadn't lost it in the melee beneath the Sistine Chapel. "Let's sit still for a minute, Brett. This pen is also a powerful mini telescope and I want to take a look at the airport gate. If nothing else, Interlink security is ruthlessly efficient. We can't put anything past them and have to stay a step of them from now on."

He held the telescope to his eye and scanned the area. He swept the gate and 100 yards along the fence in both directions. "What do you see?" asked Brett. "Has Interlink figured out where we are?"

"Not yet. If they knew where we were, we would be in custody already. Evidently, they haven't pulled Antonio over yet and figured out that we have his Fiat. Once they do that, our shit's in the wind."

"Are we going in to lease your Learjet?"

"Nope. I recognize the car, and two of the men at the gate appear to be Interlink security. They don't have our number yet, but they are covering all the bases. Klatch is smart and doesn't miss much. So, the airport's out."

"Now what, Cameron?"

Cameron swiveled his neck toward the steering wheel and peered at the gas gauge. "First, we're going to get gas. There's nowhere near enough in the car. We've got a bit of a drive ahead of us. You are going to have to drive slowly. We don't want to get stopped. There will be the Italian equivalent to an all-points bulletin out on my carcass by now. You don't have a driver's license, and I am not able to drive. If we get stopped, you are my son, and I'm teaching you to drive."

Cameron Fry was ruminating. He had removed his wallet from the glove compartment and the briefcase of cash from the spare tire compartment of the Grecale. It's a good thing I had that. It was the only way I could pay Antonio. I have plenty of cash. It's a good thing; I don't dare use my credit card at a point-of-sale. That'll be a red flag as to my location. “Pull into that Esso station, Brett. Do you speak Italian?"

“Fluent.”

"That gas station is not self-serve. Tell the attendant to fill it up and check the oil. Give him a 350,000-lira tip. It sounds like a lot, but it's only about 10 bucks. I have the money in this briefcase. While you’re at it, buy a detailed roadmap of southern Italy. I'm not sure exactly where we are, but I know exactly where we are going. "

"Where are we going, anyway?"

"Salerno. It's probably four hours from here, maybe a little less."

"I know where it is on the map. Why Salerno? You must have friends there. Before we set out on the highway, I should take a look at that stab wound. I have significant medical training, Cameron. I won't make any mistakes."

"Okay, there's a shopping plaza over there, and it probably has a pharmacy. We can come back to this park, and you can take a look."

Twenty-five minutes later, they were parked under a tree in the park. "Cough some phlegm up from as deep as you can in your lungs into this gauze, Cameron; I want to take a look at it. Breathe deeply and make note of the pain when you inhale and when you exhale. Figure it on a scale of 1 to 10. There's a trail of dried blood down your back, but it isn't significant. There is also clear liquid suppurating from the edges of the knife wound. You have been moving around, and the knife has moved also. The wound has been enlarged, and no serious amount of bleeding is apparent.”

“I think you are out of the woods, and I can remove the knife, but you still need a doctor's attention. I'm going to squeeze the wound open and pour iodine in. I have a 15% solution and that'll get you out of infection trouble for now. Then, I will pack it with gauze and tape. At least you should be comfortable. Hold your breath and grit your teeth; this is going to hurt a little and it will bleed again. Apparently, you missed the good stuff and didn’t have a lung puncture."

"You **are** pretty good. All of you, Marcus's are amazing. Where did you learn all this stuff?"

"Melanie is a board-certified internal medicine doctor and geneticist with a ton of other specialties. She is a fountain and never stops gushing information." He laughed. "We probably have more medical jargon crammed into our skulls than most doctors. So, what's the route, Cameron?"

"We are headed south on E45 until we pass Naples. There will be a bunch of small and medium-sized towns along the way. Once we get through the Naples traffic, it will be easy to drive right into Salerno. We'll get off the highway east of Salerno and follow the shoreline until we get to a little town called Positano. My cousin, Rosa, lives on a large fishing boat that I would almost call a yacht with her husband, Alfonzo Battaglia, and their two kids. He owns a small fishing fleet. He's a good friend, and he will help us."

"Are you positive? What about Interlink? Do they know of your cousin, Rosa?"

"Probably. Let's hope they haven't found Antonio yet. When we arrive at Positano, you must let me drive. The city, or town, is a resort community. The shoreline is comprised of steep, medium-height mountains and cliffs with lots of vegetation. There are roads between the tightly packed architecture of homes, shops, and restaurants etc. You have to know your way around to get through the maze. The roads don't lead completely to the water, but one goes to the villa they own, which is right above their moorings. Sometimes, they rent it; other times, the family stays there.

"I'm sorry you are in this much trouble because of me, Cameron. If I could, I would make it go away. It's obvious this has been in the planning stage for a long time and Interlink is not going to give up without pulling out all the stops. They have the entire Italian government, their own resources, and a ton of technology to try to get ahead of us. I'm worried for your sake, sir. The police may have already been there. How loyal is your cousin's husband, Alfonzo?"

"I have known Alfonzo for 22 years. My bank lent him the money to buy most of his fishing boats. He does business with us, and I believe he is old-school. I don't think we have anything to worry about from that quarter."

Cameron was driving. They drove along the coast to a promontory on the edge of a cliff above Positano with the quaint cliffside charm of a typical Mediterranean coastal town. He stopped the car and walked across the road to the guardrail, pulling out his mini telescope. Three minutes later, he returned to the car and winced in pain as he squeezed into the driver's seat. "It doesn't look like anything's going on, but you can't see much because of the congestion of the architecture. I can see their boats plain enough, and their residential boat is at the mooring. The problem is, I can only see the rooftop of the villa from this vantage point because of the trees and other buildings. I guess we're going to have to go down there. It looks quiet."

Fry drove slowly down the winding road and streets nestled between chalets, stone-clad shops, homes, and wind-swept trees until he stopped a quarter mile from his cousin's villa. Everything appeared to be quiet. How long it would stay that way was anybody's guess. It wouldn't take interlink long to put two and two together and wind up in Positano. It was a logical choice they would make. "I think we should leave the car back here, Brett, and walk the quarter mile to the villa. What do you think?"

"What do I think? I think this is your territory, Cameron. You make the call and lead... I'll follow."

No one answered their knock. "The place is empty, Brett. It's a bit of a walk, but let's go to the shore. There are some small punts on the beach they use to get to the main boat. They are motorized and in boat houses. Are you feeling well enough, after the drugs, to take this Fiat about 1/4 mile up the hill and park it under that small canopy of trees we passed?"

"No problem. Wait for me here. I'm feeling great. I can run."

"Leave the keys in the ignition, Brett. Antonio left the pen and notebook in the backseat. Leave a big note on the dashboard: 'TAKE ME. I'M FREE.' Maybe someone will take us up on it and create another diversion.

The punt motor started immediately, and they headed for the houseboat. Fry could see Alfonso standing in the stern, hands on hips, watching them approach. They pulled up to the boarding platform and he tossed them a line. They climbed aboard and approached Alfonso as Rosa exited the cabin.

Rosa hugged her cousin. "Whatever in God's name are you involved in, Cameron! A bunch of police were here in vehicles and then a police boat. They say you murdered two people at the Vatican. That's so hard to believe. Why would you ever kill anyone? They told us If you came here, we were to call them immediately, or we would be breaking the law also as accomplices!"

Other than shaking Cameron Fry's hand, Alfonso hadn't said anything. He knew Cameron Fry as the man who had helped him build a business and a life. Fry had lent him substantial interest-free money to build his fishing fleet and tourist company. Cameron Fry did not do that often, and Alfonso was in his debt. "Did you kill two people, Cameron? I would like to hear why, just from curiosity."

Cameron Fry emitted a brief chuckle. He was never one to shortchange the truth or color reality. "Yeah, I did exactly that last evening. You must want to know why, of course. The man standing next to me is the son of Iggy Marcus and the greatest figure skater in history."

Alfonso returned the chuckle. "I recognized him for a couple of reasons, believe it or not. He's wearing the same skating outfit he wore in London two days ago. Rosa and I watched it. This is bizarre, Cameron. So, what happened?"

"Short and sweet, Alfonso. I belong to Interlink, but I am a benign member who doesn't particularly want to rule the world. Interlink, however, absolutely wants to rule the world, and Iggy Marcus is the only man who can stop them."

"I see. You killed two people to save this man's life. That's obvious." He paused for a few minutes, gazing at the horizon. "You know the police were here. They will be back, that's a given. We must do this very subtly. I have 14 boats. Nine of them are fishing scows and five of them are tourist charter fishing boats. It's late, but we often fish at night when the mackerel are running."

"What do you have in mind, Alfonso?"

"You must leave before the police come back. I have a friend in town. Rosa will go and get some accoutrements. He is a makeup artist and a barber. You and Mr. Marcus need mustaches. You will fit right in with the crew of a fishing vessel on its way to Greece. How does that sound?"

He turned to Rosa, "You heard what I just said, Rosa; hop to it, these men don't have much time."

"Can they be trusted, Alfonso?"

"Implicitly, Cameron. They were smugglers I rescued from prison and gave them honest jobs. They like their new life but still hate the authorities passionately. They would rather die than talk to the police. You'll be safe with them."

"When do we leave?"

Alphonso laughed, "As soon as Rosa returns with your face decorations. You have to get out of here. "I'm going to send four boats out fishing. Two will go in one direction, west and then north. Two will go south. You will be aboard the two going south. My suggestion would be that you both go on different vessels. But that's up to you."

"There is one more thing, Alfonso."

"Oh."

"The car. It's a cheap Fiat that I traded my Maserati for. It sits halfway up the hill under the canopy of trees. You know the ones. It's definitely a marker."

"Hmmm, I see. Yes, that's a marker, all right. There is a solution. One of my men who exponentially hates authority would enjoy pulling the wool over their eyes and will probably be happy to do this... and he gets a free Fiat out of it."

Cameron Fry laughed. "I'll make up a bill of sale immediately. He can tell the authorities that Cameron Fry sold him the car. If he likes to pull the wool over their eyes, he doesn't have to tell them he works for you. That should create enough of a delay to give us all the time needed to get the hell out of here."

***

Iggy spent the last four hours on the bottom floor of the new hospital wing. He was eighty feet underground, where his entire team was gathered with Hansel and Gretel, separated, and encapsulated within the magnetic shield technology. The entire wing of the hospital was designed as a Faraday cage, impervious to EMF penetration. This was the most illustrious group of physicists, medical scientists, and doctors who had ever assembled in one place dedicated to a single goal.

Melanie, Dave and Sylvia Peterson, Dr. Marcos Boli, his colleague and wife, Surgeon General Allison MacLeod, and twenty-nine brilliant doctors who comprised the staff of Marcus General Hospital were assembled for the greatest medical crusade in history.

They would attempt to unravel an extraterrestrial and predominantly alien genetic metabolic code. Their mission to save the alien species from its own self-induced genetic destruction was the requirement to save the lives of more than 10,000 human children who existed in an alien petri dish for the harvesting of DNA.

Many of the assembled team had spent the previous twenty-five years at Marcus Hospital unlocking the secrets of the human genome and seeking answers to the enigma of death.

Iggy Marcus was the catalyst, but they were all brilliant. He had unlocked them all, many of them hundreds of times. Not only did that create a team of people dedicated to working together instead of for self-aggrandizement, but it also elevated their intellect, often as much as 100%. This team of doctors was unlocking the secret of aging. They had already cloned animals. Apparently, they would be able to eventually replicate a human being and transport his or her consciousness into a new vessel at the first moment of awareness.

Cancer was a rarity now, and cardiovascular disease was being reversed on a regular basis by clinical means. That did not alleviate the requirement for people to live a healthy lifestyle, but it brought the sick and dying to square one for a fresh start. All these things were more than simple science. They were miracles relieving pain and suffering everywhere. That had effectively stripped away the authoritarian cudgel used by organized curative medicine to bludgeon humanity into acceptance of their ivory towers of blistering authority.

So, the authoritarians pulled out all the stops. This was their last stand and Interlink was the head of the snake coiled around the tree of life. They represented the philosophy incumbent on every totalitarian monster who had tortured humanity for a power position. The Bible expressed the poetry, but the monsters brought the abomination of evil to life. They sought, in their anger and self-contempt, the destruction of autonomy and justice for all. They associated themselves with their own kind, but in the end, they believed in their unachievable delusion that only one entity should be left standing… supreme and immortal… themself. That was the philosophical root of every despot, and it was the characterization of insanity that Iggy called the God complex.

Men had struggled with the **concept of morality** since the dawn of history when they first became aware it was defined by the struggle between good and evil.

This God complex, or the desire to enslave all other creatures, was not indigenous to man alone. Of the trillions of occupants throughout existence, many had succumbed to the same arrogance and lust for self-definition through the acquisition of absolute power. The struggle between good and evil had besieged many species throughout the galaxies of the universe, and it always precipitated war. This was war on a scale far above anything Homo sapiens could create, but the roots were identical... The God complex.

Men always subliminally understood the composition of their character was a reflection of both extremes but instead of internalizing and admitting the truth, they externalized both good and evil and assigned them icons for convenience. Good was the tree of life and the reality that all must live by to prosper. Though self-evident and indigenous to the soul, it was placed on an external pedestal as an entity subject to the vagaries of choice, providing an excuse for the weak in character.

The externalization of evil was the serpent wrapped around the tree of life. Evil was also self-evident and indigenous to the soul, but men created the icon to place their inherent character flaws outside their superego for convenience. They defined character weakness and their subscription to a code of death as temptation from an external source. In other words, it wasn't their fault. The devil made them do it.

This allowed men to pursue self-aggrandizement at the expense of their brothers, then consequently fling aside the guilt emerging from the depravity of their own souls. The God complex made posturing for position and the destruction of their fellow men an acceptable trade-off to self-awareness and the acknowledgment of morality.

This was the plight of all autonomous individuals. It had emerged over and over throughout the history of every sentient civilization that had ever populated the universe. There had been several vibrant societies and several die-offs in human history. The reasons for their demise were irrelevant. This society of Homo sapiens existed now, and Iggy Marcus had been sent to clean up their act.

***

"Okay, everybody," Iggy addressed the entire team. "You all know what's at stake here. You don't need any lectures. The only one I'll give you is that you all have your specialties and I'm quite sure you will work together to find a way to deal with this and save those kids. Hansel and Gretel here are isolated from our thoughts even though they possess telepathic powers. I have set up the force field, a barrier, encapsulating them to micro-vibrate across the entire electromagnetic spectrum, which you all know is the vehicle for thoughts. You will have to question them, and I suggest asking them for their assistance. Hopefully, they will cooperate when they understand the mission. If they believe we are here to help them solve their problem for the sake of the children they have kidnapped, they just might."

They were in the lobby adjacent to the cafeteria, having coffee as Iggy delivered his little soliloquy. The elevator chime drew everyone's attention as the door slid open. Tom Rickert rushed into the room. Everyone could see it, and Iggy felt Tom Rickart's extreme anxiety. "What's up, Tom? You don't look so happy." Iggy said, starting to worry.

"You gotta come now, boss! It's Brett. He and Luke went to London to skate. That bastard, Klatch, and a dozen men grabbed him."

Iggy was calm, waiting for Tom to finish. He never let himself fly off the handle. That always precipitated mistakes, some of them unrecoverable.

"And?"

"Evidently, Klatch planned this for a long time because he orchestrated it beautifully. They were all at the Lee arena. Apparently, two of Klatch's men ran out onto the ice with machine guns and began shooting at the ceiling. Of course, you know what happened then: 8000 people went berserk trying to get to the exits, running and trampling each other like madmen. Someone tackled Luke, when he got up off the floor, he beat the crap out of the guy. It was one of Klatch's men. Then he looked for Brett, but he was gone. They had this figured pretty well, Iggy."

"Go on, Tom, but first, how did you get this information?"

"Believe it or not, from a couple of people. One of them is a fisherman who owns several ships. His name is Alfonso Battaglia. He's married to Cameron Fry's cousin, Rosa."

Iggy smiled. Somehow, if Cameron Fry was involved, Brett would be okay. "Don't stop now, Tom Rickart. Who are the other people? You can tell me as you continue."

"This is the story as best as I can put it together. You got out of there with the aliens. Cameron Fry remained. You already know Klatch was not there. That's the reason you didn't grab him. Well, he showed up 30 minutes or so after you were gone. Two guards dragged Brett to the conference room. He was drugged. Evidently, Cameron Fry did not wait more than a minute. You know the old expression, strike while the iron is hot. He pulled out a 9 mm pistol from his ankle holster and put a bullet in the left eye of each guard. It seemed he was taking no chances. Apparently, he blew blood and brains all over Pope Innocent the 14th, and even apologized."

He pressed a button on his watch... "Junior, I need you in the Daedalus hanger. Brett has been kidnapped, and we've got to bail him out. We are headed for the coast of Italy."

He turned to Tom again. "How did you get that little piece of information?"

Rickart laughed. "Believe it or not, I have a very good friend who is French Secret Service. Apparently, one of the heads of state present at the meeting was a Frenchman. Well, when all of this lunacy was over, the story got around."

"I personally talked to one of the valets at the Vatican. His name is Antonio. Apparently, Cameron Fry liked him and vice versa." Tom started laughing again; he traded Antonio his Maserati Grecale for Antonio's 2004 Fiat. Then he gave Antonio 350 million lire and told him to drive to Florence slowly. Evidently, they wrote up a bill of sale. He said when the cops stopped him on the way to Florence, he showed them the bill of sale and explained that Cameron Fry had traded their cars. Antonio gets to keep the Maserati, and the cops didn't do anything to him because he was not a willing accessory."

"Don't stop now, Tom." Iggy patiently waited.

"Cameron Fry dragged Brett to the elevator and pushed him inside just as Klatch threw a knife and stuck it in Fry's back. After he and Antonio traded cars, they headed for the airport in the Fiat. Apparently, Interlink was already there, so they headed south to Salerno where Fry has a cousin with a husband who borrowed money from his bank to start his business. I spoke to him. That's the Alfonso fellow. He's the one who gave me most of the story. This is what you have to do immediately, boss."

"Take Daedalus to the Italian coastline. Apparently, Battaglia's wife put mustaches on both Brett and Cameron Fry. They left Positano In two fishing boats headed for Greece. Battaglia sent two boats west and north as distractions. It was nighttime, which gives them a little more cover since they often fish at night when the mackerel are running. Battaglia called our gatehouse, believe it or not. He used his own cell phone, and Brett gave him your sat phone number as well as the number at the gatehouse."

"Hmm, these two," he said, pointing to Hansel and Gretel, "are the reason no one can get through on my sat phone. We are down here 80 feet underground. We've all been discussing our approach to experimenting with them to find out if we can cure their DNA problem. Damn, I could've hooked the phone up to an antenna, but I just didn't bother. Okay, let's get out of here now. It appears we've got to find two fishing boats on their way down the Italian coastline in the middle of the night."

"We've got another useful tool, Iggy. Evidently, Alfonso Battaglia gave Cameron Fry his cell phone. I have the number, and we can call them as soon as we show up and home in on their signal."

As soon as they hit the surface, Iggy pressed a button on his watch. "Liam, I need you to get to the Daedalus hanger right away and bring Lori and Gloria. We've got an emergency. Brett was kidnapped, and he's headed south on two fishing boats off the coast of Italy. It's night and I'll be able to use your abilities to tell the difference between a target and a decoy."

"I'm on my way, Dad. See you in about five minutes."

Iggy pressed another button... "Junior, I need you on Daedalus in five minutes. Brett has been kidnapped, and we're headed to Italy to rescue him."

"Hot dog, Pop. Just what I needed: an adventure. See you momentarily."

"I've gotta tell you, boss, those two, crack me up. It just never stops. Some nights, I laugh myself to sleep, thinking about Junior and Baby's antics. Evelyn asks me what I'm laughing about. I tell her, and she chuckles. I keep telling her you just gotta be there. "Those two are hilarious."

Ten minutes later, Daedalus hovered over the Italian coastline, about a hundred miles south of Salerno. Iggy had added four windows to Daedalus so Liam could get a look outside without suiting up.

"Oh, Oh, Dad! Interlopers. There are our two fishing boats. They're surrounded by five Italian Coast Guard ships, and there are two helicopters hovering above. The ships are stopped. No one is moving."

" Can you see Brett? You don't know what Cameron Fry looks like, but he won't look like he belongs. He'll have a mustache probably unless he ripped it off. He's smart enough to figure that one out. Maybe he did so we can recognize him."

"So, what's on the agenda?" asked Tom

"Can you see Brett, Liam?"

"Yup, he's on the deck of the boat closest to the shore." Apparently, there are a bunch of uniformed Coast Guard sailors on the deck now also."

"Junior, you fly. Tom, when we bring Daedalus over the ship with Brett, we'll be 10 feet off the deck. Do you think you can jump 10 feet?"

"No problem."

"Good. When you get on the deck, encapsulate yourself and Brett... nobody else. Wait until I'm on the other boat with Cameron Fry. We'll come back and pick you both up. Just protect yourself. They can't touch you if you keep the shield up."

Iggy gathered his three children around him. "Okay, gang, here's the plan. Gloria, you are going to link the four of us together telepathically. Liam, you are going to place the visual image of the exact location of the two choppers in Lori's mind. Lori, we have experimented, and I know you can do this. Both of those choppers are amphibious. They are each hovering over a ship. One at a time, you are to take the helicopters out of the sky and set them on the water half a mile away. We know you have the range. Then we'll pick up Brett. Daedalus must hover over the ships, and the choppers are in the way. We could ask them to move, but that would undoubtedly precipitate a confrontation in which several people could be injured or killed. I'm sure they would never acquiesce to that request."

Five minutes later, they were listening to the chopper radios explode in frantic Italian as the choppers were transported by some bizarre external power to a place half a mile away and set on the water. Lori was smiling. "I never really get to do anything fun like this. All I ever do is move small things around to amuse myself. This is really cool."

Iggy couldn't keep himself from laughing at Lori's comment as Yosemite Sam appeared with both guns drawn, surrounding both Tom and Brett.

There were soldiers on the other boat with Cameron Fry. He was actually the subject of arrest since he had shot two Interlink security men. Daedalus moved over the second boat, and Iggy jumped to the deck. "Well, hello there, Cameron Fry. Fancy meeting you here. Who's your favorite cartoon character?"

Cameron Fry exploded with laughter. "Nice entrance, Iggy. My favorite cartoon character? Actually, I was always partial to Quick Draw McGraw; why?" Fry said, still laughing.

"Ask, and you shall receive, Cameron. Meet quick draw McGraw."

Fry was still laughing. "Iggy Marcus, I can't remember a time in my life that I had as much fun as hanging around with you. Let's get out of here."

Iggy hugged Brett after everyone was hoisted aboard. "I guess we're going to have to be more careful from now on, at least for a while. Interlink will suffer termination soon. They will have nowhere to go. I tried to give them every chance to change and join the human race as benevolent citizens. They just can't bring themselves to abandon their ivory tower thrones. Oh well, one can only offer."

CHAPTER XIV

REVELATION AND AMNESTY

"It isn't necessary for you to go deep. The simple suggestion of Heinrich Klatch and the vault should do the trick. That will bring the next meeting immediately to mind, and you can harvest that information. Heinrich Goebbels Klatch is enjoying his last days of notoriety. It is time for him to retire to the South Pacific."

"We also must consider the fact that Klatch knows we are aware of their meeting location. They will change that. Then, you might get nothing from Pope Innocent the 14th. At least we will come to terms with that issue when we become aware of Interlink's plans.

Gloria nodded. "Yes, I'll have Baby drop me off at St. Peter's Square around five AM tomorrow morning. I'll wait up front until nine, so I will be close to the pulpit. There are often close to ten thousand people there. It becomes difficult for me to filter out that much mental gray noise. If I'm far away from the subject, the beta and gamma brain waves weaken and are hard to separate from the noise. You only want the information about the meeting if it exists, am I correct?"

"That's all. Don't leave any footprints, and there is nothing else there that we require. All I need is a date and time."

Gloria stood between the obelisk and the balcony Pope Innocent XIV would make his address from. Baby had procured Gloria's ticket the day before. Pope Innocent XIV stepped onto the balcony, and Gloria had the information within 20 seconds.

One hour later, she sat in the living room with her mother and father. "Apparently, they're not going to have meetings in the vault again. I believe they had no comprehension that we knew of the vault and their meetings. We obviously knew because we showed up to kidnap Hansel and Gretel. Now they realize Cameron Fry is no longer a member of Interlink in good standing." Gloria laughed. "That's too bad because he made a great double agent."

"Yes, he did. He still has some connections within Interlink. Not everybody in the organization subscribes to Heinrich Klatch's authority and his designs for the future. Cameron is putting feelers out to find out where their next meeting will be held. They may do this from remote locations for a while but will eventually get together in one venue. I will be there waiting, and Heinrich Klatch is coming with me. It's time to end his illustrious career."

Gloria was a little apprehensive. "When are we going to meet all those Altairians, Dad?"

Iggy grinned, "Tomorrow. I have other business today. Our medical team is analyzing our captives and I want some information before we go to the Lagrange points. Why? Nervous?"

"A little."

The following morning, Junior, Gloria, Lori, and Liam boarded Daedalus for a trip to the earth/moon Lagrange point, where the Altairian ship floated. "Seriously, Dad, do you expect these people from wherever their planet is to cooperate? Why should they? They're obviously not benevolent. They have thousands of human children, and they're scraping the DNA out of their stomach lining." Gloria was a skeptic. "Frankly, these creatures from Altair frighten me." They are obviously more advanced than humanity, so they must have powerful technology. She trusted her father but was still worried.

"I understand, Gloria. There are always consequences when we act. The key to success is to always assess the odds and then choose a course of action that is most likely to succeed, even if it is not the most desirable one. We must do this or walk away from it."

Junior listened to the exchange. He was ambivalent, or whatever a completely unemotional but sentient robot would be. Iggy had given Junior and Baby a kind of unique programming that merged with their autonomous sentience. The cleverness of Iggy's vision and efforts manifested itself in two living beings who were completely inorganic assemblies, yet with the ability to interact with human beings so well that their mechanical essence was completely disguised. "You worry too much, Gloria. I am younger than you, and I'm not worried," Junior said with a smile that was as human appearing as Gloria's.

"That's because you are a mechanical man who doesn't know how to worry. You are like a brother to me, but you will live forever while I age and eventually perish."

It was time for Iggy to jump in. "Okay, kids, enough banter. We are going to park next to their ship and attempt to communicate. That's on you, Gloria, for starters. I tried to communicate with Hensel and Gretel, but they withdrew and refused. I was able to sense they were frightened or at least apprehensive. If we had more time, I would've had you try to commune with them, Gloria. This is a priority, however. We must communicate and let their friends know our intentions before they attempt anything dramatic."

Daedalus sat 100 yards off the apparent starboard side of the football stadium-sized alien vessel while Gloria attempted to communicate telepathically. She said nothing for about ten minutes, but her face was an exhibition of emotion. She was obviously communicating with them. She broke away and turned to her father.

"They are very different from us, Dad. But I told you that when I communicated with Hansel and Gretel coming home from Rome. They are very different than the shepherds also. Their minds work in an odd fashion. They are logical, but they exist in a hive mentality. I felt like I was speaking to hundreds of them simultaneously. They are all interconnected, unlike us, who live separate lives. I didn't see it the other day with only the two of them, but it is blatantly obvious now. If we can convince them of our intentions, they will all understand it, and there will likely be no obfuscation."

"I see," Iggy responded. "Speak to them again, Gloria, and take me in with you. Can you do that?"

Absolutely, that would be easy. They communicate in images telepathically, but they know our languages. They are very intellectually advanced collectively, yet quite regressive as individuals... even more so than humans."

"Okay, Gloria. Let's go." Iggy felt his daughter enter his mind and sweep his consciousness into a seemingly surreal illusion until he touched the mind of the hive. They existed there, with no output or reproach to his attempt at communication. They were waiting to see exactly what this creature would herald. He could read the images of their thoughts. It wasn't just the thoughts of the creatures aboard this ship. He was sensing the entire hive consisting of thousands of Altairians aboard the other 30 ships. They were curious and somewhat alarmed, unsuspecting of this human technical and psychological prowess. Iggy presented his picture of intent. They seemed to understand his mission to create a source of DNA that would solve their problem and release the thousands of children they kept in a catatonic state, but it also seemed as if they were catatonic themselves. He received no answer.

Iggy and his daughter receded from contact. Iggy was mentally back on Daedalus. "That didn't seem to accomplish anything much. I don't think it made matters worse, however. Nowhere did I sense they missed Hansel and Gretel. There is no way they can communicate with Hansel and Gretel because of our EMF barrier. I'm getting the distinct impression that this hive mentality of theirs negates individual autonomy to some degree."

Gloria interrupted. "Nowhere did I sense emotion, Dad. They may have it hidden somewhere, but it wasn't obvious. That makes them completely different from us and more like Junior and Baby. They think with a hive mentality, have very limited emotional needs or consequences, and it seems they don't have priorities based on morality. I don't think they love or hate. I don't think they even feel. If they do, it's minimal. That sort of takes the worry of them being angry about Hansel and Gretel off the table."

"Perhaps... perhaps not. What it may take off the table is their incentive to cooperate with us. We are going to go great guns to solve their anatomical conundrum and get them a source of DNA, so they don't need to keep our children in a DNA bank. Their ambivalence might make our efforts irrelevant. It's almost impossible to say unless we succeed and present them with the results. Then, perhaps they will alter their modus operandi."

"Do you mind if I get into this?" Quipped Junior. "I have a slightly different perspective since I'm not big on emotion either."

Iggy chuckled. "Sure, Junior. Come on in. The water's fine."

"Ooooo, small talk. I love it," Junior laughed, mimicking Iggy's laugh. "While you were sailing around in their alien minds, Dad, I was interfacing with their onboard computer. I got a good look at their history, their society, and everything that supports their existence. You are all quite correct. They are dying, and it began centuries ago, just as you believe. This is not the only place they mine DNA. This species consists of trillions of beings scattered throughout the galaxy, and they all exist within the hive mentality. They are not in contact with others of their kind who are light years away, but they do communally exist and think together in this kind of situation. They have been around for a million years but nearly destroyed themselves centuries ago. They must all mine DNA to survive now, and that has become an acceptable part of their routine existence since then. We are not the only species victimized by their hunger for an external source of DNA. There are many. I have downloaded every file in their computer, and I know where everyone who belongs to this species is at this moment. So, Dad," Junior displayed a broad grin mimicking Iggy's, "I have some suggestions."

"Oh? Like what?"

"I'll explain at the ranch, Dad. I don't know if this will help yet. I must conduct experiments with our guests. Anyway, you have an appointment with Cameron Fry shortly. I believe he knows where Heinrich Klatch intends to surface."

Iggy smiled. "Well, I guess you are now a fugitive, Cameron. I thank you, and Brett, thanks you. That was a long way to stick your neck out, and it is appreciated. Heinrich Klatch is a madman, and there's no telling what he would've done. Killing my son would have removed his tool for coercion.

But I don't think torture would have been off the table. It is time to retire the son of Joseph Goebbels, alias Heinrich Klatch."

Cameron Fry laughed. "Yeah, I guess I'm a fugitive. There is an international warrant out for my arrest by Interpol. I guess I'm going to need to hire your sister. She and her husband are top-shelf international lawyers. I can hang out here for a while, but I still must conduct business elsewhere. Anyway, I had my ear to the ground. I heard where they're going to have a meeting from the craziest source. Someone heard Klatch and Saphra Rothman speaking of a meeting in Switzerland coming up this week. I believe it will be in the secure subterranean underground conference room of Swiss Heritage Bank. Interlink uses their conference room often... especially after you showed up at Interlink headquarters in Belgium a few years ago and arrested everyone."

"Who was the eavesdropper?" Iggy wanted to know. "I'm sure it was someone unexpected because no one knew how or where to contact you."

"Very unexpected. I was a little worried that a friend of mine who did your son and I a huge favor might be in a little trouble. If he was in trouble, I would pay his lawyer. He is a valet driver named Antonio. Come to find out, he overheard Klatch and Rothman as he delivered their Rolls-Royce. It's obvious they can't use the Vatican anymore."

"How does that get us the date and time?"

"Easy, Iggy. Interlink has no idea that I suspect when and where the next meeting will be. I know the location now. I have friends of friends who will make discreet inquiries for me. When Swiss Heritage allows the use of their subterranean conference room, it's closed during that function. It's rarely used for anything other than discrete or secret meetings. There will be a clandestine calendar date. My friends will find out next week's calendar dates and times it will be used and how many are expected to attend. The meeting is supposed to be next week. Then, depending on how many meetings are being held there, we should be able to get a good idea. The only problem I see is getting inside. There are two underground conference rooms, one large and one small. Access to both is through a 2-foot-thick vault door at the surface."

"No problem, Cameron. I don't have to get inside. As long as Klatch attends, I will scoop him up outside, but after the meeting. It will happen so fast that no one will even understand how. Daedalus is virtually invisible, and my men are the best trained in the world.

"I just received a call, Iggy. Evidently, the meeting is tonight. My contacts say that it is definitely an Interlink meeting. The other conference room has been closed, so there is no one else in the building. I'm sorry that it is such short notice."

"It's 4 p.m. in Geneva. What time do the meetings usually begin?"

"Usually at six, but I can't guarantee that. You're a burr under their saddle and have disrupted any schedules they normally have."

"Okay, Cameron, thanks." He pressed a button on his watch. "Junior, I want you to get everyone assembled. We are heading to Switzerland ASAP."

"The same people?"

"No, Paul Billings is not here. He's back in Washington. Gloria, and especially Brett, can assist with the arrest of Heinrich Klatch. Baby, Tom Rickart, and Cameron Fry will accompany us. We are delivering Klatch to his associates, who we arrested in Brussels a few years ago."

"Got it, Pop. Sounds like a fun evening. I can't wait."

Cameron Fry looked at Iggy with a huge grin. "Can you build me one of those? I find Junior is more interesting to have around than most human beings I've met. I wouldn't mind having him as a companion."

Iggy returned his smile. "Why don't you ask Junior? He might build you one. You must understand Junior is not a servant; he is a person. All metal and silicone with some electrical components thrown in for good measure, but he's alive and sentient."

"So, you're telling me he could go off on his own if he felt like it. What would be the point of me investing in that?"

"Can't really say, Cameron. His personality is a combination of programming and autonomy. He won't have desires, so I would imagine if he had a reason to stay, he'll hang around." Iggy continued to laugh, "he will be low maintenance, and you'll never have to buy him dinner.

The meeting was already in progress as Daedalus settled onto a grassy area on a knoll in the park surrounding Schweizerische Heimatbank. There were several helicopters parked at the heliport, including Heinrich Klatch's Euro X3.

"I guess we've come to the right place at the right time," said Junior. "There certainly are a lot of choppers here. Shall I let everyone see Daedalus?"

"No," Iggy replied. "Apparently, the meeting will continue for a while yet. When it's concluded, my guess is that everyone will exit through different doors to avoid attracting attention. We'll have to wait and see where Klatch exits. As soon as Klatch comes through the door, Brett, you, and Cameron have the honors." Iggy smiled. "I'll bet Heinrich Klatch isn't expecting the two of you for dinner."

"I'll really enjoy putting a run in his stockings," replied Cameron Fry. "I owe the bastard for the knife in my back."

"You brought me along for a reason, Dad."

"Yes, Gloria. I don't know how far underground they are but see if you can probe the meeting and come up with something. I'm interested in the agenda. "

"Sure thing. I don't mind eavesdropping on this bunch." Gloria began reporting the thoughts she was able to perceive. "I'll give you snippets of conversations. A man named Carrington is speaking. He wants to know why Klatch trusted Cameron Fry. Apparently, he really ruined he day for them. Klatch is talking now. He said he had no idea that Fry had a gun and would betray Interlink. He's one of the wealthiest members. Carrington says that we should have expected it. Fry was never a participant in the psychological operations Interlink is involved in. He just said they have been trying to subvert societies in every country, and that is detrimental to the international banks, which rains on Fry's parade as well. Whoops! Klatch just said he was going to put a contract out on Cameron Fry and use the Russian mafia."

"Good luck with that. It will work really well for them, trying to find someone in the Russian mafia." Junior's sarcasm brought everyone a smile. "Maybe we should give them the location of the Isle of No Return."

Gloria continued, "Lawrence Howe agrees with Klatch. He doesn't care how much it costs; somebody has to kill Cameron Fry and do it quickly. He knows too much." Gloria raised her eyebrows and shrugged. "Apparently, they are pretty angry. I guess Cameron needs a watch and a shield."

The meeting lasted another two hours. "They are talking about Hansel and Gretel. They have no idea what happened to them other than they have been abducted by you. Heinrich Klatch repeated his vendetta to choke you several times. They are discussing the subterfuge and manipulation of societies. Lawrence Howe has the floor. He intends to fast-forward their plans to crash world economies and societies." She laughed, "He just said they can't let that SOB, Marcus, continue to hold the upper hand. Ransom Hornburg couldn't make this meeting, but the two of them are working together to expedite everything covered tonight. The next meeting will be here in two weeks."

"I can just imagine how deliriously happy they would be if they knew you were eavesdropping," said Junior.

"They don't realize we are here yet. When they realize we have come for Klatch and they see Daedalus, they are all going to run like hell for the choppers and limos.

"Brett and Cameron Fry are going to have the pleasure of arresting Heinrich Klatch. Do you both think you want to manage that? These are the people at the top of Interlink. The only other people who have any say in the tragedy that is happening to the world are the people from Altair Four. They are all going on notice today."

The outer doors opened. Forty-six Interlink members and thirty-two state executives from various countries in Europe and the Middle East began exiting the building. Cameron Fry, Lori, and Brett arrived to confront them. Iggy was right. Everyone saw Daedalus and abandoned composure, running for their vehicles and aircraft. The looks of abject fear on their faces were evident. None of them had ever received a challenge to their authority.

Everyone froze in mid-stride as a giant Yosemite Sam materialized, surrounding the heliport and parking space containing the limousines. No one moved. They were reminded of the staggering power their adversaries wielded. Cameron Fry and Brett faced Heinrich Klatch.

"We are taking you to the only place appropriate for a man like you. You drugged me, intending to use me as a weapon against my father, but you failed. This is your last day with Interlink. You are a killer. Your father, Joseph Goebbels, was a killer also. The apple didn't fall far from the tree, obviously. There is no rehabilitation for you today. Such is the nature of my father. The man who defeated you is not a killer; he is a healer. Maybe someday he can bring sanity to you. But for now, you are coming with us."

Cameron Fry listened to Brett's announcement. He decided against commenting as he observed the spectacle of how minuscule these people of interlink actually were. They had money, just as he had money, but to them, it was not just a tool. They worshiped it because it was the definition of their stature and their God. Fry had discovered true human beings in the Marcus family. These people of Interlink weren't worth the bother."

Iggy turned slowly, staring at all the people immobilized by the turn of events and Yosemite Sam encircling the escape vehicles. "I delivered this little speech to you several years ago in Brussels. Many of you were there. I recognize you. You do not all subscribe to the new world order designed by your leaders. Those of you who lust for your new world order are typical of every tyrant and murdering monster that has enslaved men since time began. You believe the position of slave master is rightfully yours. Your wealth underwrites your station in life to rule others. That requires everyone else to become your subjects… Yes, Lawrence Howe, I am speaking to you, and anyone else present who thinks they have the right to enslave men."

Iggy projected his thoughts directly into the mind of Lawrence Howe, who quickly averted his eyes. He subliminally invaded Howe's inner persona and displayed the nature of the universe and man's true place in it.

"You think your money entitles you to power over others, but you are not benevolent; you are a killer. You must subjugate or destroy your adversaries to define and live with your own lack of character. It's your nature, Mr. Howe, along with everyone here who is of the same mind, including your buddy, Ransom Hornburg. Though you demand all men kneel to your supremacy, you are not yet beyond redemption. As long as a man lives, he can be saved, but not as a tyrant. You will either abandon tyranny here and now, or you will join Heinrich Klatch, the leaders of the CCP, the Russian oligarchs, and all the other tyrants who are now living their lives on deserted islands in the Pacific. That will be your sentence, Mr. Howe. Either learn to live with men as equals, or you will be removed from them forever."

"You and your entrenched oligarchs attempt to rule as Kings, and you are using socialism as the vehicle to get you there. You are a purveyor of filth. Your indoctrination of the youth will accomplish exactly what you want it to. You propagate death and destruction by stoking hatred and violence, using men to kill each other because you believe that once they kill each other and the smoke clears, you will be left standing, holding the reins of your new world order. Much of the damage you have instigated is done and beyond reclamation or mitigation. Society will have to contend with the residue of your actions. One thing is for sure; you will not remain here to hold the reins. You will be given a new home in the middle of the Pacific where you can no longer harm society."

"You have enlisted the aid of people from another star system. They were at a meeting in the Vatican weeks ago. I removed them and brought them to Lightning Ranch, where they are now." He turned to Klatch again. "You are particularly despicable, Heinrich Goebbels Klatch, and clinically insane, as well. You have been working with extraterrestrials to supply them with DNA from human children. So, you contracted with them and assisted them with kidnapping children from around the world in exchange for a governor's position. To put it plainly, the jig is up. Your party is over. We have seen to that. We will solve the alien genetics problem for them but without a price tag other than releasing the children. You, Mr. Klatch, are going to meet the other tyrants on Gilligan's Island."

Iggy turned full circle, making eye contact with each man and woman. You have the same offer to redeem yourselves. Every individual must be given the chance to atone. If you do not take this opportunity, you will be removed from society when you continue to pursue tyranny. Take heed of the offer. It is only being made once… today."

Iggy turned to Klatch. You are coming with us, Heinrich Goebbels. You will either walk onto the ship with dignity or we will carry you. The choice is yours."

Iggy followed Heinrich Klatch onto the ship. Baby was grinning. "That was quite a speech, Dad. Better than most. Was it from memory, or did you ad-lib?" Gloria roared.

Heinrich Klatch followed Brett down the island path past two Chinamen sitting at a picnic table in front of a bungalow, playing cribbage. Junior followed with a 4' x 4' crate perfectly balanced on his head.

"Just where are we, Marcus? And who are the two Chinamen we just walked past."

" I'm surprised you didn't recognize them." Brett replied. "They are Fun Chou Dung and General Li Shen Rishi, the two people who provided your organization with five nuclear weapons to kill my father three years ago." Brett smiled wickedly. "They are your neighbors, Heinrich. I would suggest you get to know them. Maybe they will invite you to a cribbage tournament. Oh yes, we are on Gilligan's Island."

"You certainly aren't much in the respect department, are you, Heinrich Klatch?" observed Junior from behind them.

Heinrich Klatch turned and glowered at Junior. He glanced upward at the 4' x 4' crate perched on Junior's head. "What's in the box? It can't be very heavy. You have been carrying it on your head for a half mile."

Brett chuckled. It weighs around 500 pounds. It contains your immediate supplies, including fresh water. Junior is my brother, you might say. He is a robot."

"A robot?" Klatch asked in disbelief. "That is no robot. Technology like that doesn't exist."

Klatch was surprised by Brett's laughter. "Okay, Junior, show the man what you've got."

"Okay, Brett, I'll play." Junior tossed the crate about ten feet in the air, spinning it, then caught it perfectly balanced in his hands before it landed on his head. "How was that Mr. Klatch?" He set the crate down in front of Klatch and pulled his trousers down far enough to expose the electrical cannon plug port in his naval and the switch below. "Try to lift it." He pointed to the crate.

Klatch tried to lift the crate, but it wouldn't budge. He looked at Junior in disbelief. "Where did **you** come from?" He asked in astonishment, his extreme curiosity setting aside his resentment over being arrested by the people he had wanted to kill.

Junior's captivating smile spread across his face, "Iggy Marcus built me... and then he woke me up. I have a sister just like me. Her name is Baby."

Heinrich Klatch stood on the jungle path, speechless. It was as if waves were washing over him. It was a tsunami of revelation becoming brilliantly apparent at that moment. All his plans, all his insecurities... in fact, everything in his life to date had been a waste. He was Joseph Goebbel's son. It was an internal psychological stigma he had unconsciously spent his entire life trying to erase. Every waking moment of his existence had been populated by self-loathing and an unknown subliminal desire to destroy himself, along with every other human being that he could take with him. It was the first glimpse of a reality he had ever experienced.

This first spectacle and his introduction to reality overwhelmed him. Reality has no extremes or opposite poles. It always is what it is and never negates itself. Most people spend their lives oblivious to it. Occasionally, however, people have an epiphany and get their first glimpse. They are forever changed. He saw the caliber of his adversary. Klatch was brilliant. Though mentally ill, he now realized this unchangeable reality existed, and Marcus was the Master of It. He had been foolish. He realized it now as he mentally reviewed the technology his adversary had created. The man was eliminating disease, had created new forms of energy, ships that would travel around the world instantly, and now this, a robot he never would have believed wasn't human. He had seen the irrefutable proof; this was his epiphany. The people of Interlink were trying to destroy a man who was indestructible. They were trying to destroy him and then destroy society and autonomy so they could rule men.

Heinrich Klatch fell to his knees with his hands covering his face and wept uncontrollably.

Brett stood there leaning on Klatch's supply crate. Sarcasm, coloring his comment, "You always have such a positive effect on people, Junior. Look at this guy. He's a wreck."

Of course, Junior couldn't feel and had no idea what emotion even tasted like, but he had every word ever written by every philosopher, psychiatrist, psychologist, and poet stored in its memory banks. That made up, quite substantially, for his lack of empathy. "You know, Brett. I know what you mean by your sarcasm. Leave the sarcasm out of this. I'm not 100% sure, but I do believe the man kneeling in front of us in tears is not the same man who began this journey."

"Hmm… Maybe you're right, Junior. Dad always said that deep within every person lurks a little bit of evil and a little bit of good. When we develop ourselves and become thinking entities, one or the other begins to dominate. He said it's like a sliding scale, and we all vacillate at times. He's right, of course. He always is. I think that you may be right also and that we should bring Heinrich Klatch back to the hospital at the ranch. I don't think leaving him here is a good idea."

Junior smiled; even though his grin was a contrivance, he knew it was the appropriate gesture considering the circumstances. "You definitely are your father's son, Brett Marcus. Just one more thing, though. As far as that little bit of evil, and little bit of good, goes, it doesn't pertain to Baby or me."

***

The medical staff worked around the clock in shifts, tireless in their mission to solve the problem of the alien's metabolic DNA degeneration. Despite the DNA similarity, the alien anatomy was vastly different from human anatomy. This was atomic biology on an unprecedented level. The Marcus staff had already been delving into the science of atomic biology as they attempted to solve the problems of human aging in a quest for immortality. Although DNA was the basic construct, the differences in the atomic interrelationships between organs and musculoskeletal integrated alien systems led the team down hundreds of rabbit holes, attempting to grasp a radically different mystery of creation. The learning curve was enormous as they unraveled the atomic and molecular arrangement of the alien metabolism and adapted their thinking to implant it in their own cognizance.

They had another problem. Marcus General Hospital had become the epicenter for medical research in the northern tier of states and afforded general health therapy for many hundreds of people in Montana. Hundreds of people suffering from various chronic illnesses also traveled from different states to avail themselves of the cures represented by their innovative approach to holistic medicine and time-tested cures for formerly fatal diseases.

Gloria explained what they were attempting to Hansel and Gretel. The aliens understood, but their intellectual and emotional makeup was very dissimilar to that of humans. Although the aliens understood the team was attempting to mitigate the DNA problem of their species, they resisted the taking of biopsies almost violently. Even after Gloria's subliminal explanation, they were resentful.

"Why do you think that is, Dad?" Gloria asked Iggy.

Iggy laughed. "You're the mind reader, Gloria. You tell me."

"I keep bumping into their hive mentality. It's an enigma. They don't feel fear like we feel fear. We are individuals, and they are a collective. We fear our own destruction; they fear the destruction of the hive."

"Well, there's your answer then, daughter. Don't you see it?"

"Oooooh, yes! You're right, Dad. That's it! When we die, we die individually. We all know what is coming and expect it. So, we live our lives without worries about our death affecting our progeny because we all must experience that. If we are under attack as individuals and destroyed, our progeny will probably live on. That depends on the circumstances, of course, but that's the theory. If someone tortures me and kills me, they have learned nothing about my offspring, and it doesn't affect them."

"When we probe one of these people from Altair, we are putting them in danger. They do not know for sure that we are acting in benevolence. So, if we destroy them, we affect the entire hive, and if we learn anything at all about a destructive methodology concerning their anatomy, the entire species becomes imperiled. Wow! Somehow, we have to explain to them what we are doing."

"Perhaps. Our explanations may not mean anything to them. They are emotionally much different than we are. I'm not sure trust is based on emotion with them. I believe we have to solve this problem quickly, so we don't give them much time for speculation. They could react in a variety of ways. I'm going to summon the shepherds."

***

"Can you help? We are not sure that we need help, but we are sure that we need time. Time may become an obstacle, depending on the people from Altair."

"You have identified the problem, Iggymarcus. Your approach is appropriate regardless of the results. Now you know what the mentality of the Altair four people consists of. You also understand

their anatomy. You have not solved the problem yet, however. Do you expect a solution?"

"Given more time, we will solve the problem. It was difficult to get past the differences in their anatomy. There was a large learning curve, and our staff has finally assimilated that. We may have a method that will solve their DNA problem. However, the solution may expand their power geometrically. We can teach them to clone our DNA in an organic vehicle but not a complete human being. The problem is that I must give them the technology for matter/energy transmutation. They do not have it now and I'm not convinced they should have it. There are over 12,000 children aboard the ships. They must be released. Coercion through all-out war is not an option."

"These are the problems we face. There is a solution; we know how to get there, but we must give them the technology. I'm looking forward to your recommendation. You have been at this longer than me," Iggy smiled.

"We have observed them for over a thousand years since their genetic experiments crippled them. They are not a violent, aggressive species. They have populated numerous planets in the galaxy but never by violence. We believe that technology will not create a desire for adversarial actions in their society."

"You say that you do not believe they will become aggressive. That is far from a guarantee. If they do become aggressive, what happens then?"

"We are not the only shepherds that exist in the galaxy. We are one of many that consist of a DNA subsystem. If they acquire the technology and attempt to use it in a destructive manner, the universe has ways to deal with it. This has happened countless times in billions of years. Your history is replete with stories that you consider mythology or ancient history. Your Bible describes the battles we are referring to. When a species evolves to a certain level and becomes arrogant, other species are called upon to intervene. That's all we can

say about this. We can assist with your timelines. Continue with your efforts, and when you have a solution, summon us."

***

Iggy's watch beeped repeatedly. "Yes, Melanie, what is it? You put it on continuous. Is there an emergency?"

"No emergency, dear. Allison and I believe we have solved the problem. Come down here as soon as you can. We may have found a way."

Five minutes later, he stood with Melanie and Allison in the lab. "Our original concept was to fabricate DNA along the lines of what we did for Alice Sledge's ovum. In Alice's case, we took living tissue extracted from Alice's ovaries. That living tissue is a product of her metabolism. It also consisted of her DNA signature. So, we were already at square one. We had Alice's DNA, and we had tissue samples from her ovaries where ova are created, even though her ovaries were stunted and would not produce ova. In her case, we had all the components sitting there waiting to be assembled. They were simply missing the atomic links to complete an ovum defined by her DNA blueprint. We supplied those links through your transmutation technology and used the template or model of my ovum's structure to complete the assembly… almost like following a set of directions when building a model of anything. Then, voilà... an ovum! The ova are normally released and descend through the fallopian tubes into the uterine gate, where they meet Mr. Sperm. Alice had no fallopian tubes. It was a genetic defect. Consequently, we implanted the ova on the uterine wall and introduced them to Bill's sperm. You know the rest.

"The process is organic, however, and it has been designed by the Creator. This is the pattern of reproduction elementary to every living creature with the DNA signature. In the Altairian's case, their reproductive system does not exactly mimic ours. Although DNA is the blueprint, the structure is radically different. So, we could not create the same scenario as Alice Sledge and expect to solve their reproductive problems. The problems were created when they tried to alter their genetics and artificially advance their evolution. When they did that, they destroyed a substantial part of their anatomy responsible for DNA production, and it was unrecoverable. What would've assisted them in the recovery of their losses was your matter/energy transmutation technology. They don't possess that, but we do. We have come to understand that there are other formats vastly different from ours than DNA, and they operate differently. The crux of this is a living biological entity must exist consisting of the DNA blueprints for the species. We then can alter the DNA or assist with creating new DNA by using your atomic transmutation technology. What we cannot do is create life. We can only alter the genome to create specific results. It just so happens that human DNA, although considerably different, is perfectly suited to supersede their deficiency."

"I see," Iggy replied. "Basically, they need fresh DNA, which they are unable to produce, implanted directly in their reproductive system to create a pattern for the reproduction of the species. Simply put, they need fresh DNA to reproduce. So that is why they appear different at different times. Human DNA is different than their DNA, and, inevitably, must physically alter them in various ways. I understand how you are approaching this. I don't see what you are using for a petri dish to create DNA for them, so they don't need our children. You've finally solved the puzzle surrounding the logistics but must still create the antidote, which appears to require a living being who will produce enough DNA. Exactly how do you intend to do that?"

Allison MacLeod was bubbling. "Your wife is a genius, Iggy. I never would have looked at this idea. She said that you are the one responsible, so maybe you can unlock me a few hundred times, too!

Melanie grabbed Iggy's hand and pulled him towards the door with a large glass window. "Look inside, dear. What do you see?"

Iggy's eyes opened wide at this macabre sight of semi-formed human children with a very small cranium and no facial features. "Wow! I didn't expect that! Tell me what you have done."

"They are actual human children, Iggy, but they are cloned from one organic source. They are identical for all intents and purposes. The reduced cranial size with no features houses a brainstem attached to the base of an artificially tiny cerebral cortex. There are no quadrants to the brain, just the stem. The brainstem is the channel through which all impulses travel to issue marching orders to the body, and that includes all involuntary instructions such as breathing, blood pressure, cardiac rhythms... In short, everything. Those signals that are instructions enabling the life process to continue originate in the brainstem. Voluntary commands from the cerebral cortex flow through the brainstem on the way to musculature, etc. to perform voluntary functions."

Allison jumped in. "The beauty of Melanie's approach, Iggy, is that these living vessels for the production of DNA are nonentities. They possess no cerebral cortex and, consequently, can never think. There are no neurons or axons, etc., which are the seat of the individual's identity. No thinking, living, and completely functional human being can exist here. A life support system must supply nutrients, oxygen, and sanitation to keep it alive and productive of DNA. If any of those systems are halted, the nonentity ceases to exist and dies. There are pain receptors because those are part of human anatomy, but there is no seat of intellect to process pain signals. Therefore, nothing is felt. It's quite complex, but I've attempted to make it sound simple."

***

Three weeks later, Poseidon floated at the Lagrange point in the center of over fifty starships. Thirty were Altairians, and the remainder belonged to the shepherds. The shepherds had intervened, and the hive was receptive. A large, heated metal vault with a glass top sat on the cargo ramp at the airlock. Junior was adjusting some last-minute settings on Lightning's sarcophagus of life before he donned his heated suit.

Junior finished the adjustments and looked up at the man who built him. "I sure wish you made my skin more resilient, Dad. Then I wouldn't need this suit. I don't need oxygen, that's for sure. In fact, oxygen is corrosive to a guy like me. One side of me will probably be two or three hundred degrees Fahrenheit, while the opposite side will be just a few degrees above absolute zero. My skin would take a heck of a beating without the suit."

"After you deliver the vault and you interface with their computer, interface with ours as well. We have solved the problem they had with reproduction, but that comes with a price. We will download their computer into ours."

The shepherds agreed to be the ambassadors. They demonstrated the efficacy of the human solution to the Altairian problem. The Altairians assessed the remedy to their centuries-long genetic enigma and agreed to release the human children when the technology was up and running. The cargo door of Poseidon opened, and the people aboard watched Junior pushing the sarcophagus across the 200-yard expanse. As he approached the closest ship, a door on the side opened, and he disappeared inside.

"Well, I guess that's that," said Gloria as the door to the other ship closed behind Junior. "What do the logistics look like, Dad?"

"The shepherds explained it to the Altairians. They understand our creation and our technology. We are going to use the systems at Lightning to manufacture what they need. They will give us back the children in stages as we assist them in building vaults to house their new DNA producers. It will be a reasonably gradual process because Rome wasn't built in a day, but within two months or so, we should have all the children in the new wing of the Marcus General Hospital and the people from Altair four will leave."

Allison MacLeod was a relative newcomer, but Melanie had given her a thorough overview of Lightning Ranch's history. She was thrilled with the children. She learned the first 369 graduates had returned to many of the places Iggy had found them when they were destitute. Their mission was to help create a new world. Now, there were 3000+ students in their learning center dedicated to the same prospect. They had radically expanded their teaching staff and format to accomplish this amazing feat. "You know, Iggy, all of this is well beyond amazing. Every time I turn around, something new surprises me. I just wonder, however, what the heck are you people going to do with 12,000 new kids who are at ground zero? They have been living in nutrition coffins, scraped of their DNA, some of them for much of their lives."

Gloria answered her. "We are buying another 12,000 acres. Lightning Ranch will be 44,000 acres when we're done. We'll have to build more buildings, find more teachers receptive to our methodology, and probably expand the garden from 400 acres to 600 acres." She grinned at Allison's look of doubt. "In all the time that I have known my father, I would guess I began to think critically at around two years old. I have never known him to overstate or understate a problem. He always said that saving humanity would never be a walk in the park."

***

Three months and eleven days later, Iggy, Junior, and Melanie watched the last of the Altairian ships leave orbit. Nine of the shepherd's ships were visible. "Well, dear, things are going to be dramatically different at Lightning Ranch in short order. All those kids need to be rehabilitated, but when they are, we're going to need a whole lot of dormitories and athletic fields, not to mention dining facilities. I know you have it figured out, but I'm having difficulty wrapping my mind around it. My parents and I are the only music teachers besides you and your siblings. 15,000 kids are a plateful for any system."

"Jack is hiring teachers and other personnel. We need more music teachers as well, but our main problem is going to be coordination. It was easy with 369 kids, but it was exponentially more difficult with 3000. I think 15,000 will multiply the problems. Nonetheless, the same principles will be applied, and the same results will occur. It will be quite a hill to climb for supervisors."

***

Iggy's immediate family and several others were hosting the Lightning Ranch Fourth of July barbecue and picnic. Over 3000 children and a thousand adults celebrated America's birthday in the 300-acre park behind the pavilion and residential center. "4000 people make quite a lot of noise, Iggy," Melanie commented. "It's a good thing we've got the kids playing music in shifts. There's just so much going on everywhere," she laughed at the spectacle. "How did you ever organize this, my husband?"

He grinned, "I didn't organize a thing, dear. Baby and Junior are in charge of the whole thing. You see them everywhere. They run around at super speed. Gloria is in the middle of the mix, also. She and Baby are inseparable friends. Well, at least that's how Gloria feels."

"Yes," Melanie observed." But I know Baby feels nothing. I think the genius of your two mechanical children is beyond even more than you thought to achieve. It's hard to determine why, but I think Baby senses a need deep inside our daughter and then fulfills it."

Iggy nodded his head and was about to speak at exactly the moment a loud whooshing noise accompanied the ship that settled on the knoll behind the park.

Baby and Gloria approached. "It's your shepherds, Dad," said Gloria.

Baby could never resist her humor programming. "They must celebrate 4 July also. I wonder if they would like the barbecued spareribs. I've never tasted them, but I understand the kitchen staff makes ribs to die for... and it *is* a holiday, after all. "

Melanie, Gloria, and Baby hopped in a Land Rover and drove around the party to the ship on the grassy knoll. The same shepherd that it seemed Iggy had dealt with in every one of their contacts emerged from their ship. As usual, Gloria translated.

"Good afternoon, Iggymarcus. We have come to say goodbye. Our intervention is required elsewhere. You have done everything you were supposed to. It appears your civilization is out of danger. You are in charge, now. That is the way of things. We have been facilitators, but it is forbidden for us to alter your destiny in any other way than advice. We are leaving, and you now know your position. We will return when it is appropriate."

He smiled, "Thank you for all your help, especially at the end with the children. They are here now, and we will mitigate the damage done to them. I hope we do run into each other down the road a piece."

"We undoubtedly will. We mentioned once before, Iggymarcus, you are a tool. Once you become a tool, you will always be a tool. We have watched your progress. You are about to unlock the secrets to immortality. Occasionally, some species do, and others are just assimilated into the Creator. Every autonomous offspring of the Creator occupies a position in infinity."

With that, the shepherd entered the ship, and they quietly left.

AXIOM: No one sees the future… But everyone writes it.

Liam Marcus

CHAPTER XV

ENDGAME BOOK II

In the beginning, there existed only pure energy, self-aware and steeped in the solitude of eternity.

That energy chose to explode into the infinite parade of existence when the first moment of time commenced. It was the Creator. Alone and infinite, the Creator was its own definition of benevolence as it created the architecture of the Universe by populating an infinite number of galaxies with an unfathomable number of its children, all destined to be part of eternity. Such was the master plan. The Creator displayed its own glory by severing fragments of itself to exist as autonomous individuals in its true image and likeness. By design, each individual spirit embarked on its immortal journey as an indestructible entity, destined to eventually rejoin its origin.

For billions of years, as the spectacle of existence unfolded, and the children of God spread throughout the universe, they were free to choose their path. Good and evil were Intrinsic to the character of each unique entity, and the choice to follow either path lay exclusively within the individual, never the collective. The problem with autonomy is that it is often the harbinger of delusion and error.

Autonomy was still the silver thread woven throughout the tapestry of existence, and by its nature, it stayed the blunt hand of God. Instead, autonomous tools were forged that became the hand of God and assumed the task of directing the traffic of the universe.

***

The roots of politics had undergone vast changes one hundred and fifty years after lightning struck the man given the task of saving humanity from itself. Fifty turbulent early years passed before the absolute power of the self-appointed authoritarian indoctrinators was finally swept away and replaced by the rebirth of autonomous individuality. The once seemingly implacable tyrants populating the halls of power throughout human history had met their match. Still… sweeping delusion under the carpet was not enough to cement humanity's epiphany in place. Iggy Marcus knew he must alter the very concepts of morality to introduce humanity to the undistorted meaning of existence.

His epiphany was not the moment of the lightning strike. As time passed, he grew into the knowledge of what the universe had in store for him. Iggy Marcus and his children had been appointed among Destiny's unique taskmasters.

They realized, even from the beginning, they must turn the character of men inside out and redefine the importance of individuality, illustrating collectivism as the death of the human spirit and autonomy.

Iggy Marcus saw every upside and downside. There were always benefits and prizes to be had, contradicted by liabilities and penalties. That was how the universal drama was set up. When God created autonomy, every individual was given the ability to choose between good or evil… life or death. The creator relinquished authority and supremacy to give every creature mastery of its own existence and the benefits from its own choices. Autonomy, by design, was free will and the opportunity to thrive, but it was also the independence to kill.

The first fifty years began the transformation. Iggy's first item of business had been the neutralization of the nuclear age and 30,000 nuclear weapons poised to murder the civilization of an entire planet. That was just the beginning. People Must be taught to think differently and relate to each other by the principal Rebecca Marcus had taught Iggy as a child, **"Never let anyone's opinion define your self-image. It cannot be given to you by others. It must come from within by mastery through achievement."**

Humanity, once on a path of self-destruction, had finally begun to learn the essence of true morality and the definition of character. It had taken over a century to reeducate people and incorporate reality into the human psyche as constant and normal. Lightning Ranch had grown more than 260,000 acres and was now structured as an independent township. Every road leading into town displayed a large sign: Welcome to Lightning Montana. The American Renaissance lives here. 170 years had passed since Iggy Marcus was struck by lightning. History considered that day the epiphany of humanity.

The remaking of the world was far from a walk in the park. The requirements to feed the people of the world and provide clean, usable energy were the priority. Iggy Marcus left the hospital after the lightning strike with a four-figure IQ. That was the gift that would provide the solutions for the dilemmas preventing humanity's march into the future.

The universe had forged its tool and Iggy Marcus looked into the future with more than a dream. It was the Utopian vision of what humanity could and should become. He knew he could implement the future with technology, but that was not enough. He must refocus the collective human mind to be worthy of the new world. It always began with the children. They were the unwritten books, malleable clay in the hands of the artist, to be formed into productive individuals. That was where he started. He was leaving today. Apparently, he had a job to do elsewhere. It had been his mission, along with his family's as well as many thousands of the child prodigies who graduated from Lightning School, to sculpt the world of tomorrow through the children. Thousands had been sent around the world to continue the process. They would teach much of humanity how to aspire and give them the tools to do it.

Technology defines men's path forward. It always had. Man's survival tools, the mind and the hand, employed technology to alter his environment to survive. It was man's only possible operating system. Technical advancement was not a license to destroy or alter his environment to the detriment of his progeny, however. There were always moral boundaries that must be defined by the integrity of the individual creator. It was essential to the preservation of the species.

Marcus General Hospital at Lightning Ranch expanded, using its new wing for research and development. It contained many of the best and brightest minds of the global medical community, and there was a never-ending line of applicants to join. The medical revelations and achievements were inspired by Iggy Marcus and his brilliant team. They had unlocked the genetic keys to forestall aging, and the average lifespan was now 300 years, as predicted over a hundred years before by Dr. David Peterson. They were on the cusp of using cloned identical duplicates of any human being to transfer consciousness from the body with extreme physical atrophy to its new host, the equivalent of a 30-year-old identical construct. That was on the horizon and only a matter of time.

Iggy and Gloria had spent enormous chunks of time wrestling with the psyches of some of the elitists he had condemned to solitary confinement on Pacific islands. Many were cured as he and Gloria dragged them back from the brink of insanity and gave them a subliminal dose of reality. Some were beyond help, but many were morally resuscitated to rejoin the world of men and live productive lives. Heinrich Klatch, once the head of Interlink and the World Socialist Progressive Council, emerged from his hereditary and environmental psychosis to become a tireless advocate for individualism and the education of children. Many of Interlink's former autocrats, given a choice between perpetual exile and rehabilitation, chose to renounce elitism and reenter the world as citizens.

The reformed members of Interlink were given the same rights and access to the scientific and medical technology created by Iggy Marcus. Those who refused to abandon autocracy were relegated to live out their lives in solitude. Promises of sincerity were not enough. They had to get past the mind of Gloria Marcus. There was no forgiveness for pedophiles. Those who destroyed children remained on Fantasy Island to live out their lives.

Iggy Marcus was the unexpected wildcard. He had transformed the world with his technology of matter and energy transmutation and discovered the universal method to enable travel to the stars. Starvation was a thing of the past, and disease had vanished from every corner of the globe. The corrupt government agencies of the FDA and CDC were no longer necessary. There was nothing or no one to protect people from. Most diseases were eradicated, and big Pharma slowly evaporated by attrition. There was no more money to be had by fleecing the public for curative, non-holistic medicines at an enormous profit. The world had become a garden, and the utopia honest men had dreamed of for centuries was no longer exclusively driven by personal wealth underlined by greed.

The biblical paradise men called the Garden of Eden was no longer wishful poetic fiction. It existed. Still, there are universal precedents necessary to preserve utopia and all things of value. Those fundamental laws preventing systemic decay are "do no harm" and "honesty and integrity must underpin everything." Although society had come a long way, and individual autonomy defined its members, not everyone had yet learned to distinguish selfishness from greed. Self-aggrandizement was still the modus operandi of enough people to jeopardize utopia. It had only been 150 years, and Homo sapiens were still in their infancy. It was a long way to childhood's end and Millennium's Gate.

Eventually, humanity would mature, leaving its inherent flaws and delusions behind when custodians would no longer be necessary. Iggy Marcus and his family had other jobs to do, unrelated to the fourth planet from Sol. Like the shepherds said, once a tool… always a tool. Iggy would leave Junior and Baby behind to mind the store.

Sunrise… midday… now comes the twilight.

We dream… yesterday's memories are left behind.

The remains are reflections of mist-blurred highlights.

Tomorrow… another sunrise and new adventure to find.

Melanie

CHAPTER XVI

SUNSET

"Jake couldn't make it?"

"Oh, he's here. He wouldn't miss this. You guys go back a couple hundred years. Anyway, it's early. Alice called me. She and Bill are flying out. I told her that we were leaving. She told Bill and he actually cried."

Melanie and Iggy finished packing the last carton as three students hauled them out to the pickup. Melanie turned to Iggy, "I hope this isn't a big deal. I know how you wanted to leave quietly, dear."

"Many of our students will be here. I spent the entire week unlocking hundreds of them. They'll be here, for sure. And there will be a lot of the people we deal with on the ranch. I finished with Brett and Luke yesterday. I unlocked those two a thousand times in a hundred years. It restructured their minds. They are now able to unlock new kids, and there are always Lori and Liam. "

"Luke, Brett, Lori, and Liam can handle this place. They will carry on just fine. You trained them, dear." Melanie smiled, thinking about all the tools he was leaving behind. "Don't forget Baby and Junior."

"They will run the show and keep the process alive. Mankind is not out of the woods yet. Civilization is near the edge but not completely free of the indoctrination hammered into it for thousands of years. It's quite a leap for them."

So, my husband, did your shepherds tell you anything? Did they say where or how long?"

"Only that this would take a long time. He said I will learn as I go. I'm sure I'll be surprised."

"Come with me, Iggy. I have a surprise for you." Melanie said with a broad grin. "Come out to the Land Rover. I'll drive. We are headed for the party field. Apparently, that's where all the kids and the people who work here are gathering. You might call this a going away party."

It was at least a five-minute drive through the hills to the pavilion and the guest apartments. The party field was named by the students. It was a stretch of pasture that extended from the rear of the guest accommodations to the foothills approaching the mountains several miles away. Large ponds and several bridge-covered streams colored the picturesque landscape with character. It had many purposes. Sometimes, it was a sports arena. Other times, it was an outdoor barbecue for thousands of kids and Lightning staff.

They rounded the corner of the furthest guest building, and the party field panorama spread out before them. Melanie looked at her husband with a tear. "They've come from everywhere, many of them from the other side of the world. They are our kids Iggy, and they came to see us off."

"Holy moly," Iggy said softly. "Why didn't you tell me? There must be a half million people here. My goodness." He almost never allowed emotion and sentiment to get the upper hand, but this was definitely one of those warm-fuzzy moments. He and Melanie sat there in the Land Rover, watching the crowd. As soon as they pulled up, the crowd went silent. There was hardly any movement. They had come to see their mentor. He had done more than just shape their individual lives. He had shaped the world and humanity's trajectory into the future.

"Three people begged me not to tell you. Tom insisted. Believe it or not, Junior and Baby were the other two. I asked them why since they had no emotions. Baby said surprises make life interesting for humans, and she would wait for you to return with a pocket full of emotions to give her."

It would be sunset in a few hours. Small clumps of trees surrounded the picnic grove directly behind the buildings. Several dozen adults were gathered there at the picnic tables. They rose as Iggy opened the door of the Land Rover and stepped onto the grass.

Melanie had tears in her eyes. "They're all here, Iggy. Everyone came. You understand why that is possible. Many of these people are almost 200 years old because of you. They love you as much as you love them. They are the beneficiaries of an incomparable treasure given to them with no strings attached. That is an amazing gift, my husband.

He approached the picnic tables where dozens of his friends stood waiting... smiling. These had been his friends. Jake Dorian was his oldest friend. He was Iggy's college roommate who eventually became president, Dr. Dave Peterson, Laura Collings, Bill and Alice Sledge, Jack Fletcher, Oniella Kengi, Richard McNerney, and dozens more.

They were smiling, but their hearts were full with this bittersweet moment, with one exception. The last person anyone would expect to see tears trickling down his cheek was Tom Rickart. He had been Iggy's friend for well over 150 years. As Iggy's security chief, he had been through all the turbulent trials and triumphs.

"When are you leaving, boss?" Iggy had always asked Tom to call him by name, which he did often but 'boss' was a term of endearment he enjoyed using.

"Tonight, Tom. Sunset will be in a few hours. I guess that's when."

"You know where you're going?"

"No."

"Will you be returning anytime soon?"

"I don't know."

"What is it that you are supposed to do when you get wherever it is you are going?"

"I don't know that yet, Tom. Apparently, according to the shepherds, I am particularly suited for some things. This is not something I must do under coercion, but it is something I must do simply because of the nature of things and the gifts I have been given. Melanie and Gloria are coming with me."

"Want another hitchhiker, boss?"

Iggy smiled at his friend. "I don't think so, Tom. We are going someplace far from here. The shepherds say I am needed. Apparently, I will be doing a lot of this kind of thing in the future. Dave Peterson and all the doctors have perfected identity transference. There is no way to test this with a viable human being. We are waiting for someone to be terminal. It will be the only way for them to survive. Then, we will try to transport their identity into a clone. If it works, no one ever has to die. We can't risk experimenting outside that scenario." He noted Tom's scowl. Don't worry, Tom, I'll be back from time to time."

Lindy, Jack, and Lucky pulled up in a ranch buggy. Lindy ran to her brother and hugged him. "I can't believe you're leaving us after all these years. I was thinking about that morning 150 years ago when you, Melanie, and I watched the sunrise from Coletta Mountain. I thought that day was something special; it was only the beginning. I'm not sad that you are leaving. This is just another adventure, and you'll be back sometime. We spoke of this a long ago, Iggy, how no one's energy ever dissipates. The universe wastes nothing. Mama and Papa are still somewhere. Maybe you can bring them back to us, Iggy; if anyone can do it, it will be you."

A large RV pulled up behind the guest buildings, and the doors opened. Amos Carmichael, his wife, and two children piled out of the back, followed by three more young adults and nine children. He strode to Iggy and wrapped his arms around him. "It's good to see you, my friend. The day we met was probably one of the best days of my life. I would like you to meet my three grandchildren, four great-grandchildren, and two great-great-grandchildren. That's quite a mouthful, wouldn't you say? It's all thanks to you. I'm 194 years old and still going strong. Thank you, my friend. We've come to see you off and wish you well. This world will not be the same without you."

Melanie gazed across the vast expanse of pasture leading to the foothills. "There are almost a million people here, Iggy. They all want to touch you one more time and say goodbye. They are all the people you have so profoundly touched over the century."

"I know," he sighed. "It's only an hour before sunset; that's when I leave. I expect visitors. I guess it will have to be a collective goodbye."

Daedalus rested a few hundred feet behind them between the guest apartments and the pasture, as the approaching sunset became the artist's hand beginning to paint the crimson fired crowns of the trees. Melanie emerged and walked toward her husband holding out her hand with a portable microphone. "Here, Iggy, you'll need this."

Melanie stood with Lindy, talking, while Iggy climbed on the Land Rover roof. "Hello back there," he said testing the microphone. Can everybody see me? How about the audio? My goodness, there's a lot of you here." He was speaking through the microphone connected to Daedalus that vibrated air molecules to produce sound. Even the people in the rear of the giant crowd heard him as if he was personally speaking quietly to them as individuals. A million people raised their hands to acknowledge his words. He surveyed the crowd. Many thousands of people were there who had been his friends and associates over the years.

They all had been affected by his actions in a thousand different ways, and each had experienced a personal epiphany. Hundreds of thousands of them were the children, now adults, whom he had rescued and educated, transforming the dregs of humanity into its brightest and finest. He had unlocked the potential of each one of them individually and gave them the intellect and fortitude to change the world. That had been the mission, and they were successful. They hadn't come to pay homage to the man. Iggy had taught them that he was just a man and their benefactor. He had always stressed the importance of their place in the future of men as individuals and not his own importance. Coupled with unlocking, however, came the deep psychic connection with each child that always precipitated love and respect. They had come to say goodbye to their hero.

"I know each one of you would like to hug me as I would like to hug you one more time. The sun is setting soon, and I must leave. I'm looking at the finest group of human beings that have ever lived. You are all the best of the best, and I am overwhelmed being in your presence. You are changing the world. You are dedicated to the process, and this is the only way humanity can address the future. I'm so proud of what you all have become."

"I know you're all thinking, 'Who will I talk to when I need advice?' I am leaving Jack, Lucky, and Lindy, as well as Brett and Luke. They will be your resources." He laughed. "And when the chips are really down, you've got Baby and Junior. They will go to the ends of the earth for you. I would wish you all good luck, but you don't need it. Wishing you luck intimates that you might fail without it. You will not fail. You can't fail as long as you remember the things you have learned here at Lightning. The old order is gone. You are the new order, and you will take your brothers and sisters through Millennium's Gate. I am not leaving forever. I will return someday."

Iggy jumped down from the roof of the vehicle, almost into the arms of Michelle Sayers. Crying, she put her arms around Iggy, speaking softly in his ear. I remember everything, Iggy. I am a savant. I didn't know that I even had a name until you saved me. I remember every moment of my life and what you have meant to me. I love you, Iggy Marcus, like I love my own parents, only even more. Every single day, I think of what my life would've been instead of what it has become. Thank you, thank you, thank you! I will miss you."

Iggy smiled and kissed her forehead. "Nor will I forget you, sweetheart. Of all my kids, you were the one I unlocked the most frequently. It took thousands of hours to remove your autism and rebuild your mind, but it was worth it. Just look at you! I am glad I had the opportunity to help you. I'll be back someday, and you'll still be here."

He turned sharply away from Michelle, hiding his own emotion, and bumped squarely into Tom Rickart. " I have to tell you, Iggy. During the past few days, I have replayed every moment of our association together in my mind. What an incredible life this has been. You are not even gone yet, and I feel this huge emptiness inside. In fact, this has been more than a life. It has been a giant fairytale-like dream that I actually got to live." A tear trickled down his cheek. "I'll see you, boss, take care of yourself and don't forget to take a lot of pictures. I want to see what's out there when you return. I love you, man. You're the brother I never had."

Melanie was in tears as she said goodbye to everyone. Then she, Gloria, and Iggy boarded Daedalus just as the shepherd's ship appeared next to them. It's time to leave, my husband."

He turned to enter Daedalus and close the hatch when he spied a lone figure pushing his way through the crowd. He turned to Gloria. "Wait! Someone is coming that I really must say goodbye to." Iggy jumped from the deck and jogged across the pasture, stopping to wait for the figure to push his way through the crowd.

They both wore huge grins but Taio Chen's eyes glistened. "Hello, Taio Chen. You have come a long way from China. Is Heng Cong with you?

"No, Uncle Iggy. One of us had to stay. Both the president and vice president of the Free People's Republic of China could not leave together. We have much going on. There are almost 3 billion people in China now. There's lots to do. So, we did what we used to do as children. We flipped a coin... I won."

Iggy smiled as Taio Chen approached and put his arms around him. "I guess you have to leave. Both Heng Cong and I have broken hearts. You and Melanie were mother and father to us and what you did for us is amazing beyond words. You raised us and made us what we are."

"No, Chen. I did not make you what you are. You made you what you are. I was just there to give you a good kick in the pants when you needed it. You know our philosophy. Become the best you can be but reach deep within yourself before you settle for second best. Anyway, Taio Chen, I'm sure you remember that first time we had contact. We had just rescued you from a park in China. I sensed even then there was greatness in you. Not everyone is born with that. Well, look at you now, president of the largest country on earth and doing a slam-bang job at it. Your sister is vice president, and you both keep your country on an even keel. I'm proud of you both, but I expected no less. You and your sister were perfect successors to Zia and Chu. You didn't have any problem winning elections either."

"Where are you going, uncle?"

"I don't know, Taio Chen. In fact, I am not even sure why. All I know is I have a job to do somewhere. It is what I have been selected for." He laughed. "I'll let you know how it went when I get back, Chen. In the meantime, you and Heng Cong must hold down the fort. You have Brett, Luke, Lori, Liam, Baby, and Junior as resources. You'll be fine."

Iggy had managed to bridle the bittersweet tears of parting all day. He kissed his protégé on the forehead, turned and quickly walked back to Daedalus. He stood in the hatchway and waved his last goodbye.

Minutes later, Daedalus drifted slowly upwards and west towards the setting sun.

Tom Rickart still had tears in his eyes. Lindy laughed. "I'm the one that is supposed to be crying, Tom. Here's my neckerchief; you need it."

"Yeah," Rickart laughed, sniffling, "I know it, but I can't help myself."

Lucky put his arm around Tom's shoulder. “I guess I did my crying yesterday. We are all going to miss him. He sure is a horse of a different color. Let's go home, Tom.”

The Author

First, I must assume that if you are reading this page, you have plodded through the first two books of this trilogy. Second, I would like to thank you for your fortitude. I hope I entertained you and delivered food for thought.

It is often said there are parallel universes, perhaps a few, perhaps a million, perhaps an infinite number. We probably will never know until the far distant future, if and when someone leads us there if we somehow manage to survive our own insanity.

Common accepted colloquial language and theory calls these parallel universes, alternate dimensions. I dispute that. Merriam-Webster says dimensions are measurements of length, width, and depth as well as the possible scope of importance.

Dimensions are measurements that define spatial coordinates. I hypothesize that the fourth dimension is electromagnetism because it defines the relationship between all forms of the manifestation of pure energy. That includes heat, light, matter, and dark matter... In short, everything in the universe, which I believe is the substance of Deity.

Time has often been called the fourth dimension. I believe that is a misnomer. It does not define spatial coordinates or particular aspects of a substance or place. It is a snapshot of existence, moment by moment, that defines the progression of the universe into the future.

Rather, I would submit to you that these parallel universes are platforms of existence. Some of them may mirror our universe exactly, some may be slightly different, and some may be dramatically opposite of the reality we exist in.

I took many liberties describing different possible concepts defining the universe, existence, and the very essence of the Creator. It is my view of one possible platform of existence, and I believe it is closer to our reality than anything I have heard to date.

Of course, men are just beginning to crack open the atom in a hopeful, controlled fashion to study the universe from the subatomic level. While this may be good, it also may be the harbinger of our demise. I'm quite sure the scientists who developed the Manhattan Project were not aware that the world would someday possess 40,000 nuclear weapons and the ability of one finger to destroy all men.

Men never stop to sit on the lid of Pandora's box. Their insatiable curiosity apparently gives them a license to eagerly lift the head of Medusa for all to see, and the consequences be damned.

Much of what I have written is somewhat controversial. Some of it will be considered heresy by many. Nonetheless, men will either march into the future with open minds or we will be crushed by our own insensitivity to reality and blind adherence to dogma. The one philosophical component I would like to leave everyone with is the product of Rebecca Marcus. She taught her children:

"NEVER LET ANYONE'S OPINION DEFINE YOUR SELF-IMAGE. A TRUE, VALID SELF-IMAGE MUST COME EXCLUSIVELY FROM WITHIN YOURSELF THROUGH MASTERY BY ACHIEVEMENT.

If all men can learn that and adopt it as a lifestyle, envy, greed, aggression, and war, which are all struggles for power position, will immediately evaporate. If we are to continue, we must adopt that moral code.

G. J. Ciccarone Jr.

Made in the USA
Columbia, SC
22 January 2024

5f1ba903-50d8-4362-a00e-9ff3109a5140R01